SAME SELF

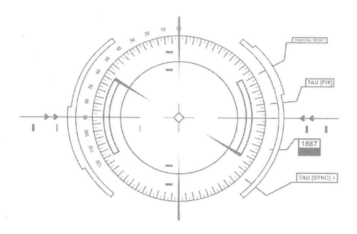

SAME SELF

Brad Raylend

Braveship
BOOKS

Aura Libertatis Spirat

SAME SELF

Copyright © 2017 by Brad Raylend

Braveship Books

www.braveshipbooks.com

Aura Libertatis Spirat

Cover Artwork & Design by Didi Wahyudi

Edited by Monique Happy Editorial Services

www.moniquehappy.com

Selected graphic elements licensed from 123RF.com

ISBN-13: 978-1-64062-014-8

Printed in the United States of America

DEDICATION

For your greatest enemy. Yourself.

ACKNOWLEDGMENTS

T.D. Cunningham — Adjusting the gain and depth of both night vision goggles, your bobbing head slowly came into focus. It was standard operating procedure to switch on the Infrared strobes strapped to the back of our helmets once we were two minutes from exiting the aircraft. However, the interior of the plane was now flashing with a bright white light amongst the dark green hue, causing everyone to start looking around in efforts to identify the source.

One would assume that you had earphones in beneath your Peltor headset; most likely playing the soundtrack to a Quentin Tarantino film. In reality, nobody ever knows what's going on in the mind of T.D. Cunningham. In the years I've known you, I have come to the conclusion that your mind continuously goes through a process of analyzing the latest scheme you have developed in order to take advantage of "the system" and/or your common man.

I am fortunate enough to be included in the great unraveling of these elaborate yet usually grounded ideas, which typically teeter between questionable morals, ideals, and fucking downright Neil McCauley bounding through the streets of LA-type shit. I reached up and flicked the switch, turning off your headache-inducing IR light. You didn't seem to notice as you continued to bob to the voices in your head.

The jump master came over the radio, informing us we had ten minutes until we were over the drop zone. Your head stopped bobbing and your hand clenched your push-to-talk button. "Yo, could you imagine if—when we landed—it was the Old West ... and there were Apache warriors charging us?"

I can't help but wonder if that was what you were thinking about the whole time. Or if that was just some crazy thought that popped in while you were planning your infiltration of the Louvre. Thank you for all your help in the last few years. You are a great writer, mentor, and friend.

Ted Nulty — You took me under your wing in the early stages of the publishing process. You had a lot on your table with the success of your own work, yet took the time to sit down and do a line-by-line read through, as well as setting me up with an editor. I have the upmost respect for you and admire your professionalism and experience. I look forward to working with you in the future.

PROLOGUE

July 14, 1967

She held her small hand out toward me, calling upon the dark figure which (for all she knew) had brought about the destruction of the world around her.

I hadn't realized that I had disengaged the cloaking system a few moments earlier, but when her eyes met mine, I could see the fear and hopelessness inside her. It was clear that she was acting out of pure desperation, or perhaps she simply didn't know what else to do.

I could end her suffering, her pain, her small and brief existence at that very moment. The ripple of her death would have no more effect on the future than pulling a blade of grass from the ground. She was not the first casualty of war I would leave to fate. If anything, it would be safer to let her die, considering that I had nothing to do with her death and perhaps she was always meant to die. However, I could at least provide her with a quick exit from this world.

I raised my weapon, the targeting reticle in my HUD leveled on her head. She didn't flinch or make a sound. I knelt beside her, pushing my rifle to the side. Her eyes widened as she saw herself in the reflection of my dark visor. Blood pooled in the creases of her dirty face. She once more reached out her hand.

I opened my visor, and she looked into my eyes. I had endured

1

the worst this world had to offer and yet her eyes made me feel a level of pity that was unshakeable, and to this day lingers in my mind. I could hear the distant thumps of the rotors of Huey helicopters. The Marines were coming to finish what they had started with their artillery bombardment. She would not be another tally-mark of a mass grave. She would live.

I carried her in my arms through the jungle for nearly three hours. The whole time, her eyes stayed locked on me. She couldn't be more than eight or nine years old.

I could hear the sound of grenades and smell the burning vegetation behind me as the Marine grunts cleared out the village. The occasional pop of a 5.56 round meant they were putting the survivors out of their misery, or at least that's what I told myself. I found a nice spot in a clear meadow where I set her down and began treating her wounds. I applied trauma gel to the large hemorrhaging wounds on her body caused by the artillery. She cried in pain as the natural clotting solution disinfected her wounds and slowly closed the broken skin. I bandaged her up and gave her some of my field rations.

She looked at the small squeeze containers containing the gooey protein-and-carbohydrate-packed food supplement with curiosity. She actually ended up liking the stuff once she finally convinced herself to eat it. I gave her the rest of my rations, I hated that shit anyway. Little did she know it would be almost sixty years before the stuff she was eating would be invented.

I pulled up some basic Vietnamese on my MTX and did my best to talk to her. I asked her what her name was. She replied "Suong."

Her voice was so damned innocent.

I held out my hand. "Hello Suong, my name is Todd."

She hesitated for a moment; the carbon-fiber-padded gloves most likely looked alien to her. Eventually, she reached up and placed her little hand in mine.

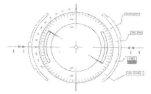

THE SECOND

Never in a million years would he ever have thought it would end this way. Todd York lay next to three of his fallen teammates, taking in the weight of his predicament and the decision he was about to make. This war was like no other. It was ending as fast as it had started, and it had taken more lives than all the conflicts of the twentieth and twenty-first centuries, combined.

One pinnacle blow to the enemy was all that was needed to turn the tide of World War III. What lay before him, however, was a choice, one that his entire life had led up to.

Nothing could have ever prepared him for this moment, but now the world and possibly all of mankind was about to reap the consequences of his actions. He thought of the people he cared for—what few of them there were—and the choice began to weigh on him heavily. He'd never hesitated before when putting his life on the line for others, never needed a push through that door to face what was on the other side. This though, was different. Nuclear devastation of this city was what it had come down to, and there was no turning back. As he laid in a pool of his own blood, mixed with that of men who had been like his brothers, everything slowed down.

His body trembled as he slowly rose to his knees. The dark reddened sky loomed over him like the eyes of a million angry souls looking down upon one of the many tools of war that had assisted in their demise. Getting his feet under him proved to be difficult, and blood streamed between his gritted teeth and clenched fists. With a blackened face, he sat back on his heels, gazing at what was left of an entire city.

Thick smoke rose into the sky, escaping the hail of bullets and explosions riddling the streets below. Dark chunks of pavement and building were scattered around him like a shrine of destruction. The cracked holographic screen of the CPD11 on his wrist displayed the status of the satellite fitted with ORMs (Orbital Rocket Munitions), which was transiting into position over the East Coast of the United States.

"00:02:02" was all that was left of the battle, the city, and Todd's life. Like every soldier, he had imagined his death many times. He foresaw his whole life flashing before his eyes, all the brief moments of happiness and joy that had occurred during his brief existence making one last appearance to assist in a peaceful sign-off. Now that he had arrived at this moment, his heart weighed heavy, for all he felt was sadness and the loneliness that he had always ignored. His mind didn't recall the smiles of good friends and loved ones that had filled his life. All he saw was a lonely broken man on his knees, surrounded by his dead comrades, beaten by the world.

"00:00:41." This man, who had accomplished the unimaginable in the opinion of a select few, had received the best training any military could offer. He had survived conflicts many had not, and although he had lived a solitary life, had done so to the best of his ability. A man he knew better than anyone and had followed so closely his entire life—himself—was now only seconds away from death.

"00:00:10." He blinked slowly, fighting back any possible tears. Moved his right hand to his left wrist, the deploy button flashing red, taunting him. He extended his index finger and it trembled above the pulsing screen. He closed his eyes, ready to accept whatever was to follow, and pressed the icon. Small objects reflected off what little light the moon could provide through the thick overcast. Like falling stars, they descended behind the D.C. skyline. He winced, ready to feel the extreme heat of a nuclear blast, but it never came. His mind went dark and drifted into a blur of memories and confusion. He felt his body slipping away into a bottomless state of unconsciousness, taking with it the fear and pain.

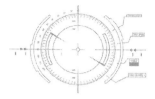

REAWAKENING

Blinding light was all he felt against his tired face as it painfully seared through his heavy eyelids. It was then that he came to grips with the reality of the pain, and the truth that was attached to it: This wasn't over.

His eyes tried to adjust, and slowly the view of an overhead light within a sleek white room came into focus. He could hear pulsing beats from an EKG; no doubt relaying his slow heartbeat. Then the sound of unfamiliar voices; nothing intelligible though, or maybe it was. The voices were whispers, sounding concerned and rushed. He tried to make out what was being said. He rolled his head slightly to the left and noticed two individuals standing at a doorway in the far wall. An older man was speaking with a young woman, both of whom stood out among the rest of the individuals gathered that were wearing white scrubs and blood-smeared latex gloves. The girl was warmly dressed, and she looked concerned and attentive.

"He ... is so much younger-looking," she said, intensely focused on Todd, who lay on an operating table, blood-stained bandages on every limb.

Todd jerked his head, trying to become more involved in the two individuals' conversation.

"He's coming around. We need to put him back under," said one of the doctors while tapping the screen of a clear holographic monitor that displayed O2 and anesthesia levels.

Todd could hear the hiss of the cool air rushing into the mask covering his nose and mouth. His eyes glazed over, but before he drifted off into the abyss, he felt the room shake slightly. It felt like an earthquake, or perhaps turbulence. He caught one last glimpse of the young woman off to his left. Her face showed sympathy, or maybe concern. He once again felt his mind and body slip into the darkness.

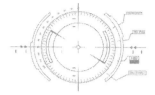

THE FACILITY

It was the discomfort in his lower back which woke him. His eyes opened to the same white light that he had seen earlier. He moved his hands to his face and rubbed his eyes. His hands froze at the soft hum of heat coming from the vents above. His vision finally came into full focus and he took in his surroundings. He found himself in a room, maybe ten by ten square feet, with dark steel walls. Filtered LED lights shone down and reflected off what was probably a two-way mirror on the far wall. A cool steel table stood before him; the chair he sat in was similar in design, and obviously not crafted with comfort in mind.

"Where the hell am I?" he asked, hearing the pain in his voice.

He looked down at his attire; he was wearing an olive-drab one-piece flight suit, similar to those worn by aircrew in the U.S. military. Thoughts began to rush into his mind. He wondered whether he had been captured. He looked at his hands and feet, noticing he was not bound or restrained in any way. He looked up at the mirror across the table and studied the few small bandages on his face.

An airlock door slid open behind him. He jolted to his feet, ready to face some Russian or Chinese soldier. Instead, standing before him was an older Caucasian man in his mid-sixties, wearing a white lab coat. He carried a large manila folder under his right arm, and a cup of coffee in his left hand.

"Good evening, Mr. York. How are you feeling?" His voice was booming, definitely not foreign, and quite possibly from the southern United States.

Todd stared at him intensely, watching every move with extreme caution. Years of training were taking over and making him feel on edge. He watched the door, waiting for more people to enter to assist with interrogation, but there were none.

"Don't be alarmed, Mr. York. You are not in any kind of danger. In fact, you are currently in the safest place in the world," the man said as he walked around to the other side of the table, eyes not meeting Todd's.

"Where would that be?" Todd asked, standing with a look of confusion and eagerness matched by his posture.

The man sat down and placed his coffee on the table along with the folder. "You are currently in what is soon to be the only free land remaining on Earth ... the North Pole," he said, removing his glasses from his face and using the collar of his coat to wipe the lenses.

Todd looked at him in disbelief. "The North Pole ... what the hell are you talking about? I was just in D.C." His anger was evident in his voice.

"Yes, you were ... and the Allied Communist Forces were invading the capital, and the United States was about to suffer its greatest loss and most definitely the war itself. You were suffering from multiple gunshot and shrapnel wounds and were moments away from your death."

Todd's eyes widened and a sick feeling crept into his stomach. "I ... don't understand."

The man put his glasses on his nose and placed his hands on the table, fingers interlocked. His eyes met Todd's with a look of utter seriousness. "What I am about tell you may be hard for you to believe."

Todd sat down in the chair, keeping his eyes locked on him. The man took a quick breath; the type of breath someone takes before they inform somebody of the loss of a loved one.

"On February 29, 2031, at 9:43 p.m. exactly, before bleeding out from a number of massively hemorrhaging wounds, you launched eleven nuclear warheads from space—destroying the entire Eastern seaboard of the United States, killing over sixty million people ...

one of them being yourself."

Todd was a statue; his eyes burned a hole through the man. His hands were tight fists in his lap, palms beginning to sweat. He tried to speak, but his mind was unable to process anything. The man finally interrupted the silence.

"You're not dead," said the man. "You are very much alive."

Todd swallowed hard then finally worked up a sentence. "Can you please stop talking in fucking riddles? Why am I here?"

The man brushed his left hand down his coat and offered his right over the table to shake Todd's hand. "I'm sorry, please excuse me for being so indirect."

Todd hesitantly reached out and returned the gesture.

"I'm Professor Brian Albrecht. I am in charge here in this facility." His massive hand swallowed Todd's.

"What exactly is this … facility?" Todd asked.

"To call it a research facility … wouldn't quite do it justice." Albrecht leaned back in his chair, placing his hands in the pockets of his white coat.

"You said we're in the North Pole?"

Brian smiled. "Yes, that's right."

Todd's face remained expressionless. "Bullshit."

Brian laughed. "That's what you said the first time." He stood up, grabbing the manila folder and his cup of coffee. "Follow me."

Todd stood, confused by the last remark and surprised at how this interrogation had not ended with him brutally beaten or water-boarded. Over twelve years of Special Operations training and never had he been sitting in a room such as this for nothing more than a friendly chat that didn't involve being slapped around by some Navy sailor trying his best to portray a Russian interrogator. Brian walked around to the airlock door and pressed a small holographic screen beside it, the door hissing as the pressurized locks released and slid open.

The two men stepped out into a long, white-walled hallway lined with large windows on each side. As he followed Brian down the long corridor he looked through the windows to his left and right.

He saw large rooms filled with holographic monitors manned by people in white coats. Professor Albrecht strolled casually, sipping his coffee. Todd trailed behind, studying the various personnel working in the rooms behind the windows. A few of them noticed him and quickly motioned for the others' attention, until nearly the entire room was staring at him as he walked past. They came to the end of the hall where a thick steel door presented a keypad. Albrecht began punching in a five-digit number, which Todd was sure to take note of.

"What exactly do you *do* here?" Todd asked, glancing back down the hallway from which they came.

The professor finished imputing his code and turned to Todd. The door hissed and slid open behind him. "We're changing the world." He smiled as wind and snow blew into the open doorway.

Albrecht moved to the side, allowing Todd to step out into the dark arctic night. The winds chilled him to the bone through his thin flight suit. What looked like blue street lights lined the horizon a few hundred meters away. A large airplane hangar was off to his left, most likely the only way in and out of this place. He shivered as the reality of the situation finally set in, as well as the extreme cold. Then suddenly something caught his eye: beautiful green and blue lights from above that faintly lit the icy floor. He looked up into the night sky to see the Aurora Borealis majestically curving amongst the millions of stars lighting up the white landscape. For a brief moment, he was lost in its beauty; the worries of the world no longer existed. It was mesmerizing as he had never witnessed it in person before.

Professor Albrecht approached him. "It never gets old," he said with a grin, his hands deep in his coat pockets, the light reflecting off his rimless glasses.

"Unreal," Todd whispered.

Professor Albrecht patted him on the shoulder. "You ain't seen nothing yet, my friend."

A few minutes later, Todd was led back into the building and into a large room with several desks occupied by a few individuals. The far wall was lined with steel bookshelves filled from top to bottom with thick books of various origins. They appeared to be mostly American history, spanning from the Revolutionary War to more current conflicts.

Professor Albrecht led Todd toward a young woman at a large glass table. Todd was shocked to realize that she was the same one he had seen when he briefly regained consciousness in the operating room. She had a petite figure, and her hair was a dark amber color, pulled back into a short pony-tail. She wore a thick blue coat with a fur collar and hood.

"Todd, I'd like you to meet Ms. Kara Dennick."

She turned quickly in her chair, looking startled at the sight of Todd.

Albrecht continued, "Kara's a historian and our subject matter expert on American history."

She stood up quickly and reached out to greet Todd. He shook her soft hand, doing his best to look pleased to meet her despite the uncertainty of the current situation. Her eyes were sharp in both appearance and in their ability to pierce through him with an intimidating beauty.

"So, what's an expert in American history doing at the North Pole?" Todd asked, pulling his hand away.

She looked as if she were about to speak, but stopped herself and looked at the professor. Albrecht motioned for Todd to sit in a chair opposite Kara's desk. He sat down and Albrecht pulled up a chair next to hers.

The professor pulled a large photo out of one of the folders and slid it across the desk. "Do you recognize this man?"

Todd picked up the photo and scanned it briefly. "Yeah, it's me …" His words caught in his throat. He grasped the photo with both hands and studied it closely. The photo was of himself, or at least someone who looked identical to him, but only if he had picked a fight with a mountain lion. The man in the photo had long, swept-back hair with several gray streaks present; longer than Todd had worn his hair within the last few years. The man looked older; his eyes were those of someone who had endured many hard years. Multiple large scars were carved into his face. One in particular spanned from his hairline and cut through his eyebrow and down his cheek. He had what looked to be several weeks of untrimmed beard.

Todd looked up at Albrecht. "Who is this?"

Kara looked at Albrecht, and then at Todd. "It's you … from an alternate course of time," she said softly.

Todd dropped the picture on the desk and rubbed his eyes. "Wait … are we talking about … time travel?"

Albrecht grinned. "Yes, what most used to believe to be only science fiction is now the greatest technological advancement mankind has ever achieved." He straightened up in his chair and used his hands to assist his words. "The world as you know it," he said, nodding at the photo, "is a direct result of this man's actions during the twentieth and twenty-first century. The past eighty years have been altered to make the future you know today."

Todd's look of confusion turned to interest and then disbelief. "Okay ..." he said.

Albrecht removed some documents from the folder and placed them on the table in front of Todd. As he separated them into stacks, he said, "Historical events such as the JFK assassination, the Vietnam War, the Cold War, and even the war in the Middle East of the early 2000s were a direct result of our own personal intervention." He picked up a document from one of the stacks and handed it to Todd. "Take a look at this, for example."

Todd scanned over the document, periodically looking back up at Albrecht and Kara. "These dates ... I'm no historian, but they look incorrect."

Albrecht nodded. "You're right, they are not accurate. Not anymore, at least."

Kara tapped the screen of the monitor in front of her and began opening files on the desktop by grasping folders with her fingers and moving them down to the glass table that displayed them in a larger format.

"After World War II, Joseph Stalin began leading Russia towards the Communist state we all know it to be. Before he died of a heart attack in 1962, he was able to absorb East Germany, Czechoslovakia, Poland, Hungary, Romania and Bulgaria all into one nation. This combined nation was what we referred to as the Eastern bloc. This expansion continued for several years as his successor Nikita Khrushchev continued west, taking over Austria, Yugoslavia, Albania, etcetera. You can see where this is going," she said.

Todd watched her go on as he did his best to keep up with the verbal data dump. Not only was it a lot of information to take in, but the fact that the information was false to him made it even more difficult. Albrecht was up and speaking quietly with one of the individuals in the room. He then walked over to a large bookcase and began pulling several books off the shelf and stacking them in his arms.

Kara continued, "They then began spreading their influence into Asian regions such as Laos, Cambodia, and Vietnam; mostly through small cell networks containing Russian advisors for the local government troops. By now, they had also moved into Cuba and were working in conjunction with Fidel Castro, preparing to use Cuba as a forward launch point for either troops or missiles. Now, this in turn led to the 'Bay of Pigs' ordeal which put President Kennedy in a tight spot with the American people and sparked the distrust between him and the Central Intelligence Agency."

She sifted through black and white imagery on her monitor as she spoke. "Kennedy could not be played for a fool again; he hung the CIA out to dry to the American public, blaming them for the failed invasion to alleviate some of the doubt that had been growing towards his administration. Thus, creating much distrust between Commander in Chief and most federal agencies who were operating in a similar independent fashion. By now it was 1965, and Kennedy's presidency was dragging on …"

Todd interrupted her. "Wait, 1965? I thought Kennedy was killed in '63?"

Albrecht sat back down and re-entered the conversation. "Remember, Todd, this is an alternate timeline … the original history, before we intervened."

A million questions came to Todd's mind. By "intervened" he now assumed that the organization he was currently being held by was in the business of killing historical figures, including U.S. Presidents. As curious and suspicious as he now was, he decided to let Kara continue before the conversation got too off topic.

"I'm sorry, go ahead," he said to Kara as he leaned back in his chair.

She smiled slightly. "Um … where was I?" she asked, looking back at the images portrayed on her monitor.

"After the Bay of Pigs invasion."

"Oh, that's right. Anyhow … President Kennedy did not want to do anything rash at this point; anything that would make us appear even more incompetent. So, when word of a growing communist influence in Vietnam began to spread, he went against his CIA leadership's advice of sending in Special Operations forces, and decided that Vietnam would not be worth the trouble. He argued that the U.S. would have a better chance fighting the Soviets through non-violent negotiations. He was now in the process of disbanding the CIA. He did not trust them, seeing them as a rogue organization within the U.S. government that played by its own rules ... which he was not entirely wrong to believe." She rolled her eyes.

"When word came out that the CIA had deployed advisors to Vietnam without the President's approval, it was the straw that broke the camel's back. He shattered the CIA into a million pieces ... as he had vowed to do. The Central Intelligence Agency, which I'm sure you are more than aware of, is an important factor in the current timeline. They have played a crucial role in every war since their early incarnation as the OSS during World War II. In essence, our first priority here at the facility was to ensure the continuation of the CIA's existence through the twentieth century. Naturally, they would eventually be re-established in the late seventies, but their absence during the crucial early years of the Cold War were inevitably fatal."

Todd scratched his head, leaning forward in his chair. "So, we never originally went to Vietnam?"

Kara shook her head. "No, Lyndon B. Johnson was in favor of sending troops, but he was only the Vice President ... and would remain in that role."

"Interesting," Todd said as he looked around the empty room. The individuals who had been working had left while he was enthralled by Kara's explanation. Albrecht stood up and walked over to one of the large bookcases and began thumbing through endless spines once more. Todd observed him, trying to get a look at the section of books he was looking at. He turned back to Kara, whose eyes were fixed upon him. She quickly dropped her gaze, returning her attention to the monitor where she tried to appear as though she were organizing her thoughts. It was obvious that she was a wealth of knowledge herself and could have given him this brief history lesson without the aid of her references. Todd couldn't help but wonder about his "other self." He was curious as to which role he had played in all this. Did he kill Stalin, and Kennedy? If so, what else could he have altered?

"I'm sure you have a million questions right now, Todd," Albrecht said, returning with a few more books. "I know this is a lot of information to take in, but we have to start from the beginning. We will explain everything in due time. For now, I think it's important that we get you up to speed on the original American history so that you have a basic understanding of how the alternate timelines can be affected."

Todd exhaled loudly and stood up. "Look, not that this alternate universe-timeline stuff isn't cool and all, but is there anything to eat around here?"

Albrecht smiled and handed him the stack of books he had accumulated. He shuffled through them; they were a variety of nineteenth century American history and fictional Westerns. Todd looked confused at the selection of books bestowed upon him.

"Come on, let's get you something to eat," Albrecht said as he led him to the door, gesturing for Kara to join them.

Todd followed Albrecht and Kara down the hall, carrying the stack of books like a kid going to school. They came to a door which opened automatically. Inside was a very clean breakroom with a few tables set out around the right side of the room. On the left was a large kitchen which looked to be straight out of the USS Enterprise. On the far wall was another door. Albrecht opened it and motioned down the hallway, which was lined with enough rooms to house the thirty- or forty-some people who appeared to occupy the facility.

"The first room on the right is yours; the kitchen is fully stocked so feel free to grab something." He walked over to the other entrance and paused as the door slid open "Get some rest. We have a lot more to discuss in the morning ... and it gets a lot crazier." He grinned and left the room.

Kara walked over to the kitchen and pulled a mug off one of the hooks above the sink as Todd set the stack of books on one of the tables. She poured herself a cup of coffee while Todd sat down at the table, rubbing his eyes and then resting his elbows on the table.

"You should eat something," Kara said as she stirred her coffee and tapped the spoon on the brim of the mug.

He leaned back in his chair, his heavy eyes staring at the ceiling. The bandages on his jaw and forehead itched and his body ached.

He unzipped the flight suit slightly to look at his beaten body beneath. His entire lower abdomen was wrapped as well as his right shoulder.

"So ... how bad was I when you guys found me?" he asked.

Kara looked surprised at the question. She walked over, holding the cup with both hands. She stood opposite him, appearing nervous to sit. "I'm no doctor ... but from what I understand, your injuries were quite severe. You had lost a large amount of blood, and there was doubt whether they would be able to stabilize you."

Todd looked down at his hands folded on the table.

"What happened to you?" she asked.

He was reluctant at first to discuss the details of his classified mission, but being that these people had known where to find him, had saved his life, and possibly had the ability to travel back in time made operational security seem irrelevant.

"My ... uh ... my team and I were tasked with a reconnaissance mission in the capital," he said, sadness present in his voice. "The communists controlled the airspace in that area so we couldn't just fly a drone over. We needed to get visual confirmation on a suspected large enemy presence in the city. They were trying to establish a permanent stronghold. There was word that over five hundred thousand communist troops would be massing on the East Coast by the end of the week." He crossed his arms, resting his elbows on the table. "We inserted the night of the 29th using the Potomac River. From there, we made our way into the city where we used various buildings as urban hide sites. We got visual confirmation on thousands of enemy troops arriving, preparing for an all-out invasion of the country. Destroying them was the only option; however, the obvious lack of air support and their overwhelming size meant we would have to use ORMs. But there were a lot of civilians still left in the city, and ..."

Kara could tell that it had been a traumatizing event for him. His eyes danced around the room as he spoke.

He sighed. "We remained undetected throughout the next day, but it all went to shit during our exfiltration the night of the 29th." He paused, stood up, and walked over to the kitchen. He paced briefly and then leaned up against the counter.

Kara said, "It's okay, we don't need to discuss it." She walked over to the door. As it slid open, she stepped out into the hallway, paused and looked back at Todd, who stood staring at the stainless-steel counter top. "I will be in the archive room if you need anything," she said and then turned as the door slid shut.

He remained standing in the kitchen for several minutes. The images of the battle continued to visit him. He quickly scrounged up some food and walked over to the door on the far wall and opened it to the dark hallway. He pressed the switch outside his room, and the door opened.

Todd flicked the switch beside the door jam and the room lit up, and he was surprised to see it looked occupied. A few black bags lay beneath the bed, and clothing was hanging in the open closet. He was about to leave to find a new room but stopped when he noticed a pair of dog tags on the nightstand. He walked over and picked them up; as he did, he noticed a small leather journal. The front cover had the initials "T.Y." stamped into it. He picked it up and studied it. The leather was old and cracked. The spine looked to have been hand sewn. He opened it up and thumbed through the pages, seeing that they were mostly small journal entries and sketches. He was much too tired to read into the notes, but paused when the pages stopped turning at a small black and white photo of a little girl. She looked to be maybe seven or eight. Her bronze skin led him to believe she was from somewhere in Southeast Asia. He flipped the photo over; a message on the back caught his eye. *"You can't change Destiny"* was written in pencil. The handwriting looked all too familiar.

He gazed out the window next to the dresser, watching as the snow was swept up by the relentless winds and blown out into the darkness. He set the journal down and looked at the dog tags. "York, Todd M." was imprinted on the top of them along with his date of birth, gas mask size, and his DOD identification number, which was different than his own. This confused him. Why wouldn't they have the same ID number? Weren't they the same person? He put the tags and the journal down and carefully stripped off his flight suit until he wore only his compression shorts. He looked at himself in the large mirror next to the dresser. Amongst the many bandages were small scabbed-over lacerations and bruises. He gingerly sprawled out on the bed, being careful with his sore body. He looked up at the ceiling, his thoughts turning to his fallen comrades. Rob, in particular. He had met Robert Ackerman during his time in the Operator Training Course (OTC) which was the rite of passage into Delta Force after completing Assessment and Selection. Rob was a hulking six-foot-three, two hundred and thirty pound African American who had spent eight years with Force Recon before making the transition to JSOC. He had been Todd's closest friend for many years, and his death weighed heavily on him.

Todd thought about the incredible information that had been disclosed to him. The possibility of time travel and the ability to change the past. He didn't understand why they had chosen him. It was all overwhelming, yet in a way it brought him a small feeling of hope. Perhaps this was a second chance. To be able to go back to the past and correct your mistakes … it was the type of second chance every man dreamed of.

*   *   *

July 18, 1967

The heat beneath the jungle canopy wafted off the lush plants and clung to my exposed face like glue. Despite the suit's internal cooling system, my body was drenched in sweat.

I sprinted through the jungle towards the sound of screams. I had been monitoring the village for the past few days, I thought the U.S. troops would pass it by as they would any other farming village, but the reports of M16s and M60s in the distance told me otherwise. I ran and slid down a mud chute that dropped me into a creek that led down to the village. The moment my feet splashed into the brown water, bullets cracked around me. I dashed down the winding creek, doing my best to stay low. Trees and vegetation exploded around me and bullets zipped past my head. I finally got to a good position behind a small embankment and tried to figure out who the hell was shooting at me.

The village was only a few hundred meters away on the other side of the ridge to my back. The people shooting at me were no doubt Americans. I had come to recognize the sound of AKs during a long career of fighting individuals wielding Soviet-made weaponry, and these were definitely not 7.62 rounds smacking the dirt. I had to get back to Suong. I had left her with the people in the village a few days prior. I could hear the soldiers to my front maneuvering towards my position. They were yelling at each other in English to push up. I shouldered my rifle and looked through the IR reflex sight. I could see multiple heat signatures. They were now only several meters away.

I couldn't run. It was uphill behind me and the cloaking system was practically useless with the amount of mud and muck caked on the suit's surface ... not to mention my dumb ass had left my helmet in my pack back at my hide sight. They were now almost on me. I shouldered my suppressed rifle and disengaged the safety. It was them or me. I saw the head of the first one and I leveled the sights on him. I squeezed off the shot and the round snapped his head backwards. The men behind him screamed out to him. I felt horrible. His brothers in arms called out to him in horror. I kept my rifle up, waiting for the next few soldiers to enter my field of fire. They began to move in on me, doing their best to confuse me by bounding forwards, alternating their forward movement while laying down suppressive fire. I could see exactly what they were trying to do, and it wasn't going to help them. Every time one would pop his head up, I would shift over, staying in a high knee, keeping my rifle firmly pressed into my shoulder. The recoil was practically nonexistent against the suit's muscular exterior. Remaining in semi auto, I continued to squeeze the trigger, my rounds mostly hitting them in the large metal helmets they wore. It made a sickening smack as it tore through the helmets and then their heads.

After taking out at least six, I dropped down into a low knee and quickly conducted a tac-reload. I had forced myself to practice retaining my empty magazines every time I reloaded. Regardless of whether or not I was in a pinch, it was vital that I didn't leave anything behind during my operations for obvious reasons, considering the lightweight plastic magazines I used were not made until 2018. I continued engaging the American soldiers, the whole time cursing under my breath. I wanted them to fall back, I didn't want to have to kill any more, but they gave me no choice.

THE NEW WORLD

The next morning, he was woken by a knock on the door. Albrecht walked in and Todd sat up, grabbing his folded-up flight suit from beneath the bed and slipping his legs into it.

"How'd you sleep, Todd?" Albrecht asked. He paused, realizing he had barged in without asking for Todd's permission. "Oh, sorry, I'll come back. Keep forgetting it's a different you." He chuckled.

Todd looked up at him as he put on a pair of Salomon hiking shoes from under the bed. "It's okay, man. You're good," he said as he zipped the flight suit up to chest level.

Todd looked around the room; the sun shone brightly through the window, lighting the room. Albrecht picked up the journal that had been sitting on the nightstand and looked at it for a moment. Todd could see the sadness in his eyes.

"What was the other me like?" Todd asked, resting his elbows on his legs.

Albrecht handed him the journal. Todd took it from him hesitantly. He looked at the cover, then back at Albrecht.

"He was a good man … and my friend," Albrecht said, looking down at the white tile floor.

Todd stood up. "Was?"

Albrecht put his hands in the pockets of his lab coat as he leaned up against the wall opposite Todd. "I don't think I will ever understand why he did what he did. I wish I could but …"

Curiosity spread over Todd's face. Throughout the night, he had pondered about the previous "him." He had never asked what had come of him. He obviously had removed himself from the original timeline in order to alter the future, but what had happened to him? Part of Todd was afraid to ask; the possibility that his other-self had been killed was the most probable possibility, which would make sense why they had returned to the future to retrieve Todd, but why all the secrecy, why not just tell him?

Albrecht sat down in the chair at the small writing desk opposite the bed. He crossed his arms and looked up at Todd, who stood with an eager expression.

"It all started when we sent him to Vietnam." He rocked slightly in the chair as he spoke, gazing out the window into the blinding white of the rising sun reflecting off the snow.

"The Vietnam War was the beginning of the end not only for the country, but it seemed to be the breaking point for York himself. The very war we created through our actions in the early stages of the Cold War; killing Stalin, and then Kennedy ... it was like we got ourselves out of one mess just to step into another."

Todd sat back down on the bed "I ... or York, killed Kennedy?" he asked.

Albrecht nodded. "Like Kara said last night, if Kennedy hadn't died, the Cold War would have escalated much quicker into WWIII. It was a necessary act of judgment in order to save millions of lives. It was my call. York was just following orders. Looking back on it now, I fear we may have made a mistake. Maybe there was another way ... maybe we could have resolved the issue abroad." Albrecht looked troubled. It was obvious he felt somewhat responsible for the state of the world.

A silence swept through the room as a million questions came to mind. He was about to speak to break the silence, but Albrecht did it for him.

"I want you to read that," he said, nodding towards the journal. "He left it here ... for his replacement, I assume. Something tells me he didn't foresee us finding you. I need you to get inside his head." Albrecht grinned. "Shouldn't be too hard, you are the same person after all." He stood and walked to the door. "Come on, Todd, we've got a lot to cover."

Todd followed Albrecht into the break room. There were about ten or so people eating breakfast and chatting quietly, but the room fell silent when Todd entered. Albrecht ended the awkward moment. "Good morning, everyone," he said cheerfully.

Several good mornings were returned, then one of the individuals approached Albrecht holding a tablet and brought something to his attention. Todd leaned in slightly to eavesdrop on their conversation. From what he gathered, the individual was informing the professor of a "recent update to timeline relevant to current work schedule." Most likely pertaining to Todd's upcoming task, he thought.

"Will you excuse me, Todd, I've got some important matters to attend to. I'll see you in a bit," Albrecht said. "Grab some breakfast." Then he walked out of the break room with the other individual.

Todd looked around and spied Kara at a table in the corner. She sat with a dark-skinned girl whose long black hair was pulled back into a ponytail. Todd moved past a group having a whispered conversation—no doubt about him—and made his way to the fridge. He grabbed a juice out of the door rack and then made himself a bowl of oatmeal. He glanced back into the break room at the several groups of individuals speaking quietly, many of whom broke eye contact at the sight of him.

He walked over to Kara's table and could hear she was talking about something history-related with the other woman. He held out his juice and oatmeal. "Mind if I sit here?"

Kara looked startled at the sight of him. A big smile broke over the other girl's face.

"Todd!" she said with excitement as she stood up and hugged him.

Todd looked at Kara in confusion.

The girl finally let go and stepped back. "It's so good to see you again, I mean … I know it's not the same you … but still it's so good to see you!"

Todd smiled slightly. "It's nice to meet you."

Kara interrupted. "Todd, this is Amber Hassan. She's a tech specialist here."

Amber smiled. "Tech specialist and your BFF!"

Todd grinned. "Thanks … can never have too many of those."

The two sat down at the table, Todd practically inhaling the oatmeal while Amber talked nonstop about her recent breakthrough with something called "IHD12," which from what he could make out was some kind of helmet. Kara and Amber chatted on for several minutes while Todd left to grab two more bowls of oatmeal. On his return the second time, Amber turned with excitement as if she was meeting him for the first time all over again.

"Todd!" she said with a big smile on her face. "Have you and Kara had time to … catch up at all?"

Kara shot Amber a look of anger mixed with embarrassment. Todd could see the redness in her cheeks. Looking back at Todd, she appeared to mask her embarrassment with a look of slight annoyance.

"Todd, I was the other Todd's … I suppose you could say counselor. Besides giving him detailed briefs on the time periods which he would travel to, I also made it my personal duty to monitor his mental health."

Todd scratched the stubble on his cheek. "So, I've gathered that the 'other me' wasn't exactly a charmer in his last days, am I right?"

Sadness came over them, and the two girls looked at each other and then at the table.

"It wasn't his fault," Kara said softly.

Todd looked at her intensely. "What do you mean?"

"I don't think right now is the best time to talk about it," she said as she finished off her glass of orange juice and set it down on her plate.

"I think you can tell me," Todd said impatiently.

People began leaving the break room, no doubt heading out into the main floors to begin their work day. Kara stood up with her plate and glass and headed over to the sink. Amber remained sitting next to Todd.

"It's so good to see you, Todd," Amber said, placing her hand on Todd's. "It's good to see you like this."

Todd looked at her and smiled. "I don't know you, but … I can tell you and I are going to be good friends."

Amber smiled. "It's good to have my badass Navy SEAL back."

Todd tilted his head in confusion. "SEAL?"

Amber rolled her eyes and smiled. "Aw, stupid time travel stuff … messes up everything."

Todd chuckled. "So the other Todd was a frogman, huh?"

The door slid open next to the kitchen and Albrecht stepped in. "Ready, Todd?" he asked.

Todd stood up, saying goodbye to Amber. As he walked out with Albrecht, he glanced over at Kara but she stood in the kitchen, her back to him.

The two men made their way down the main hall and stopped at the door labeled R&D. Albrecht punched in a five-digit code. There was a slight beeping noise, then the door slid open. The lab was occupied by a few workers, most of whom were gathered around the tables near the center of the room which had a variety of weaponry laid out. Albrecht walked up to one of the individuals in the corner who was manning a work station with a holographic monitor.

Todd stopped at a table where an overweight man in a lab coat seemed to be putting the final touches on a small microchip with a soldering needle. On the table next to him was a .300 Blackout rifle. It was a high-end AR-style weapon popular among the Operators in his unit. Todd noticed it was quite unique in its design. The outer skin of the rifle was also unique, as it resembled a carbon fiber weave.

A large hand presented itself to Todd. "How do you do, Mr. York," said the thick man in the white coat. He had a scruffy beard that extended down his neck and nearly met with his chest hair protruding from the collar of his Glock t-shirt.

Todd returned the greeting. "I'm guessing like everyone else you're well acquainted with me already?"

The man smiled. "Not you, but the other York, sure. Name's Kevin Burns. I'm the weapons expert here."

Todd nodded with a slight grin. "My kind of guy."

Kevin crossed his arms over the large gut that stuck out of his lab coat. "Not sure what they will be having you do this time around, but I can assure you, you will be well prepared to utilize any weaponry that you encounter during your missions." He looked over at the table and grabbed a heavily modified Sig Sauer pistol off the table "So in your timeline ... you still with DEVGRU?" He was referring to the other name for Seal Team Six.

Todd shook his head "No, CAG."

Kevin looked intrigued at this news. He placed the Sig back

down on the table and picked up a 1911 that lay beside the rifle. "As far as I know, you D-boys still pack the good old 1911, am I right?" he said as he racked the slide back on the pistol and locked it into place using the slide lock. He looked in the chamber, then handed it to Todd.

Todd smiled as he held the pistol. "Some of us do."

The 1911 had been his sidearm of choice for as long as he could remember. The gun had saved his life on multiple occasions during his time with the unit, proving to be one of the most reliable weapons he had ever used. Though it had been heavily modified with a custom-threaded barrel, built-in light and laser in the lower receiver, and a small flip-up tritium reflex sight on the rear of the slide, which when flipped down became standard iron sights, the overall mechanics of the weapon had remained basically the same since its birth nearly a hundred and twenty years ago. Not even John M. Browning himself would have been able to predict that his legendary firearm would stay in service until the end of time.

Todd gripped the pistol, his hands wrapped around its carbon fiber grip comfortably. He found an empty side of the room and presented the weapon up, aiming down the sights. His firing hand thumb rested atop the safety, his other thumb just below, both oriented towards his target. The fingers of his left hand rested in between the fingers on his right. Making sure he was applying equal pressure on the grip, he moved his finger from the lower receiver down to the trigger. Without budging, he disengaged the safety with his thumb and squeezed the trigger. The hammer clunked forward without any rattle in the gun, and the sights didn't budge from his target which was a small warning sign on the wall.

Todd smiled. "Perfect."

Albrecht approached the two men. "Todd," he said, motioning him over.

Todd racked the slide and clicked the ambidextrous safety back up. He handed the pistol to Kevin, who was smiling ear to ear.

Todd joined Albrecht, who stood beside Amber. She was adjusting an armored suit worn by a silver manikin. Two metal pillars with lights running down the insides were on each side of the manikin, illuminating the complex outfit. The majority of the suit was made up of large flexible armor plates that resembled the human muscular system. The plates were separated by a tough nylon-type material that was located on most of the joints and between the plates. A system of small transparent cables or wires about a centimeter in diameter ran down the extremities of the body on the edges of the plates. On the wrist was a dual connection port for something that its wearer would attach to most likely operate the entire system. Over all, between the weapons and the suit, the equipment they had at this facility was far more advanced than what Todd had used back at his unit.

Albrecht placed his hands in his pockets. "Well, I'm sure you've been wondering … this is it."

Todd looked at the suit, then back at Albrecht. "This is what?" he said in confusion.

"The key to the past," Albrecht said as his eyes scanned over the complex skin of the black suit.

"This?" Todd said, pointing at the suit. "This is the time machine?"

Albrecht turned to him and nodded. "Yes … not what you were expecting, I'm sure."

Todd chuckled. "Well I wasn't expecting to see a DeLorean parked in the garage … but this definitely is not what I expected. Where's the cape and cowl?"

Albrecht laughed.

"So, you just put the suit on and press a button?" Todd asked with a look of disbelief.

Albrecht looked at Amber, who was holding a clipboard in front of her.

"Essentially yes … but there is a little more that goes into it. The suit itself is not what produces the energy necessary to initiate the sequence, it is these cables that line it," she said as she pointed to the thin transparent cables that ran down the sides of the armor plates on the suit like veins. "These cables, when activated, create a massive amount of energy which creates a window. This window … is what some might call a wormhole. Together, the cables generate a spherical energy field with a radius of about three meters. Which when directed by the MTX sends whatever is within that radius to whatever year specified."

"This wormhole … how does it work?" Todd asked, scratching

his chin.

Amber brushed a stray hair behind her ear, "Man first began to grasp the idea of time travel when we first left Earth. It was discovered that time in space was slower than time down on Earth. I'm sure you've heard of the theory of relativity. It was theorized for many years that this could be a small example of time travel, but that notion was swept under the rug. Until 2015, that is." She looked over at Albrecht, who grinned and stepped towards the suit.

"I had been working for the Department of Defense for almost six years when I made a breakthrough in my studies in quantum physics. In late 2015, I was working on a machine in Virginia that was used to study the effects of accelerating protons many times faster than they already travel and colliding them at a single point. This machine was similar in purpose to a machine in Switzerland known as the Large Hadron Collider. Only ours was one hundred times smaller." He chuckled. "We discovered that the collisions made by the protons formed strange energy pockets which we assumed were black holes. They were open only for a small period of time and were about the size of a marble." He pushed his glasses to the bridge of his nose with his middle finger. "We are talking milliseconds that these things were open. So, the idea was to calculate the proper speed and the correct number of protons needed to create a large enough reaction upon collision in order to form a reasonably sized black hole. A few months later, we found it, when I received a letter on my desk describing the exact calculations to create a sufficient-sized wormhole. The letter had been signed by myself a year in the future."

Todd rubbed his hand over his mouth and looked at the suit. "That's incredible." He frowned. "Wait, you say the colliding protons generate massive amounts of energy, right? So, what about the explosion?"

"Similar to an aircraft breaking the sound barrier, there is an audible boom when the wearer initiates the sequence. But the process itself is practically seamless to our perception ... and painless, of course."

Todd nodded at his semi grasp of the science behind it. He was immediately beginning to regret asking about the science of the technology, as he was finding himself daydreaming through the briefing.

"I'm sure you are familiar with micro imaging cloaking tech? Being in a Tier One unit and all, am I right?" Amber said.

Todd nodded, staring at the suit. "Huh … oh yeah, I'm familiar with it, I've used it before but I've always thought the tech was a little too ahead of its time. Seemed like every time we used it, it wasn't as handy as one would think because our missions are usually conducted at night and I'm hiding behind something anyway. Being somewhat invisible just made it harder to keep track of my team."

Amber appeared slightly insulted by this. "Well I can assure you that the tech in this suit is top of the line. When activated, and the user is completely still, there is less than five percent image displacement. So you don't see that effect that looks similar to looking through an odd-shaped vase of water, and with the armor plating," she said, pointing at the many black plates, "you are nearly bullet proof as well."

Todd nodded, fascinated. "So what controls it all?"

Amber walked over to a small cell-phone-looking device and picked it up off a table. She walked back to Todd and handed it to him.

"This device controls the amount of energy put out by the cables. The more power put out, the farther back in time you go … to put it bluntly," she said. "Specifying exactly what year you intend to travel to is just a conversion of the calculations for the wormhole. Selecting the year is really just determining how long the wormhole is open. Because the calculations are so expansive, and the time frame in which it is open is so fast, we cannot specify the exact month or day you travel to. You merely arrive in the past at the same time and day … if that makes sense."

Amber made a sphere shape with her hands. "Whatever is within the radius of the explosion is sent into the wormhole. This makes the whole traveling process a much-planned event. With the possibility of sending pieces of the environment along with you back in time, not to mention the displacement theory … going back in time can be extremely dangerous."

Todd shrugged. "Displacement theory?"

Albrecht stepped into the conversation once more. "Well it's not a theory anymore, but basically it is the idea that going back in time to a random location could prove to be catastrophic, considering that the place where you might initiate it may have undergone major geological transformations between the time span from where you are and where you're going."

Todd raised an eyebrow in confusion. "Can you dumb that down for me?"

Albrecht grinned. "Okay, let's say you are standing in a desert in present time, and you initiate the sequence. Whatever year you travel to, there could have been a damn tree where you are standing."

Todd swallowed. "Shit."

Amber laughed. "Don't worry though, we have found the best method for initiating the sequence."

"Which is?" Todd asked.

Albrecht looked at him. "Well I believe you Delta Force guys use it quite a bit to get into places you're not supposed to be."

Todd smiled. "You mean HALO?"

Albrecht nodded, "At thirty thousand feet you have more than enough time to initiate the sequence, which mind you is only a split second, then land at a safe location. This also allows you to get into places unseen. Which is sort of important when you are wearing millions of dollars of high tech equipment and you come flying into some ancient civilization." He shook his head and laughed. "I don't even want to think about the headache of resetting a mistake like that again."

"You mean that's happened?" Todd asked.

Albrecht let out a sigh. "Let's just say there is a reason why we chose to send elite military operators into the past, and not clumsy scientists."

A smile broke over Todd's face.

Albrecht walked over to an empty desk and sat down. He tapped the screen of the monitor and it began powering up. Todd pulled up a chair opposite the desk.

"So, I get how you go back in time but … how do you get back to the present?"

Albrecht nodded. "Good question. We were wondering the same thing for a long time, and it ended up being about as stupid of an answer as you could get."

Humor spread across Todd's face. "Which was?"

Albrecht chuckled. "Jump off a bridge."

Todd leaned back in his chair. "You talking about base jumping … or committing suicide?"

Albrecht grinned. "At first we thought base jumping would be the best bet. With modern parachute technology, it's not hard to carry around the retractable one-hundred-square-foot chute during an operation and deploy it for extraction; keeping in mind that base jumping in itself is quite a gamble with a lot of unpredictable variables. So, on one operation in Vietnam, York lost his chute in an explosion in Hué City. He radioed us, informing us of what happened. We were worried that he wouldn't be able to make it back, but the clever bastard did the simplest thing that totally made us rethink our methods."

"Which was …?" Todd asked.

Albrecht smiled big. "He hopped up in the air and pressed the button. When he came back down he was in present day Vietnam standing in the middle of a street."

Todd laughed and shook his head. "I could see me trying something like that."

"Once we get the Operator back to the present, we then just simply pick him up," Albrecht said as he typed away.

Todd leaned back in his chair and watched the workers around the room as they tampered with devices and took notes. He studied the various individuals; most of them besides Kevin appeared to be in their mid-twenties, most likely right out of college.

"How did you get all these people out here?" he asked.

Albrecht glanced around at the studious individuals, and a slight smile broke over his face. "Most of them were my students at the University I taught at when I wasn't being the government's favorite lab rat. They all showed such great potential; they were all promising minds for the future." His face turned stern. "A future that had no place for great minds, or good people."

Todd could see the sadness in his eyes. He ignored the fact that the professor had danced around the question. "You were there, weren't you? You were in the original timeline."

Albrecht nodded. "Yes, in the original timeline the war began in

December of 2019. We were safe from it for about four years. I was fortunate enough to have a way out, however, when things got really bad. The key to salvation. Others ... were not so fortunate," he said, shaking his head.

Todd leaned forward and motioned to the students around the room. "So you saved all these people?"

Albrecht rubbed his eyes then placed his glasses back on his face. "You can't save everyone, Todd ... but yeah, I promised I would take care of them."

Todd pondered on this for a moment. It was obvious there was something Albrecht wasn't willing to share. Perhaps he had lost someone dear to him. Todd found it somewhat depressing that even with the power of time travel, someone would still be saddened by the past.

Kara walked into the R&D lab holding a large folder and clipboard. She looked at Todd, then at Albrecht. Albrecht turned to her and nodded.

"Alright Todd, time for you and Kara to get reacquainted," he said as he turned to his monitor and began typing away on the keyboard displayed on the touch screen table.

Kara was wearing a white turtleneck sweater, and her long bangs were brushed back and clipped above her ear. As Todd approached her, he realized his bandaged chest was showing. He zipped up his flight suit to collar bone level.

"Follow me, Mr. York," she said softly as she turned and walked out into the main hallway.

He followed her past the large windows, past the break room and restrooms, to the very end of the main corridor where a staircase turned left at the landing and led to another large hallway. They walked past several doors; most of them appeared to be single offices. At the very end of the hall, Kara entered a code into a key pad and the metal door slid open. Inside was a large, carpeted room, dimly lit by a few LED lamps. The floor dropped down a foot near the far wall and presented enormous windows that stretched from the base of the floor up, curving towards the middle of the ceiling. In the center of the room was a large pillar which seemed to separate the room into what was both her office and her bedroom. She walked over to her desk and set down the folder.

Todd paced around the room for a moment. Her bed was against the far wall, neatly made. Next to it was a nightstand with a picture on it, but he couldn't make out the individual in the photo because of the glare from the lamp above it. He restrained himself from nosing around any further.

"You have quite the view here," he said, looking out the massive windows into the white landscape outside. It appeared as though he were on another planet as the setting looked so surreal.

She turned in her chair. "Professor Albrecht insisted that I have this room. I feel selfish to have the best room in the facility, but I must say it is well worth it when the Northern Lights are out."

"I bet," he said as he turned and made his way over to the desk, where he pulled up a chair. "So, what exactly are we going to talk about?"

"You," she said as she powered on her monitor and opened the folder. "Shall we start from the beginning? Most of the information I have from the previous York should be accurate; however, considering you two took different career paths in the military, there is no telling how much is different." She scanned through the documents which appeared to be everything from his medical records and financial records, all of which were side by side with York's personal information. Todd noticed the military service records beside each other, York's being labeled "Department of the Navy." Todd nodded and she began reading out loud the information on each page.

"You were born Todd Michael York, October 3rd, year 2000, in Seattle, Washington?"

"Yes."

"Your parents were Michael and Ann York?"

"Yes."

She paused for a moment, then straightened in her chair. "Your father … you had a difficult relationship with him during your childhood?"

Todd answered slowly, "Uh … yeah, what little time I did see him; he wasn't exactly the fatherly type."

"Can you clarify?" she asked, scribbling notes.

"Honestly, I don't really remember him that well. When he wasn't slapping me and my mother around he was sleeping at some bar. I found out later that he had been in deep with drug dealers when he was a kid living in Miami. This information was brought to my attention during the extensive background checks conducted on me when I was trying out for CAG. I don't think he was into drugs anymore when I was around, but I guess you never really can escape your past. From what I could tell, my mother had been his way out; she opened his eyes and helped him out of that life. Unfortunately, I never saw the 'good side' that my mother often spoke of. Finally, she gave him the slip and took me to Colorado. I never saw him again."

Kara looked up at him, then back down at her notes. She continued writing down something. "Can you tell me about your mother?"

"She was kind and caring. She was no saint, but she was a good mother, and I seemed to be the only thing she cared about." He paused and thought hard, trying to recall as much as he could about her, but he seemed to be at a loss for words. "She passed away when I was a year into my military career. She was killed in a car accident one night on her way back from work."

Kara looked saddened by this. She shook her head and kept writing. "Tell me about your military career."

Todd leaned back in his chair. "Jeez, uh, well, I joined the Army in 2018. After basic training, I went to Ranger assessment, then went to the 75th Ranger Regiment. I spent nearly six years in the 'Bat usually pulling security for Delta Force. We fought the early communist movements in Eastern Europe. Before all that, we did a lot of work in Africa." He rocked in his chair, looking up at the ceiling as he recalled his history.

"When did you become a member of Combat Applications Group?" she asked.

He exhaled "20 … 2023, I passed selection and began OTC. I became fully active the next year. After that, I deployed … everywhere."

"How do you like being a soldier?" she asked in a way that seemed as if she were asking out of her own curiosity rather than to evaluate him.

Todd took in a deep breath through his nose, then let it out quickly. "It's not a very rewarding life."

"Why?" she asked gingerly.

"The biggest payoff at the end of each day is usually self-gratitude. You spend your whole career itching towards an end state, whether that be some high-speed unit, a qualification, or some higher billet. And when you finally get there, you are reminded that nothing is ever what it seems and that you are never satisfied."

"Then why do you do it?"

"I ask myself the same question every day, and honestly … I can't answer it. I guess it's just what I was meant to be. The only thing I was ever good at."

Kara looked troubled by his explanation. "Friends?"

He rubbed his forehead. "Sooner or later you part ways with them."

"How so?" she asked.

"They either move on, get out, or die right next to you. In the end the job leaves you the exact way you started out …"

Todd and Kara both simultaneously said the last word, "Alone."

He looked up to find her eyes locked on his. He looked back down at the table. She continued with her questions.

"So, when did World War III begin?"

He scratched the stubble below his jaw. "Officially, it began in the summer of 2030. Unofficially … it started several years earlier."

"What do you mean?" she asked

"For the regular military and the U.S. citizens, 2030 is when we started fighting them, but I was killing Chinese and Russian soldiers as early as 2025."

Her sharp eyes moved from the desk to his and cut through him; whatever arrogance he felt from relaying his extensive military past was immediately obliterated by her potent gaze. It felt like she was looking into his soul, through all the boasting and temerity. She was the type of person it would be impossible to lie to; if her eyes didn't get you, her pure kindness and almost childlike sensibility would. Her confidence was a result of her intelligence; what she lacked in sociability she made up for with her crisp, educated demeanor.

"How are you feeling since the event in D.C.?" she asked

He didn't want to talk about it, truthfully, but he didn't want to insult her by not letting her do her job. "It's not exactly easy seeing your friends dead around you, and feeling somewhat responsible."

She stopped writing, set down her pen, and looked at him. "It's not your fault … you can't control who lives or dies," she said.

Todd didn't look up from the table. He didn't want to be comforted, he just wanted to fix what had happened. "Hmm, coming from the people who can travel back in time. You want to know something funny?" He quickly breathed out through his nose and shook his head. "I woke up last night … and for a moment truly believed I was dead … that this was the afterlife and that my mind had created this entire situation. You know what finally convinced me that this was actually all real? If I were dead, why would I be doing the same exact shit I have been doing my whole life? Answering these types of questions, receiving briefings, training … I may not be dead, but I think I am destined to do this type of thing forever."

Kara looked at him intensely. She felt something gnawing at her within; there was so much she wanted to tell him, but she feared what it could do. The man in front of her was not the man she had known for the past five years. He didn't bear the same level of mental and physical scars, but she feared that soon, he would. That was the last thing she wanted for him.

"Does this mean you do not want to help us?"

Todd sighed. "I don't even know what you want me to do exactly, but I don't really see any other option."

THE COMPANY MAN

Todd walked into the break room and grabbed a soda out of the fridge. He turned to see a man sitting at one of the tables who was obviously different from everyone else.

He was grizzled-looking and tall with a muscular frame. He lounged in his chair, legs straight in front of him, one resting atop the other, wearing a familiar brand of hiking shoes that were popular among Special Operators. He was drinking a cup of coffee and reading something on a touch screen tablet.

"How you hold'n up, man?" he said. His eyes didn't leave the transparent screen which displayed several paragraphs of text.

"I don't think we've met," Todd replied.

The man set the tablet down on the table and stood, extending his hand towards Todd. "My name's Steven Bohden. I'm the one who extracted you from D.C."

Todd's face displayed his surprise. "So you're the one I have to thank ... I really appreciate it."

Todd had been wondering who saved his life that night. He shook Bohden's hand and then cracked open the soda and drank nearly the entire can in one tip. The carbonated drink was sweet and brought him back to reality.

"How are you handling all this?" Bohden asked, crossing his muscular arms. He appeared to be in his late forties, having gray hair near his temples. He wore a black polo shirt and coyote cargo pants, an oddly familiar fashion sense to the government and contractor types that Todd often worked with.

"It's a lot to take in, but I think I'm handling it as good as anyone could."

Bohden sat back down in his chair. "So CAG huh?" he said with a grin. "Never took you for the Army type. The last guy was about as SEAL as they come. He was with Development Group." His deep voice carried a weight to it that gave him a menacing presence.

"Yeah, I was surprised when they told me that. I had never even considered the Navy when I was younger. I'm not sure how that difference happened," Todd said as he took a seat at the adjacent table.

He began studying Bohden's appearance and demeanor. "You're no scientist, and to be able to find me in D.C. in the middle of a war zone … and survive, would have required at the very least some sort of training."

Bohden nodded. "No, I'm no scientist. I'm with Langley … or, at least I used to be. I was a paramilitary operative during the early days of the War; that's when I met a brilliant scientist who had just made the greatest scientific breakthrough in the history of mankind. I then became the CIA liaison for this project."

Todd tilted his head. "So … is this facility run by the CIA, or at least funded by them? Because I thought the CIA was disbanded by Kennedy in the original timeline."

Bohden snickered. "Well it was, but when you shatter something into a million pieces, chances are eventually those pieces are going to come together. It wasn't until 1978, during the Carter Administration, that the need for a covert agency was once again seen as a necessary asset in order to combat a new type of enemy."

"How do you guys get all the tech? How do you sustain the place, the people?" Todd asked, motioning around the room.

Bohden sipped his coffee and licked his lips. "Let's just say we're not exactly a law-abiding organization. Much like the CIA, we do what we must do to succeed and survive. So, if we have to visit the future or the past every once in a while and grab resources from various places around the world, we do it."

Todd raised an eyebrow and stood up. "Well, I guess you do what you have to in the apocalypse." He walked over to the door that led to the rooms but stopped when Bohden spoke.

"I'll be seeing you around. Do your best to get rested and back in shape; we have some important matters to attend to very soon. We're going to need your help."

Todd nodded with a raised eyebrow, somewhat irritated with Bohden's apparent lack of patience towards his recovery. He had just survived a traumatizing event and was already being prepped for what felt like a deployment work-up. The door closed behind him as he went to his room.

Todd sat on his bed, looking out the window. He took in what he had learned that day. He still was in disbelief. The whole situation was surreal, but he had a good feeling about Albrecht and the students. Todd had a knack for spotting people who were phony early on. He could tell this was a good bunch. The only one he was unsure about was his new acquaintance, Bohden. Maybe he was a little pre-judgmental of him because of his lack of trust towards the Agency. He had been hung out to dry on several occasions by CIA guys like Bohden during operations in Africa and Europe. Todd would keep his guard up around him, but he would also give him a chance. Like the rest of the people here, the man was trapped in an alternate timeline, hiding from his future. Chances were he had cut all ties with the CIA, and possibly everyone and everything he knew, much like the rest of the individuals here.

During his briefings that day, Todd had been informed that the year he currently resided in was 2016. This information was enough to make his head spin. The facility was literally hiding from the future in the North Pole. Todd continued to try and wrap his head around the multiple timeline situation. Since it was the year 2016, it meant there were now three Todd Yorks in existence. York, the original, if he was indeed still alive. Todd, himself; and a 16-year-old Todd York attending high school in Colorado.

Todd was about to lay down when he noticed the journal sitting on the nightstand. He stared at it for a moment, then picked it up. He opened it to one of the early entries.

November 22, 1963

The cheers of the crowd escalated in the distance, which meant the time was drawing near. The warm Texas weather was beginning to get on my nerves, or perhaps it was my own eagerness. Amber had just put in the new cooling system in the suit, but I think too much of her attention went to the upper body.

My groin was on fire. I felt like I was sitting in a pool of my own sweat. It didn't matter anymore though; I had been sitting on the roof of the book depository for the past twelve hours and it was about to pay off. I checked and rechecked my weapon.

For this op, I'd chosen the suppressed 308 semi-automatic, courtesy of Kev. I wasn't planning on missing, but having a few extra rounds in the magazine would come in handy if the Secret Service somehow caught on to me (but the chances of that were slim to none, plus I'd have that dipshit downstairs to draw their attention). The new improvements on the cloaking system were ten times that of the tech I had used back at ST6. If it hadn't been for the impressive tech, I would have never agreed to do this op. I didn't like that it was midday, but Kara had explained that after Lee Harvey Oswald's attempt on this day, his security tightened up exponentially for the remainder of his time in office.

Kevin had applied an outer coating of the micro imagining system on the DMR, which made it almost as invisible as I was. Although it was extremely effective, I had to make sure to keep my rifle attached to me at all times so that I didn't lose it. I could hear the motorcade now. I looked back down the road to the L-shaped intersection.

I could see the black vehicles and police bikes rounding the corner. The sidewalks were filled with civilians waving American flags and cheering. The cheers grew louder as the vehicles came closer. I checked the cable lanyard on my belt; the small carabineer was set to release in thirty seconds once I began putting tension on the system. I pulled the line out a few inches, ensuring there were no obstructions to keep it from letting out slack. I did a few last checks on my gear, making sure everything was still attached to me. I wore a chest rig on the outside of the suit, which carried spare mags and a few extra gadgets courtesy of the boys and girls at the facility. I also wore a lightweight climbing harness which carried my side arm, and I had the lanyard system on my lower back. Thirty seconds and he would be in the right spot.

I did a chamber check really quick and shouldered the weapon. Although the targeting system displayed in the visor of my helmet was extremely effective, I preferred the old-fashioned way. My rifle was equipped with a 20-power scope that automatically made adjustments based on range and wind.

Twenty seconds. He was lucky he got away with riding with no top on the first time. If Oswald had been worth a damn the first time around, I wouldn't even need to be here.

He was worthless as a sniper, but he'd end up proving his value when he took the rap for the assassination. The percussive sound of my time jump exit would pass as an un-suppressed gunshot. They'd be all over Oswald before he even had a chance to scratch.

Ten seconds. I glanced back and could see the open top Lincoln with the six individuals inside it. His wife was wearing all pink, and I knew she was sitting next to him. It would make it easier to acquire my target. The limo was now on the final stretch of the road. I pressed the rifle tight into my shoulder and peered through the scope. The crosshairs danced on his head. He wasn't making any drastic movements that complicate the shot.

I waited for a lull. Once he stopped waving to the crowd, I let out a smooth breath and squeezed the trigger.

The round barely made a sound as it left the suppressor, but it hit a little lower than I had intended. FUCK!

The other people in the car could tell something was up. He was hunched over and his wife was at his side. It would be only moments before they realized he had been shot and the limo would take off.

I leveled the crosshairs on him once more, this time taking extra time to use all the fundamentals. I ensured there was no scope shadow by adjusting my cheek weld. I rotated my shoulders forward, ensuring my body had complete control over the weapon system. Using the very tip of my trigger finger, I squeezed the trigger. The round hit him in the head, erupting a pink mist. A kill shot no doubt. I could hear Oswald beneath me cranking out multiple rounds with his Carcano rifle.

He'd take the heat just like he had the first time, only now they would pin him with actually killing the man rather than just attempting. I didn't stop to see how it panned out; I'm sure it would be easy to find the event on the internet back in the future.

I slung my weapon to my back and sprinted to the east side of the roof. Reaching back, I pulled out the line on the cable lanyard and looped it around a steam pipe that stuck up from the roof. I locked the carabineer to the line. The locking nut began clicking counter-clockwise and would unlock in thirty seconds. I ran to the side of the building. I did one last check on the line before I leapt off. The retention system hissed as it let out the line and I plummeted to the earth. When I was stable in midair, I pressed the initiation button on the MTX. One moment I was falling towards a small patch of grass on a sunny Texas day, and the next moment I landed in a puddle.

It was now a dark rainy day in the year 2011. I radioed D for extraction. I was pulled out a few hours later. Although the mission was a success, it still bothers me to this day how I missed that first shot. That was some amateur shit. I better spend some time with Kevin and sharpen my long-range skills. From time to time I think about him, and how his death was necessary. I look at the skeletons in his closet to help ease my mind. The man had cheated on his wife multiple times with a celebrity whore. He was a politician; men of that caliber would sell their own mother to stay in office. I think of these things, and it helps me look past it.

TRAINING

The next morning, Todd conversed with several of the workers during breakfast and found most of them to be quite charming individuals who were pleased to speak with him. It was obvious the last York had established good relationships with the men and women at the facility. From what he had gathered, the first York had charisma, and possibly even a sense of humor.

He started the morning talking to Corey, a twenty-nine-year-old Californian who had been one of Albrecht's students for less than a year when they began the project. Todd was amazed to hear of Albrecht's dedication to his students. They were like his family. He and the forty-some-odd men and women were part of the original timeline which saw the war begin in 2019. Albrecht used the technology he and his students had created to escape their dark future, and together they had continued working in an effort to alter the events that forced them into hiding. What started as a conversation with one, became two, then three.

An hour later nearly the entire staff was all in the break room asking questions and sharing jokes with Todd. Kara was not among them. However, it was obvious she was held in high regard among them. Many of the students called her the brains behind the operation. Whenever they were about to send York back to a period of time, they would consult with her about the time frame. She had a Master's degree in American history, which led Todd to wonder how she had gotten caught up with a bunch of theoretical physicists.

None of the students could give him a straight answer as to how Kara had gotten involved in the program.

Amber was among the group, and she seemed excited that Todd was asking about Kara. Kara couldn't have been much older than twenty-five. He didn't think she and the previous York could have had a relationship, or at least he hoped he wouldn't have done such a thing. He was thirty years old. It was his understanding that the other York was also thirty when they found him, and he was with the facility for a little over five years which meant she would have been in her early twenties. Whether they did or didn't have something, he made it a point to keep a distance from her and to keep it strictly professional. He wasn't about to lead the young woman on.

"Has she always been so … apprehensive?" he asked Amber quietly.

"I've known her for six years, and for as long as I can remember she has always been that way."

Todd leaned forward. "Do you people get out much, take some kind of leave?"

She sighed heavily at the question. "No, not really."

Todd shook his head in disbelief. "You're telling me you have been here for six years … in this metal building?"

She nodded and smiled slightly. "I've seen the outside world. I was there when the Communist forces invaded the U.S. If living at Santa's Workshop means I don't have to see people thrown out into the streets and killed ever again, then I'm okay with it."

Todd was amazed by her frankness. "The year is 2016, though. The war isn't going on yet. Are you guys stuck up here?"

Amber looked confused at the question and she shook her head. "Oh God no. We can leave at any time. We choose to stay. I can't tell you how many times the professor has thrown out his offer to have us flown out of here. In a day, we could be anywhere in the world. However, we must take into consideration that we all have a same-self in existence."

"You guys must have one hell of a plane out there," Todd said, pointing in the direction of the front entrance with his thumb.

"Oh yeah, Odin. It's an old military C17 that has been heavily modified. It's not the most glamorous plane, but it gets the job done." She laughed. "It has enough living space for everyone in the facility. It also has the medical bay on board."

"Hmm, so that's where I woke up after you guys found me," Todd said, recalling the events from a few days earlier. "Who flies it?"

"That would be me!" said a man in the kitchen.

Todd turned to see a tall, lanky man leaning against the sink. He was an older fellow who had clearly given up on his receding hairline and was now bald. He wore a flight suit that was zipped down with the sleeves tied around his waist, showing a faded Star Wars t-shirt.

"Name's Shawn Dietrich, but everyone just calls me "D." I'm the pilot, and co-pilot, and pretty much everything else here at the workshop." He winked at Amber. He had a slight Boston accent that had most likely dissipated a bit due to years of immersion amongst the students.

Amber laughed and rolled her eyes. "He's also the group nerd."

"Were you military?" Todd asked, nodding at the flight suit.

"Eh, I was, then I got the hell out and tried putting my degree to proper use. That's how I met Brian."

"How'd you get ahold of Odin?" Todd asked

"Ah … yeah, ask Bohden. He did his G-man thing and pulled one out of his ass before we started the program."

Todd nodded with a slight grin. "You named the plane after the god of war?"

D chuckled. "With the exception of Mr. Grumpy Bohden, we prefer the Odin as the god of wisdom and knowledge."

Everyone remaining in the room let out a laugh. It was now 8:30 a.m. and they began cleaning their dishes and headed out into the work areas. Todd was one of the last. Amber stayed with him. They both washed off their plates and headed to the R&D lab. Amber talked the entire time.

He was met by Albrecht and Kevin in the R&D lab. Kevin bounced from foot to foot in excitement about something.

"What's going on?" Todd asked as he approached them.

"I think it's time you start prepping for your first mission, Todd." Kevin had his hands deep in his pockets. He rocked back on his heels. "We don't have much time to get you ready, so we need to start knocking out the checklist."

"Checklist?" Todd shrugged.

"We can't send you back in time and expect you to just fit in to the local populace." Albrecht made his way over to his desk and tapped the table, making the keyboard to his monitor come to life. "I thought it would be good for you to start with something you might enjoy. Kevin here will assist you."

Todd was led out into the hallway and down to the front entrance where Kevin opened the main door. Todd squinted as the sun reflected off the white surface. Kevin stepped outside and pulled a pair of ballistic sunglasses out of his pocket, handing them to Todd, who was quite familiar with the brand.

"Thanks," he said as he placed them over his eyes.

The clear lenses automatically darkened into a comfortable setting. An Internal Heads up Display in the top left corner of the lens displayed the time, temperature, and elevation. Kevin led Todd to a single-story building next to the main facility. He punched in a code on the keypad beside the door and it slid open. Todd took a moment to look at the exterior of the facility. It looked enormous in the daylight. The outside looked far less state of the art than the inside. On the roof stood a giant metal antenna at least a hundred feet tall. The assembly was supported by cables that ran out diagonally towards the ground several hundred yards around the perimeter of the building. The aircraft hangar was vast and appeared as though it were capable of holding multiple large aircraft. The runway was a single long strip that stretched so far out across the white landscape that it was lost in the glare of the sun. Kevin led Todd over to the second building that lay between the main structure and the hangar.

The two of them stepped inside and were greeted by a rush of warm air. Kevin closed the door behind them and turned on the crisp LED lights. They reflected off the polished grated steel walls of the warehouse. There were two rooms, one on each side of the warehouse. Against the far wall was an indoor shooting range complete with a track system on the ceiling for setting up moving targets. The back wall held a large bullet trap. Next to the shooting range was a large rubber mat with a few weight machines and a bench and a rack filled with dumbbells. Kevin walked over to the room on the right and opened the door. He motioned Todd over with a big smile. Todd stepped into the room as Kevin called out to the automated lights. The room lit up and Todd's jaw dropped.

Three of the walls in the square room had guns displayed from floor to the ceiling. Five large gun racks were in the center of the room and were packed to the brim with every small arm Todd had ever seen. Every year starting from the fourteenth century all the way to the year 2036 was displayed on plaques above the weapons. Beneath each year were up to twenty or thirty weapons. Rifles and long guns were on the racks and walls, and pistols were laid out on the tables below. Kevin led Todd over to the back-left corner to the year "1887" and began pulling weapons off the wall.

"Grab the cart, would ya," he said, nodding at a steel cart by the front door.

Todd pulled it over to the corner and Kevin began stacking nineteenth century firearms on it. The group of weapons consisted of mostly lever action rifles and revolvers. Once there were enough guns to nearly break the wheels of the cart, Kevin pushed it out of the room and down to the shooting range, Todd following closely behind.

"You guys could start up a firearms museum with all that hardware," Todd said as he helped Kevin lay the weapons out on a table next to the firing line.

Kevin chuckled. "Yeah, basically any weapon you can think of from any time period, we got it."

He separated the rifles, shotguns, and pistols. He opened the chambers on all the weapons and began pulling out ammo cans from a large cage against the wall.

"So, the majority of these weapons are small caliber such as .45 and .44." He set the ammo can down and began pulling out boxes of rounds and pouring out the ammunition. "We're not going to waste time and go through every weapon of the time period, but I just want to cover the heavy hitters such as the Colt Peacemaker, the Henry rifle, and a few other popular ones."

Todd looked at the large stack of weapons, and then at Kevin. "Something tells me I'll be traveling to the Wild West."

Kevin grinned. "Well we won't go in depth with them all, but shooting 'em all sounds like a good time, right?"

He handed Todd the Colt Peacemaker. It felt like a brick compared to the side arms he was use to wielding, which were made mostly of polymer. Kevin showed him how to clear and load the weapon. He then showed him the proper revolver carry, where he wrapped the thumb of his support hand over the other.

Todd put about forty rounds through the pistol. It felt primitive compared to the weapons of the future, which could spit out ammo as fast you could pull the trigger. The revolver required the user to cock the hammer back fully before each shot and made Todd really focus on his shooting fundamentals every time he pulled the trigger.

Next was the Henry repeater. Todd started off a little sloppy with it, but less than an hour later he was shooting key holes on the paper target at fifty yards. He also worked on reloading the weapon. Loading one round at a time into the tubular magazine was time-consuming and made him miss the luxury of box magazines. Kevin lent him a leather shooter's belt which had slots for rounds around the entire belt. Todd would crank out every round in the magazine then reload the weapon as fast and as smoothly as possible, doing his best not to go too fast which could make him fumble with the loading process.

The Sharps model 1867, the Spencer Rifle, the Winchester 1866, the Henry repeater, the Schofield Revolver, and the Double Barrel Coach Gun were all covered in great depth. The history of each weapon, disassembly, and troubleshooting procedures were all covered. Todd became especially acquainted with the Schofield Revolver. The break action feature shaved off valuable seconds on his reload times. During each drill, Todd would have Kevin time him while he fired six well-aimed shots, then reloaded the weapon and fired six more. The very last weapon Todd was shown was the 1887 lever action shotgun. He smiled when Kevin handed it to him. He recognized the weapon from seeing Arnold Schwarzenegger wield it on a Harley in Terminator 2. The first thing Todd asked was how to cock it with one hand. Kevin was more than happy to show him the technique known as spin cocking. Todd spent the next hour or so firing large slugs into the paper targets and spin cocking the gun while impersonating Arnold Schwarzenegger.

*   *   *

For the next two weeks, Todd would wake up, eat with the staff, then take part in whatever training Albrecht had organized for the day. After lunch, Todd would head over to the warehouse where he would work out and get some range time with whatever weapon appealed to his interest that day. Albrecht urged him to stick with nineteenth century weapons, but sometimes he just felt like going through a few belts of ammunition with a light machine gun; other times would work on his speed with some of the modern AR style weapons, all the while trading stories and techniques with Kevin, who was always intrigued to learn about his time in Delta.

Todd would spend his evenings in the archive room studying American history with Kara, who was always excited about discussing historical events. It seemed like the future had little meaning to her. On several occasions, she said that the "real greatness in the world lies within the past." Todd didn't necessarily agree with her view, but he enjoyed seeing just how passionate she was about history. The lessons started with a broad scope of the entire nineteenth century.

As the days passed, the lessons became more specific until they were covering individual days that took place in the year 1887. Todd knew this was the year that he would be traveling to, but he still didn't have much of an idea as to why. He tried to squeeze hints out of Albrecht and D during the mess hours, but Albrecht told him, "Bohden will explain everything at the mission briefing in a few days."

Todd didn't like being left in the dark on such things that he would later put his life on the line for. He was beginning to feel like they were withholding information from him because they didn't fully trust him.

The first time Todd put the suit on, earlier in the week, it had taken nearly three hours for Amber to convince him to finally take it off. The suit made the wearer look like a mix between a superhero and a futuristic ninja. When wearing the full-face helmet with it, it made the wearer appear to be inhuman, like a space soldier out of a video game. The cloaking system was also quite addictive. Amber immediately regretted showing him how to activate it when within the first ten minutes of learning how to use the tech, Todd was sneaking around the building scaring the hell out of students. He nearly gave Kevin a heart attack when he snuck up on him in the bathroom.

Todd was also introduced to the Phoenix parachute system. It had a one hundred-foot-square canopy made of a lightweight yet durable material. The suspension lines were a flexible rubbery-like cordage that became rigid when a small electric current ran through them, greatly reducing the chance of entangled lines. After being deployed, the chute could be retracted back into the container using a switch on the hip strap. This made it extremely helpful for reusing the chute on extraction. Unfortunately, it was far too cold in the North Pole, and the winds were extremely unpredictable. So, he wouldn't be able to get any practice jumps in before the actual mission. This made Todd uneasy. He came from a line of work where it required hours upon hours of rehearsals and practice to master something new.

On an op in Africa during his early days with the Unit, his team had gone into a small village dressed as militiamen. They rode in a small Toyota pickup and they spent countless hours practicing piling out of the vehicle and taking up a three-hundred-and-sixty-degree defensive posture around the vehicle. In Todd's opinion, it was attention to detail such as this that separated amateurs from the professionals.

Throughout his time spent at the facility, Todd didn't see much of Bohden. The few encounters he did have with him were usually in the archive room, or briefly during lunch. Bohden seemed to be like most CIA operatives. He was shady, mysterious, and awkward to talk to. He was always preoccupied, whether he was reading something, typing away on a monitor, or putting rounds through his Five Seven pistol in the warehouse. Todd walked into the warehouse one morning to find Bohden down range doing speed drills from the holster. He was quick; Todd timed him on one run without him knowing. Bohden drew his pistol and put two well-aimed shots into the chest of a target ten yards away in 1.02 seconds. After Bohden left, Todd stayed in the warehouse for several hours trying to beat his time. The closest he got was 1.11 seconds. Any faster and his shot groups started to spread out too much. He decided he would continue to work on this for the next few days.

*   *   *

It was now only two days until the mission brief. Todd sat in the lounge eating dinner with Amber and D. The conversation was humorous and consisted of the two poking fun at D's obsession with movies. Earlier that week, D had shown Todd his extensive movie collection, which was made up entirely of hard copies. Todd asked him why he didn't just keep them all on a digital file like the rest of the world. D then explained how that was equivalent to theft to him, and that as a true movie buff, he thought it was only right to own a hard copy of a motion picture. His movies were organized alphabetically and made up the entire side of the wall in his room. Although Todd gave D a lot of grief over his unorthodox habit, he was caught on several occasions borrowing movies from him, most of them being Westerns and an occasional action flick.

Kara walked into the break room. Todd looked up to see her approach him hesitantly. Her hands fumbled in front of her as she asked, "Todd ... can I speak with you in private?" She nervously brushed back her hair. Her blue eyes stayed locked on Todd, telling him that it was important. From what Todd had gathered, she had no doubt seen little of the outside world, resulting in her overall quiet presence. What little time she may have spent in the outside world was most likely spent alone. It was like part of her was the kind-hearted, shy, childish girl who was fascinated by her studies, while the other was deeply troubled and lonely, longing for something more in life. He had felt the urge to talk to her, to try and understand and maybe help her, but he didn't want her to think he was hitting on her. So, he kept his distance when they weren't going over the history lessons.

"Sure, Kara," he said as he got up from the table and followed her out into the hall.

She led him to the archive room, which was empty, and they sat down at her desk.

"Is something wrong?" he asked, keeping his words firm.

"No, it's just ... I know the professor and Mr. Bohden will inform you of everything during your mission brief, but I think you need to know about your same-self. He was ... troubled, to say the least. I think I knew him better than anyone." She brushed her long bangs behind her ear. Her eyes moved from the table to his.

Todd avoided bringing up his suspicions of her possible relationship and stated the obvious. "I'm sure you spoke to him quite a bit after his missions."

Kara didn't answer, she just stared at him.

"So … what was he like … I mean, obviously, he was the same guy, but he must've had some particular attributes that made him unique, right?"

She pondered for a moment. "In the beginning, he was just like you. He seemed confident and overall positive, which was hard to believe considering what he had gone through. I was only twenty-two when I first met him. I felt like a small child when talking to him during our sessions. Like you, he was also troubled. He had endured a lot before Bohden and Albrecht brought him here, yet he was so sincere and caring."

Todd sat up in his chair. "So why exactly did you choose me … or him, in the first place?" He shook his head and grinned. "I'm sure there are many more qualified guys out there."

"It was Bohden who selected the individual to conduct the operations here."

Todd shrugged. "He seems capable enough, why didn't he just do it himself?"

"He did. He was the original operative the professor sent back in time. However, Bohden feels he has grown too old to continue. He now acts as the operations coordinator. Between you and me, I believe he and the professor are not in sync with each other anymore. It seems they carry very different dispositions towards the operation."

Todd breathed out heavily through his nose and rubbed his chin against his shoulder. "So how'd they find York?"

"York saved Bohden's life during a mission in China a long time ago."

Todd raised an eyebrow at this. "Whoa, I didn't expect that. I guess I could see why he felt obligated to pick me, though. Do you know any details about what happened?"

She shook her head. "No, you would have to ask Bohden." She paused for a moment, then let out a quick breath. She was about to speak when Todd interrupted.

"Is my same-self dead?" he snapped. The question had been lingering on his mind for the past few days. He thought they had been holding the truth from him to keep him from having doubts about the operation. Either way, he had accepted that as the truth, being the only logical explanation as to why "he" wasn't here anymore. He could see the sadness in her eyes. He prepared himself for whatever came next.

"No … he's alive," she said quietly.

Todd's eyes widened. A million questions came to mind. If he was still alive, why would they have retrieved Todd from his timeline? Were they using him until he was all out of juice and then throw him out into the wind? Going through an endless assembly line of Todd Yorks?

"Then why isn't he here?" Anger was present in his voice. He was tired of all the smoke and mirrors. He assumed the worst. His impatience intimidated her, and she pulled away from the table slightly.

"He ran," she said.

Todd shook his head. "What do you mean, he ran?"

"He used time travel to escape to the past." Her eyes didn't leave the dark glass of the table. "It became apparent to me that there was something wrong during his time in Vietnam. Every time he came back from that horrible place, he seemed more and more like a different person. He was … colder. I couldn't bear to watch him lose himself in this war that we created. He was so determined to change the future, so set on fixing the mistakes made by others, that he never took the time to take care of himself."

She paused for a moment and rubbed her forehead. "Or those who …"

He watched as she fought back tears talking about this man. A man that he knew better than anyone: himself. It was strange to listen to her talk about him like this. Todd had many friends as he grew up in the military, but being a part of an elite unit tends to breed a certain type of person and usually contains a limited amount of personalities. Most of them being type-A. Which meant you rarely saw men pouring out their hearts and souls to each other. Most men will keep their feelings buried deep inside them for a long period of time, only to finally let it out many years later when they are no longer in that environment. It's not that they necessarily feel that it is weakness to express their feelings, but rather selfish, and self-centered. It comes hand in hand with the humble mindset carried by most elite Operators. So, the end result is a bunch of strong, closely knit individuals who, although they are closer than family and know each other like brothers, still can't help wondering what the others truly think of them.

Todd did his best to work around the obvious question. "Was he a good friend of yours?" he asked, doing his best not to dig too deep.

She hesitated for a while. Finally, she replied softly, "I think so."

Her answer relieved him. He dreaded a more intimate answer. "What happened to him in Vietnam?"

She answered with anger in her voice. "I think he lost something … a piece of himself. He never came back unscathed."

"I guess that explains the scars on his face."

Kara shook her head in disapproval. "It seemed like every century left its mark on him. He nearly lost his left arm in Pakistan. It was barely attached when we were finally able to rescue him."

Todd looked surprised. "What year was that?"

"Um," she thought for a moment, "it was his last mission here. 2011, I believe."

The fact that she couldn't remember the exact year gave a hint as to just how many operations York had conducted during his five-year stint at the facility. It was obvious that Kara disapproved of York fighting the wars of the past, or maybe she disapproved of the entire operation. Todd tried to lighten the mood. He could tell Kara was having a tough time talking about York.

He snickered. "Jeez, 2011. I was in the fifth grade."

Kara smiled. "I guess you could look at it that way. This was only two years ago."

Todd laughed and ran his fingers through his hair, which had grown quite a bit in the last few weeks. He planned to continue letting it grow in order to better fit into the Old West.

"So, every time you go back in time, do you create another timeline?"

"It depends on who you ask. The way I see it, there is only one timeline. However, the moment you leave it and don't return to your present, you've essentially cloned yourself … given of course that you are in a year that you actually existed. If you ask Amber, she sees it as parallel universes. The timeline we saved you from is still going, we are just not a part of it."

Todd thought about this for a moment. "What if I travelled back to yesterday? Would I meet myself in the break room?"

Kara seemed to enjoy his curiosity. "Yes, that's why we have strict procedures on how we conduct time travel, and where and when you leave and return. If you ran into your younger self in the past, the consequences could be catastrophic."

Todd laughed in disbelief once more. It then dawned on him how complex the entire operation was, and how altering the future could affect the very second he was in.

"So, let's say I went back to yesterday, and took a pair of scissors to your hair while you were eating. You would know of it when it happened, but what happens if I jumped back to the present?"

Kara's cheeks reddened and she giggled. "Well, I wouldn't notice anything until the moment you did your horrible deed in the past, and then ... in a blink of an eye, I would have a bad hair day and would have no idea that something was awry. I would have been led to believe that that was what always happened during that dreadful lunch break yesterday." She rested her head on her hand. "Regardless, I would be coming to you for an explanation."

Todd couldn't help but smile. It was good to see her in high spirits; it was the first time he had seen her smile since they had met.

"That's interesting," he said, looking into her gorgeous eyes.

Before he knew it, he realized he had been staring for a little longer than intended. He quickly changed the subject. "So, what do you people do for fun up here?"

Her face turned back to its usual rigidity. "Honestly, besides the occasional get-togethers we have out in the rec room, our work is our life."

"Rec room?" he asked, a puzzled look on his face.

She looked surprised. "I thought you had been given the grand tour already?"

"Me too," Todd said.

She jumped up and led Todd downstairs. The workstations were dark and the R&D lab had already been locked up. They strolled down the hall towards the front entrance. Kara walked beside him, zipping up her thick blue coat. Todd had finally decided the flight suit was a little too "POW" for him and had started wearing some of York's clothes. It came as no surprise that they were a perfect fit. He wore a dark, long-sleeved shirt rolled up to his forearms and black hiking pants. The jacket he threw on was commonly used for HALO and HAHO operations. He zipped it up while Kara pulled a white beanie hat on and opened the door. The wind rushed in and bit his cheeks.

"It's in the warehouse. Come on," she said as she strode out into the painful cold.

Todd followed close behind. It was too cold to even bother looking up for the Northern Lights. He stayed directly beside her petite figure as she did her best not to slip on the uneven surface. As they neared the warehouse, a gust of wind howled in from the darkness and hit them from the side. Todd kept his feet under him and grabbed Kara around the waist before she was swept off her feet. He thought he heard her say "Thank you" as she reached up and straightened her fur hood. He let go of her as soon as he knew she was stable and headed for the door. He punched in the code "1911" and the door slid open. The two pushed inside and Todd quickly closed the door.

Kara pulled off her beanie and ruffled her hair. Todd looked around the warehouse. He had been here a hundred times in the past two weeks and yet he'd never thought of checking out what was in the room to the right of the entrance. He had just been far too preoccupied by all the weapons and the weights to ever bother looking into what he had assumed was a room full of cleaning supplies.

Kara opened the door and called on the lights. The room lit up to reveal a fully stocked bar on the far wall. Blue lights ran along the glass shelves stacked with bottles of liquor. The bar itself was a rich, dark-stained wood that that stretched across the entire far side of the room. A few circular wood tables were set out in the middle of the room. On the right side was a blue felt pool table, and a circular poker table stood on the left. On each wall was a sixty-inch transparent television.

"Whoa!" Todd said, taking in the room.

Kara giggled. "Why didn't Kevin show you this place earlier?"

"Yeah, what the hell?" Todd grunted. "This place is awesome."

Kara walked over to the bar and sat down on one of the stools. Todd headed behind the bar as if he were going to ask her what she'd have. He looked at the massive amount of alcohol that stood on the shelves like a shrine. He thought back to his early days with the Unit, when the guys would get together after an Op and talk shop at the local bar.

Todd grabbed a bottle of Makers Mark from the shelf and dropped a few cubes of ice into one of the small glasses below the bar. Kara seemed to be daydreaming as he poured the bourbon. "Want some?" he asked, holding up the bottle.

"No thank you," she said softly.

Todd screwed the cap back on and put the bottle back on the shelf. "Don't drink?" he asked as he took a sip.

Kara smiled. "Only on special occasions."

"Me too, that's why I'm drinking."

She looked at him curiously. "This is a special occasion?"

"Sure," he said as he set the glass down. "I mean, we're alive, aren't we? Hell, I know I'm supposed to be dead right now. Kevin lost three pounds this week, and I'm point two seconds closer to beating Bohden's time with the quick draw." He smiled as he took another swig of bourbon. "What else could you ask for? Except for maybe some warm weather every once in a while."

Kara was amused by his optimism. She sat in front of him, brushing her hair back behind her ear, lost in thought. He could tell that something was on her mind, something that she had been dwelling on since they had first met. He wasn't about to get nosy, but he found it irritating how hard it was to hold a conversation with her.

"Is something wrong?"

She shook her head slowly "No ... I just ... sometimes I wonder."

"What?"

"I wonder if what we're doing here is right. Part of me believes in our mission, part of me questions whether we should control the fate of millions of people's lives."

Todd looked at the cubes of ice floating in the glass. "And what does the other part of you think?"

She looked up at him, her eyes narrowed. "That some things were just meant to be."

Todd thought about this for a moment. He mostly agreed that fate was set and what happened in this world was always meant to happen, and was always going to happen. Then again, his same-self had altered the future by killing Kennedy. Perhaps his notion of fate would be changed, as he soon would have first-hand experience in altering what people believed as fate.

"Either way ... you're still alive, Kara."

Kara smiled. She picked up his glass of bourbon, finished it off, and set it back down in front of him. Surprised by this, he smiled and refilled his glass.

Todd and Kara talked an hour longer, mostly about the other students and life at the facility. Eventually they headed back. Todd stopped at the entrance to the break room as Kara paused before heading down the hall to the stairs.

"Thank you ... for talking with me," she said.

"No problem, Kara, I'll see you tomorrow," he said.

He turned and entered the room, and the door closed behind him. Kara stood in the hall for a moment. She wanted to talk more, but she didn't want to hinder him from getting his rest before the big day tomorrow. She walked down the hall and went up to her room.

Todd sat down on his bed, looking out the window at the flakes of snow rushing past. He picked up York's journal and began reading where he had left off.

July 18, 1967

The bodies of young American soldiers lay in front of me. I couldn't believe what I had done. I kept telling myself that it was either them or me. I had never run into this problem before during my time travel operations. I was usually too far behind enemy lines to even see "friendly forces." I thought about getting hold of their PRC 77 radio and using it to call in a mass casualty, but my thoughts turned to Suong. I sprinted up the steep ridge, using trees and plants to pull myself up. When I reached the top, I could see the black smoke rising from the heap of burning hooches. "Oh God, Suong!" I thought.

I ran as fast as I could through the rice paddies that lay on the outskirts of the village. When I finally reached it, I felt a sickening feeling in my gut as I looked at the mutilated bodies of men, women, and children who lay in the dirt. I couldn't help myself, I began to panic as I flipped over the bodies of dead little girls, trying to find Suong. I searched every small body that lay blackened by flames and riddled with bullets. My heart pounded in my chest as I looked at each one's lifeless face. I started searching the insides of the hooches, and when I came to the last hooch, my heart felt like it stopped. I walked inside what was left of the small house and saw her long hair tangled around her. She had not been burned nor had she been shot. Her clothes had been ripped apart and her head had been smashed by either a boot or by the stock of a weapon.

As I grasped what had happened, I began to feel a level of anger and hatred that I had never felt before. These animals, these fucking savages who were supposed to be protecting these people, had massacred the entire village, and had had their way with an eight-year-old girl. My hands began to shake. My breathing became sporadic and my body trembled with anger. This innocent little girl, whom I had taken care of, had been given a second chance at life, and then cheated out of it by these pieces of shit who called themselves soldiers. I would make them pay.

I looked at the MTX. Even with all its power, there was no way I could go back just twenty minutes so that I might save her. There was no way Albrecht would allow such a thing ... not for one irrelevant life. Plus, it would be practically suicidal to attack them like this. It was mid-day, and there were nearly thirty of them. I understood the strict rules regarding time travel. My personal feelings could not get in the way of the fate of mankind. I searched the village and found a large group of footprints that led back into the jungle. Like a ghost, I crept along the trail. The footprints were widely spaced and deep, and the trail was wide and had broken through massive amounts of vegetation. This meant that it was most likely a heavy infantry platoon. They were no doubt sloppy, poorly trained, and there was a good chance that over half of them were draftees and didn't want to be here in the first place. This was good for me. I would wait until night, until they let down their guard for a few hours of sleep. They would most likely leave a guy from each element awake on watch while the others slept, so they would be the first to go.

I finally found them several hundred meters in, and I stalked their patrol until nightfall. I knelt behind some thick plants and watched through my visor in infrared as their bodies slowly began to cool down as they started to settle in for the night. They left four guys awake on the outskirts of their little patrol base in small sandbag bunkers which they had made a few hours earlier. I watched them for an hour, and at the top of the hour, the men in the bunkers would leave and grab somebody else to take their shift. It was a key vulnerable moment when they were waking up the next watch. I waited for the top of the next hour, and right on cue, the four individuals left the bunkers and walked over to the mass of men sleeping under small ponchos in the center. Quietly, I slipped into one of the bunkers and waited for the groggy soldier to take his post. I saw a kid come stumbling over. He put his metal helmet on and carried his M16A1 under his arm.

I knelt with my back against the sandbags as he stopped only inches from me. I didn't move a muscle. He stood there for nearly thirty minutes until he decided to take a seat on a steel ammunition box. I was so close, I could see his eyelids begin to shut. It took me the next ten minutes to slowly move my hand to my lower back and pull my knife out without making a sound. Once I could feel the sleek polymer grip in my hand, I brought it up to my hip. These sick fucks didn't deserve the luxury of modern weaponry. A bullet was far too civilized for them. They were going to suffer a slow horrible death, every last one of them.

I waited for him to drift off once more, and I grabbed him, placing my left hand over his mouth. I plunged the knife into the back of his neck. I then rotated the blade laterally and drove the knife out the front of his throat. His body squirmed and flailed and blood poured out from his almost decapitated head. I dropped him and looked back at the three others who were awake. I made my way over to each one and gave them a similar outing. Once the four on watch were dead. I snuck into the middle of the masses who lay against their packs. The ones who had left their rifles out of arms reach were left alone. Those who slept with their weapon, I killed in their sleep by severing their spinal column. The rest, I decided to have a little fun with. I wanted them to experience what it was like to be overpowered, to have no control over what came next.

As it started to rain, I took all the weapons and set them in one of the bunkers, ensuring that there wasn't a single firearm accessible to them. Miraculously, none of them woke up as I did this. The rain had picked up and provided me with good sound cover. Once all the remaining soldiers were unarmed, I drew my pistol and fired several shots in the air. The soldiers all sat up quickly and began yelling at each other in confusion. Most of them were on their hands and knees trying to find their guns. One of them, a young kid, crawled right into me. He looked up and saw a shimmering transparent figure drenched with rain. He screamed and started crawling backwards. I stepped towards him and he screamed louder. His comrades began calling to him. I disengaged the cloaking system. The sleek black suit was hard to see at night, but the large dark figure that they saw was enough to cause them to panic. One by one I tackled them and stabbed them multiple times until they stopped squirming. A bigger soldier charged me and delivered a big right hook to my head. His hand cracked into my helmet, causing a brief moment of static in my HUD. He grunted in pain and held his hand. I kicked him in the chest, causing him to fall backwards. I drew my pistol and fired two rounds into his head. I looked up and saw the remaining three soldiers running into the woods. I quickly did a mag exchange and holstered my pistol, then pulled my rifle around and shouldered it. The targeting reticle automatically came to life in my HUD and I put it on the farthest guy. I fired four rounds into his back and he collapsed. I shifted over and did the same to the second.

The last one continued running deep into the jungle. I slung my rifle and raced after him. He got to a steep hill and started crawling his way up, breathing heavily, clawing at the thick mud. I grabbed his foot and pulled him back down the slippery embankment. He rolled over and looked at me and screamed in horror. I grabbed him by the throat and threw him into a small creek that was at the base of the hill. He splashed into it. As he tried to get up, I tackled him and began punching him in the head repeatedly.

I remember feeling absolutely nothing as I beat the life out him. He tried to fight back and I would just hit him harder. The hard padded gloves I wore tore his face open with every blow. When he finally was too weak to fight back, I shoved his head into the water and held him there until the bubbles stopped rising to the surface and his body went limp. I let go and his body floated face down in the dark water. I fell back and sat in the creek for a moment. I remember I was breathing so heavily that I ripped my helmet off and gasped for air. I looked up at the night sky that loomed over the dark canopy.

From that moment, everything changed.

THE MISSION

Todd walked into the R&D lab at 0900. He brought with him a notebook to write down important aspects of the mission brief. He had no idea as to what they would have him doing.

He had been doing research on the era and was starting to wonder if he was going to be tasked with killing someone important from that era. Maybe someone like Theodore Roosevelt, who would be living in New York during that time period. He thought back to what he had read so far in the journal from the previous Todd York. He was having a tough time believing that the man who wrote it was the same man he saw in the mirror every morning. He didn't necessarily disagree with what he had done in the past, but he wondered if he could actually go through with such things like killing a U.S. President and brutally taking out an entire platoon of U.S. soldiers.

Albrecht was sitting at his desk with Bohden and the two were conversing quietly when Todd approached them.

"Good morning, Todd," Albrecht said.

Bohden just gave him a nod and stood up. "Alright, let's get down to business," he said as he walked out of the R&D lab.

Albrecht and Todd followed him down the hall to another large door that was near the stairwell. Bohden entered a code and the door hissed open. The three men stepped inside. The room was almost as big as the R&D lab. A few workstations sat in rows across the room orientated towards a large holographic screen that took up the entire back wall. Displayed was a satellite image of the entire western portion of the United States. Several key personnel manned the stations. D, Kevin, and Kara were sitting in chairs near the front of the room. Next to them were two empty chairs where Todd and Albrecht sat down. Bohden walked up to the screen and tapped it. Latitude and longitude lines appeared on the map, and system data was displayed on the top of the screen.

Bohden cleared his throat and began. "Okay, Todd, this will be your area of operations." He tapped the state of Colorado and the screen zoomed in and enhanced.

Todd sat back in his chair. He couldn't believe that they were sending him to his home state.

Bohden tapped the southern portion of Colorado and the screen magnified close enough for roads and buildings to be distinguishable. Todd recognized the area very well. Bohden dragged the image with his fingers and stopped at a city just forty kilometers west of Todd's hometown of Bayfield. "This is ..."

"Durango," Todd interrupted.

"Yes," Bohden said, appearing slightly irritated by the interruption. "Let's start from the top. The situation: On the third of last month. Todd York ... the first one, that is, was about to insert into the year 2014 to combat ISIS forces in Iraq. At takeoff, he ordered D at gunpoint to fly to the United States."

Todd looked at D, who scratched the back of his head in embarrassment.

Bohden continued. "D then piloted the eight-hour flight to the U.S. Once they were over Colorado, York opened the ramp and inserted via freefall somewhere in the vicinity of Durango. The year he inserted was 1887."

Todd jotted down notes as Bohden spoke. He was having a tough time believing this mission brief. He restrained himself from asking questions, knowing that there would be time for that at the end. He wondered if they were going to have him try and kill his same-self. The idea of killing what was basically his clone was absolutely surreal.

"Your mission," Bohden said. He tapped the bottom corner of the screen. A large face shot of York enlarged and took up half of the screen, along with a detailed physical description and Bio. "Is to find Todd York, and or his MTX, and ensure that he cannot use time travel at his own accord. I don't think Todd would try and do anything that could have negative effects on the future, but having that technology floating around in the past is extremely dangerous. So again, your mission is to simply retrieve the technology."

Bohden swiped his hand across the screen, removing the image of York. He then pressed the top left-hand corner of the screen which had a small minimized image. The image enlarged and overlaid the map with grid lines and flight patterns for Odin. There were also wind calculations for the present time.

"Execution: Tomorrow at 2300, you will insert via HALO into the outskirts of the city of Durango. From there you will make your way into town and attempt to find York. If he has already left ... which he most likely has, you will need to speak with the people in the town and try to find out where he has gone."

Kara chimed in, "The population of Durango in 1887 was approximately three hundred. If he has passed through, chances are people in the town will know of him, or would have at least seen him. Plus, you shouldn't have a difficult time describing what he looks like."

Todd smiled at her sarcasm and looked back at Bohden, who stood off to the side of the large screen with his arms crossed.

"As far as logistics and command and signal go ..." he said as he pulled up a chair and sat down, "that will be handled from here at the facility. We will monitor your status by EUHF texts and voice memos from your MTX. You will also use this to contact us for extraction, or in the case of an emergency."

Todd glanced around the room at the others with a look of confusion. "So ... how is it possible that I can send messages to you when you're almost a hundred and thirty years in the future?"

Albrecht stood up and called on the lights. He walked over to the large screen and cleared it out and selected an option on the desktop that opened a clear white screen with a toolbar on the bottom. He then drew a large circle.

"Have you ever heard of ghost frequencies?" he asked as he drew several more layers of circles around the original.

Todd shook his head and shrugged.

"Believe it or not, our grand method for communicating with the past was actually a big hobby for many years. People would come up here to the North Pole and use basic frequency transmission equipment to listen to lost frequencies transmitted from the past. Individuals had claimed to have heard voice transmissions from the Vietnam War. All we did was take it to the next step."

"How does that work?" asked Todd.

Albrecht then drew continents on the middle circle, and a little antenna on the top of what was his illustration of the Earth. "Among the five layers of the Earth's atmosphere is the Ionosphere. It's called the Ionosphere because solar radiation from the sun is ionized in this layer. Think of it as a giant invisible ocean of electrons floating around and crashing into each other about a kilometer above the Earth's surface." He drew squiggly lines originating from South America; they went up and rode in between one of the layers of his atmosphere. "So, when a radio transmission is sent from … let's say South America, 1970. The invisible wavelengths travel up to this 'ocean' and get caught amongst the other infinite amounts of radio waves floating around. Like a large body of water, these frequencies get caught in a current that ends up at the North axis of the planet where they are intercepted by us many years later."

Todd chuckled. "How do you catch only my transmissions and not the millions of others headed here?"

"We use a special frequency range known as Enhanced Ultra High Frequencies, or EUHF. It has a much greater range than UHF, which is about three hundred megahertz. EUHF has nearly a thousand, which makes it a much stronger signal and makes it easy to pick out from the rest."

Bohden gave Todd a look which made it clear that he was concerned whether Todd was grasping the information. "Regardless of how the tech works, it is important that you fully understand the mission first," said Bohden.

Todd nodded in agreement.

Albrecht cleared out the screen and the monitor displayed the satellite image once more. Bohden stood up and placed his right hand in his pocket, and with his left, he scratched his dark facial hair. "Do you have any questions?" he asked.

Todd thought for a moment, then asked, "If I don't find him, how long do I keep up with this search?"

Bohden let out a shallow breath. "If you can't find him within a week, and you have not a single lead as to where he might be, radio us for extraction."

"What equipment will I be taking with me?" Todd asked. "A futuristic combat suit and a suppressed assault rifle won't be exactly incognito in this time period."

Bohden chuckled. "You will be going in unarmed on this one. Any weaponry needed must be procured on site. The suit, however will need to stay on you, or at least in a safe place where you can retrieve it at any time." He put his other hand in his pocket and rocked on his heels. "If it were me, I would go cloaked for the entire mission. We are just coming into the spring months so it shouldn't be too hot there. The suit's built-in temperature control will come in handy on the cold nights and warm days, and your helmet's HUD is very useful for night vision, thermal, and land navigation. There is a good chance that York has not moved very far since his arrival because of the lack of transportation in that era. There aren't exactly city buses cruising around back then."

Todd pondered for a moment, then licked his lips. "So ... if, and when I find him, if he is hostile towards me and I have to ..." He looked over at Kara, who was staring at him intensely. " ... take him out. Will anything happen to me?"

Albrecht shook his head. "No, you and him are two separate beings. The moment you step out of the timeline, you in essence create another you."

"But what if I were to kill my seventeen-year-old self who is in Colorado right now?" Todd asked.

Albrecht rubbed the back of his neck. "Then theoretically, yes ... you would cease to exist the moment his heart stopped. As far as we know, and assume ... the seventeen-year-old Todd York living in Colorado is living an identical life as you, meaning he will make every decision that leads him to the same conclusion. However, that will most likely change after a few operations here."

Todd shook his head in disbelief, having a hard time grasping the complexity of time travel. He looked at the others, who were staring at him, waiting for him to speak. D's mouth clicked as he obnoxiously chewed on a large wad of gum. Kara sat with her legs crossed, holding a clear tablet. Next to her was Kevin wearing black rimmed reading glasses, tapping his heel on the floor, his hands crossed in his lap. Todd looked at the three and couldn't help but feel uncomfortable for even bringing up the possibility of killing a friend of theirs. After reading through the rest of the York's journal, Todd had concluded that York was most definitely a threat, possibly even unstable. He could see in her eyes that Kara was deeply troubled.

Bohden headed to the back of the room towards the room entrance. "Wheels up at 1300 tomorrow. Let me know if you have any more questions."

Kevin stood up and patted Todd on the shoulder as he turned and left the room with D right behind him.

Kara stared at the smoky linoleum flooring lit up by the giant monitor. Todd stood up and cracked his neck and stretched out his legs. The clock on the left wall was about to hit 11 a.m. He looked over at Kara, trying to figure out the right words to possibly help ease her nerves. He was about to ask her if she was okay, but she stood and walked out. Todd stood in the dark room with Albrecht sitting in the chair next to him. Todd exhaled and scratched the back of his head.

"You doing alright, Todd?" asked Albrecht.

Todd paced around the front of the room for a moment with his hands on his hips, his dark figure moving slowly in front of the bright monitor. He noticed the eyes of multiple students manning the workstations in the room, watching him.

Todd looked over at Albrecht who sat with his left leg perched across his right. He had in his hands a large cup of coffee that rested atop his tablet. Overall, Todd felt that the mission prep and the brief itself had been uncomfortably rushed. He had only been at the facility for a little over two weeks, and he still felt much like a stranger among the students. The combination of his uncertainty, the lack of solid intel on the target's location, and the fact that this was without a doubt the most complex mission he had ever conducted gave him an uneasy feeling in his stomach. Todd's restlessness made Albrecht uneasy. He knew him far better than Todd realized, and he was all too familiar with his silent disapproval of such matters.

"I don't know, it just sounds dicey to me. This guy could be anywhere in the world, and at any time in history," Todd said, shaking his head.

Albrecht took a sip of his coffee, then leaned back in his chair. "This is the reason why we found you, Todd, and not some other elite soldier. Put yourself in his shoes. If you were going to run away, to any place or time in history ... where would you go?"

Todd rotated his jaw as he stared at the dark floor, trying his best to answer the question as honestly as possible. He thought back to his childhood and recalled his days as a young boy venturing out into the vast Colorado landscape. Growing up, he had developed quite the sense of adventure. He had fallen in love with the sheer size and beauty of yet a dangerous world around him. His mother had gotten used to having a large stock of Band-Aids ready for him upon his return from his adventures. Although his untamable spirit deeply worried her, it brought her happiness to see him so enthralled with life.

It was common knowledge amongst the residences of Bayfield that Durango was established in the late 1800s, just south of Animas City. Many of the old buildings had been replaced by modern structures, and it seemed as if the entire history of the town had been swept under the rug to make way for a technology-driven era. However, a few buildings from the nineteenth century remained to remind the population of a history long lost. Todd and his friends from school would spend hours playing cowboys and Indians out in the many acres surrounding their homes, shooting at each other with cap guns and chewing bubble gum and pretending it was tobacco. Something about the Wild West had fascinated him his entire life.

To Todd, the remains of the buildings were not just that of an old town, but a symbol of something long forgotten. Something very few still held onto in the United States in the year 2030. He could not put it into words, but if he had to, he would call it the human spirit. People of that time weren't given anything. They had to work to survive, constantly struggling through the hardships of living out west. Whole families could die if the man of the house was not able to provide for them, and in order to do that, it called for back-breaking manual labor.

The one thing he fantasized the most about was the freedom of the old world. Even though life was hard in those days, people were truly free. The world and all its beauty were open to them to explore without limitation. In today's world it seemed like there were limitations and regulations put in place to keep people in check. Laws, boundaries, and forms of accountability that were intrusions of people's privacy were implemented due to the rising threat of terrorism, communism, and the overall growing reliance of technology. The way Todd saw it, the modern world had become too easy for everyone, and far less interesting, as everybody channeled down the same linear path towards mediocracy. Perhaps this explained his career choice, as he most likely viewed combating evil around the world as the only true adventure left. There was no shortage of evil.

"I'd go where he went," Todd said.

Albrecht nodded. "Every time the MTX is utilized, we receive the data on the time initiated. The last time he activated it was when he went to '87. It hasn't been used since then. So, we know he is still there."

Todd cocked his head "What if he lost it?"

Albrecht looked at him and chuckled. "That would be extremely dangerous. As you know, the device is locked with an entry code, but still … if some prospector came across it lying in the desert … God knows what could be altered. York is no idiot. I don't think he would allow such a thing to happen."

Todd breathed out heavily and scratched the back of his head again. The crucial need for success on the op was beginning to set in. The tingling sensation in his stomach picked up as it did before he conducted any mission. It was never necessarily the danger that worried him, but rather the overall scope, and the always present uncertainty. He dropped his arm and slapped the side of his leg,

"I'm going to go prep my gear," he said as he headed for the door. The eyes of the students in the room dropped to their monitors as he passed them.

*   *   *

July 20, 2012

I sat on the closed ramp of Odin with my head in my hands. I watched my tears drip onto the cold steel of the cargo area floor and disappear into the dark spacings. It was another six hours before we

would reach the North Pole. The flight felt like an eternity as the memory of Suong's corpse was burned into my mind. I had failed her. Why hadn't I stayed close enough to the village to protect her?

My original mission had to been to kill Soviet operatives who were supplying and training the Vietcong. I could give two shits about the Vietnam War. I had conducted several ops there and it was obvious there was no winning that conflict. The country's leadership was spineless, the civilians were divided, and the conventional troops were out of their element. I had a hard enough time keeping a low profile in the jungle just by myself with modern technology. I couldn't imagine walking around with a bunch of dumb ass grunts who didn't want to be there in the first place.

I heard soft footsteps. I looked up and saw Kara standing in the doorway leading to the pressurized cabin. She looked saddened at the sight of me breaking down. She walked over and sat next to me. Hugging her knees, I looked up at her, tears pooling in my reddened eyes and streaking down my cheeks. Her eyes became glossy at the sight. She placed her hand on my forearm and I leaned into her, resting my head in her lap. Her other arm cradled my head, and she stroked her fingers through my hair. We sat there for the next hour. She was warm, and comforting. I never told her about what happened with Suong or the soldiers.

I didn't want her to think less of me, nor did I want to expose her to the evil that I had seen ... and done.

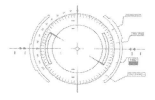

THE NIGHT BEFORE THE OP

Todd stood in his room, viewing himself in the mirror. He was wearing the armored suit and felt like he was looking at a poster for some futuristic action movie. His gear was laid out on his bed behind him. He wasn't bringing much for the op. His helmet and web gear/parachute were stretched out with each pouch open so he could check the contents inside.

He carried in his kit a small number of rations, med gear, hundred-foot cable lanyard, some anesthetic agents, and York's journal. He practically felt naked taking such little equipment. He was especially uncomfortable with going in unarmed. He wasn't expecting it to be the O.K. Corral everywhere he went, but it was the Wild West, after all.

A knock on the door startled him and shook him out of his daydreaming. He opened it to find Amber standing with her hands folded to her front. She rocked slightly up and down on her toes.

"What's up?" Todd asked.

"Todd, I know you're extremely busy right now, but could you come give me and Kevin a hand in the warehouse?" she said with a slight grin.

"Yeah, no problem," he said, "just let me change really quick."

He squeezed out of the tight suit and quickly put on some of York's old clothes. He then followed Amber out of the hallway and through the mess room. They walked down the main corridor past the large windows. The rooms were empty and not a single student was at a monitor or work station.

"Where is everyone?" Todd asked, looking around the building and into doorways as they passed.

Amber continued walking towards the main entrance and answered without looking back. "It's an early day tomorrow for everyone, so they called it around five."

He shivered as they made their way over to the warehouse. "For the love of God! You guys really need to connect the two buildings!" he yelled over the howling winds.

Amber laughed and opened the warehouse door. The winds were quickly drowned out by loud thumping music from inside. Todd walked in and was immediately greeted by a large group of students standing in the main area of the warehouse. The rec room's bar was lined with the older males of the bunch while the tables and open areas were occupied by the remainder of them. Some were dancing with each other to the loud electronic music that made the steel walls vibrate.

Amber smiled and yelled over the music, "I lied!"

Todd grinned, shaking his head. He walked into the rec room and was greeted once more, this time by several raised glasses. He waved and made his way to the bar where Kevin was serving drinks. Kevin smiled at the sight of him and began pouring him something that resembled lemonade.

"So, this is what you guys do for fun, huh?" Todd said, looking around the room.

Kevin chuckled and handed him the large drink. "Told you I'd get you back for the bathroom thing. They may be a bunch of science nerds living in the North Pole, but they are still college students at heart."

Todd sipped the drink and licked his lips. He rotated the glass in his hand and looked at it in surprise. "Damn, this is good!" he said, taking another drink.

"Had a feeling you'd like it," Kevin said.

The lemony alcoholic beverage left a sweet taste on his tongue. "Let me guess ..."

Kevin smiled and nodded. "Yeah, it took me a while to find a drink that York liked that wasn't just bourbon."

Todd leaned up against the bar and looked out into the

warehouse. He saw D dancing like a goofball with Amber next to him, laughing. Albrecht was in the middle of a circle of students talking to them with a beer in his hand. Todd could tell that the students had great respect for Albrecht. When he spoke, they listened intensely, like their lives depended on it. He wondered how it must have been before they traveled back in time, as a government scientist and college professor teaching forty-some odd students about quantum physics. He realized then how close they must have been before they made the jump. How much trust and faith they must have had towards him to abandon everything to follow him to the North Pole on a crazy assumption that they had the ability to alter the dark course of time. Using technology that many would never believe or even know existed. The thing that gave him the most admiration towards the students, however, was the sad truth that they could never be a part of the future they altered. Each and every one of them had already been replaced by the younger version of themselves, who would assume their lives with their families in happiness. Meanwhile the originals would spend the remainder of their days in this arctic wasteland.

Bohden walked into the rec room and spotted Todd. He gave him a nod as he approached him. "You ready to roll, man?" he said as he motioned Kevin for his usual glass of scotch.

Todd took a sip of his drink and watched a student break on a game of pool. "Yeah … I'm set," he said through his teeth. "My gear is all prepped and I've already coordinated primary and alternate extraction points with D."

Bohden just nodded and sipped his drink. Todd looked over at Bohden, who eyed the students around the room. It didn't make much sense why he was so distant from everyone. He had been a part of the facility from the beginning; meeting Albrecht before he had even fully developed the technology. One would think he would be more outgoing considering he was going to have to accept the predicament he was in and try and make the best of his new life. Perhaps Bohden didn't exactly agree with the upcoming mission, maybe he still cared for York, who had saved his life a long time ago. Maybe he saw Todd as a sorry replacement for a great warrior he had held in high regard.

Todd asked, "How close were you and York?"

Bohden took another drink, blinked slowly and licked his lips. "We were good friends for a long time. The first time I met him was in the original timeline in 2023. I was in mainland Japan during the ACS invasion helping fend off endless waves of Chinese forces to protect the evacuation ports. He and a few other guys from Team Six were operating with a Force Recon platoon in Okinawa. When we got pushed back south far enough, we finally ran into each other."

Todd noted that he didn't mention York saving his life and left it at that. Albrecht walked into the rec room and smiled when he saw Todd.

"How you doing, Todd? Do you have everything you need?"

Todd's mouth curved up and he nodded, raising his glass slightly. "I've never gone back in time before, but I'm pretty sure I'm ready to go," he said humorously.

Albrecht chuckled. "Trust me; you're ready."

Todd replied, "I guess you would know. Since you've pretty much already done this."

Albrecht looked over at Bohden, who was slumped against the bar. "What's the matter, Steven?" he said in an almost fatherly way.

Bohden said something back to him that Todd didn't catch. He was too preoccupied trying to get an idea as to what Amber and Kara were having an argument about out in the warehouse. Amber was making large dramatic movements with her arms and shaking her head, obviously trying to prove some kind of point to Kara, who stood with her arms crossed, looking down at the ground. He couldn't hear what they were saying over the loud music. He looked over at Albrecht and Bohden, who were having a quiet conversation, and then over at Kevin, who was watching the same thing he was. Kevin looked at him, then back at the two girls. He set his empty glass down on the bar and started walking to the door. Kara didn't see him coming. She was still listening to Amber, who was yelling. She rolled her eyes and stormed out the door into the cold darkness. Amber crossed her arms and shook her head in anger.

"What's the matter?" Todd asked.

Amber looked at him as she breathed out heavily and rolled her eyes. Todd quirked an eyebrow. "Is it just girl stuff or something?" he asked.

"You need to talk to Kara," she said in his ear.

"About what?"

She pulled back and glared at him.

"Alright, alright," he said. He turned and squeezed through a group of students and headed to the door.

"Where ya goin', man?" one of the students yelled over the music.

"I'll be back in a minute!" Todd replied. He opened the door and ran to the main building, hunched over with his hands in the crooks of his arms. He got to the main building and shook off the clinging flakes of snow. Looking down the main corridor, he saw that the lights in the workstations were still off. He made his way to the end of the hall, briefly checking the archive room to see if Kara was at her desk. The Communications room and the R&D lab were both closed and locked. He headed up the stairs to the second floor and saw that her door at the end of the hall was open. He walked towards it and noticed the lights were off in her room. He could faintly see movement reflecting off the walls. When he got to her door he peered in and saw her standing down in the landing at the base of the large windows, her arms crossed, as she stood motionless, gazing out into the night sky. The Northern Lights shone through her windows and danced on the dark walls of the room. It appeared as if she were looking into an aquarium. He knocked softly on the steel jam of the door. She didn't respond in any way.

He entered the room, walking softly, yet loud enough so she could hear him approach. The beautiful shades of turquoise lit up the smooth features of her face and reflected off her sharp eyes. He came to her side, but she didn't look at him. He turned and looked out into the breathtaking horizon. He didn't know what to say. He had concluded that she and York had been in a relationship and, like Bohden, she saw Todd as merely a lookalike. Nothing more than a reminder of the loss of a dear friend ... or perhaps in her case a loved one. He exhaled through his nose, shaking his head slightly.

"Please ... just go," she said without looking at him.

He turned and took a few steps towards the door, then looked at the photo on her nightstand. It was a photo of York, most likely before he was a member of DEVGRU. He was wearing an old Ops-core helmet, which led Todd to believe that the picture had been taken around 2018-2019. He was smiling in the photo, and his face was cleanshaven and clear of scars. He looked like a different person. He looked like Todd. He turned back towards her, his heart rate picking up as the words left his mouth.

"Were you … in love with him?"

Her head lowered, and her arms remained crossed.

"No more games, Kara." He stepped towards her. "When I find this man … there is no telling what will happen, but I can guarantee we won't be hugging each other and swapping stories. If I have to kill him … I need to know what went on between the two of you." He came to her side. "I'm not planning on staying there after I complete this mission. I need to know."

Her eyes portrayed a look of sorrow, their beauty adding to the effect. They left his, and went to the floor. "I … no, there was nothing … no matter how much I wanted there to be. He was older, and far too preoccupied to pay any attention to a foolish girl with a crush." She looked back out the window. "But I'm over it, I've put aside childish things. All that matters is making a better world to live in, good enough for all the people here to have real lives again, and if that means you having to kill him, then so be it."

He turned towards the window and scratched the stubble on his face. He looked over and saw her eyes were filling with tears. There was nothing more to say. He would either end up killing York, or condemn him to the nineteenth century. Either way, she would hate Todd for it.

He walked away, stopping at the door to glance back at her.

"Someone who gives up their entire life in order save millions of people isn't foolish." He shook his head and said, "Goodbye, Kara."

He left the main building and returned to the party where he spent the remainder of the night drinking and conversing with the students.

*   *   *

September 3, 2013

As I sit in my room looking out into the endless white, I can't help but wonder if what I'm doing is worth it. I had seen where the world was heading near the end of the original timeline; the fall of the

United States was no doubt eminent, but what about the rest of the world? Many say that the end of the U.S. means the end for everything. To an American, that may seem so. As one of three global superpowers, we are the only one who still maintains a level of democracy and diplomacy which aids in our false sense of self-righteousness. We have a well-funded military full of young degenerates who truly believe that everything they are doing is for the continuation of their God given freedom, for their families and fellow countryman. Only few grasp the situation and reality of their purpose, which is not much more than being cannon fodder and a show of force. Yet they are sent to fight an enemy that knows true suffering, knows what it is to starve, has felt the unforgiving brutality of a harsh environment, and has adapted to live in it, thrive in it, and use it to their advantage.

In this war, both sides are fighting for "freedom," but only one was actually fighting for their home, their families, everything they knew. How could we possibly beat that? I know how, but unfortunately there is only so much I can do, and I sure as fuck can't win a war with just an invisible suit. After ten long and painful operations in Vietnam, the end result was over fifty thousand casualties for the U.S., a withdrawal from the country, and multiple scars for myself. I had predicted that the war would leave the country in turmoil, so I'll chalk this one up as a win ... considering the substantial delay in the Soviet Union's rise to power.

After each op, Bohden, Albrecht, Kara, and I sit down and review the consequences of my actions and how they have affected the present. We do this by simply using the internet. It's always interesting to see how much was changed by my actions alone, and how I was the only one who was aware of the past which no longer existed. I had to document everything so that we could compare the present to the altered past. LBJ's sorry ass quit, which I thought was funny considering the chances of his reelection were about as good as JFK's. The U.S. went into a kind of recovery period for the next ten years after Nam; meanwhile the USSR continued expanding both geologically and economically while side-stepping a major conflict in Afghanistan. Eventually, they looked to China just like they had originally and began putting plans in the works to engage the U.S. directly.

It was 2013 and WWIII was still on the horizon. We needed to hit the Russians at home, we needed to cripple them in order to buy ourselves some time to work our way out of the pathetic state of limbo we were currently in (which was the mid-'70s). We started looking to events of the late '70s all the way to the '80s, trying to find a key moment where we could inflict a crippling blow. We started looking at them industrially, and our research finally led us to a nuclear power plant on the outskirts of Pripyat. Our research showed that, in the late '90s, the plant was closed due to multiple accidents that were direct results of poor maintenance and the many cut corners that were done while they were designing the reactors themselves. This led to a negative impact on their economy. If I could sabotage only one of the reactors, the plant would turn a large portion of Ukraine into an apocalyptic wasteland.

As Bohden and I started putting plans together for the operation, my mind briefly went to the civilians of Pripyat. Did they deserve this? The region would most likely suffer from the effects of fallout for many years to come if we went through with this.

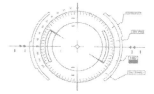

THE BIG DAY

The next morning, Todd ate breakfast with the students and headed out to the warehouse to get a few hours of range time and run a few miles on the treadmill.

Around 11 a.m., he gathered up all his gear and loaded it into one of the few 4x4s tucked away out back of the warehouse. He then rode with Bohden over to the hangar where he was met by D, who was obviously not a morning person, and/or had too much to drink the night prior. His eyes were heavy and he stumbled around with a cup of coffee in his hand.

Todd laughed at the man's lethargic state. "You gonna be able to handle the eight-hour flight?" He chuckled as D plopped down into a chair in the hangar's kitchen.

D simply nodded as he took a sip of his coffee and leaned back in his chair.

Todd stood in the kitchen with Bohden, who continued to drop extra bits of intelligence that he had gathered throughout the previous week. Most of it concerning the reported weather from that time frame, and the social state of the area regarding criminal activity. The weather was supposed to be fairly nice during that time frame, but there were not hard facts and for all Todd knew he could be jumping into a snow storm.

A few more students showed up who had been trained by D and Bohden to assist as the flight crew. The group then walked out onto the catwalk, which lined the walls of the hangar and overlooked

Odin's massive presence. The giant LED flood lights reflected off the slick grey skin of Odin's hull. The wings were so large, and they stretched so far, that they appeared to be almost a second level of the building. The back ramp was open and the cargo section lights were lit, presenting a very military-looking area that was very familiar to Todd. The crew made their way down the steel steps of the catwalk and walked to the back ramp, passing beneath the aircraft's tail. The crew set down their bags and began going over a checklist of pre-flight inspections. D made his way up to the cockpit, where he pulled out a tablet and began flicking different switches and knobs which activated different lights and displays on the console.

Todd pulled the armor suit out of the large duffle bag he carried and began undressing. Bohden walked up the ramp carrying his web gear and parachute and set them down on the red cargo netting bench next to Todd, who now had the lower body of the suit pulled on and was pulling his t-shirt off.

He heard Amber whistling at him.

"Whatta hunk!" she yelled, her voice echoing throughout the hangar and making Todd blush.

Albrecht came in behind her with Kara and Kevin. The four made their way to the plane carrying personal carry-on bags for the long sixteen hours they would spend on Odin. Todd had finished getting his arm through the tight sleeve of the suit when Albrecht came up to him and patted him on the shoulder.

"Ready, son?" he said.

Todd breathed out and cocked his head to the side. "We'll find out soon enough."

Kara didn't look at Todd as she passed him and made her way to the mid-section of the plane where the onboard kitchen and lounge were. He thought about their conversation the previous night and he felt more awkward now than he did when he asked her. He decided that he would just leave it alone. Maybe York would prove him wrong and would comply. Hell, maybe he would end up deciding to come back with him. The thought of this brought Todd hope. Maybe he could salvage what was left of the good in York and return him to the only people in the world who cared about him. He tried to put himself in the other Todd's shoes. What would he do if he was approached by his same-self and told to relinquish the technology that gave him the power to manipulate time? He wouldn't fight ... at least he didn't think so. The only reason that York would fight him was if he was mentally unstable, which Todd believed was possible.

Todd sat on the netting chair and tapped the screen of his MTX, making it come to life, displaying a pass code entry screen. He typed in his code and the screen changed to a main menu with multiple applications including the time travel settings, history records, communications, navigation, and system settings. He tapped the time travel app and it opened the screen showing the multiple wheels labeled in years. Using his index finger, he rotated the digital wheel to the specified date and pressed "set" at the bottom of the screen. He then shut off the device and leaned back in his chair. His mind raced through endless possibilities of scenarios that could present themselves to him upon his insert. He did his best to stay positive and keep his mind straight. He looked down at his helmet beside him; its sleek black visor showed his distorted reflection on its smooth curved surface. He thought about what could happen if he was seen in the Western days wearing such attire. How could somebody from back then even describe what they saw? It was absolutely imperative that he remain undetected, or at least ensure that his suit was not seen. He would have to do a good job at adopting the lingo of the day. He went through the mission in his head at its simplest form. Get in, blend in, find York, and retrieve the tech. It all sounded far too simple when put this way, but it was the only way he could think about it without believing that the entire task was lunacy.

It was now almost 1300. Todd had dozed off in the back of the plane, and he was woken by Albrecht, who patted him on the shoulder. "We are about to take off, Todd. We're all up in the lounge if you would like to join us," he said, motioning his head towards the nose of the plane.

Todd rubbed his eyes and looked at the clock on the top right corner of the MTX. "I'll be up there in a second," he said as he stretched out his legs. Albrecht nodded and headed upstairs. Todd took a few seconds to take in the moment sitting in the cargo area. It felt all too familiar, yet it was new to him. Ordinarily he would be accompanied by several other Operators who would be hanging up hammocks or sprawling out in the plane either reading, or watching movies on tablets. Rob would be cracking jokes or sharing his trail mix with Todd as they watched a movie. The thought brought a smile to his face.

D's voice came over the plane's intercom, "Everyone, find a seat. We'll begin taxiing out to the runway; takeoff in five minutes."

The plane began humming to life, and moments later Todd could feel it moving forward out of the hangar. He stood up and walked towards the front sections of the aircraft, past the med room, in which he had first regained consciousness after almost dying.

Albrecht, Kara, Amber, Bohden, and Kevin sat around a long table in the lounge. Kevin was telling a humorous story about their days back in college that had Amber laughing. Albrecht was typing something on his tablet, and Kara was next to him reading a book. To no surprise, Bohden was sitting on the far side of the table doing something on a laptop. He looked up and saw Todd and motioned him to come over.

Todd sat down in the large chair next to Bohden and fumbled for the seatbelt connections. Bohden rotated his laptop so it faced Todd and he pointed out a few images on the screen. They were grainy black and white shots of Durango. Todd nodded like he was paying attention, but as far as he was concerned, any Intel Bohden thought he had was no good. He would just have to wait until he got there to figure out the situation.

The plane was now picking up speed. Todd looked out of the window behind Bohden and saw the white ground speeding past. The sky was clear and the sun reflected off the snow and was nearly blinding. Todd could feel the wheels of the plane leave the earth's surface and the brief drop sensation as the plane left the ground.

D came over the intercom. "Good afternoon, ladies and gentlemen, this is your captain speaking. It will be about eight long … painful … boring hours until we reach Colorado, where we will drop off Mr. Hotshot back there; then it will be another eight hours back to our freezing little paradise." He did his best to sound like a typical commercial airliner pilot. "Our flight attendant Ms. Bohden will be coming by with drinks momentarily; please sit back and enjoy the flight."

Bohden grinned and shook his head. Amber was laughing at D's sarcasm. Todd breathed out slowly and closed his eyes. He opened them and saw Kara looking at him.

"Todd," Albrecht said, smiling.

He looked over at him and raised his eyebrows to say, "What is it"?

Albrecht was grinning. "You know you don't have be dressed for a while," he said, looking at the suit.

Todd looked down at himself and realized how he had been over-prepared by getting dressed eight hours early. Regardless, the suit was actually extremely comfortable, even though it was tight and form-fitting. The inner temperature control made it the perfect environment to sit in. He realized how ridiculous it was that he was sitting at a table with five people staring at him. He stood up and looked dumbly at himself. There were a few chuckles.

"Yeah … I'll go change." He came back moments later wearing a t-shirt and cargo pants. He chatted with the five of them and they ate dinner together. All the while he said nothing to Kara. He didn't want her to hate him. She was without a doubt the sincerest person he had ever met. He didn't understand why, but the thought of her despising him brought a deep discomfort to him.

*   *   *

December 9, 2013

I had a session with Kara last night. She kept prying about the last op in Nam. I dodged around the true answer, I just kept giving her bullshit explanations about encounters with "Charlie" and the horrors of war. I had earned yet another scar from a firefight a few hours after I smoked that American platoon. It was the largest of them, spanning from my cheek, down my jaw, and damn near my throat. It now had twenty stitches in it and I noticed Kara continued to look at it in a way that showed disapproval. I think she didn't agree with what I was doing in the past. Her entire life had been dedicated to learning and understanding history, and here I was altering it. Maybe she felt that I was an anomaly. No matter how I felt though, I still thought that it was going to work. All we needed to do was stop the Communists in the past and preserve the future. But one thing still troubled me.

During dinner one night I was talking with Brian and I had an epiphany. What if I did end up stopping them, and in doing so prevented Brian from ever inventing the technology, which meant he would have never gone to the North Pole, therefore he would have never found me. Would I one moment be in some random place and time, and then in a blink of an eye be back in Virginia with ST6? I brought this thought to Brian's attention and he thought about it for a moment. He told me that the war had no effect on his studies, and that he would have invented time travel anyway. The only thing that would change was his exodus with Bohden and his students to the North Pole. I told myself that no matter the result, WWIII had to be prevented. I was so blind.

Kara ended our session with one last question, one that made me really think. She asked me, "Are you afraid?" I thought about this for a moment. Although I had felt fear in combat and during my inserts and extracts, I had not felt the same level of fear that I had felt during my time with the SEALs. I almost felt invincible, with the ability to alter the future and be invisible. My answer was an effort to ease her worries. "No, I'm not scared, the mission is too important for any weakness on my end to hinder its success," I said in a confident way. Those eyes of hers showed me that she could see through my bullshit, but she didn't pry.

TIME TRAVEL

Todd stood at the hinge of Odin's ramp, the outline of his dark figure only distinguishable by the internal red lighting of the aircraft. He ensured the straps of his web gear and parachute were firmly tightened, enough to support him comfortably for when he would be beneath canopy. He double-checked all the metal buckles on his kit and ensured they were properly seated. He arched his back and put his hands up in the air to practice his free-fall body position. He chuckled when he reached back to do a practice touch on his pilot chute, remembering that he hadn't used the old system since he was a young Ranger.

The new systems were always activated via control unit such as the wrist device, or in this case the MTX. In the corner of his eye he saw a group massing behind the large window behind him.

He put his arms down and turned to see Albrecht approach him.

"Thank you for doing this, Todd; this couldn't be easy for anyone," he said as he extended a hand towards him.

Todd looked at his hand and grasped it firmly. The visor of his helmet slid up and he looked Albrecht in the eyes and replied, "Thank you ... for giving me a second chance."

Albrecht smiled slightly and nodded, shaking his hand. He turned and walked back to the front and Amber and Kevin approached Todd. Amber had tears in her eyes, and she wrapped her arms around him. He chuckled and assured her that he would be fine. Kevin shook his hand; he pulled Todd in close and placed something in the side pouch of his pack, ending the maneuver by patting Todd in the shoulder.

"Be safe out there buddy!" He said.

Todd nodded and returned a pat to his shoulder. "Will do, my friend," he said as Kevin and Amber stepped back into the adjacent room with the others. The door sealed the pressurized room so that the ramp could be opened.

He stepped to the skin of the aircraft and flicked a switch. The ramp announced its opening with a loud hissing noise. It continued to lower, presenting a growing black opening. It was a clear night; there wasn't a single cloud in the sky. He stepped to the edge of the ramp and peered twenty-nine thousand feet down at the earth's surface, seeing the small lights of modern civilization. He looked back at the group behind the window; their eyes were all trained on him. He then saw Kara standing in the corner behind the group. She wore a familiar look of worry that troubled him. Knowing that she knew he was looking at her, he grinned and winked, then the visor of his helmet slid shut. Her eyes lit up slightly and the edges of her mouth curved up. Behind the dark visor, Todd smiled ear to ear. The O2 hissed with every breath within his helmet. He stepped to the edge of the ramp and looked out into the black abyss. His heart thumped in his chest. He looked down at the MTX; 1887 was set in the time wheel. A large button pulsed beneath it displaying "Initiate."

He took a deep breath and dove out of the aircraft. The relative wind caught his extended arms and leveled him out on his belly. He moved one arm to his chest and flipped over on his back to watch Odin become smaller and smaller in the moonlight, but was unable to see the aircraft as it flew away. Assuming it was too dark due to the lack of a full moon, he thought nothing of it and rotated back over to his belly and glanced at his current altitude displayed in his HUD. "27,484 feet AGL" was quickly scrolling down as he plummeted to the earth. Todd relaxed his body and took in the massive scope and the surreal clarity of his current situation. The ground beneath him was covered in thousands of lights from cars, street lights, and buildings. He looked back at his altitude. "22,875 feet AGL." It was taking a little longer than expected so he slowly moved his arms from out front to his sides until his body was in a tracking position. The altitude began dropping quicker as he dove head first through the air like a missile.

Todd held this position for a few more seconds until he was around fifteen thousand feet. He then leveled off and brought his arms back to his front with his MTX in front of his face; his other hand held on to his left wrist. He moved his right index finger over the "Initiate" button. His heart began pounding in his chest. He was about to go back in time! He could hardly believe it. He pressed the button. The cables lining the suit lit up with a bright white light and then a loud crack made his ears ring. Suddenly, the lights of the modern civilization below all simultaneously went dark, and heavy clouds appeared out of nowhere all around him. The moonlight shone off the top of the heavy cloud coverage.

He passed through the clouds and entered heavy rain that streaked off his visor as he met the falling drops. Todd was in awe at what had just happened. One moment it was a clear night, the next it was a heavy storm. He continued falling, staring at the ground below, far too awestruck to look at his altitude, which was dangerously dropping. The word "DEPLOY!" began flashing in front of his face. He glanced at his altitude. "4,000 feet AGL" scrolled down his helmet, highlighted in red.

"Shit!" he yelled. He pressed the Deploy button on the MTX and felt the opening shock of his canopy inflating above him. He reached up and grabbed ahold of the steering toggles and began manipulating his parachute.

The rain and the lack of illumination made it hard to see the ground. Not a single light was present for as far as he could see. He used night vision to find a suitable landing area. He pulled his left toggle hard and began spinning downward. Once he was about twenty feet from the ground, he leveled off and swooped across the dark grass. Once Todd's feet touched the ground, he jogged out of the momentum until he could drop down to a knee. The rain began to die down. He flipped the small Velcro-encased switch on his hip and his parachute retracted back into its container.

He stood up and looked around at the dark landscape. A bolt of lightning lit up the dark plains around him and was followed with a cracking boom a few seconds later. He pulled up a digital map on his MTX and placed a waypoint on Durango. His HUD highlighted the terrain before him and showed a large beacon up in the sky pointing down at the earth where the town was. The distance that displayed next to the beacon was "4.8 kilometers." It would be daylight before he reached the town. He started walking towards it in the cool dead of night.

The rain finally stopped about an hour later. The clouds began to pull back, revealing a star-filled sky. Todd stayed vigilant as he strolled along the rolling landscape. Several minutes later, the clouds had completely disappeared and left the night once again beautifully illuminated by the moon. He remembered that Kevin had slipped something in his pack before he jumped, and he unclipped the pack from his shoulders and hips. He set it down in front of him and unzipped the side pocket. Inside was a small black pouch, about the size of a large book. He pulled it out; it was hefty and contained several items. He unzipped it and smiled at the contents. The custom 1911 pistol, its Kydex holster, a sound suppressor, and four eight-round magazines were inside. Todd looked up into the sky and grinned.

"Thanks, Kevin."

He screwed on the stubby suppressor and inserted one of the mags, then racked the slide. He continued walking, holding the weapon down low. He moved softly through the night, a warrior of the twenty-first century prowling the dark landscape of the nineteenth. He felt like an alien who had just crash landed.

THE OLD WEST

The sun began to emit pink rays of light over the horizon and the land around him presented its breathtaking range. Dark purple mountains lined the distant horizon like an unreachable barrier that teased exploration. Footprints appeared one by one in the grass as Todd's transparent figure walked across the endless plain.

He grasped the 1911, not sure what he might run into. To his front was a large grass hill that hid the sun and its soft mixture of colors behind it. He sighed at the sight and began huffing his way up. When he was nearly to the top, he was stopped in his tracks by a thunderous noise on the other side. He crouched down and slowly crept to the top of the hill as the rumbling noise becoming more and more present.

When he reached the peak, his body froze, and his heart felt as if it had skipped a beat. He slowly rose to his feet, removing his helmet and disengaging the cloaking system. The sweet familiar tinge of sage brush lingered in his nostrils. The sun peeked over the shallow clouds and lit the thousands of buffalo that trotted through the valley beneath him like a thundering river of fur and power. The sight put a lump in his throat and a smile on his face. The last time he had seen the U.S., it was a burning heap of concrete and glass; a dark reminiscence of an arrogant civilization meeting its end. Yet now, it was a wild and free place of natural beauty. The bison continued shuffling down the valley in an orchestrated manner. Todd knelt down and activated the "Communications" option on his

MTX. He checked the Link Quality Analysis and found it was sixty-eight percent; good enough to send a text to the North Pole. He began typing on the digital keyboard on his wrist.

-SITREP-

I have successfully inserted into the Old West. My gear is all accounted for and operational. I will reach the town in less than an hour where I will begin my search for York. I will send another transmission in four hours. Let Kev know I said thank you.

P.S. Buffalo. Lots and lots of Buffalo.

He continued walking towards the town, occasionally looking back at the distant herd of bison. He saw wooden buildings two hundred meters in front of him and he began walking softly, fully cloaked. He could faintly hear and see people inside the town going about their early morning activities.

Todd reached the backside of one of the buildings, pressed up against it and peered around the side. He was in awe. Real Western folk on horses were moving around the town, wearing nineteenth century garb. He felt like he was in the set of a movie. A wagon drawn by two horses pulled in next to the building in front of Todd.

"Whoa!" the man controlling them said as the horses came to a stop. The man wore a light red blouse with a leather vest, and a short-brimmed hat was pulled low on his forehead. He had a thick mustache that nearly stretched to below his chin. He climbed down the wheel of the wagon and walked to the back, where he opened the tailgate and pulled off what appeared to be a bag of rice. He threw it over his shoulder and walked past Todd, only inches from nudging him.

The man went back for a second bag, and Todd took advantage of his absence and darted to the adjacent building. It had a low roof and it was near the center of town. Todd decided to get to the roof and try to get a better look at his surroundings. He stepped up on a wooden barrel at the base of the wall, jumped up and grabbed the corner of the roof. His shoulder muscles tightened as he pulled himself up, throwing a leg to the roof. The man unloading the bags paid no attention to his blatant disregard for noise discipline.

In a low squat, Todd crept to the edge of the building and surveyed the town. It consisted of approximately thirty buildings, all of which were similar in design. They all had a large front that made the structure seem larger than they really were. Wooden porches skirted each building, separated at various levels from the different sized buildings next to each one. Hitching posts and waters troughs were set outside next to the support posts of most establishments. He counted six individuals who were outside and going about their own business. As time passed, more and more people would be out and about, making his sneaking around much more difficult.

His first priority was to obtain a disguise. For obvious reasons, the general store was out of the question, but he would need to borrow some clothes. At the corner of the street was the saloon, the largest of all the buildings in town. He figured there would be hotel rooms on the second floor for all-nighters. Perhaps he could acquire something to wear from an unoccupied room.

Todd hopped down from the roof and ran down the backside of the buildings, checking around the corners before he crossed each time. He hopped over several small wooden fences and did his best to do so quietly. He came to a square corral with three large horses slowly pacing back and forth inside. He hopped the gate and tiptoed past the large animals. He was only several feet from the other gate when one of the horses began rearing on its back legs. Startled by this, Todd backed up slowly. The horse continued to pounce on its hind legs, bringing its front hooves up and slamming them back down into the loose dirt, neighing loudly.

An older man with a gray beard and a floppy brown hat came running out of the barn in front of the corral. He opened the gate and put his hands out in front of him. He approached the spooked horse from an angle and talked to it calmly.

"Easy … easy," he said as he softly placed his hand on the horse's long face.

The horse shook its head and snorted as if to let the man know that something was awry. Todd watched as the man eased the powerful animal's nerves. He wondered if it had somehow sensed his presence. He took note of this and continued towards the saloon.

It was now almost 7 a.m. The sun was climbing higher in the sky and more people were walking around the quiet town. Todd peered around the corner at what he believed to be the doctor's office and spotted the saloon. He chuckled at the sight of the cliché double swinging doors at the entrance. Using thermal vision, he looked inside over the top of the double doors. He magnified the image, seeing at least two individuals inside. He imagined busting in through the doors, causing the typical piano tune to stop mid play and every drunk cowboy to look up in disapproval, slowly reaching for their six shooters. The humorous thought eased his mind and helped him think of a more realistic alternative. He noticed a parked wagon on the side of the building full of wooden crates. He could climb up this and use it to get to the roof where he would sneak into a window on the balcony. Hopefully he could snag something to wear out of a dresser or closet of one of the guest rooms. As for his suit, he would have to cloak it and stuff it in a barrel or crate outside.

Todd was about to get up and make his way to the side of the saloon when a tall man wearing a brown duster coat and black felt hat came stumbling out of the double doors. Todd observed him as he stopped at the hitching post and leaned over it, dry heaving without any payoff.

Todd laughed inside his helmet. "Good God, it's seven in the morning, bud." The man stumbled out into the main road and walked over to the side of the building where the wagon was hitched. Todd watched him as he struggled to climb up on the wagon with little success. The wagon itself had no horses connected to it, and Todd doubted it even belonged to him. Todd got up very calmly and strolled across the street to the drunk man, who was picking himself up from his second attempt to ascend the wagon. Todd walked up to him, so close that he could see his eyes drifting off as he stood up, his upper body making small orbiting motions.

Todd removed a small anesthetic injector from his kit and grasped it with his right hand; with his left, he pulled down the man's collar, giving himself some room to work with. He stuck the injector in his neck and the man grunted and fell over unconscious. Todd looked around to ensure nobody had seen the man's sudden collapse; then he dragged him by his arms to the back of the wagon. He felt a hint of pity as he removed the man's coat and boots. He pulled off the dark duster and held it up; it was a little too small to try and throw it over the armored suit. He removed his helmet and placed it on the bed of the wagon, using the lens as a mirror. It was still far too obvious that he was wearing the suit underneath. He sighed and looked down at the man. He wore a light blue blouse with a loose bandana around his neck, and over his trousers he wore leather chaps.

Todd realized that he was going to have to take it all in order to fit in. A few minutes later, the man lay beneath the wagon with nothing but his long johns. Todd stood looking at himself in the reflection of the helmet. He looked like a real cowboy, with the exception of the modern-day pistol that he wore back behind his hip, hidden by the long duster coat. The only thing he didn't like was the hat. It was obnoxiously large and the front curved up in a way that he imaged an old dusty prospector would wear it. He returned the hat to the man, placing it over his face. He connected the helmet to the neck of the suit and activated the cloaked mode. He then placed them in a wooden crate on the back of the wagon. He messed up his hair a bit, to better look the part, and headed for the double doors of the saloon.

The long spurs on the boots he wore jingled with every thunderous step made by the heavy boots. He grinned at this. He pushed through the double doors to reveal the interior of the saloon. As he did so, every person in the saloon stopped talking and looked at him. He walked up to the bar and scanned behind it for the bartender, who was nowhere to be found. He could sense the eyes of the three individuals sitting at the bar to his left. He looked around the interior of the saloon, pretending not to notice the men staring at him. The bar was a polished oak with dark stains across it. The shelves behind the bar were shallow and held a small variety of drinks that ranged from bourbon, scotch, and what he assumed to be tequila. There were a few circular wooden tables set out in the middle of the saloon and a group of men sat at one of them playing cards. A man who Todd assumed was the bartender, since he was wearing a white dress shirt with a thin bow tie and bands on his arms above the elbows, was taking the chairs off the remaining tables. The man either didn't notice him, or didn't bother looking up.

"Excuse me!" Todd said strongly, trying to intimidate the men at the bar with his commanding voice.

Without looking up, the bartender replied, "What can I do ya for?"

Todd froze for a second; it was the first time he had heard someone from this time period say anything and he marveled in the moment.

"Uh, I was wondering if you could help me find someone," he said, trying to maintain his commanding demeanor.

The bartender was in the midst of placing a chair on the ground when he met Todd's eyes. He dropped the wooden chair on the hard floor. "Look, Mister," he said, putting his hands in the air as if to keep Todd calm. "I don't want no trouble …"

Todd looked at him with his eyebrow cocked. "No trouble, I just need your help finding some—"

One of the men at the bar interrupted. "You said you'd be gone, after the last time," the man said, a small stream of tobacco leaking from the corner of his mouth into his thick beard.

Todd looked at him in confusion for a moment. He then began to grasp the situation and tried to find a way out of it.

"My older … twin brother came through here a while back. I reckon you must've heard something as to where he might've been going." Todd did his best to sound Western-like.

The man continued to glare at him. "Your older twin brother?" he said in disbelief.

Todd cursed in his head for not having planned his story better, then came back with a quick rebuttal. "Uh yeah, he came out of my ma a few minutes before me, so technically he's the older one."

The bearded man spat a wad of tobacco into the tin at his feet. "Have scars on his face, did he?"

"Yup, he got those while fighting a Chinese feller by the name of Jackie Chan, during his work on the railroads." Todd was doing his best to maintain a serious expression.

The man looked back at the two sitting next to him. They nodded at each other, then he turned back to Todd, who was standing with his thumbs in his belt buckle.

"Goddamn Chinamen," he said, shaking his head, "carved that brother of yours up pretty good."

Todd smiled. "Any idea where he went? Ma and Pa are worried."

One of the other men answered. "He said he was headin' west, last time I seen him. He had just finished a tussle with one them Moore boys who rustle cattle a few miles of here." The man took a swig of his dark drink and winced. "That'd been about ..." He looked over to one of his companions, "whaddaya you say? Two ... three weeks ago?"

The two others nodded in agreement and looked back at Todd, who was displeased with this news. He was hoping to have only missed him by a few days. Several weeks, and he could be hundreds of miles in any direction by now. And finding him in this day and age would require primitive techniques and a lot of asking locals.

He looked back at the bearded man, who still had his gaze on him. "Who're these Moores you mentioned?" Todd asked.

"There's four of 'em; they're ah bunch of assholes. Four rotten brothers, runnin' around with a group of fellow rustlers from all over. They're no Stockton gang, but a bad bunch for sure."

"How many of them are there?"

The man pondered for a moment then replied, "Ah, I reckon thirteen or so. Maybe only twelve now."

"Why's that?"

The man chuckled. "Well, that brother of yours busted up the younger one, Winston, pretty bad the last night he was here. The little shit had been gettin' rough with one of the workin' girls and your brother knocked nearly all his teeth out. Busted up his nose real bad too."

Todd breathed out quickly through his nose, humored slightly. The bartender was behind the bar now, leaning up against it. He chimed into the conversation. "You look a lot alike, you and him ... besides all the scars he's got."

Todd nodded. "Yeah, I get that a lot."

The three men chuckled. Todd thought about the change to the mission that had just presented itself. He not only would have to track his same-self through nineteenth century America, he now had an outlaw gang out looking for him. If they even saw Todd, they would most likely mistake him for York.

Todd got as much information out of the three men as he could. He asked them about the weather he would most likely encounter as well as best methods of travel and what areas to avoid. From what he had gathered, York had most likely traveled west to a nearby town.

"Do you know where I can get a horse?"

The bearded man looked confused. "You ain't got a horse?" He chuckled. "What'd you do, fall out of the darn sky?"

Todd grinned and shook his head. "My horse was stolen. I'm looking to find another so I can start headin' west."

The three men pondered for a moment, then the third man at the end who had been the least talkative spoke. "There's a rancher by the name of McWilliams, he lives about a day's ride south of here. He breaks in wild horses for a livin'. Maybe he could help ya."

Todd nodded, then thought about the statement "a day's ride." What the hell was a day's ride? Twenty, thirty miles? He sure as hell wasn't about to go on foot, but he also wasn't about to ask these men for a lift. He decided to end the conversation here. He thanked the three men for their help and said goodbye. He headed back out into the town, which was much livelier. People were all around, strolling down the streets and sitting on porch chairs. The sun was high in the sky, shining down on the town like a movie set. Todd placed his hand over his eyes to shield them from the sun. The air was crisp and cool, and it swept past him with a hint of sage that brought him back to his childhood. He thought about what his next move would be. He needed to get ahold of a horse so he could start tracking down York, but Todd had never even ridden a horse. He decided he would need to find the Mr. McWilliams the men had mentioned. As for learning to ride, Todd had always been a hands-on learner anyway.

*　　*　　*

April 26, 1986

I stood on the roof of a small building on the outskirts of Pripyat. Three klicks away, I could see Chernobyl's large chimney looming over the dark facility. The night was cool and clear, and crickets scraped their legs, giving a peaceful soundtrack to the moonlit setting. Ukraine had turned out to be quite lovely actually. I inserted during the late afternoon, giving me time to scout out a suitable observation point within the city, where I would detonate. I planted the explosives in Reactor 4 around midnight. It had been a smooth operation, up until that point. I encountered two individuals.

The first caught me as I was planting the explosives. He came up behind me and noticed a strange device that was being tampered with by a transparent figure. I whipped around, causing him to stumble backwards in fear. I drew my pistol and put two rounds in his chest, then one more in his head just to make sure. I continued setting the charge, then pulled his body close to it so that he would be completely vaporized in the blast. The second guy I took out as I was leaving. I was creeping down a long corridor, heading for the door, when he emerged from a side room, reading some notes on a clipboard. He seemed rushed. Apparently, they were running tests of some kind that night. I clocked almost forty workers who were running tests within the facility; fortunately the majority of them were all co-located. I leveled the sights of my suppressed Sig on him, but thought and stopped myself from pulling the trigger. I couldn't shoot him. If there was any reason to believe that the incident had been a covert operation, the entire event could be used as an act of war, bringing a much quicker WWIII. And even if the operation went as smoothly as intended, the possibilities of conspiracy theories were almost guaranteed.

I holstered my pistol and sprinted towards him. He looked up just in time to see me come out of the cloak and grab him. He screamed in confusion as I muscled him up against the wall. He began to fight back, throwing wild blows to my helmet and kicking sporadically. He was moving around far too much to finish him with a blood choke. Grabbing him by his long hair, I smashed his face into the wall over and over until there was a chunky splotch of blood oozing down it. His nose seemed to disappear into the red mush that was once his face. The explosion would no doubt level this portion of the building, so I didn't worry about forensics. I dropped him to the ground and continued out into the night.

For the next hour, I ran towards the lights of the populated city of Pripyat, hopping over small fences and running across open fields. When I reached the city, I ascended the fire escape of the building I'd chosen for my OP. I chose to detonate from such a far distance for obvious reasons. I knew the fallout would affect a substantial portion of the region, but had no idea just how devastating it would end up being. I looked down at the MTX; the connection to the explosives was still live. The time was 1:23 a.m. I looked back out into the city behind me that was home to over fifty thousand civilians, all sleeping peacefully, unaware that their world was about to fall apart. My mind went to a familiar place of anger and confusion because there I was, once again ready to sacrifice the lives of possibly thousands so that a generation a few decades from now may live longer than they originally had. I had spent so much time fearing the future that it had become like a cancer within me. For a time, I felt like it was just waiting to resurface and claim my life as it was always intended to do. I looked back down at the MTX. It was now 1:24. I pressed "Detonate."

I heard the distant boom of the explosion within the reactor and then saw the large orange ball of flames erupt from the top of the facility. I quickly hopped up into the air and pressed "INITIATE" and the explosion disappeared, taking with it the beauty of this place. It was now 2014 and heavy clouds loomed over the dark landscape. I turned and a chill ran up my spine.

There wasn't a single light on throughout the city. The buildings were a dark gray, overgrown with vegetation and cluttered with rust. Light snow and debris from the endlessly flaking walls blanketed the now untamed ground full of shrubs and the rusty carcasses of vehicles. I scanned the eerie, post-apocalyptic metropolis. It was like nothing I had ever seen before. It was a real-life nightmare.

The howl of wild dogs let me know of what life remained in the distance. I was now responsible for the deaths of thousands. I would later look over the images of mutilated men, women, and children affected by the radiation.

The images haunt me to this day.

A DAY'S RIDE

Todd walked down the center of the main road like Wyatt Earp on his way to the O.K. Corral. He walked with a purposeful stride that made several heads turn as he passed. The trail to York was about as hot as a day in the North Pole, and Todd was still no closer to obtaining a horse. He checked out the remainder of the town, looking at the different establishments and briefly conversing with the local populace.

The people of this time period, or at least this town, were extremely polite. Every person he met greeted him with a "Hello," or a "Mornin', Mister." He was slightly disappointed that he had yet to receive a "Howdy, Partner." At the far end of the main road, opposite the saloon, he came to a train station labeled "Silverton Railroad" with a single teller inside. She was an older woman, and she wore a dark blue dress that closed tightly around her neck right under her jawline. She sat behind the wooden desk, a pair of glasses perched on her nose, reading a dusty leather-bound book. Todd walked into the small room and scanned it, then walked over to her.

"Excuse me," he said calmly. "When is the next train due?"

Without looking up from her book, she answered slowly, "Next train isn't due until next week. Got held up down south in Farmington."

"Shit," Todd mumbled.

"Watch your mouth, young man!" she said, once again without

looking up from her book.

"Sorry," Todd said, feeling somewhat embarrassed.

He left the train station and walked back down the street towards the saloon. He was beginning to feel like his options were running out. He was already a week or so behind York, and he didn't have a method of transportation. The townsfolk continued going along with their daily routines as Todd calmly walked to the side of saloon where he found his drunken friend still unconscious beneath the wagon. He chuckled to himself, then hopped up on top of the wagon and opened the crate that contained his invisible suit. He pulled it out and set it on the bed of the wagon and began undressing, keeping an eye out for passersby. His body seemed to disappear into thin air as he eased into the suit. Once he was fully in, he felt around the back of the wagon until he found his helmet and put it on. He stuffed his "borrowed" clothes into the large pouch on his pack and clipped it back on to his web gear. Staying vigilant, he softly made his way back down the backside of the buildings towards the south side of town. It proved to be quite difficult as there were many more people he had to tiptoe past. It was fascinating to him to see people of this era living and interacting with each other. They seemed much more vocal and polite to each other than the people of his time.

He reached the end of town and looked at the road that curved southwest out through the mountain pass. He pondered for a moment, thinking about walking. He still was unsure as to what a day's ride was, and he pulled up the "Navigation" option on the MTX. The large hills surrounding the town imposed a feeling of hopelessness that began to set in on him. Even with the knowledge of the future, and the most advanced technology on his side, he couldn't escape the hardship of time. He was about to just start walking when he heard the loud patter of hooves coming down the road towards him. He ducked behind a small shrub and saw a wagon being pulled by two horses making its way out of town. Two men sat on the bench, the one on the right holding the reins connected to the bit within the animal's mouths. Todd studied the contents in the back of the wagon. There were a few crates, along with some personal effects. He could see room back towards the tailgate. If he could do so quietly, he could hop in the back and just ride along for a few miles.

The wagon passed him and he stood up and ran after it. The man with the reins cracked them and the wagon lurched forward. Todd began to run faster and he placed a hand on the side of the wagon, struggling to keep up. He waited for a smooth patch in the road and used it to throw a leg up over the side. His heel smacked the solid wood inside the bed, making a loud thud. The man riding shotgun looked back briefly and then turned back around. Todd slowly worked the rest of his body up into the bed of the wagon and sat with his legs crossed, his knees against the tailgate. He bounced up and down as he watched the land pass by. He smiled at the odd situation he had now found himself in.

The wagon jounced around along the uneven road for nearly two hours. Todd's head began to bob down to his chest, but he was quickly woken when the wagon hit a rock in the road. It became clear to him very quickly that traveling during this day and age was extremely unpleasant. The hard, steel-rimmed wagon wheels sent the rider a report of every hard feature along the earth's surface.

The two men on the bench chatted loudly almost the entire ride. Todd eavesdropped on their conversation for several hours and learned a great deal about them. The man controlling the reins was Henry, who was the local shopkeeper in Durango. He was somewhere in his late fifties and seemed to be extremely religious judging by "the Lord's" constant involvement in his conversations. The other one was Calvin, who apparently worked for Henry and couldn't have been older than seventeen. He asked more questions than he answered, and usually his questions were answered very wisely by Henry, who clearly served as a mentor role. Their conversation started with the store and its current importance to the town, and somehow led to the ever-changing nature of modern civilization and the dying spirituality and faith in society. It was interesting to hear them talk about the future, and how technology was a force that was rapidly consuming the western world. Technological achievements such as the train were an outstanding example of how the world of the future was becoming more accessible to common folk, who more and more would become dependent on machines. Todd only wished they could see the rail trains in Los Angeles from his time.

Todd looked at the time displayed in his HUD. It had been nearly four hours since they left Durango. The land around them was beginning to flatten out, slowly becoming an arid desert with hills and large buttes lining the distant horizon. The roads became softer and flatter as the sand became softer. Todd took advantage of this and adjusted the contents in the back of the wagon, clearing a space for himself so he could curl up. He ensured Henry and Calvin didn't notice the crates being moved around and, using some empty burlap sacks as a pillow, he curled up with his knees tucked up to his stomach. Before going to sleep, he tapped the MTX and sent a quick transmission to the future.

-SITREP-

I'm en route to a local rancher "a day's ride" south of Durango. Once I am able to obtain a horse, I will continue on with my search for York who was last seen heading west.

He closed his eyes and felt his mind drift off into much-needed rest.

*   *   *

June 3, 2014

The images are burned in my mind. So many lives lost because of me, so many places scarred because of my actions. I'm having a hard time sleeping, having a hard time looking in the mirror. I don't recognize the man I see anymore. This scarred-up monster in the reflection isn't the boy who grew up in Bayfield, Colorado with his sweet mother. I'm not the quiet seventeen-year-old who skipped prom night because he was too shy to ask anyone to go with him. Didn't do drugs because he was afraid he would turn out to be like his father. All I saw was the bastard who was responsible for the deaths of thousands. A fool blinded by his own wants and agenda ... who had sacrificed innocent civilians to achieve them.

I don't think I want to do this anymore. I can't watch innocent people die by my own hands and just shrug it off like they never existed anyway. I'm not like Bohden, I can't just lie to myself and pretend that things didn't happen. Who am I to decide what is best for mankind? Why should I single-handedly have the right to choose who lives or dies, who gets to live in the future and who gets their entire world torn apart around them? If it wasn't for Kara and Brian, I would have left already. They're the only reason I continue on. I want them to be able to return to the real world. They deserve real lives again. Especially Kara. There is nothing I want more than for her to be happy.

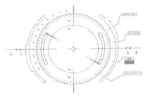

JACK

Todd woke when the wagon made an abrupt stop. He sat up quickly and saw the two men hopping down from the bench seat. His mind took a second to regain its bearings. It was now dark and the animals throughout the desert called out to the night, making for a peaceful scene.

Henry walked to the back of the wagon and pulled down the tailgate. Todd hopped off the side of the wagon and landed softly on the desert floor. He looked back to ensure the two hadn't heard him. While Henry pulled off blankets and some cooking materials, Calvin began preparing some kindling for a fire. A few minutes later, the two settled around the fire and began cooking some beans in a pan over the open flame. Todd realized how hungry he was and unclipped his pack; he pulled out one of his rations and squeezed all the contents into his mouth, turning his head so there was no possibility of them seeing his exposed face. He cringed at the artificial taste, wanting to eat some actual food. He contemplated stealing some, but it was all gone before he mustered up the courage to act upon his urges.

The two men stared into the hypnotizing flames, saying nothing to each other for a long while. The sparks flew up into the dark night and disappeared as they cooled amongst the stars. Todd slowly crept closer to the fire and settled between two smooth boulders a few feet from the campsite. The full moon lit the desert around them as the horses snorted companionably to each other next to the wagon. Todd felt an odd security from the peaceful setting; he felt his eyes becoming heavy and his mind began to wander. He wished he could take off the suit and feel the natural warmth of the flame. He lay on his back looking up at the stars, ignoring his HUD which was trying to accurately display the temperature while being affected by the hot fire. He missed camping, he missed nature. Technology had consumed his life for the past twenty years and it seemed to have become a necessity. It was strange to see Henry and Calvin sit for hours without pulling out a cellphone. It felt freeing to be in such a raw environment.

The sun shined through his visor and his eyes slowly blinked open. He sat up slowly and stretched out, but froze when he noticed the wagon was no longer behind him. He stood up and looked around. The fire had been kicked out and there was no sign of Calvin and Henry. Although they had never even been aware of his presence, he felt like they had abandoned him.

"Shit!" He couldn't believe he had overslept. Looking at the ground and shaking his head, he began thinking of options. He looked up and scanned the horizon. His HUD was actively searching for anything that resembled something manmade. It finally locked onto an object off in the distance. He squinted and canted his head at something dark that was blurry from the mirage on the horizon, so far away it looked like a small pebble. "6.5 kilometers" was displayed beneath the highlighted object. He rolled his eyes and began walking towards it, cursing every other step.

One kilometer remained and the object in the distance was beginning to take shape. He began to speed up was what was clearly a house grew in his view. He started to run but then stopped and thought for a moment. He quickly unclipped his pack and pulled out his disguise and began undressing. His skin breathed in the warm air and he paused for a moment to take it in. He held the cloaked suit and took in a long breath; the warm, dusty air was intoxicating. He looked down at his depressed pads of his fingertips bearing the weight of the invisible hard plates. Over to his right a few feet away was a distinct rock formation that rose above the shrubs like a natural pillar. He walked over, placed the suit at the base of it and began piling stones over it like an ancient burial.

He set the last stone on the large pile and stood up to admire the incognito cache spot. He would leave it here until he could get a horse and start on York's trail. He didn't feel entirely comfortable about leaving a billion-dollar suit out in the desert, but he didn't see any other option. He pulled off the MTX and put it in the duster's pocket. He also removed his 1911 and its spare magazines.

"Whatcha doin', Mister?" a little voice from above called out.

Todd jump backwards, his heart pounding in his chest. He looked around in confusion, then a shadow from above engulfed him. Sitting on top of the rock formation was a small boy wearing a flat-brimmed hat. His legs dangled down and kicked curiously.

"What the, I, uh ..." Todd fumbled with his words.

"How come you have no clothes on?" the boy asked.

Todd looked up at him in confusion, then down at himself. He was wearing only his synthetic polyester briefs. He cringed at the sight of them. In one instant, the entire timeline could be corrupted because a little boy had seen his future underwear. He felt a sickening feeling spread in his stomach. The boy canted his head and looked confused, and he pointed his little index finger down at Todd.

"Why you have such fancy britches?"

Todd thought for a second then replied, "They're uh ... silk, from England."

"Hmm, I heard 'bout England, don't they talk funny there?" he asked, his voice high-pitched and adorable.

Todd chuckled, knowing that he was in the clear. "Yes, they talk funny."

The little boy stood up and put his hands on his hips, looking down at Todd like a comic book character atop a building. "Why you out here all 'lone, Mister?"

Todd smiled up at the little boy. Placing his hand over his eyes to shield them from the sun, he said, "I was going to ask you the same question."

The boy looked out into the hills confidently. "I'm gonna find gold up on them hills, and live by myself," he said in a defiant way.

Todd laughed. "You're a little young to be living by yourself, little man. Where's your parents?"

The boy disappeared behind the ledge of the chimney, then Todd heard the sound of his small feet hit the rock landing a few feet below the peak. He came around the chimney and looked at Todd, who was at eye level with him now.

"I'm a man now, I don't need to live with my parents anymore."

Todd looked at him with a humorous expression on his face. The boy wore a dirty button-up shirt with the sleeves rolled up to his scuffed elbows, and overalls that were covered with the orange powder from the rock. He had long blonde hair that crept in front of his eyes beneath his hat. He smiled at Todd. He still had all his baby teeth, which led Todd to believe he was about five or maybe six years old. Todd looked at him with a grin, placing his hands on his hips to combat his confident posture.

"Them your clothes?" the boy asked, pointing at the long duster and the rest of his disguise sitting next to a small sage brush.

"Yup, I uh ... was trying to get some ants out of my clothes."

The boy laughed hysterically and cradled his little belly. "You can't sleep in the dirt, dumb dumb, you have tuh put somethin' below ya!"

Todd smiled. "You're smart," he said over the boy's laughter. "Your father teach you that?"

The boy stopped laughing and exhaled, shrugging his shoulders and throwing his arms down in an overly dramatic fashion. "Yeah ... Papa is mean and I hate him."

"He's mean? How mean?" Todd asked, his face going stern.

"He's always makin' me do chores and not letting me do what I want," the boy said, as he paced atop the boulder.

"Sounds like he cares about you," Todd said, as he walked over to his clothes and began dressing.

The little boy began rambling on about how his father was always strict and was very stern with him. Todd had never had much of a father, and he found the boy's complaints quite humorous. From what he gathered, his father seemed like a caring man, maybe a little harsh, but he only wanted what was best for his son. The boy's complaints were completely understandable. It was no surprise that a child would find rules unfair or see chores as punishment. Todd wondered what his father did for a living.

Todd finished dressing and threw on the long duster, tying the scarf around his neck. The boy looked at him in awe. He was unsure what it was the boy found so fascinating about him.

Todd looked down at himself then back at the boy. "What?" he asked.

The boy smiled, his little upper teeth covering his lower lip. Todd hadn't been around children much in his life. He rarely even saw kids in his line of work, and he didn't particularly even like children. This kid however reminded him of himself when he was a boy. The two looked at each other in silence for a while.

"What's your name, kid?" Todd asked.

The boy stepped to the edge of the rock, close to Todd, and presented a dirty hand. "Jack McWilliams, Mister."

Todd smiled kindly and grasped the boy's small hand. "Nice to meet you, Jack, my name is Todd."

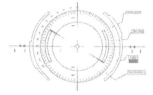

THE STRANGER

Luke McWilliams stood on the porch overlooking the vast acres that surrounded the ranch. He felt troubled inside; it wasn't the first time this had happened. He blamed himself for his son's attitude towards him. Being a father had proven to be one of the most difficult feats he had ever undergone. He had spent most of his life living outside the law, living the way most considered unworldly. Making ends meet by the skin of his teeth, day by day.

He saw his son going down the same cursed path as himself, and it was his greatest fear that Jack would one day end up being anything like him. He found it odd that he wanted his son to be the complete opposite person he was. He wondered if other fathers dealt with similar issues regarding their children. Maybe he didn't deserve a child. Jack sure as hell didn't deserve him; he deserved better.

He stepped off the porch towards the corral. His steps were thunderous as he stormed towards his saddle that sat on the post of the corral. He reached over and was about to throw it up on his shoulder when he saw something from the corner of his eye. About two hands beneath the dropping sun were two figures approaching from the northwest. He tilted his head down, using the long brim of his tall hat to shield his eyes from the sun. He could spot little Jack's proud walk from a mile away. He was with a broad-shouldered man wearing a long duster. Luke stepped away from the log fence and studied the man beside his son. They were coming close now and he could see the man's features. He had short, messy hair that blew in the wind, and he had a week or so of stubble. His dark eyes were shaded by his hard brow.

The two walked onto the soft grass surrounding the house and Luke looked the man in the eyes. Trust was something that very few individuals had earned from Luke McWilliams. He looked down at Jack very sternly. Jack looked down at his feet.

"Jack!" a voice called out from the house. A tall, slender woman came running out, holding her long skirt and apron above her feet. She came to Jack and dropped down to him, hugging him tightly. She pulled away and looked at him intensely. "Where have you been. I've been worried sick!"

Jack's eyes became teary and he refused to look up. "I'm … sorry, Mama," he said quietly.

Her anger quickly faded and she hugged him again. Luke looked back up at the stranger, who held out his hand towards him. He grabbed it, noticing a firm grip.

"Luke McWilliams," he said. His voice was deep and complemented his large stature.

"Todd … Mitchel."

"Thank you for bringing him back, he … tends to venture off every now and then."

They watched as Jack and his mother walked back to the house. Luke noticed how Todd looked around the ranch in a very strange way. As If he were making sure he wasn't being watched, or was scanning for predators. Luke looked around and then back at him.

"Where ya from, stranger?" Luke asked.

Todd was about to answer but stopped himself briefly. "I'm from … Durango. I'm heading west, trying to find my twin brother."

"This brother of yours … he in some kind of trouble?" Luke asked grimly, his arms crossed.

"Luke! I think our guest could use something to eat," said Sarah McWilliams, who approached her husband, placing her thin fingers on his shoulder.

He looked over his shoulder at her and his hardened expression eased; she was the voice of reason in his life, and she could ease all the pain and anger within him with just a look or touch. He looked back at Todd, and his thick mustache and goatee raised on his face as he broke a smile. "Come on in, Mr. Mitchel, let's have some supper and talk about this brother of yours."

Luke, Todd, and Jack sat in the dining room of the McWilliams house as Sarah placed plates of beef and vegetables in front of them. Jack, who was fresh from a bath, went straight for the beef. Sarah gave him a quick glare and he stabbed his fork into some veggies angrily. Todd seemed to stop himself from devouring the plate. He looked quite parched, and his hands shook slightly as he slowly brought his fork up to his mouth.

"So, what brings you out here, Mr. Mitchel?" Luke asked without looking up from his plate.

Todd wiped his mouth and was about to answer but was beaten by Sarah.

"Thank you, Mr. Mitchel, for finding our son. Luke and I are very grateful." She fixed herself a plate and sat down next to Luke. "He had been gone since early this morning, and had me and Luke on the fritz"

The corner of Todd's mouth curved up and he nodded. "Glad I could help," he said.

"So, what brings you way out here, Mr. Mitchel?" she asked very kindly.

Todd raised his eyebrows briefly then exhaled, as if he were already tired of a journey he had yet to really begin. "Well ... like I told your husband, I'm heading west in search of my brother."

Sarah looked over at Luke, who stared at Todd with a look that said he either didn't like him, or was using his eyes rather than his voice to figure out what kind of man he was. She shot him a quick glare by widening her eyes. He adjusted in his seat and cleared his throat.

"I noticed you approached without a horse. Are you in need of one?" he asked.

Todd's eyes lit up slightly "Yes! I ... came out here in hopes of acquiring one actually. I was referred to you back in town."

"Well you might be in luck, son, I've got a few fresh horses out in the corral in need of breaking in."

Todd looked confused by this phrase, but nodded in agreement. "How much do your horses go for?"

Luke looked over at Sarah, who raised her eyebrows at him. He looked back at Todd and replied in a way that displayed some discomfort. "Well uh ... I figure you bringing my boy home ought to cover it."

Sarah smiled big at her husband and looked back at Todd, who pondered for a moment. He was uneasy about this, but a smile crept on to his face.

"I can't tell you how grateful I would be."

Luke grinned then continued cutting into the meat on his plate. Todd looked over at Jack, who appeared to have been staring at him the entire time.

"Jack!" his mother snapped. "It's not polite to stare." She looked over at Todd and giggled. "I'm sorry, Mr. Mitchel, he shares his father's curious gaze."

Todd smiled at the boy. "It's alright Mrs. McWilliams, and please ... call me Todd."

The four quietly ate for the next few minutes. When they were finished, Sarah took their plates into the kitchen, and Jack followed her, leaving Luke and Todd sitting at the table. Todd appeared troubled. His eyes rarely held their fix on anything. He sat in silence for a while, staring at his hands folded on the table.

"Tell me about this brother of yours," Luke said, his booming voice now soft and sincere.

Todd rotated his jaw. Without looking up, he answered slowly. "He's ... in a lot of trouble."

"How so?"

"He's running from some bad people and a worse past."

Luke's hard gaze eased and he leaned forward slightly. "How do you mean?"

"Him and I have had our fair share of run-ins with death and the evil that usually accompanies it. He more so than myself." He paused for a moment, then looked up at Luke, who sat on the edges of the lantern's reach. Todd went on. "There are people who care for him back where I come from. I want to make sure he returns to them safely."

"Who's after him?" Luke asked.

"Some cattle rustlers by the name of Moore. You know them?"

Luke nodded solemnly at him. "I know of them. They're a young bunch ... amateurs if you ask me. But dangerous nonetheless."

Todd breathed out quickly "Well he busted up one of them pretty bad then left town. I'm not really sure where he is heading."

"Does he know you're comin'?"

Todd shook his head. "He has no idea."

Luke nodded and ran his thumb over his lips beneath his thick mustache. "Your brother ... he a fighter?"

Todd raised an eyebrow and nodded. "A warrior," he said firmly.

"And you?" Luke asked; his eyes looked hard, lit by the dim lantern that hung above the table.

"He and I are more alike than I'd care to admit."

Luke studied Todd. He didn't want to let his feelings sway his firm demeanor or judgment. But he felt an odd connection with Todd. He was like a split image of his younger self just before he had made a turn for the worse. He could also sense that Todd was telling the truth, and his reasons for his presence at his home were no doubt noble.

Luke stood up. He towered over Todd, and his slick black hair nearly touched the ceiling. His hardened expression eased, and his brow raised. "I'll help you find him."

Todd looked down. "I couldn't accept your help, sir. You have a family to take care of and this journey will no doubt be dangerous."

Luke snickered in a way that displayed he was all too familiar with dangerous situations. He placed his large hand on Todd's shoulder and smiled. "Danger is a lot like women. You're better off without one in your life, but sooner or later you find you need one. Besides, my family can take care of themselves for a few days."

Todd seemed like he wanted to argue further but stopped himself and just nodded up at the man.

"I'll fix ya a pallet out in the large room. It's going to be an early mornin' tomorrow."

Todd watched him walk over to Sarah and began wiping down dishes. She looked up at him and smiled.

Luke looked down at Jack, who seemed timid around his father. He placed his large hand on top of his head. "Little outlaw," he snickered.

Jack looked up and smiled. Luke chuckled and ruffled his long hair.

Todd felt a warm feeling inside him growing at the sight of this family. He wondered if this was what a family was. He wondered how his life would have turned out if he would have had a father like Luke. No matter how mad Jack had been at his dad a few hours prior, he now showed nothing but admiration.

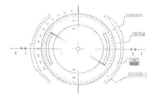

YOUNG DOG, OLD TRICKS

Luke's large boot kicked Todd in the leg, jolting him awake. He rolled over and looked up at Luke, who seemed like a giant standing above him.

He wore long chaps with leather fringes. The sleeves of his dark blue blouse were rolled up to his elbows, baring his large, muscular forearms. His tall white hat gave several more inches to his intimidating stature. Todd rolled out of the fur pallet and stood up. Luke smiled and walked to the door, his booming steps and the large spurs making an imposing noise as he walked across the wood floor. He opened the door and stepped out into the cool morning.

Todd slipped on his boots and began pulling on his leather chaps. Sarah came into the room holding a plate of eggs and bacon.

"Here you go, Todd. Forgive Luke for his morning impatience. He likes to get an early start on things," she said. Her golden blonde hair gleamed in the sun peeping through the window.

He rubbed his tired eyes and smiled. "Thank you, ma'am."

"Please, call me Sarah," she said kindly. She turned and walked into the kitchen. Her stride was confident, her head up and her steps firm. She seemed like a strong woman. Yet she'd have to be, to be able to woo a man like Luke. Todd admired this family. His time with them had been brief but he had a great deal of respect towards them.

He bit off a large piece of bacon and set the plate on a small reading table beside the fireplace, then tucked his pistol and the

MTX into his rolled-up duster coat. Todd looked up to see Jack staring at him from the hall that led down to his room. He looked as if he were in a trance, clearly not entirely awake yet. Todd picked up the bandana and tied it around his neck, then shot him a quick glare jokingly. Jack quickly ducked into the kitchen.

"Well, you're actually here … I'm surprised you hadn't gone and run off to the North Pole or something," said his mother, who was working in the kitchen.

Todd chuckled to himself as he continued eating.

"You're sure up early."

"Pa walks too loud!" he said angrily, scratching his messy hair.

"Well your father is a large man," she replied. "You better eat; your father will need your help today."

Jack let out an obnoxious sigh and stormed out into the living room where Todd side-stepped him to hand Sarah the empty plate.

"Good morning, Mister," Jack said bashfully. His long blonde hair stood up on his head like a rooster's comb.

Todd still felt groggy and didn't think through his words before he said them. "What's up, dude," he said as he opened the door and stepped outside, closing the door behind him.

Jack's face displayed his confusion. He looked at his mother, who stood in the kitchen with a similar look on her face.

"Mama, what's uh 'dude'?"

Sarah shook her head, putting her hands on her hips. "I have no idea."

Luke stood next to the corral, looking at the rising sun pouring its light through the winding valleys of the hills surrounding his land. A smooth stream of smoke rose out of his nostrils and teeth as he puffed on a thin cigar. As Todd approached, he stopped and admired the image before him: the tall cowboy gazing at the sunrise warming the cool desert scene. It looked like a painting. He stepped beside Luke and they watched the sunrise together. The two men said nothing. Luke breathed in and let it out quickly. Todd sensed something about him; he could tell a troubled past was following close behind him and, like most men of his caliber had buried it deep inside himself.

The horses in the corral paced around impatiently, as if they yearned to run freely throughout the massive land on the other side of the fence. Luke looked over at them and breathed out a large cloud of smoke.

"You see that black one? The one that stands alone from the others," he said, nodding over to a large horse with a white diamond on its forehead.

Todd nodded, watching as the jet-black animal quietly sniffed the ground.

Luke pulled his smoke from his lips and leaned his elbows up against the fence. His large hat cut shadows through the orange sunlight. "You can always tell which ones weren't meant to be tamed. The ones who will always be wild and free, no matter how much you govern their life. They may comply, or even appear to have been converted into something they are not, but deep down there will always be a burning desire to live outside the fine lines that simple men draw in the sand."

The horse raised its head as if it knew the men were talking about it. Its black eyes met Todd's.

"You and this horse ... I believe have a lot in common. You're searching for something that you feel you may never grasp." He spat a thin stream of tobacco-filled saliva into the dirt.

"What am I looking for?" Todd asked.

"You say you're looking for your brother, but I think you're really looking for yourself."

Todd held back a grin at the irony of this statement.

"I could see it in your eyes when I first saw you. You got the eyes of an outlaw. Violent men can spot their type a mile away."

Todd wondered what kind of man Luke had been before his family had become his life. He was speaking to Todd from personal experience and from a mutual outlook on things. Nobody in the future would make such statements to a stranger. No one in the future could judge someone accordingly. They would look at the way they walked, or the clothes they wore.

Luke continued. "I found her out in the hills several miles north west of here. She was all alone, grazing out in the open. When she spotted me, she didn't run ... not at first. She watched me, studying my every move. Her curiosity of the unknown overtook her natural instinct to simply run. When I tried to lasso her, she burst into a gallop. It took me nearly an hour to finally get her to comply." He looked over at Todd and grinned. "I've had her for almost a year, and I have yet to be able to break her in. Perhaps I'm not the right person."

Todd's eyes widened. "You mean like ... ride her, right?" he asked, his hand scratching his chin.

Luke let out a hearty laugh. He looked down at Todd, cocking an eyebrow. "Man, I knew you would be green, but I didn't figure you for a city dweller."

Todd just smiled and shrugged. Luke chuckled. "Well, I guess there is a first time for everything."

Todd backed up slightly, shaking his head. "Whoa, I can't just hop on her and try and ride. I've never even ridden a horse. You're the pro. If you couldn't do it then I sure as hell can't."

"Do you think just because a man fishes a lot, means he catches a bigger fish? Sure ... he may know some tricks of the trade, or know the best spots to cast out ... but at the end of the day it was either meant to be ... or it wasn't."

Todd gestured towards Luke. "Look how big you are! She'll destroy me."

Luke laughed. "Look, I'm all out of metaphors ... so just take my word for it."

Todd smiled and shook his head. He looked back over to the horse, his tongue in his cheek. "What breed is it?"

He looked at Todd and nodded towards the horse. "Mustang."

The word brought a different form of transportation to mind. The defined muscles on the horse's body flexed with every movement. He felt uneasy about what was to come in his near future regarding the mustang.

"You're at least going to show me how it's done ... right?"

Luke smiled. "Yeah, I sure can't have you dying on my ranch."

He walked over to the gate, lifted the locking bar and stepped inside. He passed several horses without paying any attention to them and went directly to a white horse with large brown splotches on its coat. He began unwinding the rope that he carried. Letting out some slack on the running end, he slowly made his way up to the horse. Very gently, he slid the loop over its nose and around its neck and tightened it. The horse immediately began to buck and rear, trying to release the loop.

"Easy!" Luke said firmly. The horse walked briskly around the edge of the fence, shaking its head sporadically.

"Does the shaking of the head mean what you'd think it means?" Todd asked.

Luke chuckled as he struggled to keep the horse calm. "Yep, means he ain't happy."

The horse continued to fight the rope as Luke led him into an alternate circular fenced-in area. He cursed as the horse fought him every step of the way. Todd watched in amazement as he overpowered the clearly stronger animal.

"You can't give 'em an inch, you do that ... they'll take a mile," he said, gritting his teeth and fighting the horse's hard jerks.

Todd moved around the outskirts of the fence, watching as Luke did his best to maintain control of the horse. It shook its head violently and kicked at the rope with its front legs. It reared back strongly and he let go of the running end of the rope. The horse felt the slack and began trotting around the fenced-in area. Luke strolled over to where Todd stood, tilting his hat up and wiping the sweat from his forehead.

"You giving up?" Todd asked in surprise.

Luke shook his head and looked back at the animal, which was slowing to a walk. "No, it takes a little while. You have to introduce them to one thing at a time. You go all at once, and you'll have the fight of your life." He walked over to the fence post where a metal bucket hung. He pulled a small cup out of it and splashed some water in his face, then removed his hat and combed his long, black hair back with both hands.

Todd watched the horse's movements slow; Luke leaned up against the thick wood and did the same.

For the next hour, Todd watched as Luke placed a blanket on the horse's back, only to remove it a few moments later. The horse seemed to notice it and disapproved at first. But as time passed, it was if the horse had no idea Luke had thrown the blanket over its large frame. He then carefully placed the saddle on the horse. The horse didn't budge as he fastened the leather straps beneath the horse's belly. He then let the horse walk around with it. He pulled out a small paper from his breast pocket and a small box of tobacco. Carefully, he filled the paper with the dark leaves and began rolling it. Licking the top edge of the paper, he sealed up the cigarette and placed it in his lips.

"Lettin' him get used to it for a while," he said, striking a match against a post, concealing the flame with his other hand to light the smoke.

"How long have you been doing this?" Todd asked, watching Luke breath out a smooth stream of smoke.

"Seven years," he replied.

Todd was surprised by his answer. He would have guessed something like ten or twenty years. He figured that men in this day in age found out what they were good at early on in their lives and held the same job until they were too old to continue. There weren't too many options as far as careers in the nineteenth century. The two men watched the horse stand without a rider in the saddle, tail flicking against the flies which gathered.

"This one will be quite easy; he's already getting the feel for it," Luke said.

He flicked his cigarette, grabbed a leather harness, and walked back into the corral. The horse snorted as he approached. Carefully, he placed the harness over the horse's head. It fought slightly, but he quickly placed the bit in its mouth and tightened down the buckle. Taking the reins, he pulled the horse toward him. It shook its head, trying to break free of Luke's grasp. In one fluid motion, Luke stepped into the stirrup and flung himself on top of the horse. It began to buck violently, trying to throw him off. He held onto the reins with one hand, the other held out, keeping his center of gravity.

"Come on!" he yelled.

Todd watched in amazement, his mouth agape, witnessing two wild souls battle it out to achieve a mutual respect for one another. Luke laughed as his upper body jerked back and forth violently. With his outstretched hand, he ensured his hat remained on his head. Jack laughed from the other side of the corral. Todd looked over to see him peering through the bottom fence post, cheering on his father as the horse breathed out heavily. Its bucks began to ease as it circled the perimeter of the corral. It stopped pouncing and went into a quick trot around in circles. Luke smiled from ear to ear.

"Nothin' to it," he said happily.

Todd shook his head, grinning. Jack came running over to him.

He put his foot up on the bottom beam, attempting to climb up, but was unsuccessful as he was too little to reach the top post. Todd reached down, placing his hands in the crooks of his arms and lifting the little boy up, placing him on the top beam. He smiled big at Todd and scooted closer to him.

"Your father is an awesome guy," Todd said.

Jack looked over at his father, who hopped down from the horse and began leading it out of the gate and into the open field. He closed the gate behind him, then mounted the horse again. Luke spurred the horse and it reared back powerfully, then exploded into a sprint out into the open field.

Jack looked up at Todd, who was watching Luke ride hard out into the sunrise.

"What's uh dude?" he asked curiously.

Todd looked down at him in confusion. "Where did you hear that?"

"You said I was a dude earlier, Mister."

Todd thought back to his brief encounter with him. It hadn't even registered when he said the word to him. He had used the term quite often and it had become part of his vocabulary.

"Shit, uh ..." Todd thought for a moment. "It means, like ... you're cool."

Jack looked puzzled. With his little hand, he reached up and touched his forehead.

Todd chuckled "No, buddy, it's like ... someone who is relaxed, easy-going, they handle themselves well."

"I dunno, Mister," Jack said shaking his head, "Mama says I'm like uh chicken who don't wanna go in its cage."

Todd laughed. "You're a just a boy, it's normal. I was a lot like you when I was a kid. Always running off into the hills, making my mother worried."

"What about your pa?" he asked.

"He was never around. My mom left him when I was very young."

Jack seemed confused by this. He had never heard of such a thing. "You didn't have a papa?"

"I guess not," Todd replied, thinking back to his actual father. He had little recollection of him. He had had many father figures in his life, most of them being team leaders or commanders. They had taught him everything from military tactics, to schooling, even to social skills. He had learned a great deal from them and over time had completely forgotten about his fatherless childhood. There was no doubt in his mind, though, that if he had had a father, his life would have been drastically different. At least it would have helped his mother. Hell, maybe she would still be alive if his father had been around.

"Everyone should have a papa," Jack said sadly.

Todd smiled. "Thought you didn't like yours."

Jack looked out at his father, who was racing across the wide-open plains. His eyes showed clear affection towards him. Todd could tell that there was admiration in the boy. He would just have to grow up a little before he realized how much he meant to Luke.

"He's just mean sometimes," he said, rolling his eyes.

"Because he cares about you, and he wants you to grow up strong and not expect the world to give you everything."

Jack did one of his obnoxious sighs. Glancing over at the house, he replied, "I guess so … it's just 'aggovating'."

Todd chuckled. "Yup, it is 'aggovating'."

Luke came riding back, a big smile spread across his face. He hopped down from the horse and opened the gate. He led the horse back in and closed it, then walked up to Todd and Jack. Dust clung to his facial hair and sun-baked face.

"You two gonna hop on any of 'em?" he asked jokingly.

"Well, I'm scared to death now," Todd chuckled.

"Eh, there's nothing to be scared of. It's just a seventeen-hand, thousand or so pound horse made of pure muscle." Luke grinned deviously.

For the next few hours, Luke ran Todd through the basics of horse knowledge. He taught him how to lasso first. Using a fence post, Todd threw the loop over and over until he ringed it. He backed up a little and tried again. Luke then went over the saddle, its nomenclature, and how to properly mount, and sit on a horse.

Todd started out on Luke's personal horse. It was a golden Quarter horse, with pearl white mane and tail. It was extremely tame and was well-used to having a rider atop it. Todd found it difficult at first to steer with the reins. It seemed as if the horse just ignored him initially. But as time passed, it started to come together, and Todd found it amazing how responsive the horse was to the slightest tugs in either direction. The first time he went into a full gallop he clinched his legs around the horse's body tightly as it sprinted across the open field. He felt timid, at the mercy of the powerful animal.

As the sun began to set, bringing an end to a long day, Todd and Luke both worked the remainder of chores around the farm. They started with the horses, grooming them, picking their hooves, and then feeding and watering them. They then went to the chicken coop behind the house and scattered feed for the obnoxious birds to pluck at. Once they were done, they made their way inside and washed up for dinner.

Sarah had made a stew with the leftovers from the prior night. Todd was extremely grateful to eat home-cooked food and was extremely happy that there was more than enough for seconds. Jack sat staring into his bowl, pushing the contents inside around with his spoon. Sarah sat up straight, eating very properly. She looked over at Todd, who was devouring the food in front of him.

"So ... Todd," she said, smiling, "do you have a lucky young lady waiting for you back East?"

He looked up, surprised at the question.

"A handsome young man like yourself must have swept some girl off her feet by now."

He looked over at Luke, who smiled, no doubt curious as to what the answer was. Todd scratched the back of his head, his cheeks reddening, and felt like he was under a microscope with the three looking at him.

"No," he replied. "There's nobody."

Sarah tilted her head to the side, looking at him in disbelief. "I find that hard to believe. Maybe you just haven't been looking hard enough." She gave him a wink.

Luke wiped his mouth and smiled at Todd, who stared at the table. "Aw to hell with that, when the times right, she'll come to you," he said with a chuckle.

Sarah looked at her husband with admiration. He placed his elbows on the table and leaned in close to Todd. "Trust me, son, the ones ya find yourself are usually the ones you regret."

Todd smiled slightly and looked down at the table again.

"Excuse me if I am being too forward," Sarah said sternly, "but … were you formerly …?"

Todd answered quickly, "No, there hasn't been anyone for as long as I can remember." He rubbed his shoulder and continued. "It seems like the last twenty years of my life have been just far too busy for things like that. Too focused, too … consuming."

"Nothing is more important than love," Sarah said.

"He's a young man, Sarah," Luke said in a hard tone, "but he knows what his priorities are."

Sarah seemed almost offended that Todd did not have a woman in his life. It was as if she expected Todd to be on track with such things as love and was unpleased with his current relationship status.

"They don't always just come to you," Sarah said to her husband with a slightly correcting tone. "No matter how big and tough some men are, they cower at the sight of a lady." She looked at Todd, and the look in her eyes eased. "Surely there must be someone you fancy?"

Todd felt ashamed of the way his relationships had always panned out. He saw himself as a lonely, self-absorbed grouch who didn't deserve the love and care of a gentle, noble woman. He tried to convince himself that he had yet to meet a true noble woman, that the majority of females he had been in relationships with only craved attention, and only showed interest because having him was like a trophy for their social status. His mind began to turn on itself, blaming himself for the loneliness that lingered in the dark corners of his heart. The loneliness that presented itself during the late hours of the night when Todd sat eating alone. He had had friends along the way to keep him company, but the void was never truly filled. His thoughts then turned to Kara. He wondered what she was doing at this very moment, if she was reading a history book, or maybe reading his messages from the past. He liked to think she was sitting in Odin, thinking of him. The idea of someone thinking about him, caring for him, maybe even missing him, put a warm feeling in his heart. It was something he had never known during his time in the military. The realist in him told him that she was thinking of York and hoping that she would soon see him again. Todd was nearly an afterthought.

"She loves someone else," he said, doing his best to fight the grimace in his face.

Sarah's eyes widened and lit up. She smiled briefly at the fact that Todd was interested in someone, but then eased her expression due to the latter part of his confession.

"Who's the dumb bastard she thinks she loves?" Luke asked, anger present in his voice.

"Luke!" Sarah snapped.

"What?" he replied sympathetically. "I want to know who is making this good man's life a livin' hell!"

"My brother ... York," Todd said with a small smile but somber eyes. "She loves him."

Luke leaned back in his chair, shaking his head angrily. He crossed his arms, breathed out and grunted. "I've never met this brother of yours, Todd, but I can tell you right now that you are twice the man he is."

Todd shook his head. "That's not true, he is a far greater warrior than me."

"I didn't say warrior," Luke said firmly, "I said man. I've met plenty of 'warriors' in my time who could kill a hundred men without breakin' a sweat, but couldn't differ right from wrong if it were staring them in the face. Some men become so enthralled with the unpleasant nature of their life, so used to killin' and survivin' ... that they lose sight of who they are."

Todd looked down. He tried to take in Luke's words and use them to help ease his troubled mind. Deep down, Todd felt that he and York were exactly the same person and would make the exact same decisions given the same circumstances.

"It's just ... the thing is ... I don't exactly disagree with his reasonings for why he ran, and I fear that we are so much alike, that given the same circumstances, I would have done the same thing," Todd said.

"You're a good man, Todd, whether you choose to believe it or not ... you are. No matter what you've done in your past, no matter how many bad things you've seen. In the end, you will be judged by who you've become, and I think you are on the right path, son."

Todd nodded and worked up a smile. Luke's large hand patted him on the shoulder and a warm feeling erupted in Todd. Sarah smiled at him and stood up to collect their plates.

For the first time in his life, Todd felt like he was part of a family. Jack laughed and fought to stay on his chair as his father tickled him relentlessly. Sarah hummed as she washed the fine china plates. Todd stood up and took some of the load off her hands. She thanked him and he thanked her for taking him in on such unusual circumstances. He felt as if he had already overstayed his welcome, but the McWilliams said they'd keep him around as long as he could stay.

As the night grew late, the conversation at the dinner table came to an end as Luke nodded off in his chair. Todd chuckled at the sight of the large man snoring with his arms crossed. Sarah walked over and gently woke him. His eyes shot open and he looked around with bloodshot eyes, not realizing he had dozed off. He stood up and said goodnight as he and Sarah walked down the dark hallway to their bedroom.

Todd walked out to the living room to lay down. It was dark in the house and he carefully felt his way to his fur pallet on the floor. He sat down and pulled his boots off. As he was about to lay down he noticed a small lump in the buffalo pelt blanket. Jack had fallen asleep during Todd and Luke's endless chatting. Very gently, he slid his arms beneath him and picked him up, doing his best to not wake him. Slowly, he rose to his feet, cradling the little boy in his arms. He walked softly down the hall towards Jack's room. As he walked toe to heel, trying not to wake him and his parents in the adjacent room, something dawned on him. A sudden realization that made him stop in the dark hallway. Holding Jack in his arms made him think of the journal entries York had written. He thought of Suong and the horrible things that had happened to her. He imaged York carrying the little girl through the dense jungle, running from her burning home. He looked down at Jack and wondered what he would do if his life was ever put in danger. A chill went up his spine as he came to terms with the dark truth. He gently set Jack down in his bed, then stepped back. Jack curled up into a little ball on his bed, his long hair splayed out on the pillow. Todd walked to the door, stopping to look back. He couldn't imagine what he would do if something bad ever happened to this little boy.

*   *   *

May 2, 2011

The city was quiet, except for the occasional bark of a dog. I moved down the street with my weapon up, scanning the doorways and corners. My HUD showed the compound was only forty meters away. My aiming reticle danced around the possible danger areas, bouncing up and down with each step. I could see the high walls surrounding the three-story building on the other side of the field that lay in front of me. The soft dirt had been plowed most likely the day prior and my feet sank deep in the soft dirt.

I pulled a small shrub out of the ground and used it as a broom to sweep over my footsteps as I sidestepped towards the compound walls. When I finally reached it, I tossed away the shrub and skirted the walls around the west side until I found a metal gate, which I used to climb up and over the wall. My feet hit the ground on the inside and I froze down on a knee, ensuring I had not been heard. I waited for the crickets to resume their noise and then I slowly rose and walked towards the small prayer room that was separate from the main structure. I was almost positive that there wouldn't be anyone in there considering it was several hours until prayer time.

I took a quick peek inside just to make sure, then made my way towards the side door of the main structure. The door was sealed with an outer gate which was firmly locked. I came out of cloak and pulled a small charge from my web gear. I had planned for this mission to go loud early on. Several teams of guys from my unit would be here shortly; originally they would suffer a helicopter crash which would have led to a significant delay resulting in Bin Laden's escape. This time, however, they would most likely take the credit for the killing of Osama bin Laden. Me and Bohden had discussed the gritty details of the mission behind closed doors at the facility.

Utilizing some of Bohden's assets, we were able to utilize satellite thermal imagery in order to predict where he was in the house. We knew that explosive breaches would have to be used in order to gain entry. Thus, making me go in cloaked was practically pointless. I stacked up on the door, my weapon against my shoulder. The MTX counted down from five. When it reached zero, the charge detonated, blasting the locking mechanism through the door jamb into the house. The door swung open and I raised my visor and burst into the house. I could already hear a woman screaming within the home and the racking of the bolts of AKs. I began clearing rooms, my movements quick and decisive.

My weapon stayed trained in front as I swept. I raised the muzzle at the ceiling in the high ready as I rounded corners and opened doors. When I reached the fifth door, I found myself looking at a man and woman, who fumbled in the dark in fear. The man reached for his rifle and I fired three rounds into his chest, then did the same to his wife.

I continued through the bottom level, encountering another couple who I put an end to quickly. I heard movement behind the last door on the first floor, and I kicked it open to find a group of children huddled together in the back corner. Anger burned inside me. Fucking Bohden! He said there wouldn't be any goddamn kids. I gritted my teeth and squeezed my rifle. My palms began to sweat and my body began to tremble. I couldn't do it, I couldn't kill them. But what did it matter? I had already smoked some of their parents. They would grow up remembering this night, and it would haunt them forever. Change them and twist them in ways that would be irreversible.

FUCK! Why ... why does it always have to be like this? Why does it always have to be innocent lives? I didn't give a fuck who they prayed to, or what they called God. I especially didn't care that they had a deep hatred for Americans. Yet here I was, torn between what was right, and what was best. The two options in front of me were blurred and I began to wonder what the difference was. The end would come anyway, the world was as fucked as it had always been. Maybe I'd delay the deaths of innocent lives by killing the man who lived two floors above where I currently stood. Did it really matter? I concluded that I was already here. People were going to die regardless, and the man I was here to kill was responsible for orchestrating the terrorist attacks on September 11th.

I stepped back to the door, staring at the tear-filled eyes of the children. They clung to each other and cried loudly, scooting deeper against the wall to further the distance between them and me. I began to sob uncontrollably. I leaned up against the door, dropping my rifle to the ground, and buried my face in my gloved hands. "FUCK!" I screamed as I punched the wall repeatedly, deepening a hole into it. I collapsed beside the door and shook as I cried. I looked up at the dark ceiling, as if to look to some higher power in hopes that my pain may be eased. I braced myself against the wall and stood up slowly. My knees shook beneath me. I looked at the children and reached for the door with tears in my eyes. "I'm sorry," I said.

I shut the door and reached down for my rifle. As I was about to stand up, the muzzle of an AK47 raked downward across my face, knocking me down to the ground. I shook my head, rattled from the hit, and looked up to see the muzzle leveling on my forehead. I shifted my head to the side quickly just as he fired off a burst of rounds. The bullets flew past my head and cut through the door, and the children on the other side screamed. I stood up quickly, grabbing the barrel of the weapon with my left hand. I forced it into the wall while with my right I smashed my elbow into his nose, causing him to release the rifle and fall backwards. I orientated the rifle into my shoulder, racked a fresh round, and fired two into his chest and one in his head. I checked down the hall for any more hostiles, then I looked back at the door that led to the children. The rounds had hit the door square in the center. I could hear the children crying in horror. I pushed the door open and my heart felt like it stopped. Two of the ten children lay dead on the ground in a pool of blood. I felt the familiar burning of anger and hatred brewing inside me. My body shook and my jaw trembled. I backed out of the room, dropping the AK. I grabbed my rifle and sprinted to the stairwell. With no regard for tactics I ran upstairs, where I encountered another man with a rifle. I rounded the corner and nearly ran into him. I hit him with the stock of my weapon and shot him multiple times. I then ran to the top level, doing a magazine exchange on the move.

There were two doors on opposite sides of the hall. I kicked in the one that led to the outer porch. After I ensured it was clear, I turned and looked at the door that had the most wanted man in the world behind it. I gritted my teeth and kicked it in. I was met by a volley of fire. Two rounds connected with my torso, knocking me backwards into the hall. I lay in the supine position and shouldered my weapon. He held his wife in front of him as a human shield, screaming in Arabic. I leveled my sights on his wife's head and I squeezed off a *round. It snapped her head backwards and she fell at his feet. I stood up and walked towards him, keeping my weapon trained on him. He stumbled backwards against the bed, dropping the rifle. I pressed the suppressor against his chest and pulled the trigger; holding it down until the thirty-round mag was empty. His body twitched and blood spilled from his mouth and the bullet wounds. I dropped to my knees, breathing heavily. Tears mixed with thick blood ran down my face and dripped on the floor. I could hear the thumps of rotors outside drawing near. I quickly snapped out of my current state and stumbled to the door. I fell several times as I tried to get out of the house as quickly as possible.*

I made my way to the entrance and the dust of the rotor wash blew into the open doorway. I fumbled to pull my visor down, and my fingers shook as I tapped the cloaking option of the MTX. I stumbled outside just in time to see an RPG round smack into the tail of one of the Blackhawk helicopters. The ear-busting boom echoed throughout the city and the helicopter began to spin out of control. It swooped down towards the building and crashed into the perimeter wall and began sliding towards me. I sprinted for the far wall as fast as I could, but felt the tail rotor slice my arm as I dove to the ground. I screamed in pain, my screams drowned out by the loud thumps of the main rotors chopping into the ground. I clutched my arm and stood up, stumbling towards the front gate. I couldn't tell if it was flesh or the suit itself that my arm remained attached by.

For the next two hours, I stumbled through the streets towards my extract point. That was it ... that was the end. The end of my time traveling. The end of my interference with the natural timeline.

I would go back to the facility, where I would spend the next several months in rehabilitation. There I would plan my escape into the past. Where I would prepare to say goodbye.

ESPRIT LIBRE

The mustang stared into Todd's eyes, waiting for him to make the first move. He stepped around it, looking for a chink in its armor. It followed him every step of the way, not allowing him to get behind it.

Jack sat on top of the fence; next to him was Luke, who smoked a thin cigar, watching as two powerful souls eyed each other. Like two masters of their domain coming face to face, trying to work past the distrust and awareness they both used to stay alive. The horse snorted loudly and shook its head. The long black mane flopped from side to side. In Todd's sweaty hands he held the saddle blanket. He breathed out slowly, his dark eyes staying trained on the horse's. His sharp jaw line flexed and he moved closer to the animal.

"Apparently we have a lot in common," Todd said softly.

The horse's ears twitched as if it were listening to his words. He released the blanket with one hand, reached up and placed his hand on the horse's sleek black side. He ran his hand down its back, talking to it very gently.

"I'm not going to try and change you, I don't want you to lose sight of what you truly are. I need your help ... to help me find another wild soul."

The horse lowered its head and sniffed the ground. Luke pulled the cigar from his lips and watched in amazement as Todd and the powerful animal interacted. He had never been able to even get close to the animal let alone touch it. Todd moved over to its head. It looked up at him and gently he ran his hand down its long nose. It moved away slightly at first, but as he pulled his hand back, it turned its head back towards him and looked into his eyes.

"I need your help. This is your element ... your environment. I need you to show me how to operate in it."

He gently caressed the horse's face and it sniffed his hands curiously. He pulled an apple from his pocket and held it up to the horse, who reached for it slightly.

"Nope," he said, pulling it away from the horse. "You've lived your entire life without having to be fed. I'm not going to change that now. You have to earn your food ... fight for it."

He put the apple back in his pocket and with both hands gently placed the blanket on the horse's back. It didn't budge an inch. He stepped back and grinned at the large animal, who was quickly adapting to the unfamiliar situation. He walked to the fence and shouldered the heavy saddle that sat atop it. He walked back over to the horse as Luke watched with wide eyes and an open mouth. A smile grew on Jack's little face. Todd breathed in, then let it out, his hard eyes glaring at the horse. Very slowly, he raised the saddle and set it on the horse's back. The mustang looked back at the weight it bore and shook its head, letting out a wet snort.

"Don't be a wimp ... I've carried much worse, and you're bigger than me," Todd snickered.

He reached down and tightened the leather straps snug against the horse's belly. Then he stood up and placed his hand on the saddle horn from which the bridle hung. He pulled it off and stretched it out. He moved to the front of the horse and held it out in front of its face.

"Worst part, okay."

He pulled it over the horse's head, placing the bit in the back of its mouth. The horse tossed its head up and down in disapproval of the bit.

"I know," Todd said.

He traced the reins back to the saddle and stood beside the mustang. He looked at the sun that peeked over the dark mountains and over the horse. He looked back at Luke and Jack, who watched in awe. Jack stared at Todd in fascination; his big green eyes stayed fixed on Todd as he grasped the reins and prepared to mount the horse. Todd grinned at Jack and winked, then turned to the saddle and placed his hand on the horn. He placed his left foot in the stirrup and stepped up, throwing his right leg over. The moment his right foot entered the stirrup, the mustang began to buck wildly, throwing her hind legs up ferociously. Todd held on tight to the reins with his left hand and his right stayed out to his side to help him keep his balance.

"Whoa, whoa!" he yelled to the mustang. "Come on girl!"

Jack cheered while Luke leaned over the railing and called out to Todd, "Stay with it, you got her!" he yelled.

Todd's body whipped back and forth violently as the horse pounced in circles around the corral, kicking up clouds of dust. "Come on!" he yelled. The mustang continued to buck and then it reared back, standing tall, silhouetting itself in the rising sun. It neighed loudly, tucking its front legs to its chest. Jack and Luke's jaws dropped at the incredible sight. The horse's front legs came back down with a loud thump and it burst into a gallop, leaping over the corral fence. Todd ducked, keeping a low center of gravity as they were airborne. The horse's hooves hit the patches of grass that led to the endless open fields and it raced out into the rising sun. Todd leaned forward as they picked up speed. The shrubs and trees shot past them as the mustang sprinted through the open field.

"Yeah!" Todd screamed. As he spurred her, she lurched forward, picking up speed.

Todd laughed excitedly as the cool wind hit his face and his heart raced. The horse snorted in short controlled bursts as it powerfully cruised through the winding trails leading to the hills. For the first time in a long time, Todd felt joy and happiness. He laughed and called to the horse, encouraging its aggressiveness.

Luke stared in shock at the dust trail leading off into the open field. He had never seen such a thing in his entire life. He didn't know what was more amazing: Todd breaking in an untamable horse, or the fact that it was on his first attempt. His eyes began to become glossy, and he blinked several times, trying to keep control of his emotions.

Jack looked up at his emotional father. He had rarely seen him so excited. Luke looked down at his son, who smiled up at him. He reached down and pulled him in closer, patting him on his back.

Todd came trotting back soon thereafter, and Luke opened the gate to the corral and led him back in. He didn't bother reaching for the horse; he let Todd hop down and take the reins to lead the horse into the stable.

"That was amazing," Luke said, his eyes wide.

Todd looked at the horse, then back at Luke and shook his head. "I don't know … I just felt like …"

"Like it was meant to be," Luke interrupted.

The two chuckled, and Luke patted him on the back and congratulated him and shook his hand firmly. Jack ran to Todd, his arms stretched out towards him, giggling happily. Todd leaned down and picked him up. The two laughed as Todd spun in circles and pulled him in and hugged him. Sarah watched from the porch, holding on to a pillar as Todd held Jack with Luke next to them laughing heartily. It felt good to see her family so happy. This stranger, a man they had not known until two days ago, had single-handedly brought this family together unintentionally. He had shown Sarah that there were good men out there who were capable of earning her grim husband's trust. His kindness had rubbed off on Luke, and his troubled past had reminded Luke of what he had overcome. Todd had not only brought their son back to them, but he had also given him a friend.

The two walked to the house with Todd carrying Jack on his shoulders. Luke continued to appraise his bravery and his natural skill. Sarah stepped down from the porch and met them.

"He's a natural," Luke said with a smile.

Sarah put her hands on her hips and shook her head. "You are one crazy man, Todd," she said in disbelief.

Todd looked up at Jack, who smiled down at him. "Beginner's luck," he chuckled.

Luke laughed. "Bullshit … fate, is what it was." He nodded his head and smiled. "So … what are you going to name her? She's your horse."

Todd looked down and pondered for a moment. Then something hit him, something he had remembered from his first Op as a young Ranger working with an ODA team in Africa. He looked back towards the stable and smiled. "Esprit Libre."

Luke canted his head at the odd name, then asked, "What's it mean?"

"Free spirit ... it's something some people I once helped used to say."

"It's a beautiful name for a beautiful animal," Sarah said.

The three made their way inside and washed up for lunch. As Todd was about to sit down, he stood up quickly and ran to the door.

"What is it?" Sarah asked.

"Be back in minute," he said as he ran outside.

He ran to the stable, hopped over the fence and walked over to Esprit Libre, who stood in her stall. He pulled the apple from his pocket and held it out to her. She leaned forward and gently took it from him, chomping down on it.

He stroked her mane and whispered, "You earned it."

*　　　*　　　*

Odin hummed softly as it continued its journey back to the North Pole. The thick cloud coverage below reflected the bright sunlight onto Kara's face. She sat alone in her private office and bunk room, gazing out at the slight curvature of the Earth. Her thoughts were of him. She missed him, and wished he would return to her; take her away from this life. There was hope inside her now, almost an excitement that she had not felt in a long time. She looked at the intercom; the speaker icon was unlit. She wished that at any moment, D would come on and announce their landing. She imagined the ramp would open and he would be standing there. Their eyes would meet, and he would step towards her, wrapping his arms around her. She rubbed her forehead, trying to put her mind on different things. A knock on the door snapped her out of her daydreaming.

"Who is it?" she called to the door softly.

"It's me."

Steven Bodhen's deep voice was unmistakable. The door opened slowly and he peeked in. She turned in the chair to face the desk squarely. He closed the door behind him and sat down in front of her, adjusting in his chair. She looked to her monitor and began scrolling through news articles. Bohden watched her, waiting for her to look at him.

"I couldn't help but notice you've been a little … 'absent' lately," he said.

Without looking up from her monitor, she rolled her eyes and replied, "What do you want, Steven? I already told you … I don't want to talk about it."

Bohden glared at her. "I know you still have feelings for him, and I want you to know I still care about him too. He was my friend, and I miss him, but you and I need to come to terms with how this is going to end."

Her eyes shifted up to him, and his hard glare eased slightly. He ran his fingers through his greying hair and exhaled loudly. "He's not coming back … never. I know him too well. I know what he's been through …" He shook his head slightly, staring at the glass table. "This new Todd … he will do the same thing. He will end up running, because they are the same person. It was a mistake to bring him into this. I told Brian before I rescued him that we should have chosen Rob Ackerman instead. Someone who knew York well enough."

Her eyes dropped and she brushed back a long stray hair that draped down to her nose.

"You know better than anyone," he said, leaning forward in his chair.

She looked up at him, her eyes saddened.

He shook his head. "We may be able to change time, but we can't change people."

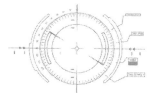

THE MAN WITH THE SCARRED FACE

He sat alone on the far end of the bar drinking a glass of bourbon, wincing slightly as the alcohol stung the open cut on his lip. The bartender didn't bother prying for conversation as he usually did with his customers. He had been around long enough to recognize when a man had no intention of making small talk. His body language was enough, but his stern face, littered with scars and the pain of hard years, was enough to make the bartender pour him another glassful and quickly walk away.

Courtney Holland was a whore. The oldest profession in the world was the only life she knew. Her mind had become numb to the idea of being a prostitute after several years of having to accept it as the only way to survive.

Her usual spot to lure in customers was the back corner of the saloon, next to the piano. She liked to listen to the pianist and daydream about being someplace else. She imagined she was somewhere green, someplace where pine trees swayed back and forth in a cool crisp breeze. She had lived in the desert her entire life and she dreamed of anywhere without dust and sand. Her daydreaming was cut short as she noticed the lonely man sitting at the end of the bar.

It was not like her to approach a man and ask him if he were interested in spending a few hours upstairs with her. Ordinarily she would wait next to the piano for a drunken imbecile to come stumbling over. This man was different. He wasn't like the other desperate cowboys looking to cheat on their poor wives who were back home with their children. He didn't look with lustful eyes at the other girls who flaunted their flesh around the saloon. He just drank quietly and stared at his hands folded atop the bar. His eyes held a dark glare, and his hands repeatedly met at his face and slowly rubbed downwards from his forehead and stopped at his chin. He remained propped up on his elbows.

She looked at herself briefly in the mirror above the bar to ensure her bright, beautiful red hair was still in its tight bundle atop her head and adjusted her breasts in the revealing dress. She made her way towards him, becoming more hesitant as she approached and his grim appearance came clearer. Behind the scars, long hair and unshaven face was a handsome man. He had dark green eyes that didn't drift from the wood of the bar. His thin lips were pulled in as if he were in pain. She turned towards the center of the main floor, towards the tables encircled with hairy men rubbing elbows and cursing each other. She went around one table in an effort to catch him by surprise. She approached him from behind, strutting daintily. He raised the glass to his lips and took a large gulp that finished it off.

"Don't bother," he said.

Although intimidating, his voice had a sincere sound to it that made her stick around for a moment to test his commitment. She sat down on the bar stool next to him, her back to the bar and her elbows resting on it. She tilted her head back and looked at him. His eyes shifted from the mirror behind the bar to hers and she felt a cold chill. He didn't intend to look angry at her, but his gaze intimidated her nonetheless. It was as if he were born looking angry, or maybe it was sadness. She wondered what had made him this way, what had given him the scars and the thousand-yard stare.

"You look like you could use some company, cowboy," she said sweetly. An almost scripted line that was commonly used by the working girls at the saloon.

He canted his nose to the side and sniffed, sounding as if he had a cold. His nose had most likely been filled with blood not too long ago. He waited patiently as the bartender poured him his third glass of bourbon and walked away. She watched him as he took a sip and set the glass down loudly in an aggravated way. She was about to get up and leave when his voice made her freeze on the edge of the stool.

"How long have you been doing this," he asked.

She was confused at the question at first, not used to being asked such a thing. "Does it matter?" she asked.

"I've seen many women in your line of work in my life. I'm just curious."

She stared at him in disbelief. She thought she saw where the conversation was going. "What do you want?" she asked. She had been lectured many times before by Bible-thumping religious nuts; their threats of an eternity in hell were no more intimidating than their abusive nature in bed.

"You know what whores all have in common," he said, looking at his glass in between his folded hands.

She rolled her eyes and stood up to storm away but stopped as he grabbed her arm. He didn't grab her in a way that said he meant to hurt her; rather his hand gently caught her arm in a way that displayed compassion. She looked at him from the corner of her eye. Not turning her head towards him.

"They're all horrible actors, as if they actually enjoy their job."

She turned her head towards him, unsure as to where he was going with this. His hard expression had eased slightly to a more somber look and his grip on her arm loosened.

"You especially." He let go of her arm and rested his forearms on the bar. "I've been in this bar for almost an hour now, and for the entire fifty-seven minutes I have been here, not once have you flaunted yourself at any of these sorry fucks who will use you and abuse you while their families are at home waiting for them."

He didn't speak like other men. His words were straight and sounded out entirely. He was firm and confident and spoke like he preplanned each sentence in his mind and then read it out loud. He didn't use filler words like um and uh. He didn't refer to people as fellers or cowboys. She assumed he must have been from far away, because nobody from around here spoke like him.

"Mister ... I ..." she fumbled with her words.

"I know," he said. "You've been over there this entire time and not once did you see me look at you. You probably half-expected to get picked up before you finally made your way over here, but were relieved that tonight you might have a customer whom you chose for yourself."

She stared at him, her eyes blinking rapidly, trying to hold back emotions that rarely made an appearance, even in the most lonesome of places.

"What do you want from me?" she asked softly.

He reached into the inside of his black felt coat and pulled out a large wad of bills that he thumbed through before dropping two bills on the bar. She was astonished at his lack of care towards his money. His drinks couldn't have cost more than a dollar, yet he dropped five dollars on the bar.

"What's your name?" he asked, folding up the bills and holding them with his right hand down at his lap. The skin of his knuckles was broken and scabbed.

"Courtney Holland," she said softly.

Men rarely asked her what her name was. They usually acted as if she wasn't a person at all. Just an object to use for an evening. She didn't know what it was about this man that was beginning to intrigue her, but she didn't want to leave.

"How long have you been doing this, Courtney?"

"Since I was fifteen," she replied.

He seemed angered by her answer, not at her but rather at the world. It was as if he blamed the society she belonged to for what she was. He looked around the saloon in disgust at the drunken cowboys laughing and yelling obnoxiously at each other. He then turned back to her.

"I'm sorry," he said sadly.

She sat down next to him, lifting the long skirt of her dress up to place her heels on the support bar of the stool.

"You don't need to be sorry ..." She hesitated then asked, "What's your name?" Her hands fumbled on the bar in front of her.

He didn't answer. He looked at the wad of bills in his hand and then up at her. "How much do you usually charge?" he asked.

She was puzzled at first and somewhat disappointed in the question. Had he given her this long speech just to make her feel better about having sex with him? She straightened up in her chair, lifting her chin up slightly. "A dollar an hour," she said.

He looked down, his jaw rotating slightly; his lips stayed sealed.

He looked back up at her and fished in his pocket once more. His hand emerged with another wad of cash and he straightened it and stacked it on top of the other one. He then set the large stack on top of the bar between them. Her eyes widened and she looked at him in disbelief.

"What? I don't ..." she mumbled.

"I want to know something, Courtney." He turned on the stool towards her and looked her in the eyes. His rigid expression made her cower slightly. "If your answer is admirable ... all this money is yours."

She looked at the large stack of money with astonished eyes, then back at him. His stare had not strayed from her, and it took every inch of bearing in her body to maintain eye contact with him.

"What's the question?" she asked.

"What do you live for? What keeps you going ... what is the end state of your years of misery?"

She blinked, then her eyes danced around him as she thought about the question. "I don't ... I don't know what you mean."

"I'm not giving you anything unless you give me something in return, a guarantee per se."

"Which is?" she asked, looking at him with fear and confusion building inside her.

"There are two kinds of people in this world." He leaned forward in his chair, resting his elbows on his legs, his hands folded in front of him. "Those who give, and those who take." He canted his head to the right and looked at her with soft eyes. "Just because you use your body to make money doesn't make you a bad person, but I would be lying if I told you that what you did didn't sadden me."

"Why?" she asked softly.

"Because I see a beautiful person in front of me who deserves better, who is here because a troubled past littered with bad people has funneled her into this life. So, I want to know ... what you are going to give to this world."

Her eyes stayed locked on him intensely as tears pooled in them. Memories of her past began to bombard her mind in an overwhelming wave of pain and sadness that brought out her emotions. She fought hard to keep them at bay but was starting to break. Nobody had ever shown sympathy towards her. Those who didn't agree with what she did usually displayed it in a hateful and disrespectful way by cursing and verbally condemning her to hell. This dark stranger had accessed emotions deep within her heart and had in just a few minutes of conversation brought her to one of the most pinnacle moments of her entire life. She thought about lying, telling him that she planned to obtain an education and become some kind of medical professional, but her lack of knowledge on the subject and her racing mind steered her away from doing so. He adjusted in his chair, looking at her intensely waiting for an answer. Tears ran down her face as she believed the sad truth would not impress him. She sat up straight, wiping the tears from her face. She rolled her eyes and shook her head, looking up at the ceiling. She wasn't going to lie to him; he was too smart and would no doubt see right through her hollow words.

"I want to move to the Northwest, near the coast. I want to see the ocean and smell the salt in the air." Her eyes dropped to the floor, and she shook her head and continued. "I want to have a child … I want to have a family." She looked up at him. "I want to tend to a house, take care of livestock and crops … cook for my family and …" She paused for a moment and scraped away a tear with her finger. She looked at him with desperate eyes. "I want to love."

His hard stare disappeared, and his eyes went soft then dropped to the floor. He breathed in slowly then let it out quick through his nose. He stood up and reached for his black hat on the bar and pulled it back onto his head. He then grabbed the stack of cash off the bar. Courtney stared at the floorboards, her vision becoming murky. She felt as if her answer was as pitiful as her existence. She looked up at the noisy saloon around her. The men at the tables yelled at each other loudly and spilled their drinks. The other prostitutes clung to them. She felt disgust and sadness. She felt a hand grasp hers. She turned quickly to see the man holding her hand in his and he placed the large stack of money in her palm and placed her other hand on top of it. She was speechless, her eyes wide. She looked up at him in complete surprise. She tried to speak but nothing legible would come out.

"I want you to have what you want … this will help get you there," he said. He then turned and walked to the swinging doors.

She stood up quickly and raced after him. She stopped on the porch outside the saloon. It was a cool, clear night. The moon lit the quiet city around them. She called out to him as he walked hastily away.

"Wait!" she said.

He turned slowly as she approached him, holding her long dress up with the large stack of money in her hand. "I don't know what to say," she said quietly.

"Don't say anything, just go do what you need to do. Live for yourself," he said as he turned and started walking towards a pale horse that stood with its reins tied to the hitching post.

"But ..." She stopped and looked down at the money then back at him. "Why? Why would you give this to a stranger?"

He looked at the ground, then turned towards her once again. "I'm not a good person, Courtney. I've done horrible things, and it's the people around me who always pay for it. I don't deserve such wealth. I don't deserve to be happy ... not after what I've done. All I can do is help someone like you who doesn't have to feel the way I do, and who deserves better than what they have."

He pondered for a moment. "I don't believe in such things ... but if hell is real I'm going there."

He untied the reins to the pale horse and traced them back. He stepped into the stirrup and lifted himself up onto the horse.

"I ... don't know who you are, and I don't know what you've done, but it doesn't have to be this way. You can always change ..." she said, looking up at him.

The horse jerked its head to the side as he pulled the reins, turning his other side to her. "You can't change who you were destined to be."

This confused her. She didn't understand this pessimistic outlook. She assumed he must have been some sort of outlaw; he must have done terrible things in order to survive, and it was this thought that made her feel somewhat attached to him.

She too had a dark past and felt an extraordinary amount of guilt because of it. She felt that maybe she could be his way out. Maybe together they could escape their dark pasts and start a new life together. The brief fantasy vanished as he began to ride away.

"Will you at least tell me your name?" she asked as he started to trot away.

He didn't look back as he answered. "My name is York." He spurred his horse, and headed out of town toward the bright moon.

STEPPING OFF

-SITREP-

I have obtained a horse and have linked up with a local who is familiar with the area. We will set out tomorrow and begin our search for York. After discussing the area with my contact, we have concluded that York is staying in a small city about thirty miles west of my current location in a small town a few miles past the Utah state line. Beyond this city is basically open desert, so there isn't really anywhere else for him to go. I will contact you tomorrow after we have set up camp. I hope everyone is doing well up there.

P.S. Tell D that my contact looks just like Mathew Quigley. He'll get a kick out of that.

Todd tucked the MTX back into the inside pocket of his duster and walked into the kitchen where Sarah was preparing dinner. He couldn't help but notice that she was always dressed very properly, no matter what time of day it was or what she was doing. Her somewhat tenacious attitude also benefited her and made it easy for Todd to see why Luke was so in love with her.

"Need any help?" Todd asked.

"Oh, no thank you, dear, it'll be ready shortly," she replied, wiping her hands on her apron.

Todd smiled and was about to walk out when she stopped him.

"Todd," she said.

He turned, raising his eyebrows. "Yes?"

She seemed almost shy as she swayed back and forth slightly, her hands fumbling in front of her. This bashfulness briefly reminded Todd of Kara.

"Are you …?"

"What?" he asked softly.

She canted her head, her eyes sympathetic. "Are you heartbroken?"

He didn't know what to say. He didn't really understand the question. He had never been asked such a question before.

"What do you mean?"

She blinked and her eyes danced. "It's just that … your brother is in trouble, you seem to be running from some kind of trouble yourself, and well … quite honestly you seem lonely. I suppose what I am trying to ask is, are you alright?"

"I wasn't," he said firmly. "Not by a long shot."

His mind went to WWIII, and he felt a sickening feeling in his gut. It seemed like yesterday he was witnessing firsthand the end of the world. Yet so much had happened since then, such incredible things that it almost seemed like a lifetime ago.

"I lost a good friend, and it weighs heavily on me. You and your family have been so good to me, you have shown me that that I don't have to dwell on the past. There is always something to hope for."

She smiled, walked over to him and hugged him. "You've been a blessing yourself. Thank you so much. There will always be a place for you here."

During dinner, the conversation was in high spirits, mostly consisting of humorous stories of the past and poking fun at each other. Todd was especially intrigued by Sarah's story of how she met Luke. They had been talking about how the weather had been beautiful lately and it led to the topic of Sarah's old family home. Naturally it branched off from there into the origins of the McWilliams family.

"I was traveling from New Mexico with my family," Sarah said. "My mother, father, and two sisters. I was the oldest of the three; I was nineteen at the time. We had been traveling north, following the Rio Grande, my father hoping to find a better piece of land for him and my mother to settle with my younger sisters. I was merely along for the ride, hoping that I might be able to set out on my own soon. We ended up finding a place that was only a few hours away from Albuquerque. My parents and sisters began getting established in a small house with a few hundred acres while I set off to town to find work."

Todd listened closely, his arms folded on the table. Jack picked at his food as he usually did. Luke ate nonstop the entire meal, taking few breaks in between bites to make a comment.

Sarah continued. "I spent the next few years taking several jobs in the area. Starting with manual labor, then finally working my way inside. By the time I was twenty-three, I was working in a library in town that was newly established. I loved the job because I spent more time reading than I did working." She giggled. "One night, I was closing up late. I had spent the entire day finishing a romance novel, one of several I had read that week. I heard a soft knock on the door. It startled me because of how late it was and the harsh weather outside. I opened the door to find a young man, drenched to the bone from the chilly rain. His clothes were shredded, and his long hair was draped in front of his eyes."

Todd looked over at Luke, who had a smug grin on his face as he ate. Todd chuckled and looked back at Sarah. "What happened?" he asked.

"Well ... ends up, he had been wandering through the desert for weeks by himself after getting turned around on his mail run. A few hours before he had found the town, he had gotten attacked by a pack of wild dogs. He had bad gashes on his arm, which I didn't notice until I finally let him in."

"Took your sweet time too," Luke chuckled.

"Well, you weren't exactly the politest person I had ever met," Sarah replied.

Luke smiled and looked over at Todd. "It was the only building with lights still on, and I was bleeding to death. This loving little flower here closed the door in my face twice."

Sarah coughed loudly as if to tell Luke to shut it. "So, after nearly begging on his hands and knees, I felt so bad that I let him in and gave him a blanket, and it was then that I noticed the blood dripping off his fingers. I didn't know much about medicine, but the sweet old man I worked for kept a secret stash of whiskey behind the counter. I grabbed it and some rags and started dabbing his wounds with it."

Luke shook his head, no doubt recalling the painful experience.

Sarah laughed. "I remember I screamed when he yelped at the first dab."

"I didn't yelp!" Luke argued.

"You let out quite the holler." Sarah laughed. "Scared me half to death."

Todd laughed. "Are you kidding? I'd probably yelp too!"

Everyone at the table laughed. Jack laughed with his mouth full and food smeared on his cheeks. Sarah looked at him and laughed again. Luke wiped the tears from his eyes.

"Clean yourself up, Jack," Luke said, holding back chuckles.

Todd finally stopped laughing and let out a sigh. "So what happened next?"

"I decided it would be best for him to stay there for the night, but I sure wasn't going to leave him there alone. So, we sat up all night, talking. I tried to ask about him, but he seemed more curious as to who I was and what I did. He seemed so interested in me, and he was so sincere. It was like he had never met a girl before."

"Not one as pretty as you that is," Luke said.

Sarah looked at him and smiled, her cheeks reddening. "It was comments like that, as well as his dashing appearance, that made me fall in love with him. That, and how shy he was. It was so adorable."

Luke leaned over and kissed Sarah on the cheek. Todd wondered if this was what true love was. It was inspiring to see a true example of something that he had believed to exist only in fairytales. He wondered if he could ever have something like this. Part of him fantasized about having a family someday. The idea was still quite foreign to him, but it was quickly becoming much more appealing.

"That was nearly twenty years ago," Sarah said softly. "If only one could go back in time. I'd love to see the first time he kissed me. Papa nearly shot him when he caught us in the hay loft." She laughed.

Jack had a puzzled look on his face. He held his fork above his plate and stared at Sarah.

"Oh, don't you give me that look," Sarah snapped.

Jack held back a smile, and they laughed once more. Todd ruffled Jack's hair and stood up to clean off his plate. He was followed by Sarah. The remainder of the night consisted of Todd asking questions about his hosts, not only to satisfy his own curiosity, but also in order to keep the conversation about them and not himself. He hated lying about his past. Every time he was asked something about his younger days, he had to choose his words carefully, converting his past in the twenty-first century into something believable.

The next morning Todd and Luke woke early and prepped their horses. They loaded their supplies into the saddlebags and tied their camping rolls to the saddles. The two then went inside and had a quick breakfast. The conversation was light and Todd could tell that Sarah and Jack were not happy to see the two of them leaving. Over the past few days, Todd had become so involved with this family that he had almost forgotten the reason why he was here. He started returning to the mission mindset. He looked over the ink map that Luke had given him and studied it religiously, taking into account key terrain features and danger areas like deep gorges and ravines. It was far from the quality of the terrain maps of the future but more useful than the MTX's imagery as it was current and had towns and trails labeled. He used York's journal to jot down a few notes about the route and put it in his pocket.

He threw on his long duster and clipped the 1911 to his leather belt just behind his right hip. He placed his spare magazine caddy on his left hip. He stuffed the MTX down into his boot and pulled his trousers over the long neck of the aged leather.

Luke walked in from the kitchen and gave him a nod.

"You ready?"

The brim of Luke's big hat curved up on the sides towards the crown and flattened out over his eyes. He wore a dark red bandana over his grey button-up blouse, and he carried two Colt peacemakers, one on each hip. Todd nodded in return and leaned down and picked the hat that Luke had given him.

The two walked out to the porch just as the sun was cresting over the horizon. Todd could see each breath in the brisk morning air. Sara and Jack stood on the porch, Sarah looking concerned. Luke kissed her and then wrapped his arm around her, his other hand holding a Winchester rifle. He pulled back and smiled at her.

"You be safe, ya hear," he said.

She smiled and said, "It's you two I'm worried about."

Luke knelt and hugged Jack. "You be good."

"I will, Papa," he said, his little arms wrapped around Luke's neck.

Sarah walked over to Todd and hugged him. "You two stay out of trouble."

Todd smiled, gently patting her on the back. "We'll be okay."

"Tell that brother of yours I said hello, and that he is more than welcome to have supper with us," Sarah said, putting her hands on her hips.

Todd smiled. "For your cooking ... he might just change his ways."

Luke walked over to his horse and untied the reins from the porch post. He then mounted it and adjusted in the saddle. Todd knelt down and held out his hand to Jack, who took it slowly, a sad expression on his face.

"When I get back, I'll teach you some more of those weird words ... okay?"

"... Okay," Jack said softly.

Todd patted him on the head and then stood up and walked over to Esprit, who was tied to the other side of the porch. He mounted the mustang and pulled the reins to the right, making the horse dance in a half-circle.

"We'll be back in two days," Luke said.

Sarah nodded, putting her arm around Jack. Then the two men rode out of the yard towards the distant buttes. They both looked back and waved to Jack and Sarah, who returned the gesture.

"I still think you should stay with your family, Luke," Todd said, bouncing up and down atop the horse alongside him.

"They'll be okay, Todd. I want to meet this asshole brother of yours."

Todd chuckled. "Well, let's go find him."

The two spurred their horses and they broke out into a gallop, racing out into the dark horizon, the rising sun at their backs.

*   *   *

January 2, 2016

I stood looking at myself in the mirror in my room. I deserved the scars, I deserved the pain.

My arm had taken months to heal from the op in Pakistan, and now that I had recuperated, it was time to make the final jump. I had spent the weeks prior to this planning a bogus op in Iraq in order to get Odin prepped. Tomorrow I will alter the course and say goodbye to this life forever. As a kid, I had always been fascinated by the Old West. It was a place where a man could truly be alone and free. I could live out the rest of my days there and not have to worry about altering the timeline ... or rather fucking it up any worse.

A knock on my door broke me out of my daydreaming. I recognized the soft knock immediately and opened the door to Kara. Those damn eyes of hers ... they could bring me back to reality no matter the circumstances.

"Yes?" I asked, sounding a little more impatient than I had intended.

"Todd ... I was hoping we could talk," she said softly. She was so damn gorgeous, I hate myself for the way I was to her. Always ignoring her, acting as if she wasn't even there half the time. I was now thirty-eight years old; she was twenty-seven. I still felt it wasn't right. I especially couldn't do that to Brian. She is like a daughter to him, and he would die for her. I think he and I both would agree she deserves the best. Not me.

"Is something wrong?" I asked, a little gentler, trying to make up for my blunt greeting.

She said, "I have this ... feeling. I don't know what it is, but I feel that if I don't do this now ... I may not have another chance." I could tell she was nervous. I wasn't sure where this was going, but my heart started to thump in my chest. "I want to show you something," she said.

I followed her out of the mess room and down the main corridor of the facility. She opened the main door and grabbed my hand, pulling me out into the frosty night. She let go of my hand and began pacing out steps, looking down as she carefully measured out her paces. I noticed then that she was wearing one of the suits beneath her long coat. Obviously, there were multiple suits in the facility in case one became damaged, but I had no idea that they had female versions. She stopped walking and turned in a tight circle to face me. She pulled off her coat and revealed the tight suit that complemented her figure. It was made entirely of the same black, flexible material that mine was beneath the armor. Hers did not have any armor plating. It seemed as if it was meant solely for time travel and not combat.

She held her hand out to me. My heart pounded in my chest as I stepped towards her. She took both of my hands and gently pulled me in close to her. She looked into my eyes and I felt the world around me slow down. She then looked down to the flexible touchscreen device that curved around her wrist. The time wheel on it was far different from the one on the MTX. Instead of four wheels that were labeled in years, it had ten wheels on it. I could faintly see the number that the wheels were set on. I counted at least nine digits.

I remember looking at her in shock as I had no idea what she was doing. She tapped "initiate" and stepped into me, taking my hands. The cables on her suit lit up with a bright light that lit her face. I could hear the familiar surge of electricity running through the cables. The light became brighter, and I heard the boom of the worm hole.

We continued staring at each other while the time changed around us in a rush of turquoise lights. The transition to the past was longer than I had ever experienced. She stared into my eyes the entire time, her hands atop mine. I ran my thumbs over the top of her soft gloved fingers. The transition stopped and the air became still, and all around us was darkness. The ground below us was too dark to see, and the horizon seamlessly blended into the star-filled sky. Her face was lit by a distant light in the sky, a single white light that looked like neither the sun nor the moon. Yet it cast a thin beam of light across the horizon. I turned back to her. I wanted this moment to never end. We stared at each other for what seemed like an eternity. The dark world; void and without form around us.

"Kara ..." I said softly. I tried to stop myself from telling her the truth, but I couldn't lie to her. It had to be done, she needed to know. "I'm leaving, Kara," I said. Her eyes instantly became saddened, and I could see the tears building up in them. It hurt, beyond anything I had ever felt. I couldn't stand the feeling of being the *reason for the look she had.*

Softly, she asked me, "Why?"

I told her. "I can't take it anymore, I can't stand to watch the world crumble around me because of my own actions. It was wrong to believe I could change what was meant to happen. No man should have that power." Tears began to roll down her cheeks as she stared at me. Her head lowered, and she closed her eyes. "I'm sorry, Kara. I wish it didn't have to be this way. I wish I could be someone else, someone you deserve. But you can't change destiny. I care for you, and I want you to be happy ... which is why I must go. It's the people I care for who always pay for my selfish actions."

I tried to hold her, to comfort her the best I could but she gently resisted, tears rolling down her face. I shook my head. I hated myself for that. I still hate myself for never telling her how I felt. It hurts to think of the last time I saw her. I wish it could have ended on a better note, but as I have so grimly learned, life has a harsh way of taking away the people you love.

This journal is for whoever Brian chooses next to wield the power of time travel, as he no doubt will find someone shortly after I leave. I wrote this so that you will know what the past will bring you, and how much responsibility will be bestowed upon you. Whoever you are, and wherever you come from, know that no matter what you do the world will never change, and honestly ... I don't think it is worth saving.

Live for yourself, don't become so fixated on changing what is, that you forget about you. I don't fear the future anymore, and not because I know I will never see it again. I feel like I never left.

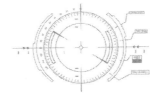

GHOST STORIES

Todd and Luke had ridden nonstop the entire day, racing through the winding hills that rose from the desert. Side by side, their horses snorted as their hooves pounded into the soft dirt. As the sun slowly dropped below the horizon, the two slowed into a trot and eventually came to a stop in a small clearing between some shrubs and boulders.

The two laid out their sleeping rolls and began building a fire. The music of the night began to amplify as they settled onto their mats around the fire. Todd stared into the flames as Luke rolled a smoke and licked the thin paper. The howl of a wild dog in the night caused Luke to look up into the star-filled night.

"Do you think we will make it to town by tomorrow?" Todd asked, trying to break the silence.

Luke didn't answer; his eyes dropped from the night and looked down at the fire. "It wasn't wild dogs," he said softly.

Todd canted his head in confusion. "Huh?"

"The night I met Sarah ... it wasn't dogs that had cut my arm open," he said as he studied the thin cigarette between his fingers.

Todd sat up, staring at Luke. The vague story from earlier that day had left him with assumptions, but he had accepted that he would never know the full story. He had sensed from the beginning that something in Luke's past was weighing heavily on his conscience.

Luke breathed out slowly, then licked his lips. "When I was a boy, my father left me and my ma to fend for ourselves deep in the Arizona desert. The heat was as harsh as the animals that lived in it. My mother passed away when I turned fourteen, and it was then that I realized just how helpless I truly was." He took a long drag on his smoke, then let it out. "I took the only good horse and began headin' north in the hopes of finding a future. I had no plan, no idea what to do. I just chased the horizon from sun up to sun down. About two weeks into my journey, my horse finally collapsed, and I continued on foot. I was a scrawny kid. My knees wobbled as I staggered through the endless desert. When I ran out of water, I ran out of hope, and I felt my mind dying with my body. I collapsed and waited for my inevitable death."

Todd listened intensely. He sat motionless, watching as Luke spoke and gazed out into the dark night. "What happened?" Todd asked.

Luke grinned and shook his head. "I remember nothing but the calm wind rustling the dry brush around me. The unforgiving sun ... blinding me through my swollen eyes. Then I heard the sound of spurs and boots drop down from a horse. I looked up, and standing above me was a grizzled-looking man with a black hat and two polished pistols. He knelt down and looked at me; his eyes were squinted hard, and he was unshaven and dirty. He held his canteen out to me and waited for me to take it. I remember leaning my head forward, waiting for him to put the canteen to my cracked lips, but he just held it there."

"Why?" Todd asked

Luke chuckled and looked up at Todd. "He stared at me with those hard eyes, not budging, and very grimly he said, 'If ya want something ... you have to take it.' It took all of my strength to reach out and take if from him, I remember nearly drowning myself with the water, and he just watched, his eyes not leaving me. As time passed I began to learn more about my new acquaintance. He was a criminal; he had been running from the law in Arizona when he found me. He took me in, taught me how to survive, how to live outside the law, how to fight. He became my mentor and my only friend. As I grew older, I became more involved with his way of life ... thieving, running, even killin'. When I was seventeen I killed my first man while robbin' a general store for something to eat. The teller tried to stop me and I shot him in cold blood. At the time, I thought nothing of it. I felt proud to be more like my mentor, but yet, he always seemed so cold and distant."

"What happened to this mentor of yours?" Todd asked.

Luke blinked then went on. "By the time I was twenty-five, he had put together quite the gang of thieves and gunfighters to assist him in his bad deeds. I was just a pawn in the posse, the bastard child of our fearless leader. I had killed many men by this time; most of them lawmen. My soul had been lost. I was an empty shell of anger and hatred. I thought with my guns and my greed. I didn't care who was affected by my actions, nor did I care for myself. I saw humanity as a bunch a' blind sheep who were enslaved by a system forced upon them." He paused for a moment, his eyes intensely trained on the fire. He sat against his saddle, his arm resting on his knee, his other hand holding his smoke down at his lap.

"It was 1867, and as usual, we were runnin' from the law. We crossed the Texas border into New Mexico to outrun their jurisdiction. We rode for days, hard into the cold dry desert. Not looking back. We had just robbed a bank in a small town on the border and had taken the lives of four men in the process. During that time, I had begun to question what we were doing. I started to see us as petty thieves who killed the innocent rather than idealistic outlaws. It was always a small peaceful town or village, and once we came through, it was left it in chaos and disarray."

Luke blinked a few times and pinched the bridge of his nose; his eyes were clamped shut. "One day, we came upon this small house. We decided to stop and try and get some food and water from whoever lived there." Tears began to pool in his eyes and he gritted his teeth. "I remember ... she reminded me of my mother. It was just her and her little boy. She knew who we were and told us to leave, waving a shotgun at us. The men in my posse drew down on her, and her child ran to her. I heard the hammers cock on their six shooters and I drew my pistols on them. I couldn't let them do it. It reminded me too much of me and my ma ... out fending for ourselves, alone in the desert. When I drew on them they laughed, and my mentor looked at me in confusion. Things escalated quickly, their confusion turned to anger, and our disagreement turned to fighting. One of 'em made a sudden movement and I started shooting. I just kept firing until both cylinders were dry, then I went for my knife. The last man standing was none other than the man who had taken me in ... had saved me. He was confused and angry. It seemed like he wasn't giving it his all. He sliced up my arm, never really going for the killing blow. I took it from him and stuck him in the gut." Tears rolled down Luke's cheeks. "I pulled back, and I'll never forget the look in his eyes. He looked as if ... he was proud of me. I dropped him to the ground, and the mother and child watched me in horror. I remember riding off without saying a word."

Todd rubbed his face, trying not to break a tear at the sight of Luke. He could see the regret and remorse that Luke felt. He wanted to try and cheer him up but couldn't find the words to do so. Luke sniffed and wiped his eyes.

"It was late that night that I found my haven. My horse was a reminder of my past and bad deeds, and I let it go, wanting not a single part of that life to follow me. I clutched my arm and stumbled through the night for many miles. It began to rain, and I began to lose hope. It was then that I realized ... it was exactly what I deserved. This life had left me the exact same way I had started ... alone and helpless." He licked his lips, blinked his teary eyes and looked up into the black horizon. "I came upon a small town. It was dark, all but one building. I remember not being able to think straight. Even if they knew who I was and turned me in, I was ready to face the consequences for the life I had lived. I knocked on the door, half-expecting it to open to the muzzle of a gun." His eyes widened and the corners of his mouth curved up. "But instead, I found myself looking at the most beautiful girl in the world. And little did I know, she would become my way out, my reason to live. She didn't just save me from the cold or my wounds ... she saved me from that life. She brought out another side of me, and I knew very quickly that I couldn't live without her."

Todd's lips tightened and his narrow eyes went to the ground, watching the firelight shift on the sand. He rubbed his sore hands that rested on his belly and took in a long breath. He found it somewhat ironic that regardless of how drastically different his and Luke's lives had been, they shared a similar guilt. Todd had struggled with it for many years. In the future, many innocent people had died because of Todd. Collateral damage was an ever-present element of war, which Todd was all too familiar with. For many years, he had been able to look past the deaths of the innocent that had occurred around him. He now however was incapable of blindly shrugging off the notion of people simply dying because of their unfortunate timing. Todd was responsible for the deaths of over sixty million people, regardless of how someone might look at his situation, since those events in the future had basically never occurred. To Todd, that had still happened, and he would have to live with it for the rest of his life.

Luke grinned and chuckled. "Sorry ... didn't mean to get all sappy on ya." He wiped the tears from his eyes.

"No ... no it's fine, Luke. Thank you for telling me that," Todd said kindly. "I know how you feel; I live with similar regrets."

"If I would have never met her, I don't think I would have ever come out of the darkness, and if I ever lost her ... I fear I would return to it."

Todd looked down, then back up at Luke. "You're a good man, Luke, and I think it's for that reason that you were given Sarah. All you needed was someone to ..." Todd stopped mid-sentence and thought for a moment. He then had an epiphany. Perhaps the only thing York needed was for someone from the outside to change his outlook on life, much like Sara had done for Luke. Maybe it was Todd who could convince him to come back into the light, or maybe it was Kara.

Luke broke the silence. "This is one of the many reasons why I came with you, Todd. I know the type of man your brother is, and I want to help you save him before he is lost forever."

Todd nodded. "Thank you, Luke. I can't tell you how much it means to me. You're a good friend."

Luke smiled and leaned back on his saddle, using it as a headrest. He breathed out slowly, looking up at the stars. "Nice night, huh?" he said.

Todd looked up at the crescent moon that glowed amongst the many stars. He felt warm inside, and for the first time in a long time he felt hope. Even with the apocalypse looming over him, he wondered if all this was meant to happen. Maybe the doomed future could be altered, just like Luke had been. He smiled and laid back, resting his head in his interlocked hands atop the saddle. "Perfect," he said softly.

*   *   *

The next morning, Luke and Todd set out early after a quick breakfast. They continued west, away from the rising sun. They yelled over the galloping horses, talking about the mission at hand and how they would go about their search for York.

Their plan was to scout out the town from afar for a while, and ensure the place was not hostile in any way. They then would go in and talk to locals at the various establishments and try to find out if they knew anything regarding York's whereabouts. They continued riding, their bandanas tied around their faces to shield them from the thick dust. They came to a small meadow and passed through it. When they reached the other side, they could see a stagecoach in the distance. They slowed their horses to a trot as the coach approached them.

As the coach neared, they could pick out an older man driving it. He wore a small billiard hat and a striped blouse and vest. Luke and Todd studied him as he drew near, watching for any sudden movements from the driver. They came up to each other along the thin road and the man called out to the four horses attached to the wagon.

"Whoa!" he said.

The horses came to a halt and he put both reins in one hand and extended his other out to Luke. Luke took it firmly and shook it.

"Howdy!" the man said cheerfully.

This was the first time Todd had heard someone say howdy, and it made him smile behind the dusty bandana.

"Were ya headed, fellas?" the man asked.

Luke nodded down the road. "Headin' into town."

"Hansen?" the man asked.

"I reckon," Luke replied, slightly impatient.

"Well you boys ain't got too much farther to go … we just came from there."

"Who's we?" Luke asked.

The door of the stagecoach opened, and the heel of a woman's boot stepped down onto the metal step of the wagon. A tall flashy white hat came out first, worn by a young woman with shiny red hair. She held up her skirt as she stepped down and pulled down the brim of her large hat to shield her eyes from the sun.

"Ma'am," Luke said as he tipped his hat towards her.

She smiled, her pale cheeks reddening, then she looked over at Todd and her expression turned to shock. Her eyes widened and her lips parted. She stared at him in silence for what seemed like minutes. Luke looked over at Todd and then back at her.

"Handsome ... isn't he?" Luke chuckled.

She stepped towards Todd, who had removed his bandana moments earlier. "You look just like him," she said softly, almost in disbelief.

"Like who?" Todd asked, already knowing who she was referring to. He felt his heart rate pick up as his search had just taken an unbelievable turn for the better.

"The man with the scars," she said.

Luke looked over at Todd, who sat in silence. "Sounds like our guy," he said with a grin.

Todd leaned forward on his horse. "You know him?"

She nodded up at Todd. "He helped me ... I'm going to Durango to take the train north, getting out of this Godforsaken desert."

"Sounds like a swell fellow," Luke said.

Todd dismounted his horse and stepped in front of her. She looked him in the eyes, then her eyes trailed down his body then back up again. She was amazed at how identical he looked minus the scars and longer hair. She leaned forward, speaking in almost a whisper.

"Are you here to help him? Is he in some kind of trouble?"

Todd looked down at the ground. "Let's just say I'm trying to keep him out of trouble. He has had enough for a lifetime."

She smiled kindly. "Please, take care of him. I could see the sadness in his eyes. Many might confuse him for an angry man, but I could tell it was sadness that was lingering in his heart."

"Was he alone?" Todd asked.

"Yes, but out of choice. He said it was what he deserved," she said, shaking her head sadly.

"What was he doing when you met him, and where was this?"

"At the saloon in town. He was sitting at the bar by himself, just minding his own business."

Todd pondered for a moment then asked, "This was …"

"Last night," Courtney interrupted.

"Was he carrying any weapons on him?" Todd asked, as he took out York's journal and jotted down some notes.

Courtney tilted her head back slightly and her eyes shifted to the sky as she tried to remember. "I don't … no, I don't believe so."

Todd nodded, looking down at his notes. Then he put the journal into the inside pocket of his duster. He looked over at Luke and shrugged. "Sounds like an easy day to me. He's unarmed, and he has no idea we are coming. Plus, I know the guy 'pretty' well, and my gut is telling me that he isn't just going to shoot at us at first sight."

Luke chuckled and his horse snorted, as if to let Todd know that it was time to get moving. Todd looked back at Courtney and asked her what her name was. She told him, and he held out his hand to shake hers. She leaned forward and kissed him on the cheek. Todd was surprised by this, and he did his best to conceal his blushing cheeks with the shade from his hat. Courtney smiled at him and quickly turned and stepped back up into the wagon. The man on the bench tipped his hat to Todd and Luke and cracked the reins on the horses who jerked forward, bringing the heavy stagecoach loaded with luggage with them. The coach became smaller as Todd and Luke began trotting down the road. Luke had a smirk on his face that made Todd do a double take.

"What?" Todd snapped.

"I'm amazed that you ain't been snatched up by some young gal," he said with a hearty chuckle.

Todd rolled his eyes and smiled. They picked up the pace and raced down the long dirt road for about two hours. Few words were spoken between the two as they rode. Todd was becoming more on edge as he continued to take in what he was about to see. He was about to be the first man in history to have ever met himself. It was unreal to think of it in such a simplistic way, and he still had a tough time believing it. In a way, he had almost convinced himself that York was in fact his brother because of how many times he had said it. He hoped that when he and York actually came face to face that York would be smart enough to play along with the "brother" cover story. Considering York's almost obsessive feelings about altering the timeline, Todd assumed that it wouldn't be a problem.

Luke could tell that Todd was getting into the mindset. He had the look of a man who was about to fight. He didn't want to disturb him during these crucial times. He knew how important it was to be alone with your thoughts when you were about to do something like this. He admired Todd's maturity, and his overall grasp of their journey. During their planning, Todd left no stone unturned as he jotted down notes in York's journal, asking about every terrain feature and town illustrated on the map. Weather, illumination, environmental hazards and even wildlife were taken into account during their map study. Luke was impressed by how thorough he was and his incredible attention to detail.

The town was beginning to come into view in the distance. The heat emitting from the baking sand and dead grass made it appear as if it were a mirage, an unreachable figment of the imagination. They spurred their horses, increasing their speed at the sight of the long-intended destination. They passed beneath several large buttes that cast long shadows down into the valleys below. Their menacing size made Todd look up them in awe. It was like he was returning to the place where it all began. They approached the outskirts of the town, and Todd prepared his mind and body for the unreal experience he believed he was about to experience.

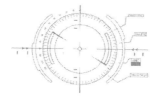

UNEXPECTED CONFRONTATION

It was a sweltering day in the city of Hansen that forced most of its occupants to stay inside or hidden beneath the shade of porches like desert animals. Like a small creek bed in the middle of the desert, the town was the only sign of life for as far as the eye could see. It was hidden between several large buttes, lying on a single road that ran east back to Colorado. It then headed west past Comb Ridge and eventually ran into Lake Powell.

The town was used often by outlaws and criminals as a place to lay low before crossing into one of the four corner states. The sun-baked road was like a frying pan, cooking the people walking across it. A few sweaty brows were shaded to view the two figures approaching from the distance. They trotted at a conservative pace as if they had been traveling for quite some time and they and their horses were parched.

Old timers of the town rocked in their wooden chairs, eyeballing their lever actions, keeping a close watch on the two strangers. They pulled down their bandanas, revealing their drastic differences in appearance. One seemed like an ordinary cowboy. He was tall and broad, with thick facial hair as most men of his age. He carried two pistols on his belt and a Winchester rifle on his saddle. The other man, however, looked like he didn't belong. He was a younger man and he seemed curious as he never stopped looking around. He studied the locals and the buildings with intrigued eyes. The two rode up to the local saloon where they dropped down from their horses and tied them to the hitching post next to the front porch.

The saloon was an old rundown building. It had two stories which seemed to be barely holding together by the dark aged wood. In big faded white lettering was the saloon's name, displayed above double swinging doors: "The Watering Hole." Todd and Luke studied the building suspiciously, then looked around the town. Todd felt anxious; at any moment he could be standing face to face with his same-self. He remained vigilante, eyeing everyone within view, studying their body movements and posture. So far, he had yet to see anyone who struck him as familiar. The two looked at each other, then ascended the two steps up onto the porch of the saloon and pushed through the swinging doors. Luke entered first, then a few seconds later Todd followed.

It was crowded inside the saloon, with crusty citizens rubbing elbows and drinking hard liquor. The piano player was playing an uplifting tune, and the prostitutes were strolling around casually in their large dresses, flicking Chinese fans in front of their faces. Luke walked to the far side of the bar and looked out into the main floor, while Todd casually approached the bartender.

"How can I help ya?" the bartender asked, not seeming to recognize him. Perhaps he was a different bartender than the one who served York the night before.

"I was hoping you could help me out," Todd said loudly over the noise of the saloon.

The bartender leaned up against the bar, leaning over to hear him more clearly.

"I'm looking for my brother. He has scars on his face. He and I are twins."

The bartender studied Todd for a moment, puckering his lips and rubbing his freshly shaved jaw. He looked around the bar then back at Todd.

"Ya know," he said, canting his head to the side, "I think I do remember the fellow … yes. I didn't bother chattin' with him for obvious reasons, he looked like a mean son of a bitch."

Todd was about to ask another question when a large mug slammed down on the bar next to him, drops of beer splashing across the wood surface and onto Todd's sleeve. Todd scooted over to make room for the individual who was obnoxiously making his presence known. He had long dirty blonde hair that was knotted and greasy. He wore a dirty short-brimmed hat that complemented his overall homeless look. He rudely asked for another drink then looked over at Todd with a devious grin which revealed his tobacco-crusted yellow teeth.

"Well, well, well," he said. "If it ain't the whore lover himself."

Todd looked over at him with a hard glare. "Do I know you?"

The man's grin turned to a scowl. "Watchya mean? We've been looking for your sorry ass for weeks. You ..." He paused, then studied Todd's face closely. "I recall you lookin' a lot uglier the last time we met."

Todd snickered. "You must be thinking of my brother. And who might you be?"

"The name's Pete Moore, and you must have lost your Goddamn mind, 'cause the last time we met, you busted up my little brother over a cheap whore," he said, pointing with his thumb over his shoulder to a group of dirty men sitting at a circular table. The youngest-looking one had a swollen nose and black eyes. His crusty lips barely concealed his tooth-absent mouth.

Todd laughed at the sight of the ugly kid, and Pete stood up quickly, knocking his bar stool down. The piano player stopped playing to see what the source of the commotion was. Every head in the bar turned to see the two men facing each other. The bartender nervously wiped down a shot glass behind the bar, and the prostitutes sat motionless in the arms of their soon to be customers. Todd reached down and picked up the barstool and gently placed it back, aligned with the others. Pete's eyes stayed locked on him, his hand hovering over his six shooter.

"Something wrong here?" Luke said as he approached from behind Pete.

"This asshole beat the shit out of my brother in Durango and ran like a chicken shit coward," said Pete, spitting a wad of tobacco onto the ground.

Todd's grin faded away and his faced hardened. He clenched his fists, waiting for him to make any sudden movement. "I told you, that was my brother. Do you see any scars on my face?" Todd said through gritted teeth.

Pete eyed his flawless skin then replied, "I don't care what kind of tricks you think you can pull. I know it's you, your disguise won't help you."

The four men sitting at the table stood up, glaring at Todd. The entire saloon was dead silent. Luke watched the four of them as they began closing in around Todd. Todd felt his hand begin to tense up as he prepared to draw his 1911.

"You sure you want to do this here?" Todd asked, looking around the room.

Pete snickered. "Why don't we step outside?"

Todd turned and walked to the swinging doors, the five rustlers following closely behind. Luke waited for them to step out before he followed. Todd and Luke had planned to not enter together to hide their partnership in case of just such an incident. As far as the Moore brothers were concerned, Luke was just an ordinary citizen who was concerned about the safety of the innocent townsfolk.

The six made their way out to the road where the five of them encircled Todd. Todd turned slowly, studying the five men around him. Each man carried a single revolver on their right hip, with the grip to the rear, meaning each man was right-handed and would no doubt lead with a wide right-handed haymaker. The chubbier one of the five held a double barrel shotgun under his arm. Pete had grabbed his coat as they left, which concealed a lever action shotgun. He held it in his left hand, down at his waist, pointing at Todd with his right.

"You've done made a big mistake fuckin' with the Moores," he said. The four others nodded in approval. "You're gonna pay for wutch ya did."

He dropped the shotgun to the ground, along with his coat, and rolled up the sleeves of his dirty shirt. Todd watched him carefully as he paced around him slowly, waiting for an opening. Luke watched from the porch, his hands resting on his dual Peacemakers. The four rustlers spread out around Todd, making an inescapable barrier.

Todd rolled his eyes. "Listen, you morons. I'm not York, okay. The guy who made a fool out of you idiots is my brother. We are looking for the same pers—."

"Shut up!" Pete yelled. "You ain't foolin' anyone."

Todd slapped his hands down to his side and sighted loudly.

"God, you guys are idiots!"

The five men circling around Todd looked at each other in confusion. Suddenly, Pete reared back with his right fist and swung at Todd. Todd quickly countered his blow by curling his arm up to his head, deflecting Pete's punch off to the left. In one smooth motion, he extended his arm, placing his hand on his chest and locking Pete's right arm between his shoulder and neck, then drove his right foot back, knocking Pete's feet out from under him and throwing him to the ground.

Todd looked down at him with an unimpressed expression. "Stay down ... and you won't get hurt."

Pete snarled then jolted up. He charged Todd, trying to tackle him to the ground by lowering his head and driving his shoulder into Todd's stomach. Todd quickly leaned forward, catching him with his chest to Pete's upper back. He held him tight, then brought down his elbow on Pete's spine, making him gasp and release his grip slightly. He then drove his knee up into Pete's face, making him stand up straight and stumble backwards. Todd quickly took advantage of his dazed state and delivered a hard right hook to his face, sending several of his yellow teeth flying out of his bloody mouth. Pete fell back onto his butt. Todd looked at the other men, who stared at him with wide eyes, their hands clutching the grips of their pistols.

"Anyone else want to lose their teeth?" Todd chuckled.

Pete crawled over to his coat and fumbled for his shotgun. The dirt in front of him exploded, causing him to back away from the lever action in a crabwalk. Todd looked over at Luke and saw the barrel of his Peacemaker smoking in his outstretched hand.

"That's enough!" Luke said firmly.

Todd gave him a grateful nod, then turned to the four rustlers around him. "I told you ... I'm not who you think I am. I am trying to find the same person as you. He is my brother. I don't want any trouble, I just want to find him and leave."

Two of the four helped get Pete back on his feet while the others backed away from Todd, their weapons drawn. Pete stumbled to his feet in the arms of his comrades. Blood poured out of his nose and mixed with frothy blood coming from his mouth.

"Fucking shoot him!" he yelled, spitting blood.

His fellow rustlers looked at him and then at Todd, unsure of what to do. Pete reached down for his six shooter and wrapped his hand around the grip. Before he was able to draw it from the holster, Todd brushed back his open duster and drew his 1911, firing three rounds into Pete's chest, causing him to fall backwards out of his brother's arms. They looked up at Todd in shock, frightened at how fast he had drawn and shot three consecutive rounds. Todd stood with his future pistol presented out. They were stunned by his odd-looking firearm, and his unusual shooting stance. Most men in this time figured only children and women held their pistols with two hands. Yet this man had obviously done so for many years and had perfected his technique. Luke was just as shocked as the rustlers. His mouth was open, eyes wide. He couldn't believe how quick Todd was. He blinked then trained his sights on the remaining rustlers, preparing for their rebuttal.

The youngest one, Winston, looked down at his dead brother in horror. Todd assumed that three of the five were actually Pete's brothers and had just seen him killed in front of them. The chubby one gritted his teeth and brought up the barrel of the shotgun. Todd quickly adjusted his sights and leveled them on him, but the man's head exploded with chunks of brain matter before Todd could pull the trigger. Luke had now drawn both pistols and was moving laterally across the porch, shooting one gun after the other at the last three rustlers who ran for cover. There were screams in the town, as the townsfolk quickly ducked into buildings and behind water trusses.

Bullets snapped and echoed through the town as the five men engaged in an aggressive firefight. Todd dove into a roll behind a wagon. Bullets ripped through the wood, sending splinters into the sand around him. He stood up with his pistol in front of him and cleared around the backside of the saloon, creeping into the adjacent alleyway. He could hear Luke still firing out on the main road. He had only twelve shots and had already fired several. He would have to reload soon and it would leave him vulnerable.

Todd quickly did a mag exchange, dropping the mag of five into his hand and inserting a fresh mag of seven. He leaned out around the building, his tritium sights combing over the area where he thought they were. Bullets smacked into the wall around him, making him duck back into the alleyway. He needed to find a new weapon, not because the .45 wasn't sufficient, but because he didn't want anybody to get a good look at the futuristic weapon. He looked out into the center of the street where Pete's lifeless body lay. Next to him was the lever action shotgun.

"Luke!" Todd screamed over the gunfire.

"Yeah?" Luke replied.

"I need covering fire so I can get that shotgun!"

There was a pause as Luke quickly finished reloading both cylinders.

"You good?" Todd yelled.

"Yeah ... go ahead!"

Todd waited for the volley of fire from Luke to force the rustlers behind cover. He then sprinted into the street, sliding like a baseball player, and grabbed the gun. He quickly jumped to his feet and ran back behind a stack of wood where Luke was hiding. Luke dropped back down behind the logs and opened the loading gates of his pistols, rotating the cylinders and dropping the empty smoking casings. Todd opened the breach of the shotgun slightly and ensured there was a shell inside.

"Tango, eleven o'clock, thirty meters," Todd said, peering over the stack of lumber.

"What?" Luke yelled.

"Never mind," Todd said. "When they stop to reload, you go around back of this building and try to catch them on their flank."

Luke shot him a confused glare. "Flank?"

Todd rolled his eyes. "Get around them ... to their blind spot."

"Gotcha," Luke said as he cocked back both hammers on his pistols.

The two men traded a grin as they found humor in each other's calmness despite the current danger. Both Todd and Luke were no strangers to gunfights.

Todd waited for a break in the rustlers' fire, then nodded to Luke. The two quickly got up and ran in their planned directions. Luke ducked into the alleyway and started making his way closer to their position from behind the buildings. Todd hopped up onto the porch of the adjacent buildings and began moving towards them, holding the shotgun at the low ready position. The moment he saw a hat pop up from behind a barrel, he fired at it, sending a load of buckshot splintering wood around him.

He quickly worked the lever and chambered another shell and fired again before ducking into the deep doorway of the laundry building. Bullets began to ricochet off different surfaces, echoing through the town. He peeked around the corner and saw Luke getting into position across the street.

Luke leaned over the top of some cover in time to see one of the rustlers making his way to his side of the street. The man hopped up onto the porch and quickly snuck into the general store. Luke holstered one pistol and crept to the back door. He peered in through a back window and saw the man hiding behind the counter. Very carefully, Luke opened the back door and stepped inside. The man cowered behind the storekeeper's desk, pointing his gun at the owner of the establishment.

"Be quiet, or I'll blow your head off," the rustler whispered.

"Please ... don't ..." the storekeeper whimpered.

The rustler was about to tell him to shut up once more when a large hand grabbed him by his long, greasy hair. Luke pulled him up over the counter, smacking his gun out of his hand. The man cursed, his legs kicking as he swung at Luke's hand. Luke pulled him off the counter and slammed him on the ground.

The man reached into his boot and pulled out a knife and tried to impale Luke in the stomach. Luke quickly caught his hand, engulfing his grip with his hand, and smashed the blade down into the rustler's chest. Blood leaked out of his mouth and his head jerked. Luke looked away, firmly holding the knife deep in his chest cavity, not wanting to feel the familiar satisfaction of a successful kill.

Bullets snapped past Todd and exploded into hard wood as he ran across the squeaky porch. A large window came up on his right and he fired a round of buckshot into it and dove through the broken glass. He quickly got up and looked out to where the last two rustlers were. They were hiding in a small barn at the edge of town, firing from the stables. Todd exited out the back door and ran down the backside of the buildings towards the barn.

Luke fired at them from down the street, drawing their attention to him. Todd crept towards the back side of the barn, trying to get the drop on them. He softly approached the large doors, his shotgun at the ready. He could hear commotion inside, cursing and movement, and then a gunshot. He reached for the door and it burst open, knocking him backwards. Winston was atop a horse bareback, sprinting out of town as fast as it would take him. Todd shook his head and watched as Winston shrank into the hot desert, a dust trail following him. He picked himself back up, turning to look inside the barn. The last rustler lay dead on the ground with a pool of blood around him. Todd walked into the barn. The sun shone through the gaps between the vertical boards of the barn's exterior and into the hay-filled room. Smoke was lingering inside, slowly rising to the ceiling where it dissipated.

The rustler lay in the blood-spattered hay, his mouth and eyes open, staring up at the dark figure that stood above him. Todd raised the shotgun at the man standing above the corpse. He was rotating the chamber of the dead man's pistol, his back to Todd.

"Drop the weapon!" Todd yelled.

The man's head shot up with surprise, not at the threat but at the man himself, or maybe it was the sound of his voice. He turned slowly to face the man aiming the shotgun at him. Todd slowly lowered his weapon as the man's face came into view beneath his black cowboy hat. A scar spanning down his cheek made Todd's eyes widen. His familiar facial structure and his unmistakable eyes made Todd nearly drop it. Todd had known this moment would arrive. He had played it out hundreds of times in his head during the days prior. Yet nothing could prepare him for what he was seeing. Standing before him was Todd Michael York. The original, the first and the oldest. Through the scars and grey hairs, and through the anger was a split image of himself. It was like he was looking at a mirror; one that showed him the future. A dark future he feared wasn't too far away.

FACE TO FACE

The two stared at each other in silence. York seemed just as surprised as Todd. Their eyes studied every inch of each other in disbelief. York seemed taller in Todd's eyes; no doubt comparing his own height by eye level. It was odd to see his own body in front of him. They stepped towards each other slowly. Todd opened his mouth, but no words came out. He held the shotgun loosely down at his side. York's lips slowly sealed shut and his eyes narrowed as he began to come to terms with the situation.

"Brian send you?" York asked softly.

His words made Todd freeze. It was unreal to hear his own voice coming from another person.

"Y—Yeah," Todd replied.

York looked down at the ground, then back up at Todd. "When are you from?"

"The future you created," Todd replied.

York blinked sadly and rubbed his fingers over his mouth. "What … what happens in the future?" he asked.

York had never found out what exactly transpired in the future that he had altered so drastically. He now was looking at a younger version of himself, his same-self who had lived his entire life reaping the consequences of York's actions. He wanted to know how much had changed, if anything was for the better. He hoped for news of a bright future, maybe even a brighter past for his younger self. However, the fact that his same-self was standing before him brought a sickening feeling to his stomach. A feeling that told him that he wouldn't be there if things had gone according to plan.

Todd breathed out slowly, shaking his head. "Nothing good," he said softly.

York looked down and closed his eyes, rubbing the bridge of his nose with his thumb and index finger. "So ... it was all for nothing," he said. "Everything I did ... everyone I hurt ... didn't change a fucking thing." His voice broke slightly.

"I'm sorry, York," Todd said. "I wish I could tell you that what you did made a difference, but I fear that this world can't be saved."

York shook his head; his voice and face were a mix of anger and sadness. "All those people ..." he said through gritted teeth.

Todd stepped towards him and placed his hand on York's shoulder. "It's not your fault ..."

York shrugged off his hand, stepping away from him. "What the fuck do you know? You think you have the slightest clue as to what I have to live with every single day of my miserable life?"

He paced around the barn slowly, looking at the empty wooden walls. "It's depressing, you know? Realizing your entire life is a paradox of futile attempts at changing human nature. I was foolish, like the people who spend every day of their lives praying to some god who they believe will save them from the inevitable. There is no hope, no hope for me ... no hope for this world. We are destined to destroy ourselves; it was always meant to be this way."

He stopped and sat down on a bale of hay, his head resting in his hands. Todd stepped over the dead rustler and leaned up against one of the empty stalls. He looked down at the ground, trying to find the right words to say. He didn't want to rush into the truth as to why he was really here. It was clear that York was unstable, and Todd had no intentions of aggravating him. Telling him that he was only here to retrieve the technology that he had stolen would no doubt stoke the fires of his anger and could possibly lead to a confrontation between the two of them. He decided he would try to convince him that he was here to simply bring him back. It saddened Todd to see York this way, as he couldn't help but wonder if this was his own future. Perhaps he was looking in a mirror in this situation, seeing the man he was soon to become.

"Why did you come here?" York asked, not looking up at Todd.

"To bring you back," Todd replied.

York shook his head. "I'm not going back."

"What about Kara?" Todd asked, stepping towards him. "She loves you ... you know she does. How could you abandon someone like her?"

"I didn't abandon her!" York yelled. "I left before I could cause any more pain for her or the rest of them. They saw their entire lives ripped apart, watched as everything they knew and loved died!" He gritted his teeth, shaking his head. "So, they put their hope and trust into me, hoping that I could change the world ... give them back what they had lost. They believed in me, and for a while I believed it too. But I couldn't, and the thing that hurts the most is that I could see it in all their faces ... they had hope."

Todd shook his head in disapproval. Though he didn't entirely understand York's refusal to return, he could however slightly relate to his overall disposition. He truly wanted to help this man. He felt for him, and in a way cared for him. The fact that Kara loved York was something that had bothered Todd since his first discussion with her. Her sadness, although subtle, was heartbreaking to Todd as he felt somewhat responsible. He wished he could be the person to bring her happiness but feared York was the only one who could.

"Please ..." Todd said softly. "At least go back for her, regardless of what has happened. She loves you so much ... she deserves to be happy."

"She won't find happiness with me, Todd. It's too late for me, I'm dead inside." York said. "She only thinks she loves me ... she's young, and she hasn't been able to see the rest of the world. It's a childish infatuation."

"You're wrong," Todd snapped. "She's not a child, she's a grown woman, and she's smart enough to know what she wants! Maybe you're too fucked up, or maybe you're just too stupid to see something good in your life. Probably the only good thing you have left, and you're going to ruin it with your self-indulged pity party."

York stood up quickly, facing Todd, his identical eyes burning a hole through his. "You go through what I had to and then tell me about the good things in life! You try watching everything around you fall apart." York jabbed his finger into Todd's chest. "You ain't me, so don't act like you understand me. You're just a replacement, a copy who inherited the easy road that I paved for you." He shook his head and scowled at Todd. "If you're so worried about her … why don't you be with her?"

Todd looked down at his feet, a frown growing on his face. He shook his head and looked up into York's eyes. "Because … like you said, we aren't the same person, and I'm not the one she wants," he said softly. He canted his head to the side, his eyes narrowed. "But don't assume you understand what I've done. I did live a different life, my own hell."

York's hard gaze eased slightly.

Todd continued. "I didn't go to Nam, I didn't kill any presidents, and I didn't cause the fucking Chernobyl meltdown."

York shook his head, reminded of the horrible events.

Todd breathed in through his nose, looking up at the sun shining through the hay loft, casting a dusty beam of light on the ground between them. "I have my own demons that I have to live with, my own memories that haunt me."

"Were you in the Teams as well?" York asked.

Todd shook his head "No, the SEALs weren't the premiere SOF unit that they were in your timeline. I assume JFK's death had something to do with that, considering he was a major player in the SEALs' creation. In my timeline, there are multiple JSOC assets."

York snickered, then looked back at Todd "So …"

"I was with the 75th when I was younger."

"When did the war start for you?" York asked.

"Officially it was 2030, but we were already conducting operations against the ACF as early as 2025."

York looked at him in disbelief. "At that level? With the Rangers?"

"No, by this time I was with CAG."

York leaned back and nodded, no doubt impressed with Todd's military history. Somehow, it made York proud that even in an alternate timeline, he would settle only for the best. A small grin formed on his face. "I guess we were always meant to be warriors, huh?"

Todd didn't reply; he continued to stare at York. He used to be proud of his accomplishments in the military, and if this conversation had taken place several years ago, Todd would have been more than happy to discuss war stories with himself. However, he now looked back on his days in the Army only as years of pain and suffering.

York grinned. "Do you remember when we fell from that tree in the backyard? That old one that Mom wanted to have removed?"

"Yeah ... I remember."

"I don't even remember falling, I just remember waking up and seeing the rock my head ... our head had hit, covered in blood, and Mom rushing us to the hospital."

Todd exhaled with a smirk. "Yeah ... apparently, Mom heard us crying from inside the house. I don't remember crying either."

"You know Mom was supposed to be at work that day? She was home because she had been laid off for a DUI. If she hadn't been there we probably would have died, just bled to death while unconscious and never would have even known. We were so young; do you remember much of life before that day? How easy would it have been if we had just slipped away; we wouldn't have had to live through what was to come? How many people would be alive right now if we had never existed past that day ... hundreds of thousands?"

"Millions ..." Todd replied softly. His eyes shot up quickly to York, immediately regretting his words.

The grin on York's face faded away, and he put his hands in the pockets of his black coat. "What were you doing when they found you?" York asked.

The question made Todd's heart skip a beat. He knew the answer would not be good news to York. He knew it was the last thing he wanted to hear. But he wasn't going to lie to him. He wasn't going to try and persuade him any longer.

"I was dying," Todd replied.

York's eyes widened and his heart sank. The slightest bit of hope that he had held onto, the thought of his younger self having a better life in a safer world, had now perished.

"H—how?" he asked, looking back up at Todd with teary eyes.

"I was suffering from several wounds, and ..."

"And what?"

" ... and I had just launched eleven nuclear missiles from outer space at the Eastern seaboard of the United States ... killing millions."

York looked at him in horror. His eyes began to dance around Todd, and his jaw flexed. "My God ... we are an abomination ... aren't we? We were destined to destroy this world. Us, not mankind, but specifically us ... me."

"York ..." Todd said firmly.

York sat down on the hay bale and continued. "In the end, it wasn't politics, it wasn't the government or the governments of others ... it wasn't an evil dictator or the scum that follow him."

"Listen, York ..." Todd pleaded.

York continued as if he didn't hear him. "In the end ... it was me. I set in motion the events that would bring an end to everything. I'm the anomaly, the glitch in the timeline that doesn't belong."

Todd knelt down in front of him. "York ... where is your suit?"

York didn't look up. "So that's why you're here, to ensure I can't travel through time. They want to make sure I can't fuck anything else up."

Todd tried to reason with him. "That's not ..."

York interrupted. "Kara, the students. They don't give a damn about me. They only want their technology back."

"No," Todd snapped. "They want *you* back."

"They only used me ... like an experiment for their science project. And now that it has failed, they want to remove me from the equation all together and start fresh. And now they will use you ... use you until you have nothing left. Until you have nothing left to give, then they will push you aside and find another."

Todd licked his lips. "You're the one who ran, York. They didn't abandon you, they didn't throw you away. They aren't trying to condemn you here ... they just want to ensure the technology doesn't end up in the wrong hands."

"I'm already condemned here," York whispered. "I destroyed the technology when I arrived. It's gone, it can't be used by anyone, anymore."

Todd let out a quick breath. He looked at York who stared at the floor. The darkness engulfing him. "Please, York. Come back with me."

York slowly looked up at Todd. "I can't go back ... I belong here."

Just then, Luke walked in through the back door of the barn. York's eyes shot up and stared at him like daggers. Luke gripped his pistol tightly.

"It's okay, Luke," Todd said, turning around and motioning towards York. "This is York ... my brother," he said, looking at York with a glare, telling him to play along.

Luke holstered his pistol and gave York a friendly nod. York looked back down at his feet.

"So, you won't come back?" Todd asked, standing above him.

"No, I deserve this," York replied softly.

Todd stepped away and walked towards Luke, who stood in the large doorway. He paused and looked back at himself. It was heartbreaking to finally meet his same-self only to find that he was a broken man, sad and alone, blaming himself for the evil in this world. There was no changing his mind; this was who he was. This was what the world had turned him into. Although Todd didn't agree with him, he also didn't blame him. How could one man bear such a difficult task? It made Todd question whether or not he wanted to continue with the mission himself. He knew once he returned, preparations would be made in order to send him back in time to continue altering the present day. Part of him knew that if he went through with it, he would end up just like York, sad and alone.

"I'm sorry, York," he said.

York stood up slowly, presenting his appearance to Luke, who couldn't believe what he was seeing. The two men were identical. York walked towards them, his walk all too familiar, yet his left arm swung slightly different than his right. No doubt a result of his injury in Pakistan. He approached Luke and Todd and stood a few feet from them.

"Don't be sorry, you go back ... continue your pointless escapade. Dedicate everything you have to it, and in the end, when you're burnt out and hate yourself ... I'll be waiting for you here."

Todd didn't respond. Luke looked at the two men, not fully understanding what they were talking about, but he understood enough to know that York was not coming with them. York clearly was not the man he used to be. Whether he was a good person before, this was who he was going to be for the rest of his life. The look in his eyes told Luke that he was beyond repair. His soul was long gone; he had permanently been lost in the darkness.

York looked Todd in the eyes intensely. "You can't change destiny, Todd. In the end, you will find yourself in the same place where you started, dying … and alone."

He stepped past him and walked out of the barn. Not looking back, not saying another word. So, this was how it would end between the two Todd Yorks. It saddened Todd to think about leaving him here, but there was no changing him. Todd looked up at Luke with sad eyes.

"I'm sorry, Todd," Luke said. "Don't blame yourself, son. That's what this world will do to people. If he has any chance of being brought back to light, it will have to be someone else who shows him the way."

Was it the fact that he had let down Kara and the students? Or was it that he feared what York had become? Maybe it was both. He couldn't believe how different of a person York was.

*   *   *

York sat atop his pale horse, looking down at the town from the hills above. His other self, Todd York, only a few hundred meters away, heading back to the saloon with his companion to retrieve their horses. He felt something inside him. Something deep and unshakable. Something that made a chill shoot through his body every time his thoughts turned to it.

He was the cause of everything he had hoped to change, and though he had planned to remain alone in the West for the remainder of his life, he felt something gnawing at him. Something needed to be done.

Todd and Luke mounted their horses and slowly began heading out of town, back east from whence they came. Todd didn't say a word to Luke. He felt an empty spot in his soul that he feared couldn't be filled. What if York was right? What if him going back in time would only further ensure the destined apocalypse? Would it bring upon his own self-destruction? He was beginning to feel like there was little reason to continue on. Why push on knowing that he would end up just like York?

Luke was deeply worried about him. He glanced over at him periodically as they road next to each other into desert. Todd's grim expression showed his apparent distraught feelings. The sun was beginning to drop behind them as the small town slowly disappeared into the orange layers of light. They quietly rode along, not saying a word. The clomping sound of hooves on the desert floor became accompanied by the sound of crickets and howls of wild dogs in the distance. Soon the sky was dark and the desert became an endless transit of thought and sounds. They continued riding for several hours in the cool night breeze, trying to decrease the distance between them and home.

MOVING ON

Todd couldn't take his mind off of York. He couldn't believe he had come all this way only to find that York was far too damaged to come back, both physically and psychologically. Like the night prior, Todd and Luke had set up camp for the night. They picked an elevated spot that was at the base of a menacing butte.

The light from the fire glowed on the walls of the orange rocks' smooth surface, casting the two men's shadows up on it like a primitive projector. The two sat in silence, listening to the dry wood pop in the hot flames. Todd stared at the glowing coals beneath the roaring fire, thinking of his future to come. He feared the coming years, beginning to feel hopeless and lost inside. Returning to the future was becoming more and more of a damnation to him. The more he thought about it, the more he concluded that there was no reason for him to return. Nobody cared for him, nobody needed him. The only people who seemed to care for him was the McWilliams' family. Why leave them when he had no reason to, no reason to return to a place that would bring him nothing? He was beginning to think that everything he needed was here.

"Luke," Todd said softly.

Luke looked up from the fire, surprised to finally hear Todd speak after an entire afternoon of silence.

"Would it be alright if I stayed with you guys … just for a little while longer? At least until I can find a place where …"

Luke smiled big, interrupting him before he could finish. "Of course, my friend."

Todd looked down at the ground. "I don't want to be a burden, it's just … I don't think there is anywhere else for me to go."

"Todd," Luke said in a fatherly tone. "My home is yours."

Todd's mouth curved up, and he nodded.

"Forget about him, Todd. He will find his way eventually, it may be many years from now … but eventually he will forgive himself and he will find happiness. It may be at his very end when it happens, but someday he will," Luke said.

"Have you ever met somebody who you believed it was simply too late to save?" Todd asked.

"Only one man," Luke said firmly.

Todd bit his lip, looking back at the flames. "What happened to him?"

Luke's smile disappeared, but his eyes remained soft. "It wasn't until I killed him that I saw something change in his eyes."

"Your mentor?" Todd asked surprised.

Luke nodded solemnly. "I thought he was the coldest man on the face of the earth. I saw something in his eyes the day I killed him. Something … good."

"If you had never met Sarah … do you think you would have ever changed?" Todd asked.

"I don't know, bud. All I know is that the man I was … was eventually going to die, one way or another."

Kara could tell that the news wasn't good. Kevin peeked into her office. She looked up quickly, hoping for news of him. Her excitement quickly faded when she noticed Kevin's expression.

"He found him, Kara," Kevin said softly.

She stood up quickly and followed him out to the main cabin, where the majority of Odin's occupants worked. The large screen at the front of the room displayed the communications screen; a recently received message was displayed on the inbox. Her heart sank as she read it.

-SITREP-

I found York. I spoke with him briefly and after several attempts at trying to change his mind, I am afraid he does not wish to return. I tried, I want him to come back as much as you all, but he is not the person he used to be.

I am sensing serious psychological issues with him, no doubt symptoms of Post-traumatic stress disorder, among many other wounds that cannot be healed in one conversation. I believe that in time he will slowly forgive himself for the horrible things he believes he is responsible for, but as of now he is a lost cause.

As for my primary objective; his suit and MTX were destroyed. He disposed of them upon his arrival in order to prevent himself, or anyone else from using it. I am beginning my journey back east towards Durango. I will keep you posted and will notify you when I am ready for extraction. I am deeply sorry everyone. I'm sorry, Kara.

~Todd

Kara turned to notice several sets of concerned eyes staring at her. They quickly dropped to their monitors as she looked around the room. Amber stared at her with a look of utter shock. She couldn't believe that her good friend had no intentions of returning to them, returning to Kara. She walked up to her slowly, wanting to comfort her. Kara turned and walked down the hallway towards her office, closing the door behind her.

HOME SWEET HOME

Luke let out a relaxed sigh as he began to recognize the familiar terrain around the two of them. The sun was setting behind them, casting long shadows that pointed towards the distant ranch. The horses sped up slightly at the familiar smell of home.

Todd leaned forward and stroked Esprit to thank her for her hard work during the past few days. She had mellowed quite noticeably through the long hours that they had spent together, yet there was no doubt she still had an ornery side to her, as she wouldn't let anyone else but Todd touch her. The night prior, she had been acting strangely as she neighed and stomped loudly, waking up Todd and Luke. It took Todd several minutes to calm her down, as she continued to snort and shake her head. "Must've seen a ghost" Luke had chuckled. She eventually settled down, allowing the two men to fall back asleep. Since then however she had seemed quite relaxed.

The two men bobbed up and down atop their horses side by side. Todd looked over at Luke, who had an uneasy demeanor.

"You okay?" Todd asked.

Luke shrugged slightly, looking forward at his vast lands. "I just feel bad for ya, bud. Ya came all this way to help your brother, only to find him not wanting any help."

"I didn't come out of this empty-handed, Luke. You are a great friend. Meeting you and your family was one of the best things that has ever happened to me." Todd's mouth curved up.

Luke grinned. "Like I said last night, you will always have a home here." His expression turned to curiosity. "What will you do next?"

"I don't know. I guess I will return to Durango eventually." Todd shook his head, not wanting to return to the future. "I made a promise to some people there."

Luke nodded. "I understand."

The two came to the back of the house and rode around the side towards the front, where the stable was. Jack had no doubt been watching from inside the house as he came running out of the house in excitement.

"Mama! They're back!" he called out as he ran towards them.

Luke stepped down from his horse. Holding the reins with one hand, he knelt and wrapped his other arm around Jack and kissed him on the top of his head. Todd smiled and led Esprit into the stable. He opened the gate to her stall and tried to pull her in, but she pulled away from him, shaking her head.

Todd chuckled. "Come on girl, it's just for the night."

She continued to pull away and started to neigh loudly, pulling against the reins relentlessly. Todd's smile disappeared as he observed her unusual behavior.

"What is it!" he snapped.

Just then, Todd noticed something from the corner of his eye. He turned slowly towards it. The fading sunlight made it hard to see. Standing in the dark corner of the barn was York. Todd's heart leaped into his throat, startled at the unexpected visitor. His dark clothes helped him blend into the shadows. Todd could faintly see the reflective surface of a polished Schofield revolver in his hand. Todd looked at the entrance to the barn; he could see that Luke had temporarily hitched his horse and had walked into the house with Jack. Todd swallowed, then spoke calmly in an effort to sound unsurprised.

"That was a good tail; had no idea you were following us," Todd said.

"Where is it?" York said coldly.

"Where is what?" Todd asked.

"Your suit."

Todd's fists clenched down at his side. He couldn't go for his 1911, York would no doubt recognize the movements and would shoot him before he would be able to draw it. He remembered that Luke had his Winchester on his saddle. He needed to get to it.

"It's in the house," Todd replied.

"Do they know you're from the future?" York asked, his voice low and sounding aggravated.

"No, I lied to them. Told them I'm from Durango, and that you're my rotten brother that I'm here to save him from himself."

York scowled and raised the revolver, pointing its black muzzle at Todd. "Give me the suit, Todd."

"What do you want with it?" Todd asked, his hands out to his sides, palms facing York.

"I have to fix this," York said softly.

Todd looked at him in confusion. What did he mean by that? Todd's heart pounded in his chest; he couldn't believe this was happening. "This isn't you, Todd. You're a better man than this. Just come back with me ..."

"It's too late for that," York interrupted. "I have to set things right, I need the suit. You're going to give it to me." His voice was low and heartless. Todd could tell that he meant what he was saying.

"Okay," Todd said, nodding. "Let me go get it."

He side-stepped to the front sliding door of the barn. He relaxed his hands and walked out of the dark building. Luke's horse partially blocked the entrance. He would use this to his advantage, act as if he was trying to move around the animal and get to its right side where the rifle was. York followed him out of the barn, holding the gun trained at his back. Todd walked around the horse; he could see the wooden stock of the Winchester in its leather sheath. Just then, Luke came out of the house, his smile fading at the sight of York. Todd's eyes widened, trying to tell Luke to stand down.

Suddenly, Luke went for his pistol. A loud gunshot from behind Todd made his ears ring and his heart stop. York had fired a single shot, his bullet striking Luke just below the collar bone and sending him toppling forwards off the front porch and onto the dirt.

"NO!" Todd screamed. He turned to face York, his eyes filled with tears. He gritted his teeth. He couldn't speak; every nerve in his body made him want to lunge towards York and beat him to death. He clenched his fists.

"Papa!" Jack cried out. He came out of the house and ran to

Luke. Luke held his arm out, wrapping it around Jack, trying to shield him from York. Blood pooled around him and streamed out of his mouth.

Todd tried to run to him but was stopped by York.

"Stop!" York yelled. "Get me the suit, or I will kill them all!" He adjusted his revolver and pointed it at Jack.

Todd's heart nearly stopped. Tears poured out of his eyes at the sight of Jack crying on his knees next to Luke. His clenched fists shook, and his body trembled with anger. He turned to York, wanting to attack him.

"How ... could you do this?" Todd said through his teeth.

"It won't matter after I fix the timeline; all of this will have never happened," York replied. Todd stared at him, anger and confusion overrunning his emotions. "Todd," York said softly, "get the suit."

Todd looked out into the dark desert to the east. The suit was still buried beneath stones at the foot of the rock chimney, almost a thousand meters away. "Its ... it's out there," Todd said, his voice shaky.

Sarah came out of the house and screamed in horror at the sight of Luke. She ran to him, kneeling next to Jack.

York looked back at Todd. "Go, Todd. He doesn't have much time."

Todd ran into the barn and mounted Esprit. "Yah!" he yelled as he spurred her. She burst into a gallop. Todd rode out of the ranch in a sprint, following the dirt road. He couldn't stop crying as he rode through the darkness. He had to calm himself in order to keep his eyes peeled for the rock chimney which would be coming up on his left sooner or later. He reached into his pocket and pulled out the MTX. Bouncing up and down on Esprit it took him several attempts to open the map application. In it he had the suit's eight-digit grid plotted on. He only had a few hundred meters to go.

The distinct rock finally came into view. The full moon lit the desert just enough for Todd to see it beside the road. He yanked back on the reins, bringing Esprit to a sliding stop. He jumped down and ran to the rock pile and began digging on his hands and knees for the invisible suit. He pulled up the MTX and disengaged the cloaking system on the suit. He brushed off the remaining sand and pebbles and threw the suit over his shoulder. He ran to Esprit, lifting the armored suit up and over and resting it on the front of the saddle, then mounted and spurred his mount. They sprinted back down the road towards the ranch house.

Todd came thundering into the yard. Activating the cloaking system, he jumped down from Esprit, hurled the suit over his shoulder and ran to York, dropping the invisible mass in front of him. Then he hurried over to Luke. Luke's eyes were beginning to wander, and his skin was pale. Todd immediately began assessing the injury.

"Sarah! I need something to pack the wound, quick!" he said.

She nodded, wiping the tears from her eyes, and ran into the house. Todd continued pressing down on the bullet wound, trying to control the bleeding the best he could. Jack cried uncontrollably next to him. Todd looked over to him. "It's going to be okay, Jack."

Sarah reappeared from the house with a few rolls of bandages. She handed them to Todd, who took them with blood-stained hands. "Okay," Todd said, "I need you to take Jack inside."

Sarah couldn't stop crying at the sight of her husband.

"Sarah!" Todd snapped.

She picked up Jack and hurried into the house. Luke watched them leave, his eyes saddened. Todd began talking to him in an effort to keep him from going into shock. "It's gonna be okay, Luke," he said as he began fishing in his pocket. "What year is it, Luke?"

Luke's gaze wandered, and tears streamed out of the corners of his eyes. His past had finally caught up with him. He felt like it had been a long time coming that someone would do to him what he had done to so many others.

"Come on, Luke!" Todd said loudly, "What year is it?" His hand emerged from his pocket with something Luke had never seen before. It looked like some sort of silver container, and it had tiny lettering on it.

"18 ... 87," Luke replied.

"Good," Todd said as he opened the cap to the silver container.

"What ... is that?" Luke asked.

Todd was now squeezing the trauma gel into his wound, and it began seeping into his body, clotting any severed arteries and stopping the bleeding. Luke gritted his teeth and closed his eyes.

"It's going to save you," Todd replied.

He had grabbed the trauma gel from his web gear when he was riding back from retrieving the suit. Luke would be too dazed to really pay close enough attention to what it was.

"Stay with me!" Todd said.

Luke was beginning to lose consciousness. Todd feared he was too late. He had lost a lot of blood, and that was something trauma gel could not help.

"You've got a little boy in there who needs you ... stay with me." Todd said, as he began wrapping up Luke's wound.

York stood a few feet away, completely invisible, watching his other-self take care of this stranger. He had shot an innocent man in order to force Todd's hand. Yet he felt no remorse as it was a necessary act; everything would return to its natural state shortly. All the wrongs he had done would be wiped clean. He walked around to the back of the house and mounted his horse. He rode out of the ranch down the main road, heading east towards Durango.

Todd heard the sound of hooves galloping down the road. He turned to see a horse with no rider sprinting off into the darkness. The moon's illumination reflected off the transparent figure riding the horse. The road only led to one place, and Todd would need to follow him as soon as possible.

*   *   *

Albrecht stood in horror as he read the message. It had been sent about a half hour prior. He and most of the crew on board had been sleeping when D came over the intercom. Kara walked into the main room, her eyes displayed her concern. Nearly everyone on Odin had been told about the message and were pouring into the main cabin to see the big screen which displayed the transmission.

EMERGENCY!

Requesting immediate CASEVAC!

Location: Vicinity of Durango, won't know exact pos until time jump is made.

Time: Approx. 12 hours from now.

Patients: 1 for sure, possibly 2.

Remarks: York has threatened innocent lives, forcing me to comply with his demands. I have given him my suit and I believe he will be making a jump back to the future. Possibly to the 2030-time frame. He said he was going to fix his mistakes ... fix the timeline. I don't know exactly what he means by this, but he will no doubt be heading east towards Durango to make his jump.

York is clearly a hostile threat and I intend to kill him. He cannot be reasoned with, and I see no other solution. If he makes the jump before I can stop him, please know that I am truly sorry that it ended this way.

Don't bother trying to come for me if I don't succeed.

~Todd

York looked at the sent messages on the MTX as he rode through the quiet night. It only took him three tries to figure out the combination to the MTX's login screen. And he was now was scrolling through Todd's transmissions, trying to gain a better understanding as to how his op had been conducted. Todd must've sent the last transmission only moments before he had given him the suit and MTX.

"Clever," York said to himself.

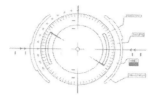

GOODBYE

$Todd$ walked out of the house and looked out into the dark desert. York had almost an hour's head start on him. He needed to follow after him as soon as possible. He was definitely heading to Durango, but where would he make his jump? There wasn't any terrain with high enough elevation for him to base-jump off anywhere near the town.

Perhaps he was planning to take the train out of Durango. Todd pulled out his map and studied the Silverton railroad that ran north almost five hundred miles past San Juan and south to Farmington, New Mexico. The terrain that skirted the railroad became more and more elevated as it continued out of the town's vicinity. It seemed like the only plausible option, and Todd was convinced that this was York's most probable course of action.

"Todd," a soft voice called out from inside the house.

Todd turned to see Sarah approach him. Her eyes and cheeks were reddened from her recent tears. Her hands fumbled in front of her as she closed the distance between them.

Todd folded the map and placed back inside his duster's pocket. He wrapped his arms around her and spoke softly, "I'm so sorry, Sarah ... I never wanted this to affect your family."

She pulled back and looked into his eyes; her mouth curved up slightly, and a tear ran down her cheek. Loud footsteps echoed through the dark house behind her. Todd looked up to see Luke emerge from the darkness. His arm was splinted to his chest with a

191

buttoned-up blouse. Blood-stained bandages engulfed his chest and shoulder. He slowly walked to the edge of the porch, using the pillar to stabilize himself. Todd stepped around Sarah and approached him.

"Luke, I ..."

Luke's deep voice stopped him from apologizing. "Todd, you have nothing to be sorry about. It was my itchy trigger finger that got me winged. You need to get goin' and catch that bastard, ya hear?"

Todd looked down at the ground. He didn't want to leave. He feared following York would only bring him nothing but trouble. "Thank you ... for everything," Todd said. He held out his hand to Luke.

Luke stepped down from the porch and hugged him with his good arm. "You be safe, okay," he said into his ear.

Todd nodded. Luke patted him on the back and stepped back. Todd turned to Sarah and hugged her once more. She smiled, rubbing the tears from her cheeks. Over her shoulder, Todd could see Jack looking at him from inside the house. He seemed frightened, like a small animal peering out of its home.

Todd held out his hand to him. "It's okay, Jack."

Jack didn't reply, just stared at him, his little eyes saddened. Todd dropped his hand to his side. He smiled at the little boy. "You take care of yourself, bud."

He looked at Luke and Sarah, their expressions similar. He gave them one last smile, then turned and walked over to Esprit, who stood near the barn. He ensured the saddle was tight, and that he had enough water for the trip. He stuck his left foot in the stirrup and placed his hand on the saddle horn to lift himself up and headed out of the yard.

"Todd!" Jack cried out from the house.

Todd turned to see him running towards him. He pulled his foot from the stirrup and hopped down from the horse. He squatted down and caught Jack in his arms, holding him tightly. Jack sniffed in his shoulder as he patted him on the back. Luke and Sarah held each other, watching as their little boy say goodbye to his best friend.

"I'm going to miss you, Jack," Todd whispered.

"Will you ever come back?" Jack's little voice broke as he asked.

Todd pulled away, his hands holding Jack's shoulders. "I promise, dude."

Through his sadness, Jack's face lit up. Todd hugged him once more, then stood up, looking down at him. Jack looked up at the man with idolization. He was different than other men; it was like he was from another world, yet completely conventional, and physically appropriate for his circumstances. Luke could see it as well, and he marveled at the sight of Todd's strong presence.

With one last pat on Jack's head, Todd mounted Esprit and spurred her. She reared back and burst into a gallop off into the darkness down the long road that led east.

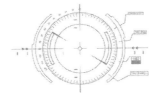

CATCHING A TRAIN

The sky was beginning to lighten as the early morning hours climbed with the rising sun. Todd had ridden hard for the past ten hours, taking only a few brief stops to keep Esprit from breaking.

She continued to push, sprinting through the cool wind as the land around them started to turn mountainous and the stars slowly disappeared into the light blue sky. Durango was not much farther, meaning neither was York. This was it, the final confrontation. Todd York, the first, was going to die today. Even if that meant Todd going down with him in the process. He had to be stopped.

A noise in the distance made Todd bring Esprit to a sliding halt on the dusty road. Only a few hundred meters away was the whistling sound of a steam engine. Its high-pitched horn echoed through the hills. Todd quickly sped towards the sound, riding through the winding hills. He came to an elevated spot in the road that looked down at Durango. The sun was shining over the purple mountains in the horizon, gleaming off the shiny features of civilization. A large trail of smoke wafted in the air as the train left the city. Its long body curved down the tracks leading south across the Animas River.

"Yah!" Todd yelled as he sped down the road towards the distant town. It took him a few minutes to reach the city; he raced down the main road, weaving in between wagons and pedestrians as he chased the shrinking tail end of the train. Esprit grunted and breathed heavily, countless heads turning to see the man riding his horse at full speed down the public street.

"Come on, Esprit! Almost there."

The town passed in a blur of dust and adrenaline as he kept his focus on the distant train, which was picking up speed as it curved around a hill just on the edge of town. Todd rode across the bridge above the river and up the long finger of the hill, cutting through the small shrubs as Esprit's breathing began to climax with snorts and grunts. As he neared the peak of the hill, the sun came into view off to his left, making him squint as he gripped the leather reins tightly. The muscles in his legs throbbed, keeping himself hovering over the shifting saddle.

The train was now just below him, off to his three o'clock position. He could feel his heart rate pick up as he readied himself for the inevitable confrontation. York had to be on this train. He would need to board it from the rear and search each section.

"Yah ... yah!" he yelled.

The mustang continued to sprint, paralleling the noisy train. Very carefully, Todd began pulling the reins towards the train, closing the gap between themselves and it. He eased up a bit, letting some of the carts pass them by. He could see folk inside the train. They looked out the windows at him with bewildered looks. He continued to hold back, waiting for the last cart to come up on his side. Suddenly, a bullet snapped past him and ricocheted off the train. Todd looked back to see a group of riders behind him, slowly closing the gap between them and him.

He reached back and pulled his .45 from his belt and with one hand started firing at them. They spread apart from their tight formation but were unharmed. It was then that Todd realized just how hard shooting on horseback was. He emptied the mag, then turned back around, placing the reins in his teeth. He ejected the mag, retaining it in his pocket, and inserted a fresh one from his belt. He pressed the slide release and fumbled to re-holster his pistol as his lower body bounced up and down.

He jerked the reins, making Esprit come uncomfortably close to the train. He pulled the lever action shotgun from the saddle and held it in his left hand. Very carefully, he pulled his right foot from the stirrup and placed it on top of the bouncing saddle. It took all of his strength and concentration to stabilize himself. In one quick movement, he leaped off the saddle with his right leg, throwing his forearms over the top of the train. It nearly knocked the wind out of him as his chest hit the corner of the train's roof. It took him a split second to regain his composure. He then attempted to throw a leg up and over in order to pull himself up.

Bullets smacked into the side of the train around him, startling him and causing him to lose his grip. He grabbed frantically for something with his free hand, but felt himself slipping off the side. Miraculously, he managed to grab ahold of the curved-up edge with his right hand. He could feel his foot hit a bar below him, and he used it as a step. He extended his left arm and fired at the approaching riders. They were close enough now for him to make out Winston Moore at the head of the pack. Todd figured they must have seen him riding through town and had saddled up to catch him. They most likely had followed Todd to Durango and had beat him there because of the stop at the McWilliams farm. Todd fired again and the buckshot managed to clip one of the lead riders, making him lurch backwards off the back of his horse. Winston looked back in horror and spurred his horse in anger.

Todd brought the shotgun in closer to his body and rotated it around his hand, spin-cocking the weapon. He aimed once more and fired, this time nailing Winston with a direct hit. He went limp and fell over the front of his horse, getting caught in between its galloping legs and causing the animal to trip over him. The rest of the riders dispersed, attempting to clear the wreckage. Todd tossed the shotgun up to the roof and reached up with his other hand, grabbing ahold of the ledge and heaving himself up on to the roof. He knelt down, looking at the many carts ahead of him, curving in unison along the fixed track. He looked off to his left and saw Esprit sprinting alongside the train. As if she had waited to ensure he had gotten on board first, she began spreading the gap between her and the train, slowly shrinking into the distance.

The powerful mustang disappeared behind the passing terrain, and Todd looked back towards the front of the train. He picked himself up and slowly began moving forward in a crouch, trying to keep a low center of gravity. He leaped over the first gap between carts, making his way up to where the passenger carts were. He looked up, and something near the front of the train briefly fixed his gaze. He saw movement near the front car, but nothing was there. His concentration was broken by bullets whizzing past him. He quickly drew his 1911 and sighted in on the riders. He flipped up the small red dot sight and pressed off multiple shots, hitting a rider multiple times. He then adjusted, shifting onto his opposite knee, and engaged the last rider. It took him multiple shots, which put him in slide lock. He reached back to his left hip to draw his last mag, but paused for a moment.

The air in front of him shifted in an unnatural way, causing him to freeze. Suddenly, he felt a hard blow hit him just above the eye. He fell backwards, catching himself from falling off. He looked back and the bright sun reflected off the transparent figure standing before him. He quickly went for a magazine but felt a pair of hands grab him by the collar of his coat. He quickly grabbed ahold of one of the invisible hands with his left hand, and with his right began using the butt of the 1911 to hammer punch York's helmet. He could feel the metal handle smashing into the helmet's visor, causing it to crack. York released his grip slightly, giving Todd the chance to break away from his hold.

Todd stood and faced him; he could see a visible crack in the transparent visor, which was causing distortion in the helmet's micro-imaging system. Todd reached for his last mag but felt nothing on his belt. It must've fallen out during the fighting.

York reached down and uncloaked himself, revealing the futuristic armored suit. The two stared at each other for a moment, then York charged.

The tough skin of the suit made his blows seem even harder and more lethal as the hard-knuckled gloves delivered bruising blows to Todd's forearms. He slowly backed up, blocking his combinations of jabs and hooks. He waited for a right hook, which he knew would be soon. It came, and Todd caught it. Thrusting his back into York, he pulled his arm over his shoulder and attempted to throw him.

However, York recognized what was coming and quickly wrapped both his arms around Todd's neck, making him roll forward onto his back atop York. York began to squeeze hard on Todd's jugular, causing his face to redden and the veins in his neck to protrude from the skin. He lowered his chin, forcing a gap just big enough to impede the choke's effectiveness. He forced York's arm up and over his head and then quickly jumping to his feet. Todd grabbed the shotgun which lay a few feet away. He cranked on the lever, sending an empty shell out of the breach and shut it, leveling the sights on York. He pulled the trigger and was greeted with a disappointing *click*.

York froze for a moment. Not at the fact of being at gunpoint, but because of how quick Todd had acted to attempt to kill him. York had no intentions of killing Todd; he had only attempted to subdue him long enough for him to make his getaway. The thought of killing his same-self had not even crossed his mind. Yet he would now be dead if Todd would have had a loaded cartridge in the shotgun. York turned to see the front of the train making its approach to his intended destination. The track curved around through a mountain pass and led to a large bridge that spanned across a deep valley, with the fast-flowing river nearly three hundred feet below. York turned back to Todd, who had ditched the shotgun and was now rechecking his belt for .45 caliber ammunition.

"You have to let me do this, Todd," York called out over the loud pistons and the screeching metal of the train.

Ensuring he had no more ammunition, Todd holstered his 1911 and stood up to face York. The wind and the shifting roof beneath them made them sway back and forth. The train rounded the bend in the tracks, passing beneath the shadow of the large hill. The firm tracks gave way as they reached a slightly more wobbly bridge span, which forced the two men to squat down in order to maintain their balance. York looked down at the MTX, then looked back up at Todd.

"It has to be this way," York said, turning and facing the side of the train, looking out over the deep valley passing beneath them.

Todd then realized what he was about to do. York steadied himself and reached back to ensure his parachute container was intact. He leaned back then lunged off of the train. Todd quickly sprinted towards the side and dove off after him. He caught him in midair and the two plummeted in a spin towards the earth's surface. Todd quickly wrapped his arms and legs around York, bracing for the opening shock. Todd quickly grabbed York's extended left arm and pressed the "Initiate" button on the MTX. There was a loud boom, then the container burst open, letting out a wad of black material that quickly caught the wind and inflated above them. There was a hard jerk upwards which forced Todd to lose his grip and slip off. Todd's eyes widened and he felt his stomach become overwhelmed with the sickening feeling of falling. He braced himself to feel his body smash into the shallow waters below. He tensed up, then felt himself become engulfed in cool water. He sank fast and yet the water was deep enough to slow his momentum before hitting the bottom.

He felt his head hit the hard river bottom and he saw stars fill his dark peripherals. The fast-moving waters yanked him for several meters down to the rocky floor before he was able to gain his bearings and reach the surface, gasping for air. He continued being pulled downstream, being splashed with white water and bumping into hard rocks below him. Todd could feel the MTX still in his hand and he grasped it firmly as he used every ounce of energy he had to begin swimming to shore. The stream mellowed for a few hundred meters and Todd took advantage of this to make his way to the side, crawl-stroking as hard as humanly possible, his heart pounding in his chest, and his limbs throbbing.

The shoreline finally came into reach and he latched onto a large rock, fighting the river's relentless pull. He crawled out and rolled over onto his back on the pebble-filled sand. He breathed heavily, coughing up the salty river water. He looked over at his hand which clutched the MTX tightly. A smile spread over his face, surprised with himself at his ability to wrench the MTX off of York's suit while in freefall, as well as maintain his grip on it during the rough ride down the river.

"Perfect," Todd grunted.

It took almost two hours for Todd to make his way out of the valley. He stumbled through the desert, trying to find any sign of civilization. Everything looked exactly the same, though he was certain that they had made a time jump. He was beginning to feel his body break down. Blood streamed down the back of his head from hitting the river bottom. He was certain that he had suffered a minor concussion, and he was now walking through an endless desert with no end in sight. He pulled the MTX out of his duster pocket and unlocked it. The screen transitioned to the time wheel, which was still set on the time which York had entered: 1986.

"What the …" Todd paused, then something on the horizon caught his eye. He walked towards it. It was large and cast a long shadow towards him. He raised his hand over his eyes to shield them from the sun. The tall object came into view, and he realized he was only looking at the thin side of it. He walked around to the front of it and the large broken neon lights presented a familiar, yet very old-looking advertisement for Coca-Cola. He canted his head in confusion at the odd-looking bottle the drink was advertised in, which appeared to be glass. Next to the sign lay an aged pavement road with faded yellow dashes running down the center of it. The road was as straight as the flat horizon and stretched as far as the eye could see.

He sat down next to the road in the shade of the Coke sign wondering what to do. He had no idea where York was and was especially confused as to why York had jumped to the '80s. Maybe it had been an accident while Todd had pulled the MTX off of his wrist while they were falling. He opened the MTX and looked at the numbered wheels. There was no way his thumb had swiped them so precisely by accident to go from the year that it had been, which was "2016" to the current year of "1986." Perhaps York had intended to come here, but why? Maybe it had something to do with the Cold War, but why would he come back? The Cold War came to an end in only five years. What could he possibly try to alter?

Todd suddenly had an epiphany; his eyes widening at his sudden grasp of what he believed to be the truth behind all this. He felt an awful feeling sweep over him as he sat on the side of the endless road. He laid back and stared up at the bright blue sky; his eyes began to feel heavy, and his aching body welcomed his motionless state. He hadn't slept in over thirteen hours and he was feeling the consequences of it. Wincing as the gash on his head touched the rough sand and pebbles below him, he rolled over to his side, staring at his outstretched hand. His eyes slowly closed as the soft winds blew over him.

Suddenly there was a large boom that made him sit up. He looked down the road to see a large wall of dust and sand coming towards him. He stood up quickly and prepared to run, but stopped when he noticed Odin's silver nose protrude through the thick cloud.

He stood in astonishment, uncertain of what his own eyes were seeing.

The plane slowed, then came to a complete stop on the wide road. Its large wingspan stretched out over the desert; its wheels lined the edges of the road. Todd stumbled towards the plane, picking up speed as he neared. It took every last bit of energy he had to walk the few hundred meters. He passed beneath the large wing and walked to the rear of the aircraft, below the tail. The ramp made a loud hissing noise, then slowly began to drop in front of him, revealing the dark, futuristic interior. The ramp touched the pavement road and the hissing stopped. Todd wobbled as he stepped towards the opening. His eyes finally adjusted, and standing at the hinge of the ramp was Albrecht and Kara. Kara's eyes widened. Todd did his best to smile, then collapsed on the edge of the ramp. He could hear Albrecht rush over to him, calling to several students.

As Todd faded out, he felt himself gently picked up and rushed into the inside of the plane.

FRAGO

An all too familiar blinding white light made him wince and his eyes slowly opened. He could feel the rough air passing beneath Odin as he lay in the examination bed of the med room. There was an uncomfortable feeling of adhesive pulling on the small hairs of his left arm. He rolled his head over to his left shoulder to see the large IV bag that was slowly distributing its life-saving fluids into the crook of his arm. He lay in only his briefs; there were bandages on multiple areas of his body covering wounds he hadn't even known were present.

There was a tight gripping feeling from the bandages wrapped around his head. He was going to raise his hands to feel it, but stopped when he realized his right hand was being held by another.

He looked over to see Kara sleeping in the chair next to the bed; her head rested on her arm, and long, stray hairs fell across her closed lids. Her extended hand was holding Todd's. A warm feeling spread throughout his body. He exhaled and laid back, feeling a sense of absolute comfort. He studied her for a moment. Her beauty was overwhelming and made him question whether or not he was truly awake. Perhaps he had died in the desert. How could they have found him so quickly, and why hadn't they told him that Odin was capable of time travel? He thought about this for a moment, then realized that they must have used the MTX to find his location. The thought of the MTX made his mind return to the epiphany he had several hours earlier. His body froze at the idea.

"Oh no ..." Todd said softly.

Kara's eyes slowly opened. She looked up to see Todd's eyes shift over to her. She quickly sat up, pulling her hand away and placing both hands in her lap. It was only then that Todd realized how cold it was on the plane.

"What ... what year is it?" Todd asked, rubbing his tired eyes.

"It's still 1986," she said softly.

She stood up from her chair and leaned over him. Her blue eyes looked down at him with a look that he hoped was affection.

"What is it?" he asked.

She shook her head "I ... can't stand to see you like this anymore." Her eyes widened. Her hands fumbled in front of her. "Every time you return ... it's like you're one step closer to death."

Todd sat up on the bed. She backed away slightly; her eyes danced to the floor, then closed.

"Please don't do this anymore. I can't bear to watch you suffer because of all this ... because of us."

"Kara ..." Todd said gently.

"No," she interrupted. "I won't be a part of this anymore. It hurts too much."

Todd spoke sympathetically, "Kara, I don't want this to affect you ... but I have to go back out there."

"Why?" she asked, her brow arced, displaying her saddened eyes. "Why do you insist on killing yourself? Why can't you just accept that you can't change fate; that what happens in the future was meant to be?" She paused for a moment, then whispered. "You're just like him."

"No!" Todd snapped angrily. "I am nothing like him ... don't ever say that again!"

She looked up at him; her timid posture revealed itself at his aggressive response. Her eyes stayed locked on him intently. She knew there had been conflict between York and Todd, but what had York done to make Todd completely despise him? What could a man possibly do to make his same-self hate him? He looked the same, but was he the same? It was the same plane, the same med room. The same bed where York had lain so many times, insisting on returning to the past. Here he was yet again insisting on returning, but this time it was different. It wasn't out of an obsessive compulsion to continue what he had started. She could tell it was more than that. It was out of desperation.

Todd looked her in the eyes as he sat up on the bed; the only thing holding him back was the IV tube taped to his arm. His hard stare eased as he looked at her.

"Kara … he's going to kill …"

Just then, Bohden came storming into the med room, waving crunched papers that were without a doubt copies of Todd's transmissions. Kara backed away from the bed, and Todd laid back down, rolling his eyes.

"Are you insane?" Bohden said at a volume just under a yell. "You have jeopardized the entire operation by making us risk being compromised in order to retrieve you!" He stopped at the foot of the bed and threw the papers down. "And it was all for nothing, considering you totally failed your primary objective by supplying York with another suit and completely losing track of him. Now we have absolutely no idea where he's going, nor do we have the slightest clue as to why we are currently flying around in U.S. airspace in 1986!"

Todd scratched the stubble on his jaw, avoiding eye contact with Bohden who was doing his best to intimidate Todd with his aggressive posture. Todd had a lot of questions himself, one being why hadn't they told him that Odin was a time machine? Though he didn't appreciate Bohden being so forward, he understood his frustration. They had invested a lot of time to make Todd ready for one mission. One mission that he had failed to complete. It made him uncomfortable; most likely they would no longer want him involved with the program as he and his same-self in reality had caused them nothing but trouble. He needed them to trust him, he needed them to give him one more chance. His entire existence could be depending on it.

"You have every right to be angry," Todd said calmly. "I have risked the lives of everyone on this plane. But you need to trust me when I tell you that you must give me another chance."

"Why the hell would I do that?" Bohden said angrily.

"Because if you don't let me go back … very soon, you and I will cease to exist."

Bohden looked at him in disbelief. "What the hell are you talking about?"

Todd sat up, pulling the IV from his arm and tearing off the medical tape. He stood up on the opposite side of the bed, instantly feeling the soreness throughout his body. He looked at Kara, then over at Bohden.

"York is going to ensure that he and I are never born ... he's going to kill our father."

Bohden stared at him in silence for what felt like several minutes. He shook his head, eyes not leaving Todd. "York's nuts. How is that my problem? At this point, I can't say I don't blame him."

Kara's beautiful eyes shot daggers at Bohden. She couldn't believe what she was hearing. Todd looked down at the floor, insulted by Bohden's words. He breathed out his nose loudly, flexing his jaw. He looked back up at Bohden and raised an eyebrow. "I think it concerns you ... because if I recall correctly, he saved your sorry ass a few years before you brought him into this."

Bohden's eyes widened and the creases in his face relaxed. As much as it pained him, he knew Todd was correct, and his recollection chilled him to the bone. York and Bohden had once been good friends. Combat had forged their close bond and it was time at the facility that had slowly eroded that bond. Their opposing beliefs had sparked much friction between the two of them and had eventually led to them never talking to one another except for when Bohden would brief him on an upcoming mission. He knew that there was no longer a friendship between him and York, and he also knew how stubborn he was. He wouldn't hesitate to act upon his plan.

Todd began dressing, a grimace on his face as he gently pulled on a t-shirt that he found folded next to the bed. He stepped into a pair of sweatpants and leaned up against the bed. Kara was silently standing in the corner, her eyes not leaving Todd.

Bohden shook his head. "How can you be so sure of this? Did he tell you?"

"No," Todd said. "He didn't have to. I know how he thinks ... and I must stop him. It's why you brought me here, right?"

Albrecht didn't seem as surprised as the others when he heard the news. Todd, Albrecht, and Bohden sat in the monitoring room in silence, all pondering Todd's idea. Albrecht had cleared the room only moments prior. The three looked at each other from across the table, waiting for someone to speak. Albrecht broke the silence by clearing his throat. "How much time do we have?" he asked.

Bohden was uneasy with the entire situation. He didn't trust Todd at all, and he didn't appreciate Albrecht immediately taking his side on the issue. Plus, the fact that his life was now on the line was beginning to make him feel detached and impatient.

"Well ..." Bohden said as he stood up and made his way over to the main screen.

He pulled up an application that displayed the CIA emblem on the back of a black page. He went up to the top right -hand corner and typed in Todd's full name, using a wireless keyboard. He pressed enter and the screen went to an extensive list of Todd Yorks throughout the world. He looked back at Todd. "Where do you live in 1986?"

"Laurinburg, North Carolina," Todd replied, thinking about his lonely off-base home, a few miles from Fort Bragg.

Bohden thinned the search and found his name. He clicked on it and a load of information about Todd popped up on the screen. Todd leaned out of his chair to try and see some of the information, but Bohden was quick to skip straight to relatives. He found Todd's father and clicked on him. A bio and police records came up along with a mug shot. Next to it was an updated photo taken in 2017, which quickly caught Todd's eye. He hadn't seen him since he was just a child and if he would have passed him on the street he would have just mistaken him for an ordinary old man.

"Here we go," Bohden said, putting his hands on his hips. "Michael C. York, lived in Coral Terrace, Miami. Which is where he ..." he paused, scrolling through the home records and police records. "Jesus Christ," he said in astonishment. "This guy was ... or should I say 'is,' in some serious trouble. Drug trafficking? I'm surprised this didn't come up during your psychological evaluation during selection."

"It did, I just didn't know enough about him to answer any questions," Todd replied shortly.

Kara walked into the room and sat down, placing a folder on the desk. She looked at Todd then at the screen. Bohden continued scrolling down through police reports, momentarily pausing to read key sections.

Kara spoke, spreading the papers out across the desk. "Your father was a suspected drug trafficker linked to the Medellin cartel during the 1980s. It was estimated that in one week the cartel could bring in over four hundred million dollars' worth through several methods of offshore importing that included boats, private planes, and even tow trucks. Your father most likely utilized one of these methods to transport enormous amounts of illegal substances into the city. Miami used to be a vacation spot for senior citizens during the '50s and '60s. After the late '70s, however, it quickly began a transformation into a fast-growing drug-dependent empire fed by millions of dollars of drug and blood money. Starting in the late 1970s, individuals who would later be referred to as the cocaine cowboys would take advantage of the almost nonexistent law on the coast, transporting large amounts of marijuana. What started as only a few small shipments of cocaine with the marijuana eventually turned cocaine into becoming the primary shipment that even blue collar Americans sought."

Todd stared at the picture of his father in disbelief. He had known that Michael had been involved with drugs when he was younger, but he'd had no idea it was to this degree. He found it hard to believe that this was the same man who had married his kind mother, but he also found it easier to understand how York would have no problem killing him, since he had been a complete screw-up his entire life.

What had Ann York seen in him? They wouldn't meet for almost another twelve years, but how much could he have changed by then? And even if he did change, it was only temporary as his mother eventually would leave him, taking three-year-old Todd York with her to Colorado.

"How come he was never convicted of trafficking?" Todd asked. "They suspected him of it ... he should have done some serious time for that."

Kara sifted through some of the papers. "Apparently, the charges were dropped due to insufficient evidence." She brushed a stray hair behind her ear. "This is odd."

"What?" Todd asked.

"Well ... during this time period, the mid '80s, a lot of traffickers are brought in, forcing a lot of big names like Escobar and Blanco to relocate due to the building pressure from government agencies such as the DEA and ATF." She shook her head, looking down at the table. "I just don't understand how he could have gotten away with it. Any evidence of affiliation would be enough to be incarcerated."

"So not only will you have to find your old man ... but you will also have to ensure that you don't ever come in direct contact with him, in order to ensure you don't affect the timeline in any way. All the while protecting him from your other self," Bohden said, licking his lips and shaking his head in disbelief.

He pulled up a map of the United States on the monitor and studied it for a moment. He began drawing a line that started on the top corner of New Mexico and ended on the edge of Florida. Pulled up a calculations and conversation menu, he then typed a few notes on his tablet. He finished and turned to Todd.

"It's almost two thousand miles from Albuquerque New Mexico to Miami. That's almost a thirty-hour drive considering he doesn't find a way to board a commercial airliner in the meantime. I wouldn't put it past him, however, but it's very unlikely."

Albrecht entered the conversation. "With your injuries, I would recommend at the very least two weeks before going back out, but since we obviously don't have that kind of time ... we need to insert you as soon as possible." He exhaled loudly. "How long do you need to prep?"

Todd sat back, rubbing his throbbing bandaged head. He thought for a moment, then answered. "I'll need a few hours to plan an insert point with D and a suitable drop zone outside the city limits. I'll need to pack light, considering I will once again need to blend in with the local populace. I will also need to be constantly updated on any information regarding his whereabouts using payment records, withdrawals, recorded phone calls ... whatever you can dig up. The FBI was obviously watching him during this time so they must have something on his daily routines."

Albrecht nodded in approval. Bohden stood in the corner with his arms crossed, lost in thought. Todd could tell he disliked the entire situation. Not only was he concerned with the timeline, but he was also depending on Todd to be successful so that his very existence may continue. He didn't like the idea of his life being in the hands of someone who he saw as possibly incompetent. He had known York for almost seven years and was aware of his abilities to complete a job. Todd, however, had proven nothing to him and had given only reasons to doubt him. If he had to place money on who would find their father first, it would be York.

"Well they don't exactly have social media right now, so finding his exact location in the next thirty hours could be extremely difficult ... but I'll see what I can do."

Albrecht rubbed his thumb over his lips in deep thought. Todd could tell something was troubling him.

"You okay, Brian?" Todd asked.

Albrecht sighed, then looked up at him. "I need to talk to you ... in private," he said, looking over at Kara and Bohden and clearly hinting for them to leave.

The two stood up and made their way to the door. Kara and Albrecht exchanged a small smile as she softly closed the door behind her. Albrecht pulled his glasses off, setting them on the table. He rubbed his eyes and leaned back in the leather chair. The aircraft hummed quietly and Todd patiently waited for him to speak. He turned in his chair and stared out into the night sky.

"Todd ... there is something you need to know. Something that I haven't had the courage to tell anyone else. Something ... I fear could make people lose hope if they knew." He inhaled, then let it out loudly. "I have been hiding from the future for six years now. Sitting ... waiting for the news that we all have been waiting for. Waiting for you to save us from it."

Todd looked at the professor questioningly. Albrecht held his soft gaze. "This world is as harsh as it is humbling," he said, shaking his head. "I started the program in early 2010; the technology was already ready for testing by then, but it would be a couple more years before the DOD finally gave Bohden the green light to start. Not long after however World War III began, they forgot about my little science project." He chuckled, then his face went stern. "It took me almost twenty years to finally crack it ... two long decades. Me and my partner."

"Partner?" Todd asked.

"Yes ... Garrett. He was the smartest man I ever knew, and he was my best friend. He was a British student attending Cambridge whose theories complemented my own, and little did I know, we would change the world together."

Todd nodded. "Was he killed in the initial attacks?"

"No ... no. He died a long time ago. Heart disease in 2003."

"I'm sorry to hear that."

Albrecht nodded. "I remember spending countless hours doing calculations with him, staying up all night arguing over whether or not it was going to work, whether we had just been wasting all those years of hard work on something that was unachievable."

He stood up, picking up his glasses and placing them back on. He stuffed his hands in his pockets and leaned up against the wall. "It's funny ... we both wanted the same result, but we disagreed on almost everything. I put my trust in science, the physics and the calculations. Why not? Why couldn't we use a worm hole to travel to the past and alter what had already happened? Garrett, on the other hand, had a different opinion. Yes, he wanted to succeed as much as me, but he disagreed with the notion of altering fate. He preferred faith as his reasoning to back his theories. He used to always say 'everything happens for a reason, Brian. No matter what we do ... the end result will always be the same.'" He shook his head. "I never wanted to believe him, especially after he died. I finally finished many years later; the power of time travel was finally at my disposal. Yet nothing could change the fact that his death was irreversible. I realized then that he was right."

He looked up at Todd, his lips pressed firmly together. "Before he died I made him a promise. That I would take care of his infant daughter, and that I would finish what we had started, give the people around me hope. Because above all else, if we lose hope, we lose everything, Todd."

"Why do you do this to them?" Todd asked. "Why don't you take the students somewhere else ... to another time; get them out of that Godforsaken frozen wasteland and let them live?"

"Because that's not what his daughter wants," Brian said firmly.

Todd canted his head and his eyes sharpened. "Kara?"

Albrecht nodded. "Yes, Garrett Dennick was a single father; she meant the world to him. Now ... she is everything to me. Everything I do is in an effort to give her a chance at being happy, to give her a better life. Everything from pursuing the alternate future, to bringing you back. I won't take her to some pre-war era where she will live out the rest of her life in solitude, reading and separating herself from everyone else. It's all she knows, but I know that's not what she wants. She deserves better."

Todd swallowed, looking down at his hands folded on top of the table. He felt an awful feeling inside of him as the words left his mouth. "York," he said. "He's what she wants."

Albrecht sat back down across from him, placing his hands on the table. "Listen, Todd. I'm not exactly sure what she wants; maybe she doesn't even quite know. But what I do know is that when you are here, something changes in her. I may be the only one who notices it because I've known Kara her entire life, but I can see it every time she looks at you. And above all else … that is why I found you and brought you here. If I were to go back a hundred times and find a hundred versions of you, you'd still be the greatest man I've ever known."

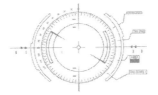

PROPOSITION

Todd walked into Kara's dark cabin to find her sleeping. He approached her, stopping beside her bed. He felt he was being too forward, and it made him uncomfortable, but he knew that he had to give it a try. She lay on her side facing him, curled up beneath the thin white blanket.

"Kara," he said softly.

Her eyes opened beneath her amber bangs, and she sat up quickly; the automated light on the nightstand turned on along with the clock, which displayed the early morning hours.

"Todd … what is it?" she asked, flicking her hair to the side and crossing her arms in the cool room. She wore only a white spaghetti-strapped top and thin black sweats.

Todd sighed. "I need to ask you something. Something that you need to really think about before you answer."

"What?" she asked in almost a whisper.

"Will you come with me … to find my father?"

Her eyes widened, and she looked at the door, then down at her hands.

"I know it sounds crazy, but I think it's the only chance we have at making York come to his senses."

"What about your father?" she asked.

"York won't do it … not if you're there." Todd knelt down, eye level with her. "He won't reconsider for me, but I guarantee he will for you."

"What makes you so sure?" she asked, raising a thin eyebrow.

"A hunch."

"But the professor ..." she proclaimed.

"I've already spoken to him," he interrupted. "He's uneasy about it, but he agrees that it will work; plus, I assume he would prefer that I don't kill York. And I think you feel the same way."

She sat motionless, deep in thought for several moments. No doubt nervous to answer either yes or no.

"Come on," he grinned. "You've spent your entire life studying history. Don't you want to experience it for yourself?"

She stared down at her folded hands resting atop her crossed legs, then rubbed her hands up and down her bare arms nervously. He leaned forward, placing his hand on hers.

"I'll keep you safe, Kara. I just need to get you to him. Because if I go alone I will kill him, no questions asked. He has hurt good people who mean a lot to me."

She looked up at him, the moonlight shining through the small cabin window glinting off her eyes. He had a tough time reading her and couldn't tell whether or not she was thinking of saying yes, or trying to find the right words to turn down his request. He pulled his hand from her shoulder and stood up, turning to face the door.

"I'll go," she said. She stood up and walked over to him on small, bare feet. "I will, I'll come with you."

He looked out the window at the bright moon partially concealed by the thick cloud cover. Suddenly he felt a rush of worry overwhelm him. He not only would have the challenging task of finding his criminal father in a pre-technological-era city ridden with crime, he also would have to protect him from York, all the while keeping Kara safe from whatever danger he would surely encounter. He wanted to ensure she understood what she was agreeing to. He turned back to her, and saw by her sharp eyes and confident stance that she'd made up her mind. Her pale skin glowed from the moonlight. There was no going back now; she was coming with him to the city with the highest homicide rate in the United States. He nodded, turned, and left the room.

*   *   *

After a few hours of deep, uninterrupted sleep, Todd awoke to the sun shining through the cabin window. He quickly got dressed and made his way out to the lounge where several familiar faces were delighted at his presence. Kevin and Amber quickly greeted him as he entered the room. He sat and ate breakfast with them, telling them of his adventures in the Old West and his encounters with York. They were surprised to hear how it had turned out, and they were saddened to find out that he would be leaving again in a few hours to continue pursuing his same-self.

Amber stood up to get a drink and Todd leaned in close to Kevin.

"Thanks again for that parting gift," he said with a grin.

Kevin smiled and patted him on the shoulder. "Come in handy, did it?"

"I wouldn't be here right now if I didn't have it."

Amber returned to the table and sat down close to Todd. He could tell she was excited about something but he wasn't sure what it was. She looked around the room with a smug expression, then back at Todd.

"So ... is it true?" she said in a whisper, her big brown eyes wide.

"What?" Todd asked.

"That you're taking her with you?"

Todd chuckled. "Man, word sure gets around. Yes, I think she is the only person on earth who could change York's mind."

She smiled excitedly and fidgeted in her chair. Todd could feel himself blushing and awkwardly looked around the room, scratching the back of his head.

"So, what was it like being in the Wild West?" Kevin asked curiously.

"Unreal," Todd smiled. "Yet very ... real. It's hard to explain it, but ... it felt like I was just visiting another place, not another time. The people were very interesting."

Todd looked up to see a large group listening in on his conversation. The students seemed intrigued by his experiences which surprised him.

"I'm sure you guys have heard it all before though," Todd said, rolling his eyes.

"No, it's actually nice," Amber said.

"Why?"

"Because," she said looking down at the table. "Nobody ever

comes back with good stories to tell." She shook her head. "There is so much good in history, yet it seems like York only visited the worst of it and came back angry."

"It's a shame that something as incredible as time travel would be used in such a way," Todd said, shaking his head. "Who knows how much we could learn with such power, yet we use it only to try and fix mistakes that we are destined to repeat."

The room fell silent for a moment as the students all pondered his dark statement. Todd looked up at them; their faces displayed the hopelessness that Albrecht had fought so hard to rid from their hearts and minds. He didn't mean to speak so earnestly, but he didn't agree with the professor when it came to giving them false hope. He knew however that it wouldn't be long before the professor finally would give up on the future. Todd wanted to slowly shift their focus to different dreams.

"If you guys could go anywhere in time ... where would it be?" Todd asked, trying to change the mood.

"Italy ... during the Renaissance period," one girl said excitedly.

"United States, during the '50s!" said an older male student who was quickly accompanied with mutual nods from his buddies.

"England, 900 AD timeframe!"

"Early Roman Empire."

Todd smiled as the students continued listing off key historical places and times that fascinated them. One student would blurt something out, and they would argue whether or not the individual was foolish in wanting to visit such a time.

"Eighteenth century Paris!" shouted one student.

"Are you insane?" an older female laughed. "You idiot, you'd be tossed on a guillotine as soon as you arrived."

The students laughed and teased each other. Todd smiled; it brought him joy to see the students in high spirits. He looked over at Kevin, who was the oldest of all the males and sat in silence.

"What about you, Kev?"

Kevin looked up at the ceiling, his eyes squinting as he scratched his beard. "Hmm ... let me think," he muttered. "I'd really have to think about that one. What about you, Amber?" he said.

"India, 1949. The year the greatest constitution in the world was passed," she said with a smile.

"That's questionable," Kevin chuckled.

Amber gave him a friendly slap on the arm. Kevin laughed and pushed her away. Todd sat in silence, his thoughts returning to the mission at hand. Knowing York, he would no doubt have already obtained a vehicle last night and would now be cruising across the country towards Florida. Todd took ease in the fact he had a huge head start on York, as Odin would be over Florida in a matter of hours. He also was fairly certain that he had more intelligence on his father than York and that gave him a crucial advantage. Of course, York had spent five years at the facility and had most likely done a fair amount of research on their father during the many hours he spent in between missions.

Just then, D walked into the lounge and a few of the students greeted him; Todd turned in his chair to see the tall pilot.

"Todd! Good to see ya man," he said, holding out his hand.

Todd stood and shook it, then sat back down at the table with the others. D pulled up a chair and squeezed in between Kevin and Amber.

"Shouldn't you be flying the plane that we are currently sitting in?" Amber asked jokingly.

"It's called auto pilot, babe! Besides, my co-pilot has flown this thing for multiple ops in the past five years."

Todd leaned close to the center of the table, looking at D closely. "I need to go over some insert planning with you when you get the chance."

"Well, we need to do it quick. We will be over Florida in a couple of hours, and you will have to insert tonight." D shook his head. "We will be bingo on fuel by early morning tomorrow, so we will have to head back to Santa's workshop as soon as possible."

Kevin canted his head in confusion, then looked over at Todd. "So, I heard we are in 1986 right now; is this true?"

The students all went silent, and everyone in the room stared at him with curious eyes. Todd exhaled loudly, then nodded. "Yes, we are in '86 right now."

"Why?" Kevin asked.

"Albrecht is a smart man. He didn't want to return to the future until he knew what had happened down there. In doing so, he most likely saved my life."

"How so?" asked Amber.

"Because the moment you return to the future ... whatever York is planning on doing will have already happened. And the consequences of his actions will be instantaneous."

Kevin blinked, his lips puckered as he thought. "So ... If he kills your father that will mean that Todd York was never born?"

Todd nodded.

"But hold on a second," Kevin said. "You and York have separated yourselves from the timeline. In essence, you two can't be affected by whatever is altered, right?" he asked, looking around the table at the concerned faces of the others.

"It's possible," Amber said somberly. "However, both Todd and York were born on the exact same day, the exact same time and from the exact same parents. That has never been altered, and neither of them have been back in time to that year making them present for their own birth. Now, you both have been to a time which was before you were born, which 'could' further prove Kevin's theory as you two are no longer a natural part of the timeline. And by killing your father, he may only prevent the birth of the third Todd York."

"But ..." Todd said, his eyebrows raised.

"Well ... I just don't know," she said, shaking her head.

"Either way," D said patting Todd on the shoulder, "you need to get down there and stop him."

Todd nodded in agreement. He and D left shortly thereafter and made their way to the cockpit where D pulled up a 3D hologram on a table. It displayed the city of Miami, as well as the flight pattern for Odin.

"So, since we are indeed flying in a plane that doesn't exist yet, I'll have to drop you outside the city limits. The plane can't be picked up on radar, but we can't risk crossing into commercial skies." He scrolled over the hologram towards the edge of the city. "Here!" he said, pointing at Highway 41 just west of Miami. The road cut straight through the Everglades towards the city. Todd could freefall from out over the open swamps and land on the road. From there he would have to acquire transportation and get into the city.

"I could drop you at a little over thirty thousand feet over the 41;

from there, you could glide east on an azimuth of ninety degrees towards the city and land on the road itself."

"Landing on a highway isn't exactly subtle," Todd said impatiently.

"Well, landing in the alligator-infested Everglades isn't exactly the proffered course of action either, my friend," D said with a grin.

"Fair enough."

"Okay," D said, clapping his hands together. "So, we will stick with the first plan. We will plan for insert to be in three hours. Hopefully that road won't be too busy and you will be able to hitch a ride into town ... keeping a low profile in the process."

"One little detail I forgot to mention," Todd said, biting his lip trying to hold back a smile.

"Oh God, what?"

"I'm gonna have a passenger with me."

D gave him a bewildered look. "A passenger? Who the hell is going with you?"

"Kara."

D's eyes widened and his head lurched back. He stared at him for a moment. Then a smile began to creep over his face. "Oka y ... so a tactical, HALO, intimate, tandem jump it is."

Todd nodded, rolling his eyes.

"You know ... this is like some real 007 shit, Todd. Christ! Nobody jumps tandem at thirty thousand feet!"

"Well I don't have much of a choice. I'm tandem qualified, so this won't be anything new to me. We will just have to ensure that she is dressed appropriately for the freezing temperatures and that she has an O2 system in order to prevent her from going hypoxic." Todd scratched the stubble on his chin. "She will no doubt be scared to death and will be breathing heavily, so we will have to ensure she has a suitable amount of oxygen, just in case."

D shook his head, grinning. "Man, you Yorks are nuts. But Goddamnit if you ain't the coolest sons of bitches I've ever met."

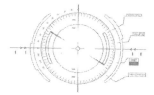

FALLING

The sun was beginning to set, filling the plane with a soft orange glow that lit the dark cargo area of the plane. All the gear he would need for the insertion, including Kara's suit, helmet, and harness were laid out on the cool steel floor. They had kept a few more suits on board in case of malfunctions during inserts and Todd would now be taking advantage of this.

His new suit looked brand new, as its black skin lacked any scars or tears in the plates or joint sections. He plugged in the MTX and the cables lit up with a brief magnificent flare. He pulled the leather journal from his pocket and wrote down everything he was taking to ensure he would not lose track of anything.

Soft footsteps approached him from the open door to the adjacent room. He turned to see Kara walking towards him. She looked down at all the equipment with an overwhelmed expression, exhaled loudly, and ran her fingers through her hair.

"It's not too late to change your mind, you know," Todd said.

She shook her head. "I would be lying if I told you I wasn't scared. But I believe it is the right thing to do."

"Look, Kara," he said, placing the journal back in his pocket. He stepped towards her, placing his hands on his hips. "I'm not going to lie to you either. Where we're going ... the people who we're going to encounter and go through to get to him ... it's not going to be pretty. I want you to be absolutely sure before we go."

"Todd, you asked me if there was something between us ... well,

I do love him. Which is why I need to do this. I know there is good in him, I know it's that 'good' in him that makes him feel responsible for what he has been through. I don't want him to die because of it."

Todd felt a sudden feeling of disappointment, or maybe it was jealousy, gnawing in his stomach. He nodded, looking at her with hard eyes and firm lips. " ... Okay," he said. He turned and knelt down, arranging the equipment. He began filling her in on the basics of high altitude parachuting and covered the nomenclature of the gear itself.

"At thirty thousand feet, the freezing temperatures accompanied with the wind chill, added with the lack of oxygen and the fact that we will be falling over one hundred and twenty miles per hour towards the earth, makes this an extremely dangerous method of insertion."

His voice was firm, emotionless. He spoke as if he were teaching a student, someone who he had no emotional attachment too. This troubled her. She was already frightened of what they were about to do, and his grim demeanor was not easing her nerves.

"Our O2 canisters will give us about forty-five minutes' worth of air, so ... if we deploy around fifteen thousand feet, we will be fine to glide the rest of the way under canopy." He thought for a moment, then wrote something down in the journal. He looked back up at Kara to see her daydreaming.

"Are you paying attention?" he asked. "It's extremely important that you understand the risks of what we are about to do."

She looked down at him, her eyes sharp and unwavering. "Yes, I understand." She stepped towards him, breathing out. "Is something troubling you?" She stood over him as he knelt down, manipulating the parachute rig. "What did he do to you?" she asked.

"He didn't do anything to me," he said angrily.

"Then wh—"

He stood up, interrupting her. "It was my fault! Because of me, I put innocent lives in danger; lives of good people who trusted me." He stared at her, breathing heavily. "He took advantage of my complacency. I won't let it happen again."

She stepped back, frightened by the resemblance she was witnessing. It sounded too familiar. He sounded like York.

He froze, no doubt hearing himself and recognizing the familiarity of his words. He knelt down, clipping the straps together on his web gear and checking for serviceability. She walked over to the red netting bench and sat down, crossing her legs and folding her hands on her lap. He continued working impatiently, his hands fumbling as he picked different things up. She could tell something was troubling him, but what was it? Was it something she had said?

"Todd, I ..."

He breathed out through his nose, looking up at her. "You better start getting dressed. We don't have much time."

Her heart began to thump in her chest and she looked out the window. The sun had disappeared, leaving only a thin sliver of purple light on the flat horizon. She stood up, grabbing her suit, and walked out of the cargo bay. Todd shook his head. Anger and confusion, assisted with his fidgeting, made him perspire. He sat back, wiping his forehead with the back of his hand. Was it the thought of York or his actions that were stressing him? Or was it what Kara had said? How could she love him after what he had become? He was almost forty years old. What could she see in him? He stood up and began undressing.

*   *   *

Kara looked at herself in the mirror. The suit did not hide her gifted figure, yet this did not even cross her mind. Fear of the unknown continued to rush through her like a frigid wind that left a consistent uneasiness. She had spent the last six years of her life in one place. A place she had come accustomed to and had eventually accepted as her home. She had grown attached to the facility, not only in its security and isolation, but because it had become part of her. In one brief conversation, she had agreed to leave behind everything she knew to venture out into an unpredictable world on a quest to find someone whom she feared to care about. Yet something inside her made her stay true to her word. Something inside her told her that this was the moment she had been waiting for so long. A chance to experience something new, a chance to maybe live.

There was a knock on the door, and she quickly grabbed her coat from her bed and threw it on over the revealing suit. "Who is it?"

she called out softly.

"It's me," said Albrecht, who peeked in. He stepped in, closing the door quietly behind him. "How are you doing?" he said, sitting down on the bed.

"I don't know," Kara replied, shaking her head and sitting down beside him. "I'm scared, yet part me feels like I have to do this ... like I don't have a choice."

Albrecht breathed out softly. "You always have a choice, Kara. It's up to you to decide the outcome of your life."

"It's just ..."

"What?" he asked, wrapping a fatherly arm around her.

"I've never been so scared." She looked out at the full moon.

He held her tight and spoke softly. "Life can be scary, Kara. It can be the most terrifying thing ... making you freeze, causing you to hesitate. It's those moments of hesitation that are the most crucial. Because that's when you are being tested, that is when you must decide whether or not you are going to overcome your fear and find what is on the other side of the unknown, or succumb to it and live the rest of your life wondering whether or not you made the right decision." He swallowed, rubbing his hand on her arm. "You remember when the first attacks came?"

She nodded, resting her head on his shoulder.

"I had never been so scared in my life," he said. "I remember I was so scared that I didn't want to move. Yet it was at that moment that I knew I had to decide. I had to decide whether or not I was going to keep your father's promise and use the technology we had created to save you and the others. I didn't know if it was going to work; I had no idea." He looked around the dark room. "Yet here we are, many years later, in the same machine that had saved us. My biggest regret is that I couldn't give you a better life. And now I must make the hardest decision of all. Do I let you go? Not knowing what might happen to the person I love most in this world, do I take a chance with the unknown, with the possibility of a better life for you on the other side? Or do I give in to my own fears and remain motionless? Keeping you here with me, not ever letting you have the possibility of something better?"

He pulled away, looking her in the eyes. "Life rarely presents us with choices with clear outcomes. But I can tell you that the easy answer is rarely the correct one."

She looked down and a single tear ran down her cheek. He placed his hand under her chin, gently lifting her head so he could look into her beautiful eyes.

"You speak as if I'm never coming back."

"Perhaps you won't want to. But I want you to know that I will always love you."

She hugged him tightly, her head on his chest. He kissed the top of her head, gently patting her on the shoulder.

*   *   *

Almost the entire population on Odin was crammed into the cargo bay. Students took turns saying their farewells to Todd. He stood there in his suit, shaking hands and giving hugs. Amber approached him, once again with tears in her eyes, but this time a smile present. She extended her arms and hugged him around the neck, making him lean down slightly.

"Good luck, bestie!" she said.

Todd chuckled. "Thank you, Amber." She let go, stepping back. Kevin approached. He held out his large hand and Todd took it, shaking it firmly.

"Sure you don't want any hardware, my friend? You know I'll be more than happy to fetch something for ya!" Kevin said, patting him on the shoulder.

"I'm sure, Kev. I can't risk it again." He placed his hand on Kevin's shoulder, pulling him in close. "You take care of all these kids, okay. They look up to you and Albrecht."

Kevin nodded, his smile fading. "I will."

The students began rustle and murmur, and everyone in the cargo bay area turned to see Albrecht and Kara approach. They parted down the center, making way for her. They stopped, and Albrecht held her hands, kissing her on the forehead. She smiled, then turned and walked up to Todd and stopped in front of him. The two were both in their suits; the dark visors of the helmets were up, revealing the only human aspect of their appearance. Her perfect figure made it hard for Todd to not stare. Her visor slid shut, and Todd looked at himself in his dark reflection.

"You ready?" he asked.

Her voice came in through his helmet via the internal radio. "Let's find out."

His visor slid shut, and the two black figures stared at each other for a moment. From the student's perspective, it appeared as though the two were talking to each other over the radio. However in reality nothing was said.

"Comm check!" said D's high-pitched voice into Todd's ear.

"I read ya loud and clear," Todd replied.

"We are ten minutes out, pal. Better get ready."

"Roger," Todd replied, looking down at his harness and ensuring the buckles were tightly fastened.

"Since we are already in 1980-whatever, there is no need for you to activate the time travel on your suit. Just sit back and enjoy the ride," D said with a sarcastic tone.

"Be sure to look up whether or not I was born when you get back to the future," Todd chuckled.

"You got it."

The students began flowing out of the cargo bay and into the adjacent room, watching from inside the pressurized cabin. Albrecht remained outside. Todd looked at Kara, giving her a hand signal to give him a moment. The visor of his helmet slid up and he walked over to Albrecht, who blinked rapidly, most likely holding back his emotions.

"You take care of her … okay," he said, his voice shaky, eyes watery.

"I will, Brian … I promise," Todd said, holding out his hand.

Brian nodded, looking back at his godchild, whom he didn't even recognize within the sleek suit. "I believe you," he said. He took Todd's hand, placing his other hand on top.

"We'll be back," Todd said confidently.

Albrecht did his best to smile, but his eyes dropped to the ground in a way that displayed his disbelief. Either way, he was happy to see her finally leaving the confines of the facility. Although he would worry for her, it would put him at ease to know she was finally free. He smiled at her, then stepped into the pressurized room. The door locked and hissed. Todd walked up to Kara, closing his helmet once more and shaking his head to ensure the visor was snug.

"Okay, the communications setting is free-flowing, so you don't have to activate a push to talk or anything of the sort in order for me to hear you. Just speak, and I'll hear you."

Her black helmet nodded timidly. He looked down at his MTX. Only six minutes remained until they were over Highway 41.

"Okay, let's hook up," he said, motioning her to turn around.

She turned, facing the closed ramp. He stepped into her, pressing his stomach against her back. He began clipping the metal D rings of her harness to his, ensuring over and over that they were firmly seated. He then pressed on her, making sure there was minimal gap between their bodies.

"Feel okay?" he asked.

Her helmet nodded once more. He chuckled within his helmet. "Don't worry, I was way more frightened the first time I jumped out of a perfectly good airplane. I think you're doing fine. If you go unconscious I'll know; I have a live feed of you inside my helmet."

"That's reassuring," she said softly.

He leaned over to the skin of the aircraft and flicked the switch to the ramp. The ramp hissed and shrieked as it slowly opened. Kara's heart began to pound in her chest as the dark sky slowly presented itself. Her wide eyes behind the visor gazed out into the cloud-splotched sky below them. Beneath the clouds, she could see the lights of a dense city. Beyond it was an endless body of water that stretched out as far as the eyes could see. She breathed out slowly, trying to calm herself.

"Thirty seconds!" D said over the radio.

Todd moved her to the edge of the ramp. Every nerve in her body made her want to crawl back inside of the plane. She swallowed hard, closing her eyes, listening to her heart race. She didn't even notice her HUD, which was actively tracking their altitude and speed. She was stricken with fear and adrenaline.

"Ten seconds!"

She breathed out once more, readying herself for the sickening feel of falling. Todd's calm voice came into her ear. "Remember, relax your body. Don't fight the wind. I'll do all the flying."

"Five … four … three … two …"

She closed her eyes tightly. Her body tensed up, then she quickly remembered what Todd had told her. Tensing up could cause them to tumble through the air, so she breathed out, relaxing every muscle in her body.

"Go!" D called out.

Todd leaned forward and she felt the ramp leave her feet as the two tipped forward and off the edge. The two dropped off the ramp head first; looking up, Kara could see the transparent belly of the plane as it flew away. She gasped, closing her eyes tightly. Todd extended his arms out past his head, catching the relative wind. Their bodies quickly leveled out and began an even descent towards the clouds.

She felt the fast air beneath her, yet she didn't feel as though she was falling. She slowly opened her eyes and looked upon the most beautiful sight she had ever seen. All around her was a clear night sky. The stars wrapped around them as if they were in space; below them, the clouds approached slowly. Beneath the clouds, the moon cast a large white reflection off the ocean, pointing towards the small city lights far below on the coastline. Her wide eyes became accompanied by a smile. Todd dipped his right arm and the two did a half-turn towards the east. The loud winds rushing past her made it impossible to hear, but she marveled in the moment.

As they continued to fall towards the earth, Kara's heart raced. She continued to look around at the rising earth. She traced the coastline up to the horizon from where the mainland separated from Miami Beach. She felt the back of her helmet bump Todd's visor.

Todd laughed. "You okay down there?" he called out over the loud winds.

She was too astonished to answer. Todd looked at his wrist and saw that the deploying altitude was approaching fast. He tucked his wrists inward, showing Kara his MTX, which displayed the pulsing DEPLOY button. She braced herself and he tapped the button. The canopy slithered out of its container and quickly inflated and the two jerked upwards. Suddenly there was silence all around them. The calm winds brushed past them as Todd gently maneuvered the canopy through the air.

"Unreal, huh!" Todd said.

"Wow!" she said excitedly.

Todd laughed and pulled down on his right toggle, gently orientating them along the long highway several thousand feet below them. She never stopped looking around as they floated through the air.

"Hang on, okay," Todd said.

He buried the left toggle, and the left side of the parachute buckled, putting them in a downward spin. Kara laughed, and Todd smiled and let up on the toggles, leveling them out.

"I ... I can't believe this is really happening," Kara said.

"It never gets old," Todd said. "There is something special about it."

She looked down at her dangling feet. The pencil-thin highway ran directly between them. She could see the lights of tiny little cars, like insects moving down the road. She giggled and looked up to see a dark cloud approaching them. Todd veered off course slightly, skirting the side of the fluffy cloud. Kara extended her hand towards it, smiling as her black gloved hand disappeared in the thick mass as they combed the side of it. Todd couldn't help but smile, seeing the joy on her face in the minimized screen in his HUD. The cloud passed, giving way to a breathtaking view of Miami to their front with the ocean just beyond it.

"Perfect," Todd said softly.

*　　　*　　　*

The students and Albrecht stared at the black opening in the back of the plane. Albrecht couldn't help but feel sadness to know that Kara wasn't with him and safe. He felt like he had the worries of a father who was releasing his child into the world. Amber came to his side, putting her arm around him and leaning her head on his shoulder.

"She'll be fine, Professor," Amber said gently.

"I know ... it was meant to be."

Just then, the back door to the room opened. Bohden stepped in, wearing one of the suits, a parachute rig fastened on him. He stormed to the front of the room, squeezing past the large crowd within the room.

"Steven! What are you doing?" Albrecht asked, following him out of the airlock room and into the cargo bay.

"Go back inside, Brian!" Bohden called out, using the electronic voice intercom within the helmet. "You will go unconscious in minutes."

"Bohden ... what are you planning to do?"

Bohden stepped to the hinge of the ramp and stared down at the large peninsula below him. He looked up at the moon, then turned towards Albrecht. "I'm not going to jeopardize everything we have accomplished by putting our lives in his hands. I'm going to ensure York doesn't kill their father."

Albrecht's eyes widened and he stepped towards him. "Please Steven, don't do this. There is still time. He will succeed, I trust him!" he yelled over the roaring winds.

"Your trust is too easy to earn," Bohden said grimly. "Kara's life ... my life, is in danger now because you trust a man you don't even fully know! I'm not going to sit back and wait to disappear from this world!"

He turned and ran to the edge of the ramp, diving off of it into the blackness. Albrecht felt dizziness overwhelming him; his vision began to darken and he started to see stars in the corners of his eyes. His brain was not getting enough oxygen and he was slowly slipping into hypoxia. He stumbled towards the airlock door, fumbling with the switch to open it. The door slid open from the inside and Kevin stepped out and grabbed him, quickly pulling him inside. He set him down against the wall, looking back into the room and yelled to the others to get an O2 system. Students quickly ran out of the room towards the med bay.

Albrecht was beginning to regain his consciousness, breathing in the oxygen within the room. "We ... we have to ..."

"Don't talk, Brian, save your oxygen," Kevin said, reaching down and picking him up.

"We ... have to warn them," he said as Kevin carried him out of the room. "Tell D to send a mess—"

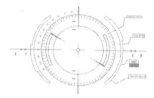

THE GOLDEN YEARS

Todd and Kara came swooping in only a few feet off the ground. The pavement below them came quick, and without Todd's night vision it would have been almost impossible to see. There was a break in between the passing cars and he took advantage of this to land on the side of the road. He landed, being careful not to trip over Kara in front of him.

"Phew!" he said over the radio, "good thing that was one of my better landings."

Todd began unclipping her from him, being conscious to not touch her inappropriately as he loosened her leg straps. She continued to stare up into the night sky, not saying a word. He looked up at the corner of his HUD at the video feed of her face. Her eyes were wide with a look of a newfound astonishment and understanding.

"You okay?" he asked.

"That was absolutely incredible," she said softly. "How many times have you done that?"

He stood up, ensuring the pouches on his web gear were secured. "Hmm," he thought for a moment, "that would have to be around four hundred and twenty jumps for me."

"Over four hundred?" she asked in amazement.

"Yeah … and believe it or not … that's very few compared to more serious jumpers." Todd chuckled, then saw a small set of headlights heading towards them. He turned towards Kara, motioning at his hand.

"Here comes a car! Quick, cloak yourself."

The two turned invisible and made their way farther off the side of the road, ducking beneath the thick trees. They watched as the car raced past them, speeding towards the city. The car itself looked ancient; it was loud and Todd scowled as it roared past them.

"Jeez!" he said.

"What?"

"Cars sure are loud here."

Kara smiled. "Well cars are all powered by gasoline during this time, and most of them are operated with manual transmissions."

"Great!" he said. "Driving is going to be a pain in the butt!"

The two sat on the side of the road, quietly talking for several minutes. Todd listened as Kara spoke of the technological transformation from gas to battery-powered cars from the twentieth to the twenty-first century. Todd then had an idea. He ran back into the woods, causing Kara to stop talking and watch curiously. She listened to him rustle around in some bushes, then she heard the crunching and snapping of tree branches. He returned, carrying a large bundle of branches and a few thin logs. He knelt down next to her, holding the lumber in his arm.

"What are you doing?" she asked.

"We need a ride," he said. "Keep a look out for a pickup, or even better, a semi."

Several cars passed by, leaving them waiting in the dark for nearly an hour. Using the magnification feature in his visor, he spotted a large semi carrying two vehicles on its flat bed. He quickly ran out into the road, placing the thick branches out on the right lane. He then ran back to Kara.

"Okay … when he slows down to go around the debris, you and I are going to hop on the back of the trailer."

She looked at him as if he were insane. She thought for a moment, then nodded in agreement.

"Stay right behind me, okay?"

She nodded once more. He looked back down the road to see the large truck approaching. The loud diesel engine roared and the brakes hissed as the driver slowed. The wheels cranked to the left and the truck began slowly pulling into the left lane.

"Now!" Todd said.

The two transparent figures ran onto the road. Todd quickly hopped up onto the trailer, grabbing ahold of a chain which secured one of the vehicles. He looked back, reaching his hand out to Kara. She reached out and he grabbed her, pulling her up to him. He assisted her up into the bed of a small pickup truck strapped to the rear of the trailer. The two sat down with their backs to the truck's cab. Todd looked back towards the front, ensuring the driver had not spotted them. The semi quickly curved back into the right lane and began speeding up down the long highway.

"Nicely done!" he said.

"Thanks," Kara said, smiling, no doubt finding excitement in all of the night's events.

The dash marks on the road flew past them in a blur in the red taillights and disappeared. The moon lay above the long stretch of highway, shining down on the body of water that paralleled the road. Kara sat with her knees up to her chest, looking out at the darkness behind them in deep thought. Todd rested his arm on the side of the truck bed. He looked over at her, only able to see her because of thermal imagining. Her body was a warm red and orange, the world around her a cool dark blue.

Part of him wanted to scoot closer to her. It was the first time he had ever had someone with him on a mission who wasn't a fellow Operator. He usually had an unwavering focus and stern demeanor while on an op. Nothing in the world could shake him from his combat mindset and his attention to detail when he was truly in it. Yet this time it was different; he felt somewhat insecure and distracted.

He was having a difficult time staying focused on the mission at hand. Ordinarily he would be going through every scenario in his head, trying to stay two steps ahead of whatever unexpected occurrence could possibly present itself to hinder the mission's success. However, no matter how hard he tried, all he could think about was her.

His mind went to York and his relationship with Kara. He wondered what would happen when she finally met him outside of the facility. Would he instantly come to his senses, drop whatever he was doing and embrace her? The thought of this made Todd feel a familiar bitterness towards the current task. It almost made him want to fail. What was he going to gain from all this? Yes, he would obviously save his own existence, but was that truly even worth it? He had almost died twice already. According to every natural law he should be dead anyway. Maybe he was as he had previously considered: an anomaly. Maybe he didn't belong. Maybe there was only room in this world for one Todd York.

A bump in the road shook him out of his daydreaming. He looked up to see Kara's dark helmet orientated towards him. The illumination from the night sky faintly refracted through her transparent figure. He turned, raising to a low crouch, and peeked over the cab of the truck. The right side of the road was dark and shielded from the moonlight by thick trees and vegetation. Off to the left, the river running alongside the road was beginning to thin out as the road began to widen and lead into a large intersection. Todd ducked down, sitting next to Kara. The street lights passed over them and the semi hissed to a stop. Todd looked around at the many cars making their way through the intersection. He couldn't help but notice how blocky the cars appeared. Off to his right, a lipstick red car that looked very sporty revved its engine. The sound of it made him stare in awe at the powerful machine. The driver had his stereo at full blast. Heavy electronic beats were heard over the engine itself.

"That's a Ferrari 308!" Kara's voice said over comm.

"That's a Ferrari?" Todd asked in disbelief. "Looks like an electric razor with wheels."

The Ferrari didn't waste time when the light turned green. It bolted through the intersection and down the long stretch of road.

Kara watched it race off, gripping the side of the truck bed.

"You're into cars?" Todd asked curiously.

The diesel engine rumbled as they continued on down the road. "Not really, I just find it fascinating how technology changes very little over time."

Todd canted his head. "How do you figure? We were pretty advanced in our time."

"It may seem that way, but think about it, Todd ... our phones may get better service, and our cars may be more efficient, but are we really that much more advanced? We can't even prove how the

Earth was created, only eight percent of the Earth's oceans have been explored, and the farthest man has made it in space is the moon." She giggled, bringing her knees up to her chest and hugging them. "If you think about it, all we really have done is made things smaller and flashier."

"Hmm." Todd looked at his MTX then back at Kara. "What about the tech you guys have made at the facility? What about time travel?"

Kara thought for a moment, she canted her head. "The world will never know it exists, nor should it ever know. Could you imagine what someone could do with such power?" She shook her head. "A single person could destroy everything we know."

They continued down the long highway talking with one another. The whole time, Todd felt a sort of enjoyment in his overall complacency for the mission. It was nice to be distracted for once.

"So ... Odin is a time machine, huh?" Todd asked.

A smile began to form on her face. She didn't answer; she was not going to try and mislead him from what he already knew. "Yes ... surely you must understand the reasons for why they didn't tell you ..."

"I know," Todd interrupted. "You didn't know if you could trust me." He paused for a moment, staring up into the night sky. "I guess I don't blame you."

She looked at him with sympathetic eyes. "Do you trust us?" she asked. "Do you ... trust me?"

Without turning towards her, he looked into her eyes on the small screen in his HUD. He could tell that she was truly curious as to what his answer was.

"I'm not going to lie ... there were a few times when I was in the Old West that it crossed my mind that you were just using me." He paused for a moment.

"What changed your mind?" she asked.

"Brian, when he told me about your father."

Her eyes sharpened, then looked down. She sat in silence, watching the cars in the adjacent lane pass by and their taillights shrink into the night.

"I'm sorry," Todd said softly.

"It's okay," she said, shaking her head. "To be quite honest, I cannot remember him."

Todd's expression softened and he rested his forearms on his knees, holding his wrist with his other hand. He looked up at the bright moon behind them, his mind faintly recalling his own father. "Seems like family is a rare thing in the future."

"What do you mean?"

He shook his head. "The future seems like it's full of nothing but broken families, and ... I don't know. When I was in the West, it felt as If there was something present there that was lacking in our time."

"What?" she asked. She scooted closer towards him curiously.

He grinned. "I don't know ... something wholesome, something ... genuine."

She blinked, looking at him closely. Her fingers fumbled timidly for a moment. A question had lingered on her mind since he had returned and part of her was anxious to ask, yet the other part was nervous to try and pry.

"What happened?" she asked, her eyes dancing around him. "When you were there?"

Todd thought for a moment, the thought of York shooting Luke, and him turning the gun on little Jack, was still burned into his mind. He thought of the good moments, the moments of joy and the great experiences he had shared with the McWilliams. A smile slowly grew on his face. "I met this little boy, Jack." He chuckled. "He was such a good kid, smart, headstrong. He reminded me of the little rascal I used to be."

Kara smiled as she watched Todd's expression lighten as he spoke. He continued to tell her about his time spent with the McWilliams, learning how to live on a nineteenth century ranch. He told her about Esprit Libre, and how he had broken in an untamable horse and forged a bond with the remarkable animal. He smiled and laughed as he recalled how on multiple occasions he had used modern day dialogue and had confused Jack. She laughed at this to his surprise, as he was most certain that she would disapprove of such carelessness.

"What did you say?" she asked.

Todd chuckled. "I called him 'Dude' on multiple occasions."

She smiled. "Well, you know the word 'Dude' originated in the late eighteen hundreds." She giggled. "Maybe you are the person who invented the term," she said with her eyebrows raised and a canted smile.

Todd grinned, shaking his head. "Man … it was unreal. You would love it there."

"I wish I could see it!" she said, staring off into the darkness.

"Maybe you will," Todd said.

Her smile faded and she looked over at him. Her heart began to thump in her chest. A feeling of excitement began to rise in her. She wanted to embrace it, but part of her insisted she kept her bearing. Never before had a time traveler returned with such remarkable stories. Never before had she even wanted to visit the past. York had always returned with yet another piece of himself lost forever. She had hated the operation for what it had done to him. Yet here was Todd, who was essentially the same person, but had experienced an entirely different side of history, up until he met his other self. It made her question whether or not time travel was a terrible thing. Perhaps in the right hands it could be used to closely study the lives of individuals of the past in order to help create a better future.

Todd adjusted himself next to her, looking at the time on his wrist. "You better get some rest. I'll stay awake in case we need to get off."

"Are you sure? You could probably use some rest yourself," she pleaded.

"I'll be fine."

She nodded and slowly lay down in the truck bed, curling her legs up and resting her head on her arm. She felt herself immediately begin to drift off. Through all the excitement, she hadn't realized how tired she had become since the adrenaline had finally worn off. Before she turned in for good, she looked back up into the night's sky, thinking of the exciting journey at hand. Although their goal was vital, and the consequences of failure were unspeakable and frightened her, she somehow was enjoying all this.

Two hours passed and Todd peeked over the cab of the truck to the front of the semi to see the city lights in the distance approaching. The buildings and street lights emitted a warm purple light that highlighted the city amongst the dark backdrop. He breathed in heavily, taking in the depth and reality of the task at hand. Reviewing the limited Intel on the MTX, he knew that his father was clocked consistently at a local night club in Miami Beach called The Palms. It was well known that drug money fueled the establishment, and big time traffickers and drug lords made frequent appearances to either flaunt their cash, discuss business propositions with other groups, or even threaten and/or intimidate competition. According to police reports and multiple futile cases, the establishment was a cesspool of coke-hungry hookers and thugs, spending their nights beneath the neon lights dropping cash on the irresistible white powder.

Before he could begin his search, he needed to get established, not only in the city, but in the time period itself. He needed a safe house, some place close to the night club yet far enough away to allow him to give a tail a runaround if he picked one up. He also needed money and clothing. Utilizing the MTX, Amber had shown him a way to hack into an older ATM. The more he thought about it, the more he realized having Kara with him was helpful, rather than a liability. She'd assist him in his cover story that he and Kara were newlyweds visiting Miami for their honeymoon. He had explained this to her while riding in the truck bed and she seemed to agree that it was a suitable explanation that could prove to assist them in the case of being questioned. They would pay for everything in cash and would use only first names. If Todd managed to get himself arrested, he would rely on Kara to break him out using her cloaking ability.

Kara rolled over and looked up at him. He was peering over the roof of the truck, his hands grasping the edge tightly above the rear window. From the inside of her helmet, she could see his body heat was burning a bright orange and red. He was uneasy about something, or perhaps he was anxious. She couldn't imagine the amount of stress that was weighing heavily on him. So much was at stake, so much was resting on his shoulders. The repercussions of his death could prove to be far worse than suspected. He had been an exceptional soldier, not only in the sense of his elite status and position, but because being in such a well-respected unit would have landed him in pinnacle operations during early WWIII. Who knows how many lives had been saved by him alone. The thought of this made her feel for him. Regardless of what Bohden had proclaimed and had suspected, Kara refused to believe that Todd was undergoing this journey out of his desperate need to survive. Instead, she believed part of him cared for the father whom he barely knew. Maybe he wanted to know him, try and learn why he had turned out to be so distant and cold. Or perhaps it wasn't his father who he was interested in. Maybe it was his internal struggle with knowing what York had done; seeing what kind of man he was, maybe he wanted to prove to himself that he and York were not the same man. Or maybe he wanted to see for himself that York couldn't go through with killing their father.

The light from the city shone over the semi, and Kara rose to her knees next to Todd. Familiar establishments passed them by as they continued towards the skyscrapers. They passed the familiar arches of the McDonald's sign and she watched as it shrank behind them. It was odd to be in a modern civilization again. She couldn't remember the last time she had been in a city like this that wasn't occupied by troops or that was cluttered from curb to curb with traffic of civilians desperately trying to escape the war. She continued to look around curiously, studying the pedestrians and their odd sense of fashion. She couldn't help but notice how everyone's hair was so long and puffy.

Most men had it swept to the sides and long in the back almost like a mullet. The women all had long hair that was wavy and large. Many had streaks of unnatural colors like pink and purple to match their brightly colored clothing and large earrings. Kara felt nervous as she began to worry that she would have trouble fitting in this time period with such short hair. She had yet to see a single woman with a bob or pixie cut. The thought of hindering Todd in any way made her feel uneasy. She looked over at him to see him tapping his finger on the MTX, switching in between screens.

"I'll let them know that we're here," Todd said, as he began typing a message to send to Odin.

He switched off the device, and looked back over the front of the truck. "It's weird ..."

"What is?" Kara asked.

Todd shook his head. "They're in 2016 now, even though they'll get this message. They already know whether or not we fail."

Kara bit her lip, looking back towards the city.

Todd looked over at her; he spoke firmly and without hesitation.

"We need to clear something up right now … if anything happens to me … if Michael dies and I just vanish, you need to get in contact with them as soon as possible so that they can come get you."

She looked at him in disbelief.

"Do you understand?" he said, his visor locked on hers.

She nodded reluctantly.

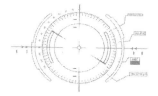

PARADISE LOST

The Spanish transmissions never seemed to stop squawking through DX-302 shortwave radio on the desk. The cables fed through the small gap in the window and led to the large antenna on the roof that could be seen from several miles down the beach. Michael had always loved the sound of the ocean just outside his window. It seemed to bring him a sort of peace which was scarce in a heavily populated city.

It had been a long day, meeting with employers and potential clients whose wealthy status was completely owed to illegal narcotics. Frankly, he had never understood the obsession with cocaine. Naturally he had tried it, as he had no shortage of opportunities; however, the numbing feeling it brought to his throat was unappealing as well as the feeling of snorting it in general. Seeing how dependent on it people became was a turn-off. He found their obsessive scouring for the powder as a pathetic weakness, but he welcomed it as it brought him plenty of revenue.

He considered himself a more modest trafficker compared to his colleagues and rivals. For simply picking up a shipment and driving it across town to the buyer he would make almost a quarter million. With several shipments a week he was doing very well for himself. Looking at his beachside estate you wouldn't take him for a millionaire, but rather a young, wealthy blue collar citizen who most likely had inherited the perfect location for a home in Miami Beach. At only twenty-five, he was living in the ideal bachelor's pad, making more than the state senator. Though he was living the life that many dreamed of, part of him disapproved of his work. He was well aware of the risks involved, yet the reward seemed to easily outweigh any doubt. Many traffickers had gotten cleverer with their methods, such as using tow trucks to transport loaded vehicles through town in order to ease any suspicion of their intentions and also give them complete deniability. Michael chose the more routine way of doing things. His car was his most prized possession, and its 7-liter V8 engine would outrun any police cruiser that made him. Of course, in his vast experience in the job it had never even come close to that. On a few occasions he had been stopped, only to detour the officer from conducting a search in his trunk by bribing him with the several thousand in cash in his pocket. All in all, he felt untouchable.

He cupped his hands over his cigarette and lit it, shielding it from the ocean breeze. The moon hid behind a few fluffy clouds, illuminating the back of his home with ambient light. He left his shirt unbuttoned, the humidity in the air overwhelmed by the consistent breeze over the crashing waves. He let out a long stream of smoke, staring at the glowing ember. A familiar feeling of loneliness began to set in. The feeling came and went on occasion. It was times such as this; completely isolated with nothing but all the money in the world, that he felt it. Something was missing in his life. He didn't know what it was, but he knew there was something awry. His nights usually consisted of partying at night clubs or clinging to the bars at noisy strip clubs, throwing his money at loose women. He was constantly surrounded by people and he devoured the night life and all that it offered, Yet he felt as if he was searching for something that he didn't quite understand, or perhaps deserve. His life was empty.

He checked his watch. It was nearly 3 a.m. on Thursday. His head was still spinning from the massive amounts of alcoholic beverages he had consumed earlier in the evening. The hangover would no doubt be vicious and would leave him immobile for most of the next day. Thankfully he didn't have any work until Saturday night when he would meet with a big-time employer. Apparently, somebody in a high place had recognized his consistency and his hard work and was going to pay him a visit at The Palms. He was uneasy about getting in too deep with the people in charge of the operation. There were plenty of horror stories floating around about the types of punishments administered by the kinds of people he was working for. It was thoughts such as this that assisted in his overall decision on getting out of the city as soon as possible. All he had to do was this last big job, and he would call it quits forever, maybe move to someplace quiet in the Pacific Northwest. There he would use the millions that he had conjured to buy some untouchable property hidden in the pine trees.

He leaned back, flicking the cigarette off the porch into the white sand. Putting his feet up on the railing, he felt himself begin to doze off.

*   *   *

Todd had nearly emptied the entire ATM trying to figure out how to extract just the right amount. He had intended on extracting only a couple thousand, but was now stuffing a little over twenty thousand dollars into his pack. He and Kara quietly made their way down the graffiti-ridden dark alley, stepping over an endless amount of discarded newspapers and plastic bags. Overflowing metal trash cans lined the walls beneath the collapsed ladders of fire escapes. The two quietly made their way to the end of the alley where it led to the street. The traffic was as scarce as it was the early morning hours. Todd and Kara ran across the street beneath the orange street lights towards the dark store on the other side. The paint-decorated windows were concealed by the metal grates used to keep out muggers. Todd studied it closely, looking for a way inside.

"Any ideas?" Kara asked, standing behind him and watching the street for any cars.

Todd leaned down and pulled on the metal gate. It began to pull back slightly, revealing a small space to the front door.

"Here ..." he said, bracing himself with his foot on the other side. "You can squeeze through, just get us enough to get us through the night."

She nodded and dropped down, squeezing through the small gap. She rose up in between the gate and the glass door to the store. "I'll be right back ... okay?"

"Okay," Todd replied. "Just get the essentials, enough for us to get a hotel without raising any suspicion."

She nodded and turned, opening the door and disappearing into the dark store. Todd knelt down as a black Mercedes drove past. He could hear Kara through his helmet as she combed through racks of clothing on metal hangars.

"Everything okay in there?" he asked.

"Yep!" she said cheerfully.

Todd began typing on his MTX and pushed send. "I'm sending you all my sizes, okay? If you can't find them don't worry about it. We just have to make it a few hours in these clothes."

"Okay," she said. He looked back into the store and he could faintly see her frantically moving around through the store with her arms full of clothing.

He could hear her giggle on the other side of the headset. "I mean ... don't make me look like an idiot ... please," he said, peering back through the window.

"I got it!" she said.

She returned to the door several minutes later, holding two bags. She squeezed through the door and pushed the two bags through the small gap that Todd was holding open. She then crawled out and retrieved them.

"Good job," Todd said with a smile.

Kara smiled and the two made their way down the street and ducked into the closest alleyway.

Todd scrolled through the 3D constructed map of Miami on his MTX as they walked. "Okay ... there is a hotel on the east corner of the airport. That is only a few miles north of here. Let's change then head over there. Maybe we can catch a cab along the way."

Kara nodded. Placing her bag on the ground, she reached up and pulled off her helmet. She inhaled, breathing in the ocean air. She rustled her hair and set her helmet down. Todd did the same, setting his helmet on the top of a metal trash can. He then reached to his upper back, loosened the concealed airtight zipper on the armored suit and proceeded to squeeze out. He stepped out of it and knelt down in his briefs, digging through the shopping bag. He pulled out the jeans and t-shirt that Kara had picked out for him. He chuckled at the shirt.

"Well ... I guess that won't be suspicious," he said, holding up the baby blue Miami Dolphins t-shirt.

Kara laughed as she began pulling her arms from her suit and pushing it down to her waist. She rocked her hips back and forth, pushing the tight suit down over her legs. Todd turned his back to her quickly to give her some privacy. He pulled the shirt over his head and began stepping into the stone-washed jeans. Kara put on a slouchy purple long-sleeved shirt that draped over one shoulder.

"So odd," she giggled.

Todd smiled and opened up the shoebox holding white high-top Nike sneakers. "Sweet!"

The two laughed as they continued dressing. When they finished, they studied themselves and each other.

"What are those?" Todd asked, pointing at the pink knitted bands around her ankles.

"Oh! They're leg warmers. I have no idea why girls wore these. But it seemed to be the popular thing to do."

Todd shrugged. "I like it, I guess."

Kara's suit and helmet were light enough so that she could place them in her shopping bag. Todd however had to hold his bag from the bottom in order to prevent the suit from tearing through. The two then casually walked down the street towards the hotel. The occasional night-dwelling pedestrian passed by. Todd and Kara greeted them. They received a few hellos in return, but Todd couldn't help but notice the obvious difference in people's mannerisms and politeness in this time period compared to the Old West. They then came across a kid who wore a jean jacket covered in metal studs. His hair was long and puffy, much like the females. He wore tight jeans and loose black boots. As he approached, Todd prepared himself for a potential fight.

"How's it going, man?" Todd said with a nod.

"Bite me!" the kid snarled.

Todd cocked an eyebrow, then looked over at Kara. "What the hell does that mean?" he asked.

"I'm almost certain he doesn't mean that in a literal sense," she replied.

The kid looked at Kara and kissed the air, then gave her a devious grin. She giggled at the odd expression, not having ever seen someone do such a thing to a total stranger.

"Get lost, you little shit!" Todd said angrily.

The kid flipped him the middle finger and continued on down the sidewalk in an uneven stride, no doubt constricted by his tight jeans. Todd felt the urge to go pummel him but was taken aback by Kara laughing.

"What?" he asked with a confused grin.

"I foresee a lot of trouble in our near future."

"Can you believe that guy? What an asshole."

They finally arrived at the hotel only about an hour later after successfully hailing a cab. The building had multiple stories and a curved pool outside. A few homeless men sat outside the perimeter fence, no doubt breathing out whatever money they had conjured on the streets in long streams of smoke that made Todd wince. He and Kara made their way through the front door and stopped at the front desk. An older man with thick glasses slumped in a chair behind the counter, snoring. Todd cleared his throat, trying to get his attention. Then once more, even louder but without success. Kara stepped around Todd and leaned up against the counter.

"Excuse me," she said very sweetly.

The man's bloodshot eyes shot open and he quickly sat up in his chair. "Yes! How can I help you?" he asked, scooting his chair up to the desk.

"We would like to get a room for the night; would that be possible?" she said, her child-like kindness no doubt getting the better of him.

"Well, yes …" The man straightened his glasses on his nose and began thumbing through his logbook. "Hmm, let me see … one bed or two?"

"Um … two."

"Okay … well, the only two-bed room I have left is on the top floor. Will that be okay for you?"

"That will be fine," Todd answered. He then pulled an unreasonable amount of cash out of his hip pocket and began thumbing through it, looking at it as if he were using currency from another country.

The man returned with two room keys and set them down on the counter.

"Will this cover it?" Todd said as he set a stack of twenty dollar bills on the counter.

The man's eyes widened and he looked up at Todd as if he were insane. "Well ... yeah, but ..."

"Perfect!" Todd said. "Keep whatever is extra." He grabbed the room key and made his way over to the elevator, looking at the oddly shaped piece of metal in his hand.

"Thank you," Kara said as she picked up her key and her bag containing the suit and met Todd just as the door of the elevator announced its opening with a ring. They stepped inside and Todd pressed the button to the fifth floor. The door slowly slid shut and he felt the floor lurch upwards. Kara looked at him as he rubbed his narrow eyes.

"You look tired ..." she said.

Todd nodded. "Yeah ... well we need to get out of here as soon as possible. York could be in the city already. We need to find Michael before he does."

"He doesn't have any more information on him than we do. If anything, we have the advantage. Tomorrow night will be our best chance at finding him."

"Seems very convenient that he would get snatched up for questioning within seventy-two hours of when we go back in time to find him ... doesn't it?" Todd asked.

The doors to the elevator opened, revealing a dark hallway with endless doors on each side. Kara followed him down the long hallway, thinking about what he had just said. It was rather perfect timing for Michael to pop up on the grid. She couldn't help but wonder if it was just a coincidence, or perhaps something far more unbelievable.

They stopped at their room number and Todd fumbled with the key in the lock. It took him several attempts to figure out which way the key went in and in what direction it needed to turn in order to release the door jam. He finally heard it click, and he pushed the door open, revealing a dark room, lit only by the lights of the city shining through the large window.

He dropped the bag at the foot of the bed and walked over to the window and gazed out at the quiet city. He could see the overpass that connected to the expressway and eventually led to Miami Beach, where his father was currently holing up. It was surreal how impossible the task at hand seemed. Yet his determination and focus helped him overlook the incredible underlying reality of his current situation. However, he was having a hard time focusing due to the lack of sleep.

He closed the blinds, instantly darkening the room, and plopped down face first on the bed. Within seconds he was asleep.

Kara remained awake for a while. She sat down on the other bed, watching Todd sleep soundly. She couldn't help but worry for him as part of her feared that he was slowly becoming York. She could see it in his eyes that something was burning inside him.

Whether it was sadness, anger, or a toxic mixture of both, she sensed that there was something missing in his life. Something that he had lost, such as close friends in the war, or the love of his only parent. Or perhaps it wasn't what he had lost, but rather what he had yet to find. Maybe meeting his father would end up giving him some sort of closure, although assuming everything went according to plan, and they might never directly meet.

She rolled onto her side, watching his shoulders slowly rise and fall, silhouetted by the dim light from the city shining through the curtains.

*   *   *

The street lights passed in a spaced rhythm, briefly lighting his scarred face in the rear-view mirror. His eyes were heavy, and the monotonous humming of the Mercedes's engine furthered induced his mind's need for sleep. He had been driving for nearly twenty straight hours and was beginning to question whether or not he could continue. He refused to turn on the radio as he didn't want to become indulged in the period. As far as he was concerned, he was simply heading to Miami to kill a target. He would blend into the local populace just enough to assist him in closing in on his target. Besides that, nothing in the world would hinder him from completing his mission. A self-induced mission that consistently had him questioning his own sanity, which he felt had been slipping long before he had set out on this escapade.

His mind continued to taunt him with the same memories that were responsible for his unshakable rage. His hatred being towards himself, and the man whose own blood ran through his veins. His mind then went to his other self.

He still found it hard to believe that he had met his same-self back in the Old West, let alone that Todd had somehow tracked him down in the nineteenth century. For a moment, seeing that his younger self appeared to be in much better condition both mentally and physically, he had hoped that maybe there was still a chance for them. However, hearing that he was committing the same horrible atrocities and living the same pointless and empty life furthered his belief that they were empty shells shaped as men. And yet, he had seen his same-self give his own life while pursuing him.

But why? Had he known what York was planning to do? Or was he simply driven by hatred and vengeance for York's shooting of the rancher?

He pulled off to the side of the road and turned off the engine, leaning back in his seat and staring up at the night sky through the tinted sunroof. He felt like an imposter in this timeline, like a cancer.

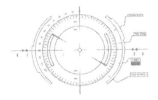

END OF THE ROAD

Todd limped down the long street cradling his abdomen; his free arm dangled at his side, blood streaming through his fingers and dripping onto the dark pavement. He took long staggering steps in an effort to convince himself that he was going to make it out of this living hell. However, the dimming light and the growing amount of blood leaking from his body was telling him it was merely hopeful thinking.

He grunted and moaned with each painful step, bracing himself against the dark concrete wall, his body riddled with bullet holes. He looked up into the dark red sky, sweat and blood running down his face.

Unmanned drones screamed as they arced across the red sky, launching missiles into the tall skyscrapers around him and sending large chunks of concrete and rebar crashing into the pavement only a few meters in front of him. He fell backwards, landing on the pale bloated body of a Chinese soldier. All around him were the faceless uniformed corpses of his enemy. Their blood pooled together, forming a seamless layer that slowly flowed towards the street gutters. The stench of death flooded his nostrils; the blood running down his extremities trickled down his legs and added to the massive pool beneath him. He cradled Jack's little body in his arms. His watery eyes and uncontrollable sobbing impeded his ability to observe his surroundings as he stumbled down the long street. To the right-hand side of the street lay a massive figure. His expressionless dead eyes stared up into the night sky. It was Luke, or maybe it was Rob. Todd fell to his knees, his arms now somehow empty. He brought them up to his face and screamed up into the air, a powerful roar of anger and anguish.

"Todd …" a soft voice called to him.

The sky above him then seemed to split in half as a trail of smoke cut vertically towards the ground. Beneath the long trail of smoke was a pointed object. He looked at it in despair, knowing all too well what it was. He sank, his head drooping over his chest, blood trickling out of his mouth.

"Todd," the voice called out again.

He lifted his head slowly, looking up to see himself standing above him. But it wasn't himself, but rather an older, scarred version who stared down at him with a look of disgust and hatred. Todd's mouth remained open slightly, bloodstained teeth concealed by broken lips. York continued to stare at him as if he blamed him for everything that was taking place. Where were they? How did it come to this? Everything Todd had done in order to prevent this had proven to be futile, and through all his efforts, he had come to realize that it was he who was directly responsible.

The small object disappeared behind the tall buildings, and then there was a blinding flash that shook the earth beneath him. The dark alleys lit up and disappeared in fire. The giant wall of flame rushed towards him, engulfing everything in front of it with a bright wave of heat and power. York continued to stare at him, the massive wall of destruction closing behind him. Todd looked into his eyes. Suddenly, he became nothing as he was vaporized in front of him.

"Todd!" the voice said louder.

Todd yelled as he sat up quickly, causing Kara to jump backwards and knock the lamp off the nightstand. He breathed heavily as he looked around the room in confusion, unsure of where he was. He looked out the window and saw the sun shining brightly behind the thin blinds. He could see the small reflection of cars driving over the overpass. He turned to see Kara, grasping the table behind her, frightened by him. It was then that he realized where he was and what had just happened. He brought his hands up to his face, running them up and over his hair to the back of his head.

"What time is it?" he asked, shaking his head.

"It's almost two in the afternoon. You were muttering and moving restlessly," she said, remaining clamped to the table. "Forgive me for startling you."

"It's okay …" He looked up at her to see her eyes locked on him, as if she were afraid to move. He slowly rotated on the bed and stood up. Walking over to the sink, he fumbled with the faucet until cool water began filling the bowl. He reached in, cupping the water in his hands and splashing his face. He looked up at the mirror, watching the beads of water run down his forehead and cheeks and pool in the overnight scruff. He exhaled and grabbed one of the folded towels on the counter and dabbed his face.

Kara refrained from coming any closer to him. She walked over to the bed and sat down slowly, her eyes never leaving him. Todd turned and made eye contact with her, which she quickly broke, turning to look out the window. It appeared to Todd that Kara didn't trust him, and that his unpredictability had her on edge. This was an issue, not only because he didn't like the idea of her being uneasy in his midst. But it could also prove to be a problem as they exercised their cover stories. He needed her to be completely comfortable around him in order to make it appear as if they had known each other for years.

"Hungry?" he asked.

She looked up at him with a curious expression. "Um … yes."

"Let's go find a place," he said as he walked over to the bed and began pulling on his sneakers.

Ten minutes later, the two made their way through the hotel lobby and up to the front desk where Todd asked the employee about rental cars. After a quick conversation as to its whereabouts, and Todd handing the man the room keys and a generous tip, Todd and Kara left the hotel and walked around the corner to the airport rental station. Todd was brief as to what vehicle he wanted. The owner seemed surprised when Todd asked him for the fastest car that he had in stock. He ended up settling on a brand-new blood-red 1985 Chevrolet Corvette convertible, which he seemed unimpressed by and was overly uncaring about dropping a thick stack of money down on the table to rent it. The large amount of cash distracted the owner, making it possible for Todd to get around having to show them a driver's license.

Kara watched in amusement as Todd struggled to operate the manual transmission. Not amused by his misfortune, but rather his aggravation towards the ancient machine was what she found adorable. He gritted his teeth as he unintentionally continued to kill the engine as the car hopelessly lurched forward towards the parking garage exit. He paused for a moment, looking at the employees who were watching him struggle from behind the large windows. He exhaled, placing his hand on the key. He held in the clutch, then turned the ignition. Kara tampered with the radio, browsing through the loud white noise and squelch until she found a clear deep voice.

"This is 99.7, all the latest and greatest hits. Coming to you live from the beautiful Miami Beach; this is one of my personal favorites ... from 'The Outfield', this is 'Your Love.'"

Todd paused for a moment as the song started. He looked over at Kara, who had a smile growing across her face. He put the shifter into first gear, then placed his right hand on the wheel. He then applied pressure to the gas while smoothly releasing the clutch. The engine revved and they gently pulled out of the parking garage and onto the main road. Todd waited for the RPMs to max, then shifted into second gear.

"I kind of like this!" he said with a grin.

"The song?" Kara asked, "Or the car?"

"Both!" he chuckled. "It feels kind of good to be ... normal."

"Yeah," she agreed. "I cannot recall the last time I rode in a car on a normal day like this."

"Me neither."

They came to a stop light, where he pressed the brake and the car stopped abruptly. "Shit, I'll have to work on that."

Kara giggled. He looked around the intersection at the other cars, ensuring he was not violating any traffic laws. "So," he tapped the steering wheel to the beat of the song. "What do you want to do today?"

Kara shot him an intrigued expression. She thought for a moment, her cheeks reddening. The light turned green and Todd accelerated through the intersection and down a long road with tall white buildings tightly lining each side. Kara's hair blew in the wind, her long bangs brushing against her face. She swept them away as she pondered for a moment. She wore a tank top and skirt, which she seemed to be uncomfortable in as she was not used to wearing such revealing clothing. However, the warm climate made it impossible to wear anything more. She held her hands down at her pressed-together legs.

"How about a movie?"

Kara smiled. "I am not very familiar with many films ... let alone from this timeframe."

Todd grinned. "Good! I believe there are a few good ones that came out this year. We'll have to find out where a theater is."

A few minutes later, Todd and Kara found themselves sitting at a table for two in a crowded restaurant. Todd nearly devoured two whole sirloins, while Kara chose a variety of seafood. They spent nearly two hours at the restaurant, mostly talking about the students and Albrecht, and how Kara hoped they were doing okay. Todd repeatedly assured her that they would be fine and were no doubt far more worried about her. Kara appreciated his reassurance and took his words to heart as she slowly began to become more cheerful as the day went on.

Next, Todd found himself following Kara through the mall for nearly an hour. She was curious more than anything, as she did not purchase much, but rather seemed to enjoy just looking and talking with Todd as they made their way from store to store. Todd took this opportunity to purchase some more suitable clothing; however, he found it difficult to find something that appealed to him. Kara wouldn't wander far when Todd would stop to look at something. He would find that she was usually within arm's reach whenever he would catch himself becoming lost in thought.

"Well ... I'm satisfied," Todd said, as he began making his way towards the mall entrance.

"I am as well," Kara replied.

After they found the car and buckled in, Todd adjusted the rear-view mirror and slowly backed out of the narrow parking space. She studied him in his deep concentration as he navigated through the tight parking lot. His eyes never ceased to study his surroundings.

"What do you think about?" she asked with an innocent curiosity. She was oriented towards him in her seat, hugging her left leg. He head was against her head-rest.

"What do you mean?" he asked, glancing over at her.

"You always appear as though you are lost in thought. As if you are always waiting for something, or something is constantly troubling you."

Todd smiled, glancing in the rear-view mirror, then over at her. "I guess it's habit. When you spend most of your life trying to stay alive by being quicker and smarter than the people trying to kill you, it can be hard to relax sometimes." He pulled out of the mall parking lot and sped down North Miami Avenue.

"That sounds exhausting," she said, tilting her head. "Certainly, you must feel at ease sometimes?"

"I do. It's funny actually ..." he looked over at her. "I feel at ease when I'm around you."

Within milliseconds after saying it, he began to wonder if his statement was inappropriate. He looked over to see her gazing out the window, and he couldn't see her expression. He immediately began feeling sick to his stomach and an overwhelming feeling of embarrassment. As they drove in silence, he continuously ran the statement through his head, looking at it from every perspective and analyzing it every way that it could be interpreted. He then began to curse at himself for his complacency. He had lost his edge for a split second and now he was paying for it. He tightened his grip on the wheel, returning to his aggressive and observant state of mind.

Todd took the exit off of the I-95 express way and onto the Julia Tuttle causeway towards Miami Beach. The sun was beginning to drop behind silhouetted buildings on the horizon. The radio station continued to play familiar tracks which gave a pleasant soundtrack to the long drive. Artists such as Phil Collins, Mr. Mister, Survivor, Pet Shop Boys, Lionel Richie, and Van Halen had Todd subtly tapping his foot at the first few songs, but by the time they were crossing the Causeway to Miami Beach, Todd was smacking the steering wheel and bobbing his head, lip syncing the lyrics to 'Burning Heart.' Kara laughed as he dramatically pointed at her as if she were part of the song.

Miami Beach was just as Todd had expected with colorful pedestrians filling the sidewalks and crowding the building corners. Limber individuals danced out of pure enjoyment, while their comrades held large boom boxes on their shoulders. Todd continued east and eventually came to the famous Ocean Drive, where he and

Kara gazed around in astonishment at the sight of the sprawling paradise. Kara stared at the ocean with a gaze that made Todd wonder if this was the first time she had ever seen it. A few moments later, multiple women wearing bathing suits stole Todd's attention from the road and he watched them as they rolled past on shoes with small wheels attached to them. Kara looked at him and then back at the road with irritation.

"I believe that was a stop sign that you just drove through," Kara said, her arms crossed.

Todd quickly turned his attention back to the windshield. He began blushing as a car behind him honked.

"Sorry, I was looking at the uh … wheel shoes or whatever those were," he said, shaking his head.

"Roller skates?" Kara suggested with a hint of sarcasm.

"That's what they're called?" he asked, scratching his jaw.

Kara looked at him with her thin eyebrow raised. He shook his head slightly and exhaled with aggravation. She wondered if perhaps she had made him feel uncomfortable for pointing out his natural curiosity.

"Are you alright?" she asked.

He placed his elbow on the door, resting his chin on his thumb, his index finger on his temple. "That was stupid," he said.

"What?"

"Me … staring at the girls … I could have gotten us into a car accident." He exhaled once more. "I'll be more careful."

"Todd, I … I did not mean to make you feel uncomfortable."

"No, you only pointed out the obvious. That I wasn't paying attention." He flexed his jaw, glancing in the rear-view mirror. His voice started low but began to rise and intensify as he spoke. "I promised Brian that I would keep you safe … that I wouldn't let anything bad happen to you. Yet here we are, and I'm putting our lives in danger because I can't focus on the fucking road!"

She stared at him, trying to understand his almost obsessive self-criticism, yet somewhat intimidated by it. She raised her hand, wanting to place it on his arm, but stopped herself out of uncertainty, brushing her bangs away from her eyes instead. "Todd … I did not intend for you to feel so badly. It is quite alright for you to be drawn to such things, and I hope you know that I do trust you."

He looked at her, his hard expression relaxing slightly. Up to this point, he had believed that she did not trust him at all and was only along for the trip out of moral responsibility. But to hear her say that she trusted him gave him a different outlook on the mission. It gave him a sense of encouragement, and a warm feeling grew inside him.

"Thanks ..." he said. He loosened his grip on the wheel, the soft sunset matching his newfound relaxed state of mind. The bright neon lights of the buildings to his right, and the fading light on the beach to his left gave a festive feeling to the already intriguing setting. The radio station announcer had changed to a louder individual who announced each song as if it were a boxer who was making his entrance into the ring. Kara smiled as Todd reached over and turned up the volume to "The Promise" by "When in Rome." Todd didn't say a word as he slowly drove south, the fading sunlight casting an orange and pink haze over the skyline. Although the sun had left, the warmth remained, as if the lights had simply been turned off and the atmosphere of the city compensated for it with neon lights and loud music.

They came to The Palms, which was a large building with blue neon lights lining the flat roof and the borders of the flashy sign. Tall palm trees neatly lined the sidewalk in front, and a long line of extravagantly dressed people eagerly awaited their access inside. Todd studied the front entrance, turning down the volume to the music. He could see video cameras posted above the front entrance and above the awning along with what appeared to be two bouncers. He slowly drove around the side of the building, looking for any possible structural and/or security shortfalls that he could exploit. He came to the back lot, which was filled with flashy cars. An emergency exit with no camera in sight was secluded in the dark corner near the alley way. He looked at Kara and grinned. "Well, if they don't just let us in ... that will be our entrance."

He then drove around the block and found a rundown five-story building with a partially broken sign displaying the flickering word "Vacancy." He pulled into the back parking lot, and he and Kara made their way to the front desk where he purchased a room for two on the top floor. The view was not as advantageous as he had hoped, being as it overlooked an old strip club across the street. He set his bag on the bed and gazed out the window at the bright pink neon lights casting horizontal shadows onto his tired face through the blinds.

"Well, I was hoping that we would have a good view of the night club, but this is the only hotel that's this close," Todd said with a look of displeasure.

"I'm am sure it will be fine, Todd," Kara said, sitting down on the adjacent bed, her hands folded in her lap.

Todd rubbed the back of his head, a grimace overtaking his face as his fingers touched the broken skin on the back of his scalp. Kara stood up and walked towards him, her hands fumbling.

"Would you … like me to take a look at your injuries?" she asked.

He moved his head side to side, working out the stiff aches from the long drive. "No, that's okay," he said, dropping his hand to his side. "I'll be fine. I don't know about you, but I could use a bite to eat."

Kara nodded, a small smile presenting itself, with a look of worry accompanying it. They left the hotel room and drove around the city in search of a restaurant that interested them. They ended up settling on fast food and then on a movie.

After the movie, Todd and Kara began making their way back to the hotel, being held up at each stop light and crosswalk. Kara didn't say much and Todd could tell something was on her mind. Although he found himself attracted to her tranquility and mysteriousness, he couldn't help but feel slightly offended by her lack of words. As time continued to pass, being that it had been almost two months since he had met her, all he wanted was for her to talk to him. It wasn't that he wanted a relationship necessarily, but rather a friendship and an understanding between them.

"You okay?" he asked.

She looked at him, her saddened eyes forcing his to become fixated on her.

"Kara …?" he said.

"May I ask you something?"

He looked at her; he could tell what she wanted him to do. He quickly turned off the road, parking on an empty space overlooking the beach. He shut off the engine and turned towards her, his heart rate slowly beginning to pick up in his chest.

"Is everything alright?" he asked.

She breathed out softly. "I want to ask you something ... something only you can answer. Something I have wanted to know since I first met you."

"What?" he asked in almost a whisper. He adjusted in his seat, palms beginning to sweat.

She brushed her bangs away from her left eye, her hands fumbling in her lap, shrugging her shoulders briefly. "You know how he thinks ..."

"Kara ..." He shook his head and chuckled. "What is it?"

She looked down at her hands, speaking in almost a whisper. "If you don't want to answer I understand, but I must know. Does ... he love me?" Her eyes left her hands and shot up to his, eagerly awaiting an answer.

Todd let out a quick breath, looking out at the dark breakers quietly crashing into the white sand. He bit his lip, doing his best to choose his words carefully. The conversation was about York, yet he felt his heart thumping in his chest for reasons he could not understand. He was about to answer when she broke the silence.

"It's just that ... I was so sure that there is ... was something between us ... that he felt it too. I have always been too afraid to ask him, I didn't want to become a hindrance in his already complicated life. Nor did I want to make him feel uncomfortable if in fact he did not share the same feelings. I have never loved anyone in such a way. He's always so kind, so ... interesting to me. I want to know what he feels. Can you tell me?"

Todd scratched his chin. He continued to watch the white foamy water crash on the beach and then disappear back into the black surf. He had to force himself to look past what York had done to Luke; he had to look past his own hatred and also his jealousy.

"Well ..." he said, raising his eyebrows and exhaling softly. "As I'm sure you know, he is a troubled person; he has seen the very few loved ones in his life taken from him. He is afraid of love ... afraid of its grasp." He continued to describe the man that he knew better than anyone, the man he had followed his entire life. "He wants to love, he wants to be happy ... but, I believe he feels that the time for that has passed. He sees it as a luxury that no longer has a place in the life of a man in his position. He blames himself for his losses, for his failures." He stared at the steering wheel, his hands tight fists in his lap. "He sees himself as the cause for all his pain." He paused for a moment, gathering his thoughts; he then turned, looking into her eyes. "He may not be very good at displaying his affection because he has never truly had anybody, and he fears that he may lose you if he lets himself become involved. But Kara, I promise you ... you are on his mind this very moment. No matter how far, or how long ago he may be ... you are all he wants in this world."

Kara's eyes widened and her breath fluttered. A smile grew on her face and she turned, her fingers covered her lips as she looked out at the dark ocean, the warm breeze softly blowing her hair. Her hopeful eyes made Todd feel a sense of warm fulfillment. Although he knew her thoughts were of York and not himself, it brought him comfort in seeing her joy. He wanted her to know the truth, to know of the dark reality of the man she loved. But her smile was rare, and he would not miss a chance to witness it.

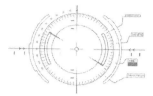

THE GOOD, THE BAD, AND THE
UNEXPECTED

The club's fire exit would make a suitable surreptitious entrance and would no doubt grant him access without hindrance. It also would help him resolve the issue of having to show any identification. Steven Bohden checked his 2014 Omega watch and saw that it was nearly midnight. The club was just now beginning to pick up, as the line continued to grow. He took note of this, since the big shots and VIP's would no doubt show up once the place was lively.

He walked across the street, passing a group of young women who shouted at him with unrealistic invitations. He ignored them as he cut through the alley, walking quietly down the dark, trash-cluttered road, his hands in the pockets of his newly acquired leather jacket. He passed through the alley and made his way to the other side of the block. He studied the buildings in the area, most of which averaged three to five stories. He would find a place to hold up for the night, then tomorrow he would stake out the club until he had positive Identification on any of the three Yorks. Only then would he make his entrance.

The '80s seemed to be a time of lax and leisure, as if the country and its citizens were enjoying the splendors of living in the most powerful nation in the world. The Cold War was still present on people's minds, but with such an aggressive leadership in the White House and no major conflict to bring upon any finger pointing, most

Americans were sleeping soundly and were seeing a bright future ahead. It had been a long time since Bohden had stepped into the past himself, not since the early operations conducted by the facility. He still did not find it as fascinating as others, but rather still viewed it as a method of waging the world's most innovative and secretive espionage. Like the host country of a target location, he saw the odd clothing and atmosphere of 1980's Miami as simply another place in the world. He would do whatever was necessary to blend in and complete his mission.

*　　　*　　　*

It took York less than two minutes to pick the lock on the sliding gate covering the sports store entrance. He glanced back to ensure nobody was near, then he slowly pushed the gate open, revealing the glass door. Using the butt of his fixed blade, he hit the lower section of the glass door on the top right corner. The glass instantly broke into large shards and fell from the aluminum frame. He stepped through, turning on the built-in LED light on the helmet's temple. He began searching for an appropriate weapon system. He busted the glass of the front counter, immediately setting off an alarm.

He looked over the handguns within the cabinet. Most were six shooters of a few varieties and some nickel-plated semi-automatic pistols, too flashy for his liking. He ended up settling on an M9 Berretta. Far from his preferred side-arm but the high capacity magazines would come in handy. He loaded up six magazines and stuffed them in the suit's web gear. He then grabbed a double barrel twelve-gauge shotgun from the rack behind the counter. Using a hand saw that he found within the store, he sawed the barrel down all the way to the hand guard; he then sawed the stock off, leaving a stubby wooden grip, all the while the alarm continuing to ring out into the night.

Blue and red lights danced outside the store and the tires of a police cruiser came squealing to a stop. York casually stepped out of the broken door and walked down the street. The cop ran in directly behind him, completely missing the transparent suspect. York chuckled as he rounded the corner into the alley where his Mercedes was parked. It was another few blocks to The Palms, but he was in no rush as he had almost another twenty-four hours before Michael would make an appearance. Starting the car, he backed out of the alleyway and drove down the street to what appeared to be an abandoned twelve-story building with the top floors not completed. Graffiti and overgrowth consumed the outer walls like the underbelly of society competing with nature to reclaim what had been abandoned by the city.

York turned off the lights and coasted to a stop next to a metal door on the side. He stepped out, softly closing the door to the Mercedes, and moved up to the door with his M9 at the ready. The door knob squeaked as he turned it, the sound echoing throughout the dark interior. He stepped inside and observed the interior through night vision. Garbage and obvious signs of life cluttered the corners of the dark walls and filled the building with a foul stench. With his pistol raised he walked softly, checking each corner and each open doorway as he passed by. He did this on each level, hastily checking each open room until he reached the fifth floor. He came to the doorway at the landing on the fire exit stairwell. The door had been replaced with a hanging rug and behind it he could faintly hear movement. The helmet amplified the surrounding ambient noise, while muting any loud noises that measured a high enough decimal that could harm the wearer's ears. Thus, making small noises like whispers and the faint rustling of movement easier to hear, yet muting gunshots and explosions.

The amplified hearing came in handy. He could make out the subtle snoring of someone inside the room and the rustling between blankets. He removed his knife from his sheath and held it against the grip of his pistol, giving him instant access to two close-quarters weapons. He very gently pulled back the rug and stepped into the room. Switching to thermal vision, he could see almost twenty heat signatures laying in pallets on the floor. He covered each body with his muzzle as he passed them, carefully taking each toe to heel step. Up against the walls, the muzzles of assorted weapons systems lay next to their owners. He proceeded even more carefully now since he had no doubt entered a criminal headquarters. He contemplated leaving but decided to stick with his plan—which was to hole up on the roof since it was the tallest building only a few blocks away from the night club. He headed up the stairs.

He leaned up against a steam pipe on the roof and looked at the time on his HUD. He would do his best to get some sleep, but with the gang of criminals a few floors below him, he felt uneasy about letting down his guard. He ensured he was cloaked and rested his pistol in his lap. The sawed-off shotgun dangled from a homemade lanyard on his shoulder. There wasn't going to be any blending into the local populace for York. He was going to enter the club once he knew his target was inside, and he would kill him. Whether or not he would be seen doing so was transparent to his success because everything would return to its natural state once Michael was killed.

*   *   *

Todd woke to the sound of honking horns in the street below. He sat up, glancing at the old clock on the nightstand. On the other side of the room,; Kara lay facing away from him, sleeping on her side beneath the thin white sheet. Rubbing his tired eyes, the reality of day began to set in. Tonight, was it; he would be forced into one of the most difficult predicaments of his life. If he succeeded, his success would no doubt be owed completely to Kara. Once she convinced York not to go through with his dark agenda, he and she would most likely say their goodbyes to Todd, and Kara would be gone, out of his life forever. Although he tried to tell himself otherwise, this was slowly becoming his greatest fear. Beyond death, and the fear of never having existed, somehow Kara had become his only priority. His focus and overall grasp on the task at hand had become blurred due to her presence.

He stood up and stretched out his arms. He walked to the bathroom and flicked on the light. Looking at his reflection in the mirror, he saw the bruising in his cheeks and lips had finally subsided, but his body still bore many scars and bruises from the fall. He began washing his face, forgetting that Kara had been sleeping only a few feet away. He quickly shut off the fast-spraying water and peeked back into the room. She was now awake and her eyes were trained on him. He pulled a towel from the rack and dried his face, briefly glancing back at her. Beneath the white sheet, he couldn't help but notice how much color her once pale skin had inherited from Florida's tropical climate. It only added to her overwhelming beauty and made it harder for him to accept the impending future, that he would not have her company much longer.

She slowly sat up, stretching out her arms above her head and turning towards the sun shining through the window. She smiled, then looked over at Todd, who stood next to his bed pulling on a shirt.

"Good morning," she said, brushing away her bangs.

Todd turned and returned her greeting with a small smile. She stood up, pulling the sheets away from her bare legs and standing on the balls of her small feet as she walked over to the bathroom. Todd couldn't help but watch her pass as he pushed his head through the neck hole of his t-shirt. She closed the door very softly behind her and he could hear the shower turn on. He continued getting dressed, running through the endless amount of scenarios in his head of how the night could play out. The more he thought about it, the more nervous he became. Any sort of confrontation in the club could alarm Michael's employers, and if they were the typical drug lord types, they wouldn't hesitate to kill Michael under the assumption that he was either unreliable, had been pinched, or that he had flipped on them. There were a lot of possible scenarios with an endless number of outcomes. It was all extraordinarily overwhelming. Never in his life had he been so nervous on an Op, and never had he felt that the stakes were so high, even when it was the fate of mankind resting on his shoulders in the dark future. Nothing compared to this.

Kara emerged from the bathroom wearing a damp tank top, her skin still speckled with beads of water. She walked over to her bed, drying her hair. Todd did his best to not watch her as he aimlessly stared at the MTX, but could not help himself as she ran the towel down her smooth legs. The more he thought about it, the more it became apparent that Kara was quickly becoming a dangerous distraction. He told himself he shouldn't have brought her along. He knew that if he had come alone, all his attention and focus would be on the mission at hand; he would only have himself to take care of. However, he couldn't lie to himself anymore, for the feelings he had described as York's the night prior were that of his own.

She looked up to see him staring at her. She looked down at herself, then back up at him. There was silence in the room, yet neither broke it Finally, Todd stood up slowly and placed his hands in his pockets.

"You know, I've been thinking …" he said.

Kara blinked, shaking her head slightly as if she were snapping herself out of a daze.

"Judging by some of the people we saw last night going into that club … I think we're going to have to do some clothes shopping," he grinned.

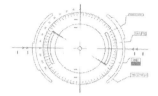

TROUBLE IN PARADISE

It had been an impatient and stressful event refueling Odin and gathering supplies back at the facility. Albrecht had been relentless with D and his aircrew as they rushed to prepare the aircraft for the long flight back to Miami. Albrecht felt an uncomfortable amount of stress, more than he usually allowed himself to feel.

The plan was to get airborne as soon as possible to time travel back to 1986 once again and send a transmission to Todd's MTX, warning him of Borden's intent. He shut off his computer in horror and briskly walked out of his office and down the hallway to the stairwell where Amber was waiting for him.

"We are just about ready, Professor," Amber said, her hands behind her back.

"Good, we need to get back to that year as soon as possible," he said, walking past her without making eye contact.

Amber lowered her head. She had rarely seen Albrecht so flustered. The last time she had seen him like this was when York had escaped to the past, and his demeanor brought a sickening feeling in her stomach. She had a feeling that something bad was about to happen. No matter how technologically advanced they had become, they couldn't change the fact that the world was an evil place. Living in the facility for so long had brought a feeling of immunity and isolation from the rest of the world. It was instances such as this that brought them back to reality.

"Brian!" she called out.

He stopped on the landing and looked back up at her. He exhaled and his eyes softened, no doubt realizing he wasn't acting like his usual self.

"Yes?" he asked softly.

She took a step down towards him. "Do you think Bohden will try to kill him ... the second Todd, that is?"

His lips pressed together firmly. "Bohden will do anything to survive. I should have let him go a long time ago. If Todd disappears ..." He fought back tears. "Then Kara will be out there all alone."

Amber took a deep breath. "Why did you let Kara go with Todd? You knew that it could be dangerous. Why would you protect her like you have for so long, only to let her go?"

He breathed out through his nose, almost sounding aggravated. "Because I have come to terms with the truth that I should have accepted a long time ago ... the future cannot be changed, and the only way for us to survive to is to get as far away from it as possible. Right now ... they are all converging on the same place, and if we don't hurry, we will not be able to warn Todd of Steven's intentions."

*   *   *

Todd sped south down Collins Avenue, feeling as if he were late to something to which he had no idea was even going to take place. He glanced over at Kara for what seemed like the hundredth time. It was painfully difficult not to stare at her in her long-sleeved silver mini dress. Her hair was flared out with sweetly smelling products and her piercing eyes were darkened and intensified, surrounded by light purple eye shadow.

It wasn't who she was, both she and Todd knew it, but it brought out a different perspective on her physical perfection. Todd wore a dark grey suit with the jacket undone and the sleeves rolled up to his forearms. Instead of a dress shirt beneath, he wore a black t-shirt. He was skeptical of this when he tried on the outfit, being that the style would never fly in his day, but the tailor had insisted and Todd finally gave in.

Although he wasn't exactly comfortable with what he was wearing, he completely forgot about the whole ordeal once Kara emerged from the women's department. The woman who did her hair had taken great pride in the finished product and seemed very interested in Kara. Naturally they had sparked conversation during the session and very quickly a mother-daughter type of friendship had formed.

He parked several blocks away due to the lack of parking near the club, and he and Kara walked the rest of the way. He continued to glance back as they walked casually down the sidewalk. He was nervous as hell, and he was having a hard time keeping a relaxed demeanor as he checked every alleyway and eyed every individual who passed them. Kara could sense his nervousness. She felt the entire world was watching them stroll down the street, side by side awkwardly.

"Todd ..." she said.

"Yep?" he replied, not making eye contact and continuing to look around as if any moment they would be attacked.

Her lips pursed as she held back a smile. She then grabbed his right arm, holding onto him the way couples would. Todd looked down at her with a shocked expression, and his pace suddenly slowed. Her smile grew, and their walk became more casual, with her clinging onto his arm and him blushing like a boy in grade school. Suddenly the world around them seemed to melt back into its natural state, as if they had finally concocted the proper camouflage to blend into their environment. His attention was now no longer on their surroundings as he stared down at the passing sidewalk, his hands in his hip pockets.

"You should relax more often," she giggled. "Not everyone is trying to catch you off guard."

"Well you just did." Todd grinned.

"I'm simply trying to help us blend in. Must you be so distant and cold all the time?" she asked with a playful scowl, trying to imitate his constant expression.

"Well ... why don't you warm me up? he said with a devious grin.

Kara's lips curved up, and she grasped his arm ever so slightly harder. Todd could feel a flurry of prickly warmth throughout his body. He pondered on her nonverbal response in silence for a while. The mission at hand completely took the backseat as his conversation with Kara now required his full attention and focus. He was now choosing words carefully, putting together a well-thought-out sentence in his head. However, she broke the silence first.

"Have you ever ... been with someone before?" she asked.

He was caught off guard by this question. He didn't want to lie and say no in order to make her pity him, but he also somewhat feared telling her the truth. The truth being that he never could keep a relationship because women found him to be too internal and eventually selfish in his apparent lack of interest towards them. The mystery that they were initially drawn to eventually subsided and very quickly became an awkward lack of sociability on his part.

He scratched his chin and snorted. "Um ..."

"Well?" Kara asked, leaning into him slightly.

He chuckled. "Jeez ... Not really. I mean ... I've gone on dates before while on leave, and well ..." he struggled to find the right words.

"What's that like?" Kara asked.

Todd was taken aback by her child-like curiosity. He looked down at her; her eyes were locked on him; eagerly awaiting an answer. "Dates? Gosh. I don't know. Usually for me they're pretty awkward."

"Why?" she asked.

Todd laughed. "I don't know ... because she and I almost always have absolutely nothing in common. I'm not really sure ... wait ..." He stopped walking and looked at her. "You're telling me that you have never ... ever been on a date with someone or at least had some sort of significant other?"

"No," she said bashfully. She brushed a hair out of her eyes. "Is that strange?'

Todd started walking again, pondering her confession. "No ..." he said, his eyebrows raised in amazement. "Not at all. Honestly, I think that is a good thing." He shook his head, almost appearing as if he were angry with himself. "So many people waste so much of their lives chasing things that in the end bring them nothing but heartbreak." He shook his head once more, pressing his lips together and staring out at the lit skyscrapers in the distance. "I wasted my entire life pursing something that I knew would one day kill me. Twelve years ... twelve years of my life given to people who never gave a damn about me, and in the end all I am left with is dead friends and worthless medals."

They stopped walking once more. Kara let go of his arm, her hands returning to their usual spot—fumbling in front of her. His self-loathing always saddened her. She had seen it enough over the past six years with York.

"But you ..." he said.

She looked up at him, becoming nervous as he spoke of her.

"You're a rare breed, Kara. Special. You are so kind, and beautiful in every way ... it kills me to see you so unhappy. You deserve everything you want in life. Someday you are going to meet someone who will give you that. And all I can hope is that he is as perfect as you are."

She looked down at her feet, her cheeks rosy and her palms beginning to sweat from gripping her hands together so tightly. She looked back up at him, finding his gaze upon her had not moved.

"What about you?" she asked.

"What about me?"

"Don't you deserve to be happy as well?" She stepped towards him slightly.

He didn't answer. As if his own bitterness had drawn his attention down the street, he sighed and looked to see the nightclub's blue neon lights glowing only a few hundred meters away.

"We better get going," he said. He turned and started down the street. She followed him, watching as his stride started to increase. She once again grabbed his arm, forcing him to slow down. This time he seemed almost irritated but complied nonetheless.

The line in front of the club was not as long as Todd had expected. It was nearing midnight and most of the attendees were most likely already inside. He decided that he and Kara would simply enter like everyone else, seeing that the wait was minimal and there was no real reason to break in unless they were denied entry. It took them a little less than half an hour to finally get in. They were greeted by a heavy-set bouncer and Michael Jacksons "Beat It" as they entered. Todd stopped near the entrance and took a quick moment to ascertain the layout of the place. Overall the place was a giant circle; the dance floor was in the dead center and heavily crowded with lavishly dressed people dancing to the blaring music.

On the outer edge of the dance floor was a silver railing which separated the dance floor from the small tables that encircled it. A clear walkway separated the tables from the booths that lined the walls with large mirrors above them, reflecting the beams of light emitting from the ceiling.

With Kara on his arm, Todd first made his way over to the bar. He skillfully pushed his way through the screaming and hollering crowd and ordered himself a glass of bourbon and a martini for Kara. The two then found an open table which overlooked the dance floor and sat down. Neither of them took a drink; instead, Kara watched as Todd scanned the entire building and all its occupants like a predator. He had no idea what his father would have looked like. For all he knew, he had a mustache and a mullet on this night.

Kara slowly and aimlessly stirred her drink, resting her head in her other hand. Todd continued to eye the crowd like a hawk, grasping his drink between both his hands on the table. He was determined to pick out Michael as quickly as possible so that he could ensure his safety. He had done personal protection detail before while with CAG and in doing so he had grown to despise it. Not only was it usually a boring assignment, it was usually also a pain in the ass, as the planning process in preparation and the coordination with outside agencies was always a difficult feat. Not to mention that individuals usually under protection were snobby politicians who didn't deserve protection in the first place.

Kara seemed almost irritated with him. She watched him as he rotated in his chair, looking at the individuals sitting in the booths behind them. Her irritation led her to finally ask the question that had been lingering on her mind since they had left Odin.

"Have I done something wrong?" she asked.

Todd turned back to face her, looking confused by the question. "Huh?" he said, shaking his head.

"It seems that every time we have a conversation about one another, you end it very sternly and abruptly," she said, her eyes narrow.

The song ended and transitioned to Cyndi Lauper's "Time After Time," making it easier to hear the exasperation in her soft voice. This intimidated him slightly, causing him to feel an almost intriguing nervousness. Rarely was she so direct with her questions, but he had come to learn that she had an almost supernatural ability to derive the truth from him using nothing more than her sincere curiosity.

He looked out into the crowd and noticed their sporadic movements had slowed exponentially in order to match the song. "I, uh ... I guess I'm just not very good at socializing with ..."

"That's not it," she said, cutting him off. "I have done something, or perhaps said something that has resulted in your bitterness towards me." Her eyes stayed fixed on him. "I want to know what that is. You brought me here, knowing the dangers that could possibly lay ahead, and knowing that I could prove to be nothing more than a hindrance. Yet you asked me. So, what have I done to cause such a disconnection between us?"

Never had she been so forward with him, and never had she been so passive-aggressive. Todd felt like a child who had been caught red-handed. He felt vulnerable and defenseless against her. He no longer felt as though he were wearing his impenetrable armor. He stared at his hands that wrapped around the small glass of bourbon. He couldn't think of a way out of this conversation that didn't result in the disclosure of his most personal feelings.

"Is it York?" she asked bluntly.

His eyes shot up to meet hers. She continued. "Is it because I told you that I love him ... or perhaps because of our conversation last night?"

Todd didn't say a word; he continued to stare at her somberly, lips pressed together, his heart pounding in his chest.

She looked down at the table, shaking her head. "I was wrong to say you and he are alike. You're two completely different people indeed. But the one thing you two have in common is your self-induced guilt. You both spend so much time criticizing and critiquing your every action so harshly ... so focused inward ..." She looked up at him, lowering her voice. "That you miss what is right in front of you."

She canted her head. "Like our conversation last night ... and how you most certainly misinterpreted it, and perhaps you have misinterpreted my love for 'him' as well." She exhaled and her eyes briefly traced around him then back to him, as if her chips had run out, forcing her to finally confess to something. "I asked you what you felt last night, but not because I am interested in what York feels towards me."

The creases on Todd's forehead disappeared, and he slowly slid back into his chair.

A small smile formed on her face, and her eyes softened. "I suppose … I too am not very good at socializing."

Todd's heart fluttered in his chest and his mind began to race, but before he could completely process her statement, a man wearing a white linen suit walked up to Kara.

"Would you like to dance?" the man asked.

Under no circumstance would Kara agree to such an offer. Especially since it was given by a stranger and was far unlike her personality. But for some odd reason, when she looked up to see the man asking the question, it appeared as if something inside her clicked, and she nodded in agreement. Todd snapped out of his motionless state and looked up at the man with irritation. Beneath his white blazer, he wore a pink shirt with the collar popped up and practically every button undone. He wore dark aviators, the rims hidden by his shaggy blonde hair. Todd felt like pummeling him for even thinking he had the right to be in Kara's presence. He felt his body begin to tense up as he scrutinized every movement he made towards her.

The man reached out his hand and she took it, seeming as if she were not acting out of her own will. She gave Todd one last look before she turned away. A look that both concerned and confused him, appearing as if she were trying to tell him something. He stood up quickly, watching as they made their way to the dance floor, the man holding her hand. Todd watched them push through the thick crowd beneath the beams of different colored light. His jaw and fists flexed. He looked up across the room, motion catching his attention. On the far wall in the private booth sat a large group of well-dressed Hispanic men. Their eyes were fixated on Kara. He leaned up against the steel railing, watching them closely.

The music changed to "What is Love" by Haddaway, and the crowd roared in excitement. Todd watched as the Hispanic men spoke in each other's ear, no doubt talking about Kara and the man who accompanied her. He began following the railing, slowly circling the dance floor, his eyes not leaving Kara's observers.

But then his attention was stolen as the man with Kara closed the gap between her and himself, dancing in a conservative manner, as if he were merely warming up to his true potential. Kara seemed nervous; she stood in front of him, watching him, her hands nervously moving from her hips to fumbling in front of her. Her hips then began swaying back and forth and she slowly ran her hands up her body. A clear sense of enjoyment seemed to present itself as her movements became more fluid.

Todd moved laterally through the observing crowd, his eyes not leaving her. His first instinct had been to go down to her, but upon seeing that she was now enjoying herself he maintained his distance and her smile brought out his own. She ran her hands up her body, then into her hair, stopping near the top of her head. She continued to sway back and forth, her hips and head flowing side to side. Her smile grew and her eyes were closed as if she would have been content being the only person dancing. There wasn't a single thing about her that Todd wasn't attracted to. Her ability to step out of her comfort zone to either blend in or make Todd jealous had him hypnotized.

The Hispanic men then chuckled to one another, and the man who was dancing with Kara gave them a quick wave. Suddenly, Todd had a realization. The men in the corner were no doubt dealers, and the man with Kara was clearly an acquaintance. Todd stepped up to the railing and looked at the man closely. As if it had been rehearsed, while continuing to move her body, in a brilliant and smooth fashion, Kara moved the man's glasses to the top of his head, combing his long hair out of his eyes at the same time. It was then that Todd realized that Kara was far more observant than even he was. The man she was with was his twenty-five-year-old father.

Todd's eyes widened as he began to recognize him. No doubt interpreting her action as attraction, Michael pulled Kara in close, holding her by the small of her back. Kara seemed slightly uncomfortable by his advance, yet she placed her hand on his abdomen between his jacket and his shirt, then ran it down to his hip.

Michael looked down at her hand and smiled. "What's your name, babe?"

Kara pulled her hand away from his hip quickly, her hand in a fist. "Kara," she said sweetly.

"Nice to meet you, Kara. So, tell me … who's the stiff you came with?" He chuckled. "Boyfriend?"

"Just a friend," she said, looking up at Todd, who observed them like a hawk. She could see his surprised expression. She desperately wanted him to come down to them.

Michael looked up at Todd with an arrogant glare. "Looks like he's a little upset."

Todd was so fixated that it took him a moment before he felt a small vibration in his pocket. He reached down, pulling the MTX from his coat. Shielding it in his hands in an effort to conceal it, he pressed the screen to see that a new message had been received.

URGENT!

TODD, BE ADVISED. BOHDEN HAS FOLLOWED YOU AND INTENDS TO INTERVENE. I'M NOT SURE WHAT HE IS PLANNING TO DO, BUT HE FEELS THAT HIS LIFE IS IN DANGER AND THERE IS NO TELLING HOW FAR HE WILL GO TO ENSURE MICHAEL'S SAFETY. PLEASE BE CAREFUL, PLEASE TAKE CARE OF KARA.

~BRIAN

Todd felt a sickening feeling in his stomach. He looked up at Kara, and their eyes met briefly. Michael turned her away from him, forcing her attention towards himself.

"Well, my name is …"

"Michael," she interrupted.

Their movements ceased, and Michael stared at her suspiciously, his dark eyes shadowed by the flashing lights. "What the … how do you know my name?"

The center of the crowd behind them seemed to stop moving in sections, as it was split down the center, someone hastily forcing their way through towards Kara and Michael.

Bohden sidestepped his way through the heart of the dancing crowd, the pink and purple lights making it difficult to maintain visual of his target. He had tracked him since he had arrived at the club and figured it was now or never. Michael had his back to him, concealing Kara. He ensured his pistol was accessible in the back of his waist band beneath his leather jacket. Once he was within arm's reach, he grabbed Michael by the shoulder and turned him around quickly.

"Michael York?" he yelled over the loud music.

Michael looked shocked; he looked at Kara and then at Bohden once more.

"Kara?" Bohden said, surprised to see her.

Michael quickly broke away from Bohden's grip and began shoving people out of his way as he headed towards the back exit. Bohden quickly turned and started after him. Todd was now forcing his way past the large group at the bar to get down to the dance floor. The large group of Hispanics stood up and yelled to one another, seeing that one of their traffickers had most likely been caught by law enforcement. One pulled a MAC 10 from his coat. Holding it down at his waist, he leveled it at Bohden who was still in the center of the crowd.

"Kara, get down!" Todd screamed.

Bohden pulled his Five Seven from his waist and quickly shot the man in the head, spraying the mirror behind him with brain matter. Screams erupted throughout the club, and people began running for the exit in a half-crouch. Bohden held his pistol at the ready, pushing people out of his way to get a clear shot at the cartel members. However, one of their posse had been at the bar during the confrontation and was now drawing a silver 1911 from his waist. Holding it in one hand, he aimed at Bohden.

Todd grabbed his arm right as he fired and forced the gun up towards the ceiling, then smashed his elbow into his nose. Todd quickly glanced back towards the dance floor, trying to find Kara, but the panicking crowd obscured his line of sight. Rotating the man's arm backwards, Todd forced the man's shoulder to the ground, prying the gun from his hand at the same time. While forcefully stepping down on the back of his neck, he quickly pulled back the slide just enough to see the brass casing of a fresh round and then fired it into the back of the man's head.

Todd turned just in time to see one of the bouncer's fists coming at him. He ducked but just slightly too late, as the man's knuckles scraped the back of his head, causing him to drop to his hands and knees. Bullets from a MAC 10 submachine gun began shattering the mirrors and bottles of liquor behind the bar and cut through the bouncer's chest and neck. A cartel member had retrieved the submachine gun from the ground and was now firing wildly. Assuming he had hit Todd, he orientated himself towards Kara, who he must have believed was undercover. Kara was picking herself up when she noticed the man aiming at her. In a matter of milliseconds Todd had seen this panning out and was on his feet, sprinting towards her. Kara gasped as the MAC 10 started spitting rounds at her. She moved her arm up to her face and flinched. Todd felt his heart stop as he was only a few feet from her and he came skidding to a stop.

The bullets seemed to spark and ricochet off of thin air in front of her. She lowered her arm, unsure of what had just happened. The sprinkler system within the building burst on, showering the interior of the flashy club. The shifting beams of light shone through the water-drenched outline of a transparent figure standing above her. Her eyes widened. Suddenly, in one smooth motion, Todd swooped her up and sprinted for the back door. The man dropped the MAC 10, staring in horror at York's wet outline. A double barrel raised towards him and unloaded both tubes into his chest. The man was sent backwards into the glass table. York looked back to see Todd carrying Kara, utter confusion causing him to freeze. Rounds sparked off the steel railing behind him. York opened the chamber, sending two smoking cartridges twirling into the air. He quickly loaded two more cartridges and another criminal opened fire on him from behind a large speaker. York quickly dove for cover.

Todd carried Kara down the back steps and rushed through the parking lot. He spotted a black Mercedes, its tires squealing as it tore out of the lot. He could just faintly see Bohden in the driver's seat.

"I'm alright," Kara said.

Todd seemed unable to let her go. His arms were like a steel frame. He knelt, still cradling her. He examined her limbs frantically, checking for wounds. Cool drops of rain began to tap the dark pavement.

"Todd ..." she said softly, "I'm okay." She smiled. "Do all your dates end this way?"

His hands stopped combing over her, and he brushed the wet hair out of her eyes. "Scared me." He exhaled, his breathing starting to slow. "We need a car ... quick!" he said, looking up at the few cars still left in the parking lot.

Kara held up a closed fist to him. She opened her fingers, revealing a set of keys. Todd looked at them and then at her in shock. Her lips pursed as she held back a smile. Todd chuckled at her cunning, realizing she had snatched Michael's keys during their dance. He took the keys from her and helped her to her feet. He examined the keys in his hand. It was a single ring with only two keys attached to it. One being a car key, the other most likely belonged to some sort of lock box. Attached to the ring was a silver horse in mid-sprint.

"Now we just have to figure out which car it belongs to," Kara said.

Todd looked up at the back of the lot. His eyes instantly fixated upon something. He didn't bother examining the other vehicles for he already knew the answer to their problem. A grin crept onto Todd's face. Kara looked at him with a confused expression, then looked where he was staring.

"Hello, Esprit," he said.

In the back corner of the lot, concealed by the shadows and assisted by its sleek black color was a 1967 Shelby Mustang. A smile grew on Todd's face, as if Esprit Libre had returned, reincarnated into this powerful machine to assist him once again only in a different era. He took Kara's hand and they ran to the car. He unlocked the door and stepped inside, Kara ran around and got in the passenger seat. He quickly turned the engine over, and it roared to life. He backed out of the enclosed lot and shifted into first gear, bolting down the road in the direction Bohden had gone. The car emitted a deep rumble as he coasted to an intersection. Traffic was scarce and he glanced to his front and to his left down the adjacent streets.

"I see him!" Kara said, looking out her window.

Todd tore through the intersection and sped down the two-lane street, weaving in between traffic on both sides. Horns blared and headlights flashed him as he swerved in and out of oncoming vehicles.

"It's a miracle you are alive. That guy must have been a terrible shot!" Todd said over the loud engine, continuing to jerk the wheel to each side and work the manual transmission.

"It was York," she said.

Todd briefly looked over at her, to the road and then at her again. "What? He was there?"

"Yes."

*   *   *

York dropped the empty shotgun and ran for the back exit. He cleared the doorway with his M9 then hopped the railing, absorbing the fall with a roll. He could hear sirens not too far off. He desperately searched for an accessible vehicle. The high-pitched whine of a street bike could be heard approaching. He sprinted to the sidewalk to see a rider speeding towards him. Balling up his fist, York lowered his center of gravity and, just as the rider passed him, he rammed his forearm into the rider's visor, knocking him off of the bike. He picked the bike up and jumped on, then sped off down the road following the multiple tire marks. He could faintly see the taillights of what he assumed was his target swerving between cars a half mile ahead of him.

He was still in disbelief that he had seen Kara. Why on earth would she be here? And who had been the man with her? Had Brian found another Todd York after the last one had died in the fall in 1887?

His mind was in utter chaos as he was overwhelmed with confusion. He also thought he had seen Bohden. What was going on?

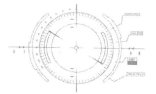

CHASE

The sirens were becoming louder in the distance, and he could faintly see the flashing of blue and red lights on the sides of buildings as he turned each tight corner in an effort to lose his pursuers. Michael was panicking in the backseat, sliding from window to window, watching for the cops.

"Man, I really owe you one," he said, gazing out the back window. "So, who are you? You work for Mrs. Blanco?"

"No," Bohden snapped. "I'm with the CIA, and I'm here to ensure your safety."

"Me?" he asked with utter confusion. "Why would the CIA want to protect me?"

"I know about what you do, Mr. York, and I'm not interested in your choice of employment. All I care about is you not getting killed tonight."

"Oh fuck ... fuck!" Michael cried out. "I knew I should have called it after the last job. Goddamnit!" he yelled, his breathing beginning to speed up to the point of nearly hyperventilating.

"Calm down!" Bohden screamed as he stepped on the gas as he came out of a turn and straightened out on a long stretch of road. "I'm not letting anything bad happen to you."

"Who were those people back there ... at the club?" Michael asked. "What do they want with me?

Bohden refrained from answering out of annoyance and considering he would have to concoct an elaborate lie to avoid the unbelievable truth. "All you need to know is I'm your best chance of survival tonight."

*   *   *

The engine's high-pitch cry echoed through the streets as York leaned side to side to achieve the tight turns that his target was making. His HUD was beginning to cut in and out with dark static. The large crack down the left side of the visor let in drops of rain, spraying his exposed eye and forced him to squint, further impairing his eyesight. The cloaking ability on the suit was no longer functioning due to the amount of external damage to the suit's outer skin. The armored chest of the suit was all but diminished due to the hail of bullets he had received in the club. He now even doubted the suit's ability to time travel. Yet it didn't matter, for he did not intend to utilize it.

His mission had not changed, yet his state of mind was not as it should be. Seeing Kara at the nightclub was all he could think about. What was she doing there? Had she come along with Bohden and the other Todd York? Even if that was so, why would Brian send three people? He was still dedicated to his agenda and would do anything to achieve his goal; however, the thought of Kara's life being put in jeopardy deeply troubled him. He gripped the throttle tightly, and the taillights of the Mustang came into view. Suddenly, his attention was drawn to his rear-view mirror above the throttle. The flashing lights of a police cruiser reflected off the circular mirror. He looked back over his shoulder briefly. He could see two police officers within the vehicle.

Drawing his M9 from his hip holster, maintaining control of the handle bars and gas with his right hand, he leaned back and presented the weapon at the car. The officers inside began to frantically adjust in their seats, attempting to draw their service pistols. York fired five rounds at the front left tire. It exploded and the cruiser was sent into a hard-left turn, the hood engulfing a light post on the sidewalk. He turned around, reclaiming both handles, and lifted the gear lever with his left toe, shifting into the next gear and speeding up along the straightaway.

*   *   *

The Mercedes rounded yet another turn; Bohden was no doubt trying to utilize the many turns to lose Todd. Todd stepped down hard on the brakes, gritting his teeth as he had missed the tight turn made by Bohden. He quickly shifted into reverse and whipped the car around, speeding after him. However, he could no longer see him on the long stretch of road. The rain streamed down the speckled windshield, causing the many lights from the city to glare off the small drops. Kara gripped the door tightly as Todd pushed the gas pedal to the floor board.

"I don't see him anymore! Why is he trying to lose us?" she said over the loud engine.

"I don't know. I'm thinking he doesn't trust either York or me," replied Todd.

Todd glanced in the rear-view mirror to see a single headlight growing behind them. He continued to look back at it as it came closer, the glare of the bright light beginning to wash out the mirror. Todd looked in the side mirror to see York whip off to the side of the Mustang. He shifted into the next gear, hoping to create a gap between them. York drew his M9 once again, holding it out to the side at Todd. He closed the gap between the bike and the car. He held the pistol at a slight cant, trying to steady his aim on Todd's head. Every imperfection on the road made it difficult for him to keep the front sight locked on him. With his free hand on the throttle, he eased the handlebars towards the car, slowly closing the gap.

He could faintly see two people inside: a driver and a passenger. However, the rain obscured his vision and he assumed Michael would be lying down in the back seat. He pulled his pistol and inched closer to the car, trying to see the back seat. Todd jerked the wheel to the left. York quickly turned to avoid the collision but was too late and the two collided. The bike was forced towards the sidewalk, the front wheel wobbled out of control, and York was thrown off the bike as it was laid down on its side. The pavement bit him hard as he crashed into it, rolling until his body smashed into a dumpster.

The Mustang took a hard left, then straightened out on a long stretch of road that skirted a narrow river. Todd peered in the rear-view mirror, then briefly over his shoulder. "Shit!" he said. "The cops are on us."

Kara was frantically tapping on the MTX, scrolling through the digital map of Miami. "He cannot be far. He was heading north on Collins Avenue ... we're currently on Indian Creek Drive. The two roads eventually merge only a few blocks from here!" she said excitedly, looking over at Todd.

"Okay," Todd replied with a small grin.

Sirens, and the slamming of doors caused York to slowly lift himself off the ground. He raised his head, blood seeping through his gritted teeth. The suit was badly damaged with abrasion-covered flesh exposed. Two police officers approached him, .357 pistols trained on him. He slowly rose to his knees, placing his hands on the top of his head.

"What the hell?" one of officers said, seeing the unworldly suit.

"Stay down!" the other yelled. "Keep your hands where I can see them!"

The officer pulled his radio from his belt, slightly dropping his fix on York. "This is Unit Six! We have a possible suspect in custody; requesting ..."

Suddenly, York lunged forward, pulling the officer's extended arm over his shoulder and throwing him to the ground. The other jumped back quickly, firing a round into the wall behind York. York quickly grabbed the weapon with both hands and forced his back to the man, prying the weapon from his hands. He quickly cocked the hammer and aimed in on the police officer who cowered on the ground at his feet. He aimed the weapon at his forehead.

"Please ... don't," the man pleaded, his hands raised.

From the open window of the squad car, York could hear the squawking sound of the department's dispatch. "All units, be advised we have a high-speed vehicle heading north on Collins avenue. Requesting any available units to intercept."

York looked back down at the man. It then occurred to him that there was no reason to kill him. Sure, whatever he did this night would be undone once Michael died, but there was no need for any more collateral damage. He dropped his aim and quickly walked to the police cruiser. He opened the door and stepped in. The car took off down the road, the sirens still echoing through the streets. He took the first left which put him on Indian Creek Drive. He pressed the gas pedal to the floor and the buildings whipped past, the wind booming through the open window. Taking one hand off the wheel, he quickly pulled the helmet off of his head and tossed it into the passenger seat. His long bangs stuck to the blood oozing from the gash above his eye. Pain throughout his body was becoming overwhelming.

Todd slowed to almost cruising speed as the Mercedes came to an abrupt stop only a few hundred meters down the road in front of him. He could see two figures rush out of the vehicle and into the tall building that loomed above them. Todd came to a quick stop, examining the building where they had entered. A few brief moments of moonlight assisted in his observation. It was a rundown-looking place. Graffiti was visible on almost every floor of the dark building. The top floor looked to have once been under construction but had never been finished as there was visible space between the roof and the floor below it.

Todd coasted to a stop next to the sidewalk. He turned off the ignition and pulled the silver 1911 from his waist. "Look ..." he said, quickly examining the magazine which only contained five rounds. "I need you to stay here. Stay out of sight." He reinserted the magazine and checked the chamber for the sixth round. He quickly opened the door and stepped out into the pouring rain.

"Todd!" Kara pleaded.

"Please, Kara," he said, looking back into the dimly lit cabin of the Mustang. Her saddened eyes caused him to question his own judgment. "I can't let anything happen to you. I have to make sure Bohden keeps Michael safe. I'll be right back."

He took one last look at her. Every part of him wished the circumstances were not as they were. He wished he could stay with her, not only in this moment, but for eternity. His heart ached in his chest, but his conscience told him to hurry and get into the building. He shut the door and sprinted to what appeared to be a fire exit in the alleyway. He popped the door open, checking the dark corners of the stairwell before him, and began ascending the stairs.

CONFRONTATION

Bohden held his breath at the landing of the fifth floor. Michael squatted behind him. Their sprint had come to an abrupt halt at the sound of yelling and movement from the floors above. They heard thunderous footsteps of multiple individuals and the banging of hardware, probably weapons.

"What have we just stumbled into?" Bohden whispered.

He slowly pulled his pistol from his jacket and crept closer to the base of the stairs leading to the next floor. Michael crept closely behind, breathing heavily, and looking around as if he were an animal being stalked.

"What is it, man?" he asked. "Are they going to kill us?"

Bohden peeked up to the next landing to see the flickering light of fire creeping through what appeared to be a thick blanket covering a doorway. Suddenly loud voices echoed through the stairwell and multiple individuals stormed out of the room, moving quickly and yelling back and forth.

"What the fuck are the cops doing here, man?" one yelled to the other. "Don't know, but we betta ice deez fools quick."

Bohden shoved Michael back down the stairs, his gun raised. "Go, go!" he whispered. The two quickly returned to the lower landing and made their way into the interior of the building. They moved down the long dark hallway before them. Bohden kept his pistol raised, briefly checking open doorways to the abandoned hotel rooms. He felt his stomach leap up into his throat when Michael stepped on a large piece of broken glass.

"They're down here!" a voice called from the stairwell.

"Go, now!" Bohden said, shoving Michael down the hall and aiming at the door behind them. The door opened and Bohden fired several shots into it. Automatic fire erupted from the stairwell, muzzle flashes and bullet sparks lighting the dark hallway.

"Run!" Bohden screamed.

*   *   *

Todd stopped and aimed his pistol up the stairwell. The loud echoes of gunfire and screaming caused him to tighten his grip and clench his jaw. He squinted in the dark, then his eyes widened as he saw two raggedy individuals come storming down the stairs with assault rifles. He quickly identified them as neither Michael nor Bohden and fired up at them. The first man dropped and rolled down the stairs; the next managed to fire off a burst before Todd emptied the rest of the mag into him. Todd reached down and grabbed the first man's CAR 15. He checked the weapon, briefly pausing as he examined the stubby twenty-round mag. He continued up the stairs with the weapon resting in his shoulder. The gunshots from above were becoming louder and more frequent. His heart pounded in his chest and adrenaline was rushing through him, making his movements quicker and his demeanor more aggressive. He arrived at the fifth floor, where he found a dead man lying on the landing. He looked up at the door and could see that he had been shot through it. He bypassed the door and continued up the stairwell.

*   *   *

York stumbled out of the squad car and towards the Mustang. He cradled his stomach, wincing as he realized his ribs felt broken. He leaned up against the car and peered inside, seeing that it was empty. He held the pump action shotgun from the squad car's cabin in his free hand. His shoulder slumped low. Looking over the roof of the Mustang, he could see an open door just down the alley that led to a stairwell access. He looked up at the building in front of him. It was the same one he had spent the night in the night prior. "Of all the places ..." he muttered. He limped down the alley, occasionally looking up as he heard the sound of gunfire. As he entered the dark building, the sounds of screams and the cracks of bullets caused him to stop at the base of the stairs. He held onto the railing, looking up into the darkness.

*   *   *

Bullets from above caused Todd to dive through the door on the sixth floor. He landed, orienting his muzzle down the long hallway. He scrambled to his feet and rushed down the hallway. He heard commotion from behind him. He whipped around quickly, dropping to a knee, and fired four shots into a gang member at the doorway. Another entered through the doorway and sprayed wildly with a Tec 9 machine pistol. Todd aimed in but the trigger felt mushy as he squeezed it and the weapon didn't fire. "Shit!" He quickly kicked in the door to an empty room as bullets zipped down the hallway behind him. He knelt down and pulled on the charging handle. It didn't budge, meaning the empty casing from the last round he'd fired was stuck in the chamber. Suddenly, a figure entered the doorway.

The man yelled, "Gotch you, you mutha …"

Todd stood up and forcefully smashed the butt stock into the man's face, simultaneously using the momentum to rip the charging handle back and extract the empty casing. The man fell to the ground, grunting in pain. Todd fired two rounds into his chest then moved back out into the hallway. He looked down both sides, then sprinted to the adjacent stairwell access. He popped open the metal door and was greeted once again by a volley of fire. He waited for a lull in the fire and then crept up the stairs, shooting four to five rounds into each man as he processed them.

The CAR 15's bolt locked back and he dropped it to the floor, picking up a UZI 9mm submachine gun. He extended the collapsible stock and continued up the stairs, firing small automatic bursts into the gang members.

Finally, he came to the ninth floor. It was cleaner than the others, as it was no doubt newer and had seen less unwelcome occupants. He burst through the door to find himself in an open floor with no walls on either side. Unfinished concrete pillars and exposed rebar made up the walls. Abandoned floor plans and construction equipment littered the floor. The rain had stopped and the sky was beginning to lighten, pink and orange light cresting over the dark waters on the horizon.

Amongst the few drops of water, Todd could hear the sound of footsteps from above. He quickly climbed a stack of rotting lumber and leapt to an open hole in the roof. Pulling himself up, he spotted Bohden, who was stripping off his leather jacket and exposing the sleek black suit beneath. Michael stood beside him, a bewildered look upon him.

"Bohden!" Todd yelled.

Bohden turned quickly and fired, the bullet striking Todd in the chest. Todd felt the wind immediately become pulled from his lungs and he fell back onto the hard concrete. He gasped for air but felt only the intensifying beat of his heart and the desperate need for oxygen. He tried to pick himself up, his hand touching a warm pool of blood forming around him. His eyes widened as he touched the burning bullet wound below his left collar bone. He trembled slightly, then looked back up at Bohden.

Bohden turned and began fixing the cable lanyard around a thin pillar near the edge of the roof. Michael watched in horror, looking at Todd in confusion. Was it the fact that he had seen him in the club only a few hours earlier? Or perhaps something much more unexplainable. Like he was looking at someone he once knew, or maybe had yet to know and would now never have the chance. He couldn't understand why this man on the ground in front of him stole his curiosity.

"Who is he?" Michael asked.

Bohden didn't answer. He continued fixing the lanyard to his harness, then switched on his MTX and began entering in a year.

Todd stared up at the sky. The clouds had pulled back to reveal what was soon to be a new day. Only a solitary star remained visible. He stared at it, gasping for air. His mind didn't race as it once had when he was near death. He didn't think of all his pain and regret. He didn't ponder the many wasted efforts, nor did he feel the guilt that had lingered on his mind his entire life. All he thought of was …

"Kara?" Bohden said, looking to the roof access from the stairwell.

Her eyes went to Todd, and the look of horror overcame her. "Todd!" she screamed. She ran to him and dropped down beside him. Her hands combed over him, stopping at his hand, which was pressed against his chest. She pulled it away to reveal the wound. She cried out, placing her hands on it and looking at him with tears streaming down her cheeks. "Oh God no. Please no!" she cried.

Todd continued to stare up at her, a gurgling sound hidden beneath each desperate gasp for air. He raised his shaking hand towards her, his trembling fingers touching her cheek. She grasped it, holding it against her face. She opened her tear-filled eyes and looked into his. His body arched up with each throaty moan, his collapsed lung causing his chest cavity to fill with air. His quivering lips slowly curved up between the shallow breaths to form a smile. She cradled his head, continuing to plead for him.

"Please don't leave me … not again," she said.

It took every bit of strength he had left for York to pull himself on to the roof. He emerged to see Bohden with his attention elsewhere, and Michael in the open. The rising orange sun peeked over the dark ocean behind him. With the handle of the pistol, he struck Bohden in the back of the head, causing him to fall to the ground. He gritted his teeth, blood running down his face and into his beard. He raised a Tec 9 at Michael, struggling to keep the front sight on him. He shook as he aimed in at his own soon to be father. Every bit of hatred, every bit of guilt, would all be wiped clean by this man's death. He would erase himself and his mistakes from existence. His final mission was about to end.

He had spent his entire life honing his knack for survival. Developing a sense of awareness and focus that would keep him alive in the most unpredictable situations. Yet his attention was stolen away by something off the side. A sight that he had daydreamed about many times during the lulls in focus. Perhaps that was why it had distracted him, being that it had been but a mere fantasy for so many years. Holding the weapon up at Michael, with his head turned to the side, he watched as Kara cradled a dying Todd York. Kara closed her eyes, leaving Todd in want of the sight of them before he perished. Yet all the pain in his body and soul was briefly vanquished when her soft lips met his. He felt a warmth overcome him, and with the strength he had left, wrapped his arm around her. She pulled away, tears still streaming down her cheeks.

York felt something inside him. Something that if given a lifetime he could not comprehend or explain. It was in that moment of heartbreak and a flurry of emotions that an entire lifetime of mistakes could be made right. With just one decisive action in the midst of his confusion, he knew he would find his redemption this day, but not in the way he had originally intended. With tears in his eyes, he turned to see Bohden rising to his feet, raising his pistol at the wounded Todd York.

"Move, Kara!" he yelled, swaying back and forth from the recent blow, leveling his sights on Todd.

Kara turned to see York standing just behind Bohden. Her eyes widened. Not in surprise to see him, but in a desperate calling for help. Michael tried to grab the gun from York, who quickly delivered a blow to his jaw, knocking the gun out of his hands and over the edge. He kicked Michael back, turning to see Bohden raise the gun at him. Bohden fired, hitting York in the abdomen. York moved forward, grabbing the barrel of the pistol and orientating it towards the ground, smashing his forehead into Bohden's nose as the same time. Bohden grunted. Stepping back, he shook his head. He seemed surprised to finally see York. They stood facing each other, the Five Seven pistol on the ground between them.

"Todd?" Bohden said. "It's you ... the real you."

"I knew I should have left you to die that day," York said. "I've always known you were a coward."

Bohden grimaced and he lunged for the weapon. York quickly kicked it away and assisted Bohden's descent towards the ground with a throw. He grabbed him by the collar of the suit and pulled him up.

"Like a rat, you'd do anything to survive," York said, pulling him up. He grabbed the cable lanyard from Bohden's belt and let go of it. It retracted back into its housing towards the pillar.

From his hip, Bohden pulled a small blade. He turned quickly and plunged the knife into York's side. York quickly grabbed Bohden's wrist as he grunted and collapsed to his knee. In a crouched scramble, he quickly retrieved his pistol and turned and aimed at York, who was clutching the knife buried in his rib cage. He raised his shaking hand to his eyes, looking at his blood-drenched, trembling fingers. He then looked up at Bohden.

"You're not going to undo everything we've fought so hard to achieve. I won't let you," Bohden said. He paused for a second, looking around for Michael, who was nowhere to be seen. He turned back towards York and pulled the trigger. *Click.* It was only then that he realized the slide of the pistol had been locked back and it was empty.

York gave him a bloody grin. "You never were that smart either." He raised his hand, revealing the MTX which he had snagged off of Bohden's wrist. Bohden snarled and in one last desperate attempt he charged him. He smashed his shoulder into York, knocking him to the ground. He reached down, pulling the MTX from his fingers. He quickly reconnected it to his wrist and tapped the screen. The "INITIATE" button was pulsing.

Breathing heavily, Bohden looked down at York and sneered. Then he walked over to the pillar, retrieved the cable lanyard, and clipped it to his harness. He strode toward the edge of the roof. He stopped, looking over at Kara, who continued to hold Todd, and then at York, who was on his knees, cradling his bloody abdomen.

Bohden chuckled. "Looks like I didn't need to be. You're both dead anyway." He turned and leapt off the roof, pressing the button once in freefall. The screen transitioned back to the year wheel which was set on 1648. Bohden's eyes widened. He looked at the ground below him which was now a dense forest a hundred feet below. The cable lanyard was no longer attached to anything, as it was now a ten-foot cable simply trailing behind him, and he fell to his death, screaming.

York looked down at his hand which was drenched in his own blood. He picked himself up and limped over to Kara, who was still holding an almost incoherent Todd. He gently pulled her away, placing his hand on Todd's chest. Only one half of his chest cavity was rising, meaning his chest cavity was filling with air and collapsing his lung. If he didn't hurry, the other could collapse as well. He reached into his web gear and pulled out a small syringe that had an electronic valve on the end of it. He grunted as he pulled the knife from his side and used it to cut open Todd's shirt.

"Please help him," Kara pleaded, tears streaming down her cheeks.

York didn't respond. He pulled a small occlusive dressing from his web gear and peeled away the backing, then stuck it over the bullet wound and ensured it wasn't slipping on Todd's bloody chest. He paused for a moment, gritting his teeth. The bullet wound Bohden had inflicted was beginning to take hold of him. It was in his low abdomen and, combined with the knife wound and the many other injuries he had, he didn't have much time.

Using his teeth, he pulled the cap off the syringe and spat it to the side. He then jabbed the needle into Todd's chest, in between the ribs. Todd's chest instantly inflated as a whoosh of air was released out of the syringe. Todd took in a deep breath, his eyes widening as he could finally breathe. York pulled the needle from the catheter, leaving it in his chest with the valve, and discarded the needle.

Todd looked up at Kara, who had the look of hope in her eyes. He then looked over at York, who was kneeling above him, blood dripping from his hands.

Studying him, York instantly could tell that it was the same person he had encountered in the Old West. He could simply see it in his eyes. York sat down and scooted backwards until he could lean up against a concrete pillar. He searched in his webbing for anything he could use to patch his own wounds but found nothing. He breathed out somberly, yet almost in a way that displayed relief, for a life of suffering was almost over.

Kara helped Todd to his feet; she put his arm around her and the two slowly walked over to where York sat propped up against the concrete pillar. Todd leaned up against a tall bundle of rebar as Kara knelt in front of York. York slowly looked at her, and he reached his hand out towards her. She took it, trying to shake the tears from her eyes.

"Kara ..." he said with a small smile. He shook his head. "You are beautiful in every way." He looked at Todd, who leaned on his arm against the rebar, holding his chest with the other arm.

"The rancher ... did he survive?" York asked.

Todd nodded.

York then turned back towards Kara. "God ... I'd give anything to be him," he said, nodding towards Todd. "Don't ever let the world change who you are."

She stood and buried her head in Todd's shoulder. Todd closed his eyes and wrapped his arms around her. York watched as his younger self held the most beautiful girl in the world, and a smile spread across his face. "Perfect," He said. His smile then faded, and his eyes began to drift.

His head slowly drooped down to his chest and he was dead.

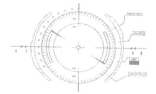

THE FUTURE

Albrecht stood on the hinge of the Odin's ramp above the slowly passing clouds. The shimmering blue of the endless ocean peeked through the scattered openings in the thick white ceiling. He looked up from the MTX which displayed the message he had just received from Kara.

He gazed out into the dawn of a new day. He felt the sadness of a man who had to let go, yet he felt the joy of someone who had found a new beginning and foresaw a bright future. He took in a deep breath of the cool air. The last forty-eight hours had been the most stressful of his entire life. Knowing that Kara's life was in danger and there was simply nothing he could do to protect her. Knowing now what Todd had done to protect her, and what York had done to save the both of them, it brought a warm feeling of reassurance that Todd York, no matter the circumstances, was not only a good man, but the right man for Kara.

Amber approached from behind him, her demeanor displaying her excitement. "Professor!" she said over the howling winds.

She came to his side, and the two gazed out into the vast skies in front of them. "What about Kara?"

"She is where she belongs," he said.

Amber looked down at the ground. "What about us?" she asked softly. "What do we do now?"

Albrecht turned towards her, took her hands, and smiled. "We go home ... our new home."

*   *   *

Michael stood in the airport terminal with only the clothes he was wearing and what cash he had left. He studied the board displaying the outgoing flights, unsure of where to go. He continued to look over his shoulder, waiting to be grabbed by somebody who knew what kind of a person he was. He had spent the early morning hours at the local police station answering a barrage of questions as to his involvement at the night club. However, due to the fact that he had been unarmed, his car had been stolen, and he had no illegal substances on his person, he was an innocent man. People passed him by as if he were a statue. In all his days, never had he yearned for a home that could bring him the isolation that he now desired. No longer did he want to live the lavish life of a selfish individual taking advantage of a loose justice system. All he wanted was the security of an honest living, and the feeling of never having to look over his shoulder everywhere he went.

"Attention all passengers for Flight 485 to Seattle. We are now boarding at Gate 3C. Please make your way to check in."

*   *   *

It had been four weeks since that night. The night when Todd's life would change forever. He had witnessed York do something that gave him a new understanding of himself. He no longer feared the future, for it was an ever-changing reality that had no set end. He had spent four weeks in a Miami hospital with a chest tube inside him. His mind had drifted in and out during his time there and it had blurred together like one painful dream. However, during his brief moments of consciousness, he would see Kara beside him. Her blue eyes never leaving him, and her smile giving him hope. She had become the reason for his existence, and he now knew what to do with the time he had.

He stood now on an isolated beach in Northern Florida, looking out at the ocean. In the hinterland behind him stood the small, unmarked grave of a man who had never existed during this time. Todd stood with his hands deep in his pockets, the crashing waves causing him to daydream and think of the many possibilities of the bright future. He took a few more moments to pay respects to a great warrior, a man he had hated, yet who had saved his life.

"Thank you," he said to himself.

He turned, a smile spreading across his face at the sight of Kara leaning against the Mustang on the side of the road. He approached her and felt warm air in his chest as she wrapped her arms around him. He kissed her, then pulled back to see her hope-filled eyes meet his. He held her for what seemed like ages. The radio behind her was emitting a deep vibrant tone that made him pause for a moment in an attempt to recognize the song that had just started.

"What now, Todd?" she asked.

The radio announcer came to life. "You're listening to 99.7. This one is for all you outlaws out there, living life day by day, always on the run. This is 'I Ran' from 'A Flock of Seagulls.'"

Todd grinned and looked out at the long stretch of road ahead of them. It then occurred to him that he had made a promise that he fully intended to keep. "I was thinking Colorado. There's a little boy I think you'd love to meet."

She smiled and kissed him once more. She then opened the passenger side door and jumped in. Todd chuckled and walked around to the back of the Mustang where the trunk was propped open. He pulled the MTX from his pocket and looked at it for a moment, contemplating the endless possibilities of the journey ahead. He dropped it inside, where it landed on both their time traveling suits.

Below the suits were multiple black cases filled with cash that Michael had no doubt intended to use for his retirement. He shut the trunk and hopped into the driver's seat, firing up the engine to the sleek black beast.

They sped down the long stretch of road with the sun rising to the east above crystal waters. The beautiful setting gave him a sense of hope that reflected a different kind of future in front of them.

A future in the past, where he would not be alone.

THE END

ABOUT THE AUTHOR

Growing up in the Pacific Northwest, Brad Raylend developed a love for the outdoors and adventure at a young age. He would eventually become a member of Marine Force Recon, and would take advantage of downtime aboard ship and on overseas deployments to write fictional stories. His extensive knowledge of firearms and combat tactics combine with his experiences in special operations to inject a level of technical authenticity into his work.

SAME SELF is his first novel. It won't be his last.

CUTTING-EDGE NAVAL THRILLERS
BY
JEFF EDWARDS

www.braveshipbooks.com

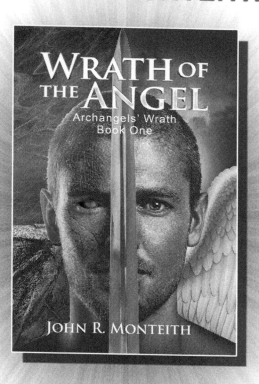

**A VICIOUS DRUG CARTEL IS ABOUT
TO LEARN THE HARD WAY...**

TED NULTY

...there's no such thing as an ex-Marine.

www.braveshipbooks.com

TRIBE. LOYALTY. LOVE

JOHN THOMAS EVERETT

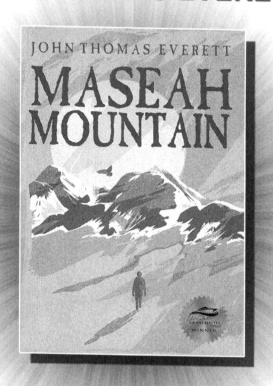

A tale of survival, adventure, and self-discovery.

www.braveshipbooks.com

**THE THOUSAND YEAR REICH MAY BE
ONLY BEGINNING...**

ALLAN LEVERONE

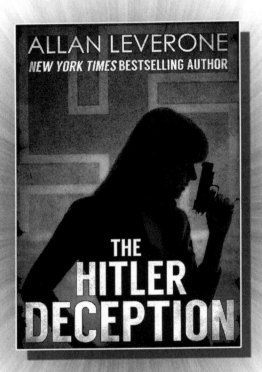

A Tracie Tanner Thriller

Made in the USA
Columbia, SC
10 July 2022